it had to be you
the gossip girl prequel

y
PBK
Von Ziegesar

by
Cecily von Ziegesar

poppy

LITTLE, BROWN AND COMPANY

Poppy
Hachette Book Group
237 Park Avenue, New York, NY 10017
For more of your favorite series, go to www.pickapoppy.com

First Paperback Edition: January 2009

Poppy is an imprint of Little, Brown Books for Young Readers.
The Poppy name and logo are trademarks of Hachette Book Group, Inc.
The characters, events, and locations in this book are fictitious. Any similarity to real persons, living or dead, is coincidental and not intended by the author.

Photo on page i and cover design by Andrea C. Uva
Cover photos by Ali Smith; Author photo by Roger Hagadone

alloyentertainment
Produced by Alloy Entertainment
151 West 26th Street, New York, NY 10001

"It Had to Be You" by Isham Jones and Gus Kahn.

"Hello Goodbye" by John Winston Lennon and Paul McCartney
(Sony/ATV Tunes, LLC). All rights reserved.

Library of Congress Cataloging-in-Publication Data

Von Ziegesar, Cecily.
   It had to be you : the Gossip Girl prequel / by Cecily von Ziegesar. — 1st ed.
      p. cm. — (Gossip Girl)
   "Poppy."
   Summary: Reveals the effects on a trio of bright, attractive, fifteen-year-old friends—
Serena van der Woodsen, Blair Waldorf, and Nate Archibald—when Serena considers
leaving their seemingly-perfect life of luxury in New York's Upper East Side for board-
ing school.
   ISBN 978-0-316-01768-8 (hc) / 978-0-316-01769-5 (pb) / 978-0-316-00827-3 (int'l)
   [1. High schools—Fiction. 2. Interpersonal relations—Fiction. 3.
Wealth—Fiction. 4. Schools—Fiction. 5. New York (N.Y.)—Fiction.] I.
Title. II. Title: Gossip Girl prequel.
   PZ7.V94Itah 2007
   [Fic]—dc21

                                                            2007037824

10 9 8 7 6 5 4 3 2 1
CWO
Printed in the United States of America

Gossip Girl novels created by Cecily von Ziegesar:

Gossip Girl
You Know You Love Me
All I Want Is Everything
Because I'm Worth It
I Like It Like That
You're The One That I Want
Nobody Does It Better
Nothing Can Keep Us Together
Only In Your Dreams
Would I Lie To You
Don't You Forget About Me
It Had To Be You
The Carlyles
You Just Can't Get Enough

If you like gossip girl, you may also enjoy:

The **Poseur** series by Rachel Maude
The **Secrets of My Hollywood Life** series by Jen Calonita
Footfree and Fancyloose by Elizabeth Craft and Sarah Fain
Haters by Alisa Valdes-Rodriguez
Betwixt by Tara Bray Smith

For my family. I was born lucky.

For nobody else, gave me a thrill—with all your faults, I love you still. It had to be you, wonderful you, it had to be you.
—As sung by Frank Sinatra

Disclaimer: All the real names of places, people, and events have been altered or abbreviated to protect the innocent. Namely, me.

hey people!

Ever have that totally freakish feeling that someone is listening in on your conversations, spying on you and your friends while you sip lattes on the ivory-colored steps of the Metropolitan Museum of Art, following you to premieres and parties, and just generally stalking you? Well, they are. Or actually, I am. And the truth is, I've been here all along, because I'm one of you. One of the Chosen Ones.

Don't get out much? Hair so processed it's fried your brain? Perhaps you're not one of us after all and you have no clue what I'm talking about or who "we" are. Allow me to expound. We're an exclusive group of indescribably beautiful people who happen to live in those majestic, green-awninged, white-glove-doorman buildings near Central Park. We attend Manhattan's most elite single-sex private schools. Our families own yachts, estates, and vineyards in various exotic locations through-out the world. We frequent all the best beaches and the most exclusive ski resorts in Austria and Utah. We're seated immediately at the finest restaurants in the chicest neighborhoods with nary a reservation. We turn heads. But don't confuse us with Hollywood actors or models or rock stars—those people you feel like you know because you read so much about them in the tabloids, but who are actually completely boring compared to the roles they play or the ballads they sing. There's nothing boring about me or my friends, and the more I tell you about us, the more you'll be dying to know. I've kept quiet until now, but something has happened, and if I don't share it with the world I'm absolutely going to burst.

the greatest story ever told

We learned in our eleventh-grade creative writing class this week that most great stories begin in one of the following fashions: someone mysteriously disappears, or a stranger comes to town. The tale I'm about to tell is of the "someone mysteriously disappears" variety.

To be specific, **S** is gone. The steps of the Met are no longer graced with her blond splendor. We are no longer distracted in Latin class by the sight of her twirling her pale locks around and around her long, slim fingers while she daydreams about a certain emerald-eyed boy.

But keep your panties on, I'll get to that in a moment.

The point is, **S** has disappeared. And in order to solve the mystery of why she's left and where she's gone, I'm going to have to backtrack to last winter—the winter of our sophomore year—when the La Mer skin cream hit the fan and our pretty pink rose-scented bubble burst. It all began with three inseparable, perfectly innocent, über-gorgeous fifteen-year-olds. Well, they're sixteen now, and let's just say that two of them are not that innocent.

An epic such as this requires an observant, quick-witted scribe. That would be me, since I *was* at the scene of every crime, and I happen to have an impeccable eye for the most outrageous details. So sit back while I unravel the past and reveal everyone's secrets, because I know everything, and what I don't know I'll invent elaborately.

Admit it, you're already falling for me.

You know I love you,

gossip girl

like most juicy stories, it started with one boy and two girls

"Truce!" Serena van der Woodsen screamed as Nate Archibald body-checked her into a three-foot-high drift of powdery white snow. Cold and wet, it tunneled into her ears and down her pants. Nate dove on top of her, all five foot eleven inches of his perfect, golden-brown-haired, glittering-green-eyed, fifteen-year-old boyness. He smelled like Downy and the L'Occitane sandalwood soap the maid stocked his bathroom with. Serena just lay there, trying to breathe with him on top of her. "My scalp is cold," she pleaded, getting a mouthful of Nate's snow-dampened, godlike curls as she spoke.

Nate sighed reluctantly, as if he could have spent the rest of the morning outside in the frigid February meat locker that was the back garden of his family's Eighty-second-Street-just-off-Park-Avenue Manhattan town house. He rolled onto his back and wriggled like Serena's long-dead golden retriever, Guppy, when she used to let him loose on the green grass of the Great Lawn in Central Park. Then he stood up, awkwardly dusting off the seat of his neatly pressed Brooks Brothers khakis. It was Saturday, but he still wore the same clothes he wore every weekday as a sophomore at the St. Jude's School for Boys over on East End Avenue. It was the unofficial Prince of the Upper East Side uniform, the same uniform he and his classmates had been wearing since they'd started nursery school together at Park Avenue Presbyterian.

Nate held out his hand to help Serena to her feet. Behind him rose the clean-looking limestone prewar luxury buildings of Park Avenue's Golden Mile, with their terraced penthouses and plate-glass windows. Still, nothing beat living in an actual house with an entire wing of one's own and a back garden with a fountain and cherry trees in it, within walking distance of one's best friends' houses, Serendipity 3, and Barneys. Serena frowned cautiously up at Nate, worried that he was only faking her out and was about to tackle her again. "I really am cold," she insisted.

He flapped his hand at her impatiently. "I know. Come on."

She pretended to pick her nose and then grabbed his hand with her faux-snotty one. "Thanks, pal." She staggered to her feet. "You're a real chum."

Nate led the way inside. The backs of his pant legs were damp and she could see the outline of his tighty-whiteys. Really, how gay of him! He held the glass-paned French doors open and stood aside to let her pass. Serena kicked off her baby blue Uggs and scuffed her bare, Urban Decay Piggy Bank Pink–toenailed feet down the long hall to the stately town house's enormous, barely used all-white Italian Modern kitchen. Nate's father, Captain Archibald, was a former sea captain–turned-banker, and his mother was a French society hostess. They were basically never home, and when they were home, they were at the opera.

"Are you hungry?" Nate asked, following her across the gleaming white marble floor. "I'm so sick of takeout. My parents have been in Venezuela or Santo Domingo or wherever for like two weeks, and I've been eating pizza or sushi every freaking night. I asked Regina to buy ham, Swiss, Pepperidge Farm white bread, Grammy Smith apples, and peanut butter. All I want is the food I ate in kindergarten." He tugged anxiously on a messy lock of wavy golden brown hair. "Maybe I'm going through some sort of midlife crisis or something."

Like his life is so stressful?

"It's Gra*nny* Smith, silly," Serena informed him fondly. She opened a glossy white cupboard and found an unopened box of cinnamon-and-brown-sugar Pop-Tarts. Ripping it open, she removed one of the packets from inside, tore it open with her neat, white teeth, and pulled out a thickly frosted pastry. She sucked on the Pop-Tart's sweet, crumbly corner and hopped up on the counter, kicking the cupboards below with her size eight-and-a-half feet. Pop-Tarts at Nate's. She'd been having them there since she was five years old. And now . . . and now . . .

"Mom and Dad want me to go to boarding school next year," she announced, her enormous, almost navy blue eyes growing huge and glassy as they welled up with unexpected tears. Go away to boarding school and leave Nate? It hurt too much even to even think about.

Nate flinched as if he'd been slapped in the face by an invisible hand. He grabbed the other Pop-Tart from the packet and hopped up on the counter next to her. "No way," he responded decisively. She couldn't leave. He wouldn't allow it.

"They want to travel more," she explained, the pink, perfect curve of her lower lip trembling dangerously. "If I'm home, they feel like they need to be home more. Like I want them around? Anyway, they've arranged for me to meet some of the deans of admissions and stuff. It's like I have no choice."

Nate scooted over a few inches and wrapped his arm around her sharply defined shoulders. "The city is going to suck if you're not here," he told her earnestly. "You can't go."

Serena took a deep, shuddering breath and rested her pale blond head on his shoulder. "I love you," she murmured without thinking. Their bodies were so close the entire Nate-side of her hummed. If she turned her head and tilted her chin just so, she could have easily kissed his warm, lovely neck. And she wanted to. She was actually dying to, because she really did love him, with all her heart.

She did? Hello? Since when?!

Maybe since ballroom-dancing school way back in fourth grade. She was tall for her age, and Nate was always such a gentleman about her lack of rhythm and the way she stepped on his insteps and jutted her bony elbows into his sides. He'd finesse it by grabbing her hand and spinning her around so that the skirt of her puffy oyster-colored satin tea-length Bonpoint dress twirled out magnificently. Their teacher, Mrs. Jaffe, who had long blue hair that she kept in place with a pearl-adorned black hairnet, worshipped Nate. So did Serena's best friend, Blair Waldorf. And so did Serena—she just hadn't realized it until now. She shivered and her perfect, still-tan-from-Christmas-in-the-Caribbean skin broke out in a rash of goosebumps. Her whole body seemed to be having an adverse reaction to the idea of revealing something she'd kept so well hidden for so long, even from herself.

Nate slipped his lacrosse-toned arms around her long, narrow waist and pulled her close, tucking her pale gold head into the crook of his neck and massaging the ruts between the ribs on her back with his fingertips. The best thing about Serena was her total lack of embarrassing flab. Her entire body was as long and lean and taut as the strings on his Prince titanium tennis racket.

It was painful having such a ridiculously hot best friend. Why couldn't his best friend be some lard-assed dude with zits and dandruff? Instead he had Serena and Blair Waldorf, hands down the two hottest girls on the Upper East Side, and maybe all of Manhattan, or even the whole world.

Serena was an absolute goddess—every guy Nate knew talked about her—but she was perplexingly unpredictable. She'd laugh for hours if she spotted a cloud shaped like a toilet seat or something equally ridiculous, and the next moment she'd be wistful and sad. It was impossible to tell what she was thinking most of the time. Sometimes Nate wondered if she would've been more comfortable in a body that was slightly less perfect, because it would've given her more *incentive*, to use an SAT vocabulary word. Like she wasn't sure what she had to *aspire* to, since she basically had everything a girl could possibly want.

Blair was petite, with a pretty, foxlike face, cobalt blue eyes, and wavy chestnut-colored hair. Way back in fifth grade, Serena had told Nate she was convinced Blair had a crush on him. He started to notice that Blair did sort of stick her chest out when she knew he was looking, and she was always either bossing him around or fixing his hair. Of course Blair never admitted that she liked him, which made him like her even more.

Nate sighed deeply. No one understood how difficult it was to be best friends with two such beautiful, impossible girls.

Like he would have been friends with them if they were awkward and butt-ugly?

He closed his eyes and breathed in the sweet scent of Serena's Frédéric Fekkai Apple Cider clarifying shampoo. He'd kissed a few girls and had even gone to third base last June with L'Wren Knowes, a very experienced older Seaton Arms School senior who really did seem to know everything. But kissing Serena would be . . . different. He loved her. It was as simple as that. She was his best friend, and he loved her.

And if you can't kiss your best friend, who *can* you kiss?

upper east side schoolgirl uncovers shocking sex scandal!

"Ew," Blair Waldorf muttered at her reflection in the full-length mirror on the back of her closet door. She liked to keep her closet organized, but not too organized. Whites with whites, off-whites with off-whites, navy with navy, black with black. But that was it. Jeans were tossed in a heap on the closet floor. And there were dozens of them. It was almost a game to close her eyes and feel around and come up with a pair that used to be too tight in the ass but fit a little loosely now that she'd cut out her daily after-dinner milk-and-Chips-Ahoy routine.

Blair looked at the mirror, scrutinizing her outfit. Her Marc by Marc Jacobs shell pink sheer cotton blouse was fine, as were her peg-legged Seven jeans. It was the fuchsia La Perla bra that was the problem. It showed right through the blouse so that she looked like a lap dancer from Scores. But she was only going to Nate's house to hang out with him and Serena. And Nate liked to talk about bras. He was genuinely curious about, for instance, what the purpose of an underwire was, or why some bras fastened in front and some fastened in back. Obviously it was a big turn-on for him, but it was also sort of sweet. He was a lonely only child, craving sisterhood.

Right.

She decided to leave the bra on for Nate's sake, hiding the whole ensemble under her favorite belted black cashmere Loro Piana cardigan, which would come off the minute she stepped into his well-heated town house. Maybe the sight of her hot pink bra would be the thing to make Nate realize that he'd been in love with her just as long as she'd been in love with him.

Maybe.

She opened her bedroom door and yelled down the long hall and across the East Seventy-second Street penthouse's vast expanse of period furniture, parquet floors, crown moldings, and French Impressionist paintings. "Mom! Dad? I'm going over to Nate's house! Serena and I are spending the night!"

When there was no reply, she clomped her way to her parents' huge master suite in her noisy Kors wooden-heeled sheepskin clogs that she'd bought on impulse at Scoop, opened their bedroom door, and made a beeline for her mom's dressing room. Eleanor Waldorf kept a tall stack of crisp emergency twenties in her lingerie drawer for Blair and her ten-year-old brother, Tyler, to parse from—for taxis, cappuccinos, and, in Blair's case, the occasional much-needed pair of Manolo Blahnik heels. Twenty, forty, sixty, eighty, one hundred. Twenty, forty, sixty, eighty, two hundred. Blair counted out the crisp bills, folding them neatly before stuffing them into her back pocket.

"If I were a cabernet," her father's playfully confidential lawyer's voice echoed out of the adjoining dressing room, "how would you describe my bouquet?"

Excusez-moi?

Blair clomped over to the chocolate brown velvet curtain that separated her mother's dressing room from her father's. "If you guys are in there together, like, doing it while I'm home, then that's really gross," she declared flatly. "Anyway, I'm going over to Nate's, so—"

Her father, Harold J. Waldorf III, Esquire, poked his head out from behind the velvet curtain, holding it firmly in his grasp so that Blair couldn't pull it aside. The one shoulder she could see appeared to be dressed in his favorite charcoal tweed Paul Smith cashmere bathrobe. But if he wasn't naked, then why wouldn't he let her open the curtain?

"Your mom's with Misty Bass looking at dishes for the Guggenheim benefit," he said, his nicely tanned, handsome face looking slightly flushed. "I thought you were out. Where are you going exactly?"

Blair glared at him and then yanked the curtain aside, catching him as he tucked his rather bulky BlackBerry into his bathrobe pocket. She shoved him aside and stood amongst his custom-tailored Valentino and Dior suits with her hands on her hips. Who had he just been talking to? His intern? His secretary? A salesgirl from Hermès, his favorite store?

"What's up, Bear?" Her father smiled tensely back at her, his crystalline blue eyes looking a little too innocent. What was he hiding?

Does she really want to know?

Her stomach roiling with bilious outrage and her blue eyes shining with angry tears, Blair stumbled out of the master suite and clomped her way across the penthouse to the foyer. She grabbed her blood-orange-colored Jimmy Choo Treasure Chest hobo and ran for the elevator.

February had been unusually cruel. Outside it was breathtakingly cold, and fat snowflakes fell at random. Usually Blair walked the twelve blocks to Nate's house, but today she had no patience for walking. She couldn't wait to see her friends and tell them what a scumbag her father was. A cab was waiting for her downstairs. Or rather, a cab was waiting for Mrs. Solomon in 4A, but when Alfie, the hunter-green-uniform-clad doorman saw the terrifying look on Blair's normally pretty face, he let her take it.

Besides, hailing cabs in the snow was probably the highlight of his day.

The stone walls bordering Central Park were blanketed in snow. A tall, elderly woman and her Yorkshire terrier, dressed in matching red Chanel quilted coats with matching black velvet bows in their white hair, crossed Seventy-second Street and entered the Ralph Lauren flagship store on the corner. Blair's cab hurtled recklessly up Madison Avenue, past Zitomer, Agnès B., and the Three Guys coffee shop where all the Constance Billard girls gathered after school, turned east on Eighty-second Street, and finally pulled up in front of Nate's town house.

"Let me in!" she yelled into the intercom outside the Archibalds' elegant wrought-iron-and-glass front door as she swatted the buzzer over and over with an impatient hand.

Nate and Serena were still cuddling in the kitchen when the buzzer rang. Serena raised her head from his shoulder and opened her eyes, as if from a dream. The kiss they'd both been fantasizing about had never actually happened, which was probably for the best.

"I think I'm warm now," Serena announced, and hopped

off the white marble countertop, composing her face so that she looked totally calm and cool, like they hadn't just had a moment. And maybe they hadn't—she couldn't be sure. She grinned at the monitor's distorted image of Blair giving her the finger. "Come on in, sweetness!" she shouted back, buzzing her other best friend in.

Nate tried to erase the disturbing thought that Blair had caught him and Serena together. They weren't together. They were just friends, hanging out, which is what friends do when they're together. There was nothing to catch. It was all in his mind.

Or was it?

"Hey hornyheads." Blair clomped into the kitchen with melting snowflakes in her shiny, shoulder-length chestnut brown hair. Her cheeks were pink with cold, her blue eyes were slightly bloodshot, and her carefully plucked dark brown eyebrows looked messy, as if she'd been crying or rubbing her eyes like crazy. "I have a fucked-up story to tell you guys." She flung her orange bag down on the floor and took a deep breath, her eyes rolling around dramatically, milking the moment for all it was worth. "As it turns out, my totally boring Mr. Lawyer father, Harold Waldorf, Esquire, is like totally having an affair. Only moments ago, I caught him talking on the phone in his closet with some random babe, saying, 'If I were a wine, how would you describe my bouquet?'"

"Whoa," Serena and Nate responded in unison.

Blair turned on the kitchen faucet and then turned it off again. Her face twisted up into a horrible grimace. "He just sounded so . . . *slimy!*" she wailed with dismay as she admired her own reflection in the polished white porcelain. She looked up and tucked her hair behind her tidily small, slightly pointed ears, waiting for her friends to say something soothing to make her feel better.

As if that were possible.

"Well, maybe he was just talking dirty to your mom," Serena suggested.

"Sure," Nate agreed. "My parents talk like that all the time," he added, feeling a little sick as he said it. His former navy admiral dad was so uptight he probably couldn't even *think* sexy *thoughts* for fear of being court-martialed.

Blair grimaced. The idea of her tennis-toned-but-still-plump, St. Barts–tanned, gold-jewelry-loving mom having any kind of sex, let alone cabernet phone sex, with her skinny, preppy, argyle-socks-wearing dad was so unlikely and so completely icky she refused to even think about it.

"No," she insisted, snatching the uneaten half of Serena's Pop-Tart off the counter and wolfing it down. "It was definitely another woman. I mean, face it," she observed, still chewing. "Dad is totally hot and dresses really well, and he's an important lawyer and everything. And my mom is totally insane and doesn't really do anything and she has varicose veins and a flabby ass. Of course he's having an affair."

Serena and Nate nodded their glossy blond heads like that made complete sense. Then Serena grabbed Blair and hugged her hard. Blair was the sister she'd never had. In fourth grade they'd pretended they were fraternal twins for an entire month. Their Constance Billard gym teacher, Ms. Etro, who'd gotten fired midyear for inappropriate touching—which she called "spotting"—during tumbling classes, had even believed them. They'd worn matching pink Izod shirts and cut their hair exactly the same length. They even wore matching gold Cartier hoop earrings, until they decided they were tacky and switched to Tiffany diamond studs.

Blair pressed her face into Serena's perfectly defined collarbone and heaved an exhausted, trembling sigh. "It's just so fucked up it makes me want to vomit."

Serena patted her back and met Nate's gaze over Blair's Elizabeth Arden Red Door Salon–glossed brown head. No way was she going to bring up the whole being-sent-away-to-boarding-school problem—not when her best friend was so upset. And she didn't want Nate to mention it either. "Come on, let's go mix martinis and watch a stupid movie or something."

Nate jumped off the counter, feeling completely confused. Suddenly all he really wanted to do was hug Blair and kiss away her tears. Was he hot for her now, too?

That's the trouble with friends who happen to be boys. You can't take the boy out of the friend.

"All we have is vodka and champagne. My parents keep all the good wine and whiskey locked up in the cabinet for when they have company," he apologized, pulling his heathered gray J.Crew sweatshirt off over his head and giving both girls a small heart attack at the sight of his bare, tanned navel.

Yum.

Serena broke away from Blair and scooted down the countertop on her bum until she reached the bread pantry, where most families would actually keep bread, but where Nate's mom stored the cartons of Gitanes cigarettes her sister sent from France via FedEx twice a month because the ones sold in the States simply did not taste fresh. She slid open the door and pulled out a royal blue carton. "I'm sure we can make do."

She ripped open the carton and stuck two cigarettes in her mouth like tusks. Then she beckoned Nate and Blair to follow her out of the kitchen and upstairs to the master suite. If anyone was an expert at changing the mood, it was Serena. That was one of the things they loved about her. "I'll show you a good time," she added goofily.

She always did.

The Archibalds' vast bedroom had been decorated by Nate's mother in the style of Louis XVI, with a giant gilt mirror over the headboard of the enormous red-and-gold-toile-upholstered four-poster bed, and heavy gold curtains in the windows. The walls were adorned with red-and-gold fleur-de-lys wallpaper and renderings of Mrs. Archibald's family's summer château near Nice. On the floor was a red, blue, and gold Persian rug rescued from the *Titanic* and bought at auction by Mrs. Archibald at Sotheby's as a gift to Mr. Archibald for their tenth wedding anniversary. The only modern exception to the room's historical décor was the circular glass skylight in the ceiling over the bed, a porthole to the stars.

"*Bus Stop? Some Like It Hot?* Or the digitally remastered version of *Some Like It Hot?*" Serena asked, flipping through Nate's parents' limited DVD collection. Obviously Captain Archibald liked Marilyn Monroe movies—a lot. Of course, Nate had his own collection of DVDs in his room, including a play-by-play of the last twenty years of America's Cup sailing races. Thanks, but no thanks. His parents' taste was far more girl-friendly. "Or we could just watch Nate play Xbox, which is always hot," she joked, although she kind of meant it.

"Only if he does it naked," Blair quipped hopefully. She sat down and bounced up and down on the end of the luxuriously huge bed.

Nate blushed. Blair loved to make him blush and he knew it. "Okay," he responded boldly, sitting down next to her.

Blair snatched a Kleenex out of the silver tissue box on Nate's mom's bedside table and blew her nose noisily. Not that she really needed to blow her nose. She just needed a distraction from the overwhelming urge to tackle Nate and rip his clothes off. He was so goddamned adorable it made her feel like she was going to explode. God, she loved him.

There had never been a time when she didn't love him. She'd loved the stupid lobster shorts he wore to the club in Newport when their dads played tennis together in the summer, back when they were, what—five? She loved the way he always had a Spider-Man Band-Aid on some part of his body until he was at least twelve, not because he'd hurt himself but because he thought it looked cool. She loved the way his whole head reflected the sunlight, glowing gold. She loved his glittering green eyes—eyes that were almost too pretty for a boy. She loved the way he so obviously knew he was hot but didn't quite know what to do about it. She loved him. Oh, how she loved him.

Oh, oh, *oh!*

Blair blew her nose with one last trumpeting snort and then grabbed a hot pink, tacky-looking DVD case from off the floor. She turned the case over, studying it. "*Breakfast at Tiffany's*. I've never seen it, but she's so beautiful." She held the DVD up so Serena could see Audrey Hepburn in her long black dress and stunning pearls. "Isn't she?"

"She is pretty," Serena agreed, still sorting through the movies.

"She looks like you," Nate observed, cocking his head and studying Blair in such an adorable way that she had to close her eyes to keep from falling off the bed.

"You think?" She tossed her dirty tissue in the general direction of the Archibalds' dainty white porcelain wastepaper basket and studied the picture on the DVD case again. A movie began to play in her head, and in it she *was* Audrey Hepburn— a fabulously dressed, wafer-thin, perfectly coiffed, beautiful, mysterious megastar. "Maybe a little," she agreed, removing her black cashmere cardigan so that her fuchsia bra was clearly visible beneath her blouse.

She turned the DVD case over and examined the pictures on the back of it. Audrey Hepburn looked like the most stylish, sophisticated woman in the world, but she also looked sort of prim and proper, like she wore sexy underwear but wouldn't let a guy see it unless he was going to marry her. Blair yanked her cardigan back on and buttoned the top button. From now on, her life's work would be to emulate Audrey Hepburn in every possible way. Nate could see her underwear, but only once she was sure that one day they'd walk down the aisle at St. Patrick's Cathedral with wedding bands on their fingers and confetti flying through the air.

That makes sense—to her.

"I watched that movie with my mom," Nate confessed, causing both girls' hearts to drip into sticky puddles on the floor. "It's kind of bizarre, actually. I think it's supposed to be romantic, but I'm not sure I even understood it."

That was all the girls needed. Blair stuck the DVD into the player while Serena mixed martinis on top of the vintage hammered steel wet bar in the adjoining library. This involved pouring Bombay Sapphire into chilled martini glasses and stirring it with a silver letter opener. It was only noon—not exactly cocktail hour—but Blair was in crisis, and Nate tended to take off his shirt when he got drunk. Besides, it was Saturday.

"There," Serena announced, as if she'd just put the finishing touches on a very complicated recipe. She handed out the glasses. "To us. Because we're worth it."

"To us," Blair and Nate chorused, glasses raised.

Bottoms up!

even cowgirls from vermont get the blues

"Whose idea was it to send me to Constance anyway?" fifteen-year-old Vanessa Abrams demanded of her nineteen-year-old sister, Ruby.

"Fuck if I know." Ruby was in the bathtub, soaking off the sweat and stench from her gig at Pete's Candy Store the night before. She was the bassist for the band SugarDaddy, the latest sensation on the Williamsburg, Brooklyn, bar scene, and she'd been up all night, rocking out. "Do you mind?"

Vanessa stood in the doorway of the bathroom while her sister floated naked in the sparsely bubbled lukewarm water, her thick black Williamsburg hipster bangs plastered to her clammy white forehead. "Is there some reason why I couldn't go to a more convenient, less materialistic, less-full-of-bitches school in, say, Brooklyn, which happens to be where I live?" Vanessa railed on.

"You know the story." Ruby hugged her pale wet knees. "Dad read an article about that woman recycling personal objects to make art in *Atlantic Monthly* and the artist's bio said she went to Constance Billard. He was so impressed that when you told him you wanted to come live here with me, he just signed you up. He doesn't care what a hassle it is to get there. And it makes him feel good that you're at this ritzy school all day. It's like he thinks the school can be your substitute parent because it's used to dealing with families where the parents are always in Gstaad or Cannes or wherever." Ruby lay on her stomach so that her flat, pink ass was in plain view. Outside the tiny, city-grime-smeared bathroom window a cargo truck rumbled by on its way to the sugar factory three blocks away. That was one of the things Vanessa loved about living in gritty Williamsburg: the air always smelled like cotton candy.

"Nice," she muttered grimly. Vanessa turned to the mirror over the sink, grabbed Ruby's green rubber hairbrush, and started to brush out her waist-length, naturally jet-black mane. Six months ago, on her first day of school at Constance Billard, the tenth-grade girls had all gone crazy over her hair, stroking it and braiding it, like Vanessa was one of those Barbie hairdressing heads or a new pony or something. It was clearly the only thing they liked about her. "Okay, so he read that article like twenty years ago. The girls in my class don't give two shits about recycling or art. All they do is get their highlights done and trade lip glosses they get in gift bags at all those fancy parties they go to. Plus, you graduated from White River High and you're making decent money without even going to college."

"I'm exceptional," Ruby replied dryly, sitting up to squirt Johnson's baby shampoo into her palm. "If I'd gone to Constance instead of some shitty high school in Vermont, I'd probably be the first woman president by now."

Vanessa examined her pores in the bathroom mirror. The bathtub was beige and the sink was scrambled-egg yellow—

typical Williamsburg—but she adored the wonky plainness of the shabby one-bedroom apartment. If only the school she attended five days a week, all day long, were equally wonky. She'd spent lunchtime alone yesterday, drinking black tea and eating saltines while at the other end of the table Kati Farkas, one of her shiny-haired, glossy-lipped classmates, complained about having to go sailing again in the Greek Isles for spring break with her parents. *"But I've already been to Corfu. It's like, can't they take us sailing somewhere in Greece with better shopping, like Milan?"* Kati had whined, blissfully ignorant of the world's geography, topography, and just about everything else, despite Constance Billard's efforts to educate her.

It wasn't as if Vanessa had tons of friends back in Vermont either. She'd spent so many years dreaming about moving to New York City and becoming an avant-garde filmmaker in the style of Ingmar Bergman, she didn't have time to socialize. Now that her parents had finally given in and let her move in with Ruby she was sort of . . . bored. Or maybe the word *empty* was more like it. It wasn't a new feeling, but she'd thought the sensation would go away when she got to New York, and it hadn't, not really. Not even when she pigged out on falafel.

"You need a project," Ruby observed from the scratched beige porcelain tub. Her parakeet, Tofu, flew into the bathroom and alighted on the soap dish, where he pooped and then started to dip his green beak into the murky bathwater.

Vanessa picked up her digital camcorder again and zoomed in on Tofu. "It's so cute how he does that," she giggled.

Ruby rolled her eyes and sank down lower in the water. "You're still relatively new in town. You need to establish your-self and make a few friends so you have something else to do besides film me naked in the bathtub, which is actually totally perverted and annoying, especially when I've been up half the night playing my tits off," she yawned. "Why don't you start a blog or something? Like, fill the homepage up with stills of parakeet shit or some such. There are a lot of people who'd be into that. Think of all the friends you'd make. You might even meet your first boyfriend that way."

Vanessa reached out with her foot and kicked the soap dish into the tub. Tofu flapped up to the shower curtain rail with a squawk. His poop floated on the surface of the bathwater like a piece of chewed Juicy Fruit gum. "Wench," Vanessa muttered before stomping out of the bathroom in the black vintage Doc Marten steel-toed combat boots she wore as a big "fuck you" to Constance Billard's "simple dark shoe" rule. There was nothing complicated about combat boots, but she was pretty sure the school was thinking of something more along the lines of a penny loafer or ballet flat. Right. Fuck that.

She flopped facedown on the plain white sheets of the unmade futon in her boxy, plain white bedroom, intending to wallow in irritation and resentment until Ruby dragged her wet ass out of the bath and turned on a movie or something. But Ruby's comment had given her an idea. Vanessa spent most of her free time at home, flipping through back issues of alternative photography and art journals and absentmindedly splitting the split ends in her long black hair. Constance Billard's photography studio was ridiculously well stocked and totally underused, and the school probably had millions of dollars in endowment money. Why not take advantage of the school's resources and start an arts magazine of her own? She could ask for submissions from her fellow Constance students and feature one of her own darkly brilliant photographs on the cover of every ingenious issue. She wouldn't get a boyfriend out of it, not that she cared, but it would keep her busy, and it might even help her get into NYU.

Of course she'd probably have to publish a lot of dumb photographs of girls' pedicured feet and poems about dead bichons frises, but she could always deface them with a fat black Sharpie in the privacy of her own home. Maybe some girl's big-deal gallery owner mom would discover her raw, intuitive, behind-the-camera eye and she'd begin her filmmaking career before she even made it to NYU film school. Maybe Ruby was right—she did need a project. Starting her own arts magazine would be the ideal way to establish herself uptown and show everyone there was more to the pale, slightly chubby, dark-tressed, Doc Martens–wearing newcomer from Vermont than they'd first thought. And while she was at it, maybe she'd do something different with her hair, something unexpected.

Here's hoping whatever she does doesn't involve parakeet poop.

psychotic stalkers come in small packages

"You remember Mom's, though, right? They're not small," twelve-and-a-half-year-old Jennifer Humphrey reminded her older brother, Daniel, as they sat at their cracked, banana-colored Formica kitchen table, eating Saturday brunch. Her tiny, four-foot-eleven-inch body tucked into the same pink fleece footie pajamas she'd been wearing since she was ten, Jenny was working her way through a giant container of peach-flavored soy yogurt in hopes that the naturally occurring estrogen in soy would increase her breast size. Everyone in her seventh-grade class at Constance Billard was blossoming—Luna Skye had gone up two cup sizes since September!—everyone except Jenny.

"Yeah, but maybe they're fake. I mean we don't know anything about Mom really," a scruffy, stained-brown-corduroys-wearing Dan pointed out. This winter he had worn only two outfits: brown corduroys and a black polo shirt with a frayed white turtleneck underneath it—all from Old Navy—or faded black Levi's paired with a mustard yellow hoodie he'd bought at a thrift store in the East Village. He'd rotate the two outfits until they turned gray and Jenny would finally break down and wash them for him in the basement laundry room of their building. That's what happened when you didn't have Mom around to do the wash, Jenny thought dolefully. Little Sister wound up doing it.

Dan spooned another heap of Folgers crystals into the green plastic Winnie-the-Pooh mug he'd been drinking coffee out of since he was six. The topic of their mother always made him squirm, and since their father, Rufus, had been away since last night, attending an all-night howl-in with his anarchist, Beat poet comrades, Jenny had been talking about Mom even more than usual.

"They're not fake. We were both breastfed, so—"

"Can we please stop discussing Mom's . . . *parts*?" Dan interrupted grumpily, feeling guilty almost instantaneously. Jenny was the only girl living with her scruffy weird father and her scruffy weird brother. She had every right to talk about her ever-absent mother. The lack of femaleness or even normalness in their decaying Upper West Side rent-controlled apartment was excruciating. Jeanette Humphrey had left Rufus and her two children when Dan was eight and Jenny was not yet six to "discover herself" with a handsome count in the Czech Republic. Dan preferred to think of their mother as a babysitter who took care of them for a few years and then got another job. He certainly never thought about how he resembled her. Clearly Jenny thought about it a lot. Or at least she'd continue to think about it until she finally got breasts and started thinking about something else. It wasn't like she missed their mother. Who could miss someone who'd abandoned her young children, never wrote or called, and sent them each a pair of lederhosen in a child's size four two Christmases in a row?

The only person Dan ruminated over obsessively was Serena van der Woodsen. *Serena van der Woodsen.* Just the thought of her *name* made him clutch his coffee mug with sweat-slicked fingers. Serena was so beautiful he felt like puking every time he allowed his thoughts to wander back to her; so perfect it was difficult to believe she existed; so entirely unattainable she might as well have been a ghost or the tooth fairy or something equally ethereal. Serena van der Woodsen was and always would be Dan's dream girl, his muse—not that he ever did anything creative that required a muse.

Never say never.

Two years ago, in a fit of insane compassion for his mother-less son, Rufus had thrown the mother of all birthday parties for thirteen-year-old Dan. There was a disco ball, Jell-O shots, a bathtub full of St. Pauli Girl, and enough Häagen Dazs coffee ice cream and Newman's Own microwave popcorn to feed the entire roster of eighth-grade boys at his school, Riverside Prep. Since Rufus was notoriously liberal and would definitely have no problem getting a bunch of eighth graders drunk, Dan's entire class came, including woman-hips-sporting Zeke Freedman, Dan's only real friend. But Riverside eighth graders weren't the only ones who'd heard about the alcohol-friendly party. The sophomores came and so did the juniors. So did twenty-odd kids from across the park who'd heard about the party from Dan's highly obnoxious Park Avenue–dwelling classmate, Chuck Bass. A few of the crashers were girls—thank God—and Serena was one of them.

She got drunk, and so did Dan—all of them did. But the eighth-grade version of Dan had been even more introspec-tive and insecure than the tenth-grade version, so he'd never mustered up the nerve to talk to her. He just sat on the worn brown leather sofa in the study, watching through the doorway while Serena played a bizarre drinking game involving a Latin textbook, a Sharpie, and a boy's bare chest with her friends down the hall in the dining room. It was Jenny who'd told him her name. Jenny was supposed to be in bed—yeah, right—but she'd slipped onto the leather sofa next to him with a pint of ice cream and two spoons and whispered those magical words in Dan's ear: "That's Serena van der Woodsen. She goes to my school. Isn't she divine?"

Absolutely divine.

Jenny was even more obsessed with Serena than he was. She cut out pictures of Serena in the society pages and drew doodles of her in the margins of her Hello Kitty diary. She memorized Serena's schedule—which was taped to the outside of Serena's locker—and followed her around school. She eavesdropped on her at recess, at lunchtime, and in the bathroom. Weekends, she trolled the Internet for pictures. Just this morning Jenny had downloaded a picture from the archives of a tiny Ridgefield, Connecticut, weekly newspaper of an eight-year-old Serena eating a cone of dripping green mint chocolate chip ice cream. Four of her front teeth were missing, but she still looked glorious.

"I've been thinking. Why don't we make a collage?" Jenny suggested now. "Like, of her whole life, as we imagine it."

"You mean of Mom?" Dan asked, his forehead furrowing worriedly. Too bad their father was totally anti-psychotherapy. His sister kind of sounded like she needed it.

"No, silly. Of Serena," Jenny clarified, holding up the ice cream cone picture.

Like that's any *less* psycho?

"What?" Dan refused to admit that it sounded like the most exciting idea he'd ever heard. "No way." He went over to the sink and filled his Winnie-the-Pooh mug with semi-hot water from the tap, stirring in the Folgers crystals with a plastic spoon. He took a sip. Perfect.

Perfectly nasty?

Jenny tapped away at the keyboard of the family's white MacBook, ignoring her brother's protestations. She'd learned that when it came to the matter of Serena van der Woodsen, Dan was utterly useless. "Oh, wow," she murmured as the new picture she'd just downloaded began to appear onscreen. She swiveled the laptop around so that Dan could see it. "Look at this. She looks like she should be on the cover of *Bride* magazine or something."

Dan planned on feigning disinterest, but it was impossible. Serena had one of those remarkable faces that even when distorted and pixilated glowed with the sort of beauty that can't be marred. Jenny could have drawn a mustache and huge eyebrows and a hairy nose over the image and the effect would have been the same: he could hardly breathe.

Serena was dressed in a long white halter dress with silver beading in the bodice, and she really did look like a bride, but not a wedding dress model. She was too beautiful to model. Her beauty was so exquisite, genuine, and priceless it was impossible to imagine anyone using it to sell anything.

Except maybe MasterCard.

"So now do you want to make a collage?" Jenny persisted, tapping away at the keyboard. "We could pretend this was like your wedding announcement photo in the Styles section of the *New York Times* and write the column underneath." She opened a new Word document. "Serena Antoinette van der Woodsen and Daniel Fartbreath Humphrey, July 12 at St. Patrick's Cathedral on Fifth Avenue. The bride met the groom when they attended Columbia University together. He had been obsessed with her for years but was too intimidated to talk to her until one day she sprained her ankle in the library after tripping over his Shakespeare anthology. He carried her back to his smelly dorm room, propped her foot up on his mini fridge, and read her boring existentialist books until she began to cry. From that day on they were inseparable. He even started to smell better. Daniel's voluptuous younger sister, Jennifer, is engaged to be married to the bride's younger brother, Miles, on Thanksgiving Day."

Dan was used to Jenny's babblings and would have half tuned her out if it weren't for the fact that what she was saying was very much like the little daydream he allowed himself to have every night before he fell asleep. "Is Antoinette really her middle name?" he demanded suspiciously.

Jenny shrugged. She had no idea what Serena's middle name was or whether or not she had a younger brother named Miles or Michael or Morty. Her middle name probably wasn't Antoinette, but it was undoubtedly something equally glamorous. Scarlett? Jessamine?

"I think you should tell this girl how smitten you are so I don't have to listen to you moon about her all day long," the voice of their father, Rufus Humphrey, boomed from the kitchen doorway. Rufus's long, frizzy salt-and-pepper-colored hair was pulled back in a low, loose ponytail tied with the yellow plastic cinch he'd removed from a Hefty bag. He was dressed in his "homeless look" best: his favorite coffee-stained purple sweatshirt, the sleeves cut off at the elbows, with QUESTION AUTHORITY emblazoned in black across the chest; a pair of tight, stretchy red ski pants that Jenny and Dan's mother had left behind in her closet; and black rubber Birkenstock clogs that did wonders for his hairy ankles. Actually, one ankle was inexplicably hidden in an orange woolen sock, while the other foot had been left bare. Obviously Dan and Jenny were used to their father, but it was still a little shocking to see him after a good night's sleep, and it was always, always totally embarrassing when he visited their respective schools. Nobody else's dad looked or acted quite like Rufus. But they still loved him fiercely, no matter what he wore.

"Nice pants, Daddy," Jenny remarked. "If you ever let me go snowboarding can I borrow them?"

Rufus smiled broadly at the compliment. "They're insulated!" he boomed. "You could take a leak in these fuckers and they wouldn't leak!"

Dan was still fixated on what his father had just said. Tell Serena he loved her? Impossible. Terrifying. Unfathomable.

Rufus slapped a shiny black leather-bound book on the kitchen table in front of his son. "Write her a letter or a poem. Tell her how you feel. Then Jenny can put it in her locker. She'll be thrilled. Everyone will be thrilled." Rufus's enormous, bristly charcoal-colored eyebrows stood up on end. He was getting excited, like he fancied himself the next Cyrano de Bergerac, which happened to be one of Dan's favorite tragicomedies. "I've even thought of a first line. I thought of it when I was putting my shoes on this morning and I could only find one sock. *I was lost like a sock but now I've found you. We are a pair.*"

Dan rolled his eyes. No wonder his father had never published any of his own writing. But maybe he could get a job at

Hallmark writing lines for greeting cards and finally hire them a housekeeper. Dan opened the black leather-bound book and grabbed a chewed-up pencil stub from the tabletop. Without thinking he began to scribble.

> *Nothing hurt until you pushed me, hard, and I fell.*
> *It's bleeding. I'm bleeding.*
> *And I'm falling still. Still falling.*
> *Can't you see me from up there? The water's clear.*

Rufus peered over his shoulder and frowned. "That's a little dark."

Jenny scooted her chair over to see. "What's a little dark? What'd you write?"

Dan slammed the book closed. He'd never really written a poem before, just letting the words pour out of him. It was kind of exciting. "I'll show it to you guys when I'm done. Maybe." Already he'd thought of another line. Actually it was just a word: *becoming*. He was becoming a poet, and Serena was becoming his muse. Even if he never actually spoke to her in person, he could write to her, or at least about her. And then if he died in a terrible fire at a tragically young age and his poetry was heralded as groundbreaking and heartwrenching, she would become famous for being his inspiration.

As if she wasn't already famous.

all dressed up with no place to go

"Isn't life just perfect?" Serena wondered aloud as she puffed on the ridiculously long black lacquered cigarette holder she'd discovered in the tiny drawer in Mrs. Archibald's gold-painted antique bedside table, along with several prescription bottles of pills and a small red-suede diary full of illegible blue felt-tipped scribbles in drunken French. *Zut alors, je déteste Misty Bass! J'adore mon nouvel chauffeur!*

"Merveilleux," Blair agreed, adjusting Mrs. Archibald's enormous black Chanel sunglasses on her nose.

The girls were lying on their backs on Nate's parents' bed, watching the stars come out through the round skylight overhead. Nate lay between them, his glittering green eyes closed. His dad's purple-and-black silk bow tie and matching cummerbund were tied around his white Polo shirt. "Hmm," he noted drunkenly. Nate was sort of a lightweight when it came to gin, but even drunk and dressed like a jackass he was still hot.

"Do you think she wore pajamas to bed?" Serena mused. "Or a nightgown?"

"Pajamas," Blair responded definitively. "White satin pajamas with black velvet trim." They'd watched *Breakfast at Tiffany's* twice in a row and neither girl could stop talking about it. They were obsessed.

"If I ever become a director, that's the kind of movie I'd like to make," Serena declared dreamily as a plane flew high above the skylight, its lights flashing. "And you two can star in it."

"Not me," Nate yawned. Acting was totally not his thing. Memorize all those lines? No, thanks. He was a sailor. He'd always be a sailor. Not that he actually sailed much during the school year, but he and his father were working on the blueprints for the awesome sailboat they were going to build up at their family compound on Mt. Desert Island, in Maine. One day he'd take Serena and Blair sailing on that boat. And one day he'd win the America's Cup with it.

In her head, Blair was already playing the movie she was going to star in. She and Nate couldn't be perfect strangers in her movie the way Fred and Holly Golightly had been. They'd known each other forever. But maybe after college they'd wind up living in the same building on the Upper East Side just like Holly and Fred. And one day, when they were both running for the same taxi, they'd bump into each other in the rain. Blair would be holding a cat, and they'd kiss and realize that they'd actually been in love their whole lives. Then they'd rush up to her apartment and have wild, passionate sex.

Or maybe that would happen right now.

Blair turned her head slightly to glance at Nate. There was a tuft of soft golden fuzz on his cheekbone that he'd missed with his electric razor. His light brown eyelashes curled so dramatically they looked fake. It was almost painful to be this close to him and not actually touch him. Boldly, she pressed her head into his chest and sighed sleepily in her best Audrey Hepburn voice, "Thank heaven for king-size beds."

On Nate's other side, Serena tapped out her cigarette in an empty martini glass, unbuttoned her still-snow-dampened Earl jeans, and slithered out of them. Then she rolled over, slipping one long, always-tanned, perfect leg around one of Nate's khaki-clad knees. He was just a great big yummy teddy bear, perfect for snuggling. And one day soon she would get up the courage to slip her hands underneath his shirt and kiss him, really kiss him.

One day soon, please.

It was a blessing he was drunk or Nate wouldn't have been able to stand it. Even with three martinis swirling around in his belly, his khakis were getting tighter and tighter in a certain zippered area. He loved both Serena and Blair, he really did, and they were both so hot. He even liked *Breakfast at Tiffany's* a little better the second time around. But one thing had occurred to him while he was watching it again: everyone seemed so repressed. All the girls wore makeup and the guys wore hats and they all stayed fully clothed the whole time. It just made him want to . . . want to . . .

Nate was fifteen going on sixteen and tired of being a virgin. Finding himself the cheddar in a Serena-Blair grilled cheese sandwich didn't help matters either—it just made him hornier than heck. But how could he choose between them? They were both so much a part of him it felt wrong to imagine one of them naked. He crossed his ankles, throwing off Serena's leg. Maybe it would be better if he remained their best friend, eunuchlike and asexual—at least as far as his two best friends were concerned—while he found some other girl to finally do it with. Just to get it out of his system.

Um, not exactly what either of them had in mind.

"Let's stay together like this forever," Serena murmured sleepily, burrowing her nose into Nate's warm neck. Then she remembered that her parents wanted to send her to boarding school next year. She squeezed her enormous navy blue eyes shut, but she no longer felt tired. Her long, nearly black eyelashes fluttered against Nate's neck as she opened her eyes again. His breathing slowed as he drifted into dreamland. Blair was already wheezing and whistling in her sleep, the way she always did when she'd been drinking and smoking. Serena lifted her head to look at them, both fast asleep in an adorable, cozy heap, like puppies that had played too hard.

In Mrs. Warwick's English class they'd been reading *The Picture of Dorian Gray* by Oscar Wilde. In it, this guy Dorian stays young and beautiful while the portrait some painter paints of him ages and gets ugly. Serena cupped her hands around her eyes and clicked her tongue, pretending to take a picture of her friends that would freeze them like this, together and forever perfect. She bent down and lightly kissed Nate's cheek, breathing in the wonderful sandalwood soap smell of him and dampening his skin with her tears. She was crying because she loved both him and Blair, and she was never happier than when she was with them. How could she leave her two best friends?

And maybe she was crying because the idea of Blair and Nate snuggling on his parents' bed *without* her was simply too much to bear.

Disclaimer: All the real names of places, people, and events have been altered or abbreviated to protect the innocent. Namely, me.

hey people!

watch out, liz smith

Much to my surprise, this tell-all business comes quite naturally to me. The only thing I cannot share is my own identity. Many of you are already clamoring for it, but alas, I operate under a strict don't-ask-don't-tell policy, so don't even bother. You might want to tell me all sorts of *other* juicy stuff, which is entirely welcome. I'm totally easy when it comes to gossip—I'll listen to anything. After all, I descend from a long line of glamorous gossips and advice columnists, including Dear Abby, Hedda Hopper, Simon Doonan, and Liz Smith. Not that I'm actually related to any of them by blood, but I can feel them in my veins. So give me the scoop!

sightings

B fighting with her dad in **Ferragamo** on **Fifth and Fifty-second Street**. She's scary when she's angry, but she finally did calm down long enough to try on and make Daddy buy six—count 'em, six—pairs of cute satin ballet flats in jewel shades. **S** with her mom in **Frette** buying Italian flannel sheets in twin size X-long. Where's she going, sleepaway camp? **N** flirting with a gaggle of French girls from **L'École** in front of that pizzeria on Eighty-sixth and Madison. Pardonnez-moi, but hands off—he's already spoken for, by more than one girl.

the *l* word

We're young, we're not completely freaking out about college yet, and we still make major fashion mistakes and social faux pas and totally get away with them. Why bother with love now when we're so footloose and fancy free? The obvious answer: boredom. We need to stir things up a little, and because we're bored, not boring, we have no qualms about telling our best friends that after all these years of friendship, all we can think about is them—naked. I know, I know, I can already hear you squealing, *Ew!* But just imagine that your best friend is **N**—who could *not* think about him with his shirt off and taking your shirt off with him? I mean, come on!

There, I've said it. I'm in love with him too. Et vous? Or am I enough for you?

You know you just can't get enough of me,

just another manic school day

"Need I remind you boys that winter is almost over and we'll soon be playing our dicks off? I don't care if you're cold. Run! Hit the fucker! Get yer stick up!" Coach Michaels shouted at the St. Jude's School for Boys' varsity lacrosse team. The boys were running drills in the corner of Sheep Meadow in Central Park beneath a gray, sunless sky. Frozen balls of ice crunched beneath their cleat-clad feet. Most of the boys wore shorts, as if to prove how studly they were, impervious to the cold.

Talk about impervious. Coach Michaels was wearing the same hunter green Lands' End windbreaker he'd worn all fall and all spring. Either he had some serious polypropylene ultra-warm, ultrathin long johns on underneath it, or he was totally insensitive to heat or cold or much else, which was most likely the case. "Archibald, just because you're my youngest player doesn't mean you can be the pansiest. Goodred, grab Archibald and do some relays. Shove your stick up his ass!"

The other boys snickered. Coach Michaels was famous for his foul mouth and absurd commands. He never said what he meant, or if he did, there was no way the boys could actually do what he said. But they got the picture. He wanted them to run hard, take command of the ball, pass accurately, and score. He was a good coach and they usually won. Plus, he recognized talent. Nate was only a sophomore, but Coach Michaels had swiped him from the junior varsity team "to give him bigger balls."

Luke Goodred, the varsity team captain, cupped Nate's crotch with the basket on the end of his beaten up Brine lacrosse stick and pretended to toss Nate's growing balls over the trees bordering the park and out onto Central Park West.

Splat!

Luke was tall and skinny with curly reddish brown hair, Mick Jagger lips, and nervous brown eyes. He would have been pegged a geek if he weren't so confident and such an ace lacrosse player. "You're wearing sweats," he observed wryly. "I bet you're still a virgin. Jesus, Archibald. How can you spend all your time with those two smokin' babes and still be a virgin?" Luke took great pride in knowing the sexual status of every player on his team and did his best to help the virgins get devirginized. "You ever talk to L'Wren anymore?"

Nate shrugged. "She's in college," he responded before chasing after the ball.

Luke ran after him. "Well, she's coming back for my party tomorrow. You coming?"

Normally it would be strange for a senior to invite a sophomore to his party, but something about Nate transcended class hierarchies. Perhaps it was the fact that he never went anywhere without his two gorgeous female friends, Blair Waldorf and Serena van der Woodsen, making him welcome basically anywhere. He was still trying to figure out exactly who he was, just like the rest of his fifteen-year-old peers, but he wasn't a dork about it. In fact, it was already sort of obvious that some of the seniors at his school worked very hard to emulate *him*.

"You girls just keep talking!" Coach Michaels yelled at them from across the grass. "Would you like me to bring you some tea and biscuits? This isn't fucking cricket, you morons!"

Luke laughed. "Hey Coach, I'm having a party tomorrow night, wanna come? It's gonna be a freaking orgy, I can already tell!"

Coach Michaels stuffed his hands into the pockets of his windbreaker. "No, thanks. I got my own orgy going on at home!" The entire team winced, their faces wrinkled in a collective grimace. Coach was always talking about himself and his wife like they were the hottest couple alive. The boys had seen Mrs. Michaels' picture on the wall of Coach's office in the gym, and they'd all agreed she looked sort of like Jennifer Aniston. Her dyed red hair was long and wavy, and she had smiling brown eyes and a nice smile. But she wore huge amounts of makeup and sported a pink windbreaker to match the coach's green one. The team's official verdict was that the Michaelses kept their windbreakers on when they did it.

Nice.

As soon as practice was over, Nate texted Serena and Blair, who were across the park, enjoying Double Photography. Double Photography was everyone's favorite. An entire hour and a half to roam around the city unmonitored under the pretense of taking photographs, when what they really did was go to sample sales, get haircuts, buy shoes, or get their eyebrows done. Why waste precious weekend time doing all that stuff when they had Double Photography?

The lights were on in the darkroom, and the lab smelled like fixer and Mr. Beckham's perpetual espresso. The teacher examined his attendance sheet, preparing to pair the girls up to venture outside with their Nikons. Serena's cell phone buzzed in her ice blue Lambertson Truex microhobo. She slipped her hand into the bag and surreptitiously read Nate's text.

COME TO A PARTY WITH ME TOMORROW NIGHT? IT'S AT MY LAX CAPTAIN'S HOUSE SO I HAVE TO GO.

Nate was so cute and helpless—he could never do anything without them.

YES, BABY. OF COURSE WE'LL COME, Serena typed in reply. DON'T FORGET, TOMORROW IS VALENTINE'S DAY.

"Don't move," Blair whispered to her, grabbing Serena's arm. "Mr. Boring is pairing us up. We have to be together," she added, like it was life or death.

"Kati Farkas and Vanessa Abrams," Mr. Beckham droned in his monotone Midwestern accent.

"No fucking way," hissed Vanessa, the strange, combat-boots-wearing girl with waist-length black hair who'd arrived in September from who-knows-where and refused to speak to any-one. "If you think I'm going to walk around taking pictures with Cootie Fungus, you're out of your fucking mind," she stated in a fairly loud voice.

Serena and Blair exploded into howls of laughter. Cootie Fungus? Now why hadn't they thought of that?

Vanessa was wearing the navy blue and white checked bloomers—yes, bloomers—the lower school girls were required to wear for gym class, over a pair of black leggings, like an Anna Sui model who'd lost her skirt.

Well, at least she was still in uniform.

"Excuse me?" Kati whined, putting her hands on her pale, exposed hips. Kati preferred to wear cropped pastel-colored Polo or Lacoste shirts paired with the same teensy-weensy uniform skirts she'd been wearing since sixth grade. She left the skirts unbuttoned and folded over at the waist, so they were super low and super short. "Mr. Beckham? Shouldn't she be, like, expelled for saying that to me or something?"

Mr. Beckham ignored her. Vanessa was the most talented photographer in his class, and he wasn't about to get her expelled or even suspended when she might very well make him famous one day. "Whatever," he sighed, as if his students' petty viciousness couldn't have bored him more. "Vanessa, you go with Blair, and Serena, you go with Kati."

"No!" Blair wailed, throwing her arms around Serena and holding on tight.

"It's all right," Serena whispered, shaking off Blair's death grip. She'd thought she might use the next two periods to finally tell Blair about boarding school next year, but Blair had been acting so jumpy ever since she'd overheard her dad talking dirty to someone in his dressing room, Serena couldn't bear to freak her out even more.

"I have to go to Barneys anyway, and you've already been there twice this week," she reminded her gently. Blair had a terrible habit of going to Barneys during lunch or immediately after school, even if it meant being late for all the extracurriculars that were supposed to be getting her into Yale, like French Club, tennis, Princeton Review, and the new Junior Board at the Guggenheim Museum of Art. Besides, Serena hated shopping with Blair because Blair was so competitive about it. Before they checked out, she'd have to compare what she was buying to what Serena was buying, and if Serena had one more skirt than she did, or a dress in an unusual print, then Blair would have to scour the racks for some equally fabulous purchase. Today Serena wanted to buy something cute to wear to the party Nate had just invited them to tomorrow night, and she didn't really want Blair to see what she picked out. Plus, it might be nice to have Kati along to hold her stuff.

Wannabes do have their uses.

"And don't forget to submit your photographs to Vanessa's new magazine," Mr. Beckham reminded them. "It's a wonderful way to showcase your talent," he added halfheartedly.

Vanessa rolled her eyes. That morning she'd taped two brown paper bags to the walls of the Constance Billard lunchroom. One of the bags was labeled ART and the other WRITING, with a sign above them that said SCHOOL ARTS MAG SUBMISSIONS. So far both bags remained empty, which was fine with her. She'd taken plenty of photographs to fill up the magazine, and maybe she could just scatter in a few random quotes, like the one scrawled on the bathroom wall of her favorite falafel restaurant in Williamsburg: *Youth is wasted on the young.*

The girls sprinted upstairs to their third-floor lockers to retrieve their coats. Constance Billard had recently redecorated its hallways in gold and silver—gold walls and silver lockers, gold carpet and silver paint on the ceilings. The idea was that the girls would spend less time on their appearance and more time on their studies if the school out-glitzed them all.

Nice try.

A carefully folded piece of paper was sticking out of one of the slats in the silver metal of Serena's locker door. She removed the piece of paper and unfolded it, hastily reading as she shrugged

on the new brown Burberry plaid wool coat her mother had
bought her in London last month.

> *Nothing hurt until you pushed me, hard, and I fell.*
> *And I'm falling still. Still falling.*
> *Can't you see me from up there? The water's clear.*
> *It's becoming—no, I'm becoming*
> *Clearer and clearer still.*
> *Can't you see me?*

"What is that?" Kati peered nosily over Serena's shoulder at
the piece of paper as she buttoned up her new orange mohair
coat that looked almost exactly like the orange cashmere Marni
coat Serena had worn the whole first part of the winter. "Did
you write that?"

"No," Serena responded, rereading the poem. "Someone left
it here for me, I think."

"Ew!" Kati shrieked, tucking her overly blow-dried strawberry blond hair behind her rather prominent ears. "That is so
scary. I would so get a bodyguard right now if I were you."

Serena shrugged her shoulders. She was used to being
admired, and it was kind of flattering to have a poem written
expressly for her, even if the poem was kind of dark and morbid
and fucked up and she had no idea who'd written it. She tucked
the white piece of paper into her pocket and slung the strap of
her Nikon camera around her neck. Then she folded the waistband of her navy blue pleated uniform skirt over, shortening
the skirt so that it barely covered her navy blue tights–clad butt
cheeks. One thing she wouldn't miss if she went to boarding
school was Constance's horrible uniforms.

"Come on, Kati, let's go find something cute in purple velvet. Every girl should own some purple velvet, don't you think?"

Kati's vaguely hazel eyes lit up with excitement. "Really?" she cried.

Definitely.

v helps b notice the little things

"It's just so pink," Vanessa observed, kneeling down on the dirty ice to get another close-up photograph of the wad of spat-out chewing gum just outside Constance Billard's massive blue-painted wooden doors.

She'd been photographing the gum for almost half an hour, and Blair wanted to strangle her. Blair could not believe she was walking around with someone wearing bloomers, which were basically puffy navy-blue-and-white-checked underwear, in public. "Our pictures are all black-and-white anyway, remember?" she snapped. "Can we go now?"

Of course Vanessa knew perfectly well what kind of film was loaded in her camera. "I just want to get it from one more angle," she replied distractedly, lying down on her back on the sidewalk and holding the camera upside down over the piece of gum. She fought back an attack of the giggles. Wow, was it fun to annoy Blair.

Will it still be fun when her camera gets chucked onto Fifth Avenue?

"Jesus," Blair muttered, yanking her vibrating cell phone from the pocket of her kelly green Marc Jacobs Jackie O coat with the gigantic tortoiseshell buttons. "Hello, Mother," she said coldly. "I'm glad you finally found the time to return my calls." Blair had left four messages for her mother since yesterday, having decided the night before last that she had to tell her about the incident with her father in his dressing room. Of course, she saw her parents nearly every morning before school—her father insisted on family breakfasts during the week—but she needed to speak to her mother alone.

"I'm sorry, honey, but you know how busy I am this time of year. Spring is coming and there are just so many benefits to plan. I wish there were three of me!" Eleanor exclaimed.

Blair rolled her eyes. There already *were* three of her. Over the past month her mother had gotten extremely fat on some ridiculous French diet which required her to eat a steak a day and an entire wheel of brie a week. Blair squatted down on the sidewalk and rummaged around in her bag for her white TSE cashmere scarf. She wasn't wearing any tights, and she was freezing her ass off. "I just thought you should know that last weekend I caught Daddy hiding in his dressing room, having this gross conversation with another woman while you were tasting food for the Guggenheim benefit," Blair blurted out. "He's having an affair. I'm sure of it."

Like most mothers and daughters, they had a complicated love-hate relationship. Blair thought her mother had a right to know what she'd seen and heard, but telling her was a sort of challenge, as if to say, "Here's the deal, Droopyass. Now what are you going to do about it?" Not that Blair really wanted her parents to fight or split up or whatever, but it would certainly add drama to her life.

And we all need drama.

"Oh, I'm sure you just misheard him, sweetie," Eleanor replied in her chirpiest "this information does not compute" voice. It was all Blair could do not to hang up on her. "Daddy has been working very hard lately. He was probably just practicing for a case or something."

Blair's father was a patent lawyer who specialized in pharmaceuticals and footwear. Blair was pretty damned sure he wasn't working on any cases for Ernest and Julio Gallo.

She found the scarf and stood up to wind it around her neck, only to find that Vanessa had left. She whirled around, her mother's overly perky voice still chattering in the background. "I thought maybe we could go to Bergdorf's after school," she was saying. "I haven't been there in weeks, and you need a new spring coat."

It was a gray, dank February day and the air smelled like cold mashed potatoes. Dirty slush crowded the curbs, and even the bright yellow taxis looked cold. It was the kind of day that made Blair want to put on her favorite Missoni knit bikini and elope with Nate to St. Barts.

Across Madison Avenue Blair caught sight of Vanessa's wide, bloomered butt sashaying down Ninety-third Street toward Park Avenue, her long jet-black hair billowing out behind her in the damp, winter wind. Blair started to follow her, walking quickly. The phone call with her mother seemed totally irrelevant since her mother wasn't listening to her anyway. It was much more important that Vanessa know that *she* was the one who was supposed to decide where they were going. She'd wanted to take pictures of the cute new baby ducklings swimming in the reservoir in Central Park, but Vanessa was walking east, away from the park.

"I gotta go, Mom. I'll see you later, unless you're going out."

"Your father's taking me to some Wagner opera. *Boring.*"

"Okay. 'Bye!" Blair cut her off and dashed across Park Avenue to chase after Vanessa. Her taupe Prada ankle boots were not exactly running shoes, and they were getting completely slush-stained. "What the fuck?" she panted, catching up to her class-mate.

"I thought your conversation sounded private," Vanessa explained without slowing down. "And I was finished with the gum."

"So now where are you going?" Blair was annoyed that she'd even followed Vanessa when what she really wanted to do was pop into Starbucks and buy a venti hot chocolate with extra whipped cream.

"I just have a quick errand," Vanessa announced vaguely as she spotted the thing she'd been looking for. She turned down Lexington Avenue, walked halfway down the block, and pushed open the door to a closet-size men's barbershop.

"What the—" Blair hesitated and then followed her inside. The barbershop smelled like air freshener and bus exhaust, and the barber was wearing oversize white nurse shoes and a weird red patent leather belt, like a serial killer who moonlighted as a clown. He draped a black polyester tablecloth-like thing over Vanessa's shoulders and sat her down on one of the two worn maroon pleather barber's chairs.

Reluctantly Blair perched on the other chair to wait. There were no magazines in the shop, not even a *Sports Illustrated.* Just one copy of some newspaper called *Il Recordo* that wasn't even in English. This better be quick. "Your hair is so healthy looking," Blair observed, making friendly conversation to keep from being completely bored out of her mind. "I was thinking you must trim it every few weeks to keep it looking like that." *But in a dump like this?*

Vanessa ignored her classmate and stared straight ahead at the mirrored wall, a smirk on her thin, red lips. The barber pumped a lever with his foot to raise the chair and then ran his hands through her thick, black waist-length hair. "Just a nice trim, miss? Two or three inches maybe?" he asked politely.

Vanessa took a deep breath. "Actually, I'd like you to shave it, please," she commanded. "Shave it all off."

Come again?

She caught Blair's shocked stare in the mirror in front of her. With her lush, tenderly cared-for chestnut locks, bright green designer coat, taupe patent leather ankle boots, expensive-looking oversize orange leather handbag, and her glossy pink pout, Blair looked completely out of place in the crummy, masculine barbershop. Even Vanessa looked out of place. But not for long.

The barber nodded and snipped the air with his scissors a few times, as if he couldn't wait to chop into all that hair. He clasped the ends with his hands and got ready to hack away.

"Stop!" Blair gasped, as if it were her own hair. "You can't do that!"

Vanessa turned halfway around in the barber's chair. "Why not? It's my hair."

Snip, snip! An enormous clump of thick black strands fell onto the gray linoleum floor.

Not anymore.

Blair stared at the hair, lying in a messy pile near the toe of the barber's ugly white lace-up shoes. She couldn't imagine chopping all her hair off like that, especially not when it was as long and luxurious as Vanessa's was. Some of it was probably her baby hair!

"You should at least save it," she advised, crossing and recrossing her legs uncomfortably. "Or give it to charity. Serena and I both got bobs at Kute Kuts on Madison in fourth grade, and if you have at least five inches of hair, they donate it to a charity that makes wigs for children with leukemia. Braid Aid I think it's called. It's a really good cause."

Vanessa's smirk wrinkled into a frown. Donating the hair wasn't a bad idea, but it kind of took away from the shock factor of shaving it off. Unless she could get Blair to shave *her* head, too. In fact, why didn't the whole class, no, the whole school shave their heads if it was such a good fucking cause? She could already picture the headline on Page Six of the *New York Post*: "Selfless Constance Billard girls shave heads for sick children!"

Like that would ever happen.

The barber spritzed Vanessa's head with water and began to buzz the thick dark hair at the nape of her neck with an electric razor. "You may as well take some pictures of this," she suggested to Blair. "It's all in the name of art."

Blair snapped away with Vanessa's digital Nikon. She really didn't need to document the event herself. It wasn't exactly something she'd forget. She had to admit, though, Vanessa did have a nice head—free of bald spots, blemishes, or scars. It almost looked . . . *good* shaved. And her eyes seemed bigger, browner, and somehow prettier now. The barber sprinkled baby powder on the back of her pale, clean-shaven neck and then whisked it off with a giant brush exactly like the one Blair used with her favorite Chanel translucent oil-blotting face powder.

"Good?" he asked, as if he could have made it look any different. She was basically hairless.

Vanessa considered her reflection in the mirror. She certainly didn't look like a Constance Billard schoolgirl now. She was just herself—totally unaccessorized, un-made-up, and unadorned. What a coup to have started her own arts magazine *and* created her very own alternative image all in one day. "It's perfect." She slipped out of the maroon chair and stood up. The barber unsnapped the black sheet, tucked it under his arm, and brushed off her black sweater with a stiff lint brush. "Would you mind sweeping up my hair and putting it into a little baggie or something?" she asked politely. "My friend here wants to donate it to charity."

Blair's mouth opened. Who the fuck did Vanessa think she was anyway? Swiftly he swept up the mound of black tresses, shoved it into a large plastic freezer bag, and tucked the Ziploc into Blair's dark orange Jimmy Choo bag like he was doing her a massive favor.

Blair followed Vanessa out of the barbershop and deposited the plastic bag in the nearest sidewalk trash bin. *Ew, ew, ew!* It looked like a dead animal. She fished around in her bag for a bottle of Purell sanitizing hand gel.

"It's all right," Vanessa assured her. "I took a shower last month, so the cooties shouldn't be too bad." She giggled and ran her hand over her freshly shorn scalp, loving the clean, bristly feel. Blair glared at her and Vanessa glared back. Making her Constance Billard classmates hate her was an intrinsic part of the image she was cultivating, and out of all the people in her class, it was very important to her that Blair Waldorf hate her the most.

Well, let's just say she's off to a brilliant start.

b-r-e-a-s-t—find out what it means to me!

They were so perfect. Even if she finally got some of her own, they'd probably never be like that. Tan and round with a little blond fuzz on them. Okay, so now she sounded like the biggest pervert in the universe, even if no one could actually hear her thoughts. But it wasn't as if she could hide it, she was totally obsessed. If only there was something she could take to make her own grow just the tiniest bit bigger. . . .

Jenny took one last, long look at the picture of Serena she'd just discovered on a Web site called Model Shoppers, featuring snapshots of models coming out of the changing rooms in stores like Barneys and Bendel's. Serena wasn't a model, but she'd certainly fooled the photographers. Wearing only a simple white triangle-top bikini, everything about her was perfect, especially her perfectly sized breasts.

Hastily, Jenny typed "bigger breasts" into the search engine at the top of the page. Serena's picture vanished, replaced by the 2,407 search results. *Bigger Breasts and a heightened libido in only three weeks. Feel better, look better, without weight gain. Low risk of side effects. The alternative to surgery!* Ignoring the totally pornographic links like seemygreattitz.net, Jenny scanned down the list, pausing when she read the words *all natural, risk-free* with a link to a site called noknockers.com. It was a stupid name but it sounded safe. She clicked on the link and read through the list of ingredients of a 100 percent organic, all-natural breast enhancement supplement called MammaGro. Yams, fenugreek, something called kavu root from Thailand, barley. They really did sound totally harmless, but MammaGro cost $300 for a four-month supply, which was how long the Web site claimed you had to take the pills for them to have their full effect. In the testimonials at the bottom of the page, some women claimed to have gotten great results in even less time. *"From a B cup to a C in two weeks! I'm so excited. So is my boyfriend!"*

Jenny's fingers hovered over the keyboard. She'd have to order them in her dad's name, because you had to be over eighteen, and she'd have to use his credit card number, which she'd memorized, because she didn't have one of her own. The Discover card was supposed to only be for emergencies, but the truth was, her lack of any sign of breasts whatsoever had reached emergency proportions.

She filled in the appropriate information and hit "order now."

Thank you!

"Jenny, may I talk to you for a minute?" someone whispered directly behind her, causing Jenny to leap out of her seat with embarrassment. Her hand flew to the little button at the bottom of the computer monitor, flicking it off before anyone could see what she'd been doing. She'd totally forgotten that she was in the computer lab at school, presumably downloading fonts for the yearbook staff who liked to use smart seventh graders like her for cheap labor.

Jenny spun around to see her art teacher, Ms. Monet, whom she despised, even though art was her favorite subject. She was convinced that Ms. Monet had become an art teacher simply because of her last name, proving that she had absolutely no imagination. The thing was, Ms. Monet knew nothing about art. She made her students paint the most boring and predictable still lifes of bananas and plums and refused to use the word *blue*, preferring the word *azure* instead. Apparently blue was just blue to her, whereas to Jenny blue was as limitless and exciting as her future.

Or the robin's egg blue Balenciaga bag in the latest Barneys catalog.

Jenny perched on the computer desk and folded her arms in front of her, affecting the completely innocent stance of someone who has not just ordered breast enhancement supplements over the Internet. "Yes?" she responded querulously.

Ms. Monet handed her a mustard-yellow sheet of paper. CONSTANCE BILLARD HYMNAL DESIGN CONTEST was typed in big bold letters at the top.

WINNER WILL BE CREDITED AS THE DESIGNER OF OUR ONE-OF-A-KIND HYMNALS TO BE USED IN WEEKLY SCHOOL ASSEMBLIES AND CHERISHED FOR GENERATIONS TO COME. ILLUSTRATE AND DESIGN THE PAGES FOR EACH HYMN. TO ENTER, CHOOSE YOUR FAVORITE HYMN TO ILLUSTRATE AND DESIGN IN THE FORM OF YOUR CHOOSING.

GRADES 9–12. DEADLINE MARCH 1. RESULTS WILL BE ANNOUNCED IN JUNE.

GOOD LUCK, GIRLS!

MRS. MCLEAN, HEADMISTRESS

The sign had been up ever since the girls returned from winter break last month. Since she was only in seventh grade, Jenny had ignored it.

"I knew at once that this was perfect for you," Ms. Monet told her in a loud whisper. The diminutive teacher was wearing a paint-splattered white men's button-down shirt over black tuxedo pants and flat black boots. She wore black Ray-Ban frames with green lenses in them and kept her gray-blond hair cropped in a severe chin-length bob. She probably thought she looked hip and artistic, but Jenny suspected she had merely copied someone else's style.

Meryl Streep in *Devil Wears Prada* meets Bono?

Jenny pursed her lips. There was a strict no-talking rule in the computer lab, and the proctor—some male math teacher with a bristly brown mustache—was frowning at them. "It says grades nine through twelve," she responded quietly. "I'm in seventh."

Ms. Monet pushed her glasses up on her long, bulbous nose and shook her head. "Don't worry about that. You're the most talented artist in this school."

"I'll think about it." Jenny tucked her curly brown hair behind her ears in the same oh-so-poised-but-casual manner she'd seen Serena van der Woodsen employ when she spoke to her teachers. Of course she was dying to enter the contest, but no way was she about to admit it.

"Well, good." Ms. Monet pushed her Ray-Bans to the top of her head as if to suggest that what she had to say was too important for glasses. "Just submit some of those wonderful angels you scribbled in the margins of that pop quiz on Dalí I gave last week. And a page of calligraphy. Your calligraphy is remarkable."

Jenny stared at her. Angels? Angels? She'd never drawn any angels. The bell rang suddenly and the girls at the desks around hers began to pack up their belongings and leave. Jenny bent down to collect her dark purple nylon Le Sportsac backpack. Angels. What angels? Then she remembered. They weren't angels, they were pictures of Serena, so blond and golden and perfect that of course she looked like an angel.

"I've got to run to my fifth-grade class." Ms. Monet smiled fakely, her chapped, lipstick-free lips sliding across her coffee-stained teeth. "I'll keep my fingers crossed for you!"

Even though she was late for English, Jenny sat down in front of the computer again. The hymnals were distributed on every girl's chair before assembly so they could read or sing along with Mrs. McLean to the Lord's Prayer or hymns like "Hark! The Herald Angels Sing." To think that her secret doodles of Serena might be printed hundreds of times over in the same hymnals that the entire student body saw almost every day was unthinkably bizarre.

But then a sudden shiver of excitement crept inside the turned-up cuffs of Jenny's black wool Old Navy V-neck sweater and wriggled its way up her arms and into her chest. Maybe she would win. And with that and bigger boobs, she just might become something one day—something more than just curly-haired, petite, and forgettable.

Don't forget ambitious. We'd be nowhere without ambition.

the only thing assholes are good for

"You better grab a copy while I still have some, man," Chuck Bass whispered loudly across the space between his desk and Dan's. He shoved a large, glossy black-and-white photograph of his own head and bare upper torso in Dan's direction. "I just got back from Berlin last night where I did this cologne ad? German chicks are fucking awesome." Charles Bartholomew Bass, the only child of Bartholomew and Misty Bass, and heir to the Bass leather and luxury goods fortune, was tall and handsome in a cheesy men's underwear or aftershave ad type of way. His carefully coiffed dark hair was thick and shiny, he sported a fake-looking tan, his cheeks were overmoisturized, and his glassy blue eyes gleamed lewdly. Chuck wore a gold monogrammed pinky ring and, in winter, a navy blue cashmere scarf with a gold monogram, as if to demonstrate to everyone that he was in love with every aspect of himself, including his own initials.

Dan was generally a very nice boy, but when this particular Riverside Prep classmate spoke to him, his automatic physical response was to wrinkle his nose in absolute disgust. He pretended to be lost in thought, dreaming up the next stanza of the new poem he was writing for Serena, even though they were in geometry, but his eyes couldn't help but wander to Chuck's annoying head shot.

"I'm serious, man, take it while it's still fresh."

Dan flashed a disparaging half-smile and tucked the photograph inside his grubby black messenger bag. "Thanks." He went back to musing on Serena's unbelievable beauty, his gnawed-on blue Bic pen poised over a fresh page in his black leather-bound notebook.

Chuck didn't get the hint. "You think if I give these out at that party tomorrow night Serena van der Woodsen will finally give in and let me see her naked? After all, tomorrow is Valentine's Day."

Dan blinked. Suddenly he didn't mind Chuck's ridiculous stench of man perfume. "What party?"

Chuck leaned his elbows on Dan's desk. "While I'm here, do you have the answers to the worksheet Miss Porkbutt handed out yesterday? I was gonna do it at lunch, but then my agent called to ask if I could shoot an ad for Axe in Reykjavík this Sunday. As if I need to work so badly I'm willing to lose my dick to frostbite."

Their geometry teacher, Miss Pohrbet, was forever leaving the room for five minutes and then coming back, either to test them or because she had some sort of bladder problem and had to go to the bathroom a lot. Presently she was out of the room. Dan handed over his completed worksheet. Saying no and then arguing with Chuck would require too much energy—and besides, it was only math. "What party?" he repeated insistently.

Chuck grabbed the worksheet. "Just some senior from St.

Jude's," he explained vaguely as he hastily copied down the answers. "But everyone will be there."

Everyone. Translation: Serena.

Dan nodded. "Do you think it would be weird if I went?"

Chuck shoved the worksheet back at him. "What the fuck do I care? You could go or not go," he growled dismissively, indicating that he was no longer interested in talking to Dan. "But if you do go, maybe you could try not wearing pants from the giveaway bin at the Salvation Army."

Dan glanced down at his faded black corduroys. They were from Old Navy and had been new once—sometime last year. Other than his brown cords and the green track pants he wore sometimes to play basketball in the park, they were the only pants he had. Rufus wasn't into shopping, and although Dan had to follow Riverside Prep's tan, black, gray, or navy blue slacks and plain collared shirts dress code, he liked that he looked a little retro and a little scruffier than his khaki-clad classmates. But would Serena be revolted by his faded clothes and generally unkempt appearance? Maybe he was just beginning the descent down a slippery slope. Before he knew it he'd be tying his hair up with twist ties or pieces of garbage bags, just like his father.

Best get himself to a department store tout de suite!

Dan pulled his cell phone out of his bag and discreetly texted his only friend in the world besides his little sister.

GOING 2 THE GAP AFTER SCHOOL WANT 2 COME? he typed hurriedly. Cell phone use was strictly forbidden in school—not that everyone and his kindergarten-age little brother didn't break that rule on a daily basis.

YES UR GAYNESS, Zeke Freedman texted back from across the room. WHAT'S THE OKSION?

Dan was about to invite Zeke to the party with him, but the fact was the other boys in their class called the big-hipped, acne-prone physics and basketball whiz Zeke the Geek. It was probably best not to advertise their friendship when his ultimate goal was to talk to Serena.

MY ASS GREW, Dan typed back, feeling guilty—but not that guilty—for neglecting to mention the party or his reason for going. He preferred to avoid being berated by Zeke for getting a haircut, shaving, and wearing new jeans for a girl who had no clue he even existed. If Serena took a chance and smiled at him, or even better, said something, Zeke would be forgotten so fast it would be as if he'd never existed anyway.

So much for loyalty.

Dan flipped open his notebook as a rush of words flooded his mind.

It's not the idea of me. It's me. Whether you know me or don't,
We're the same sameness.
So pretend. It's just pretend. Pretend that you know me.
That we're in love. Just pretend. That's the idea.
That's it.

Blushing as his pen flew across the page, Dan felt his palms grow more and more damp and he bit his lower lip. He was the next e. e. cummings! The next Robert Frost! The next Wallace Stevens. Of course he'd never let Serena read this one. *Pretend that we're in love?* He'd rather be thrown into a pit full of vipers first. But he could pretend that she'd read it when he saw her at the party. It would be his own little Valentine to himself.

Which is slightly sad, but also extremely cute.

it's not a party without a hairless crasher

Did you ever wonder what happens after a pet dies? Well, my family's German shorthaired pointer died last week of stomach cancer and it was really sad. I know it sounds dumb but I believe in dog heaven. Stella visits me in my sleep and licks my hand. And then I give her one of her favorite treats: caviar on a water biscuit. She also loved white wine and she used to eat the cigar butts out of my dad's ashtray, which was how she got stomach cancer. . . .

At first Vanessa was going to ditch the story but then she decided to keep it in the "yes" pile. After all, the girl who had written it was only in eighth grade. And so far it was the only written submission besides a poem by a junior, which she absolutely refused to publish.

> *My Boyfriend*
> *He makes me laugh and tells me I'm pretty*
> *And I feel even prettier each time*
> *He is so funny I can't stop laughing*
> *I'm even laughing now*

We went to the beach and he said I was pretty
We went ice-skating and he said I was pretty
He fell down and then I fell down
And we were laughing and then he kissed me

She couldn't decide whether the so-called poet was a complete idiot or exquisitely profound. Regardless, the poem was so annoying it was the perfect first entry for what was bound to be a great big reject pile. Vanessa tossed the poem in the "no" pile on top of a pathetic drawing of some girl's foot that looked more like a chicken leg. She stood up from the dust-moted floor of her bedroom and threw open the grimy window, letting in a cold blast of sugar-factory air. Happy cheeseball bullshit like that poem made her blood boil. She felt completely full of . . . rancor. The dark baby fuzz of hair on top of her newly shorn head stood on end, and a slow smile spread across her bitter mouth. *Rancor.* It was a perfect name for her magazine—angry, unusual, and slightly intimidating.

Kind of like someone we know.

She shoved the slim pile of papers back into her black canvas backpack and headed into the bathroom. Anyway, what was she doing working on a Friday night when she had a party to go to?

Standing in front of the soap-scum-smeared bathroom mirror, she squirted Bed Head antifrizz gel on her hand and rubbed it on her nearly bald head just for fun. She hated Valentine's Day and hadn't planned on going to any sort of party tonight, but yesterday Blair had gotten five text messages about tonight's festivities while they were out taking pictures in Double Photography, and the idea of showing up unexpectedly just to shock and piss off her coolest classmates was so delightful that she couldn't resist.

Technically, Vanessa had never been to a party in the city before. Parties in Vermont consisted of a bunch of losers in football jerseys drinking skunky Busch beer out of a keg in somebody's moldy basement rec room or out in a field. A Manhattan Upper East Side private school party was probably exactly the same, except for the surroundings, the clothes, and the beer. Actually, there probably wouldn't be any beer, just vintage scotch and 100-proof vodka. But Vanessa wasn't much of a drinker anyway. She'd only gotten drunk once, with her sister, and she'd wound up sleeping in the bathtub, facedown in a puddle of her own yuckiness.

Of course, she was going under the premise that she was taking her camera. She'd do a photomontage for the magazine—"Assholes in Paradise." A profile of teen excess.

And be honest, who wouldn't want to star in *that*?

you know it's a good cocktail if you can't taste the booze

"What's so funny?" Nate demanded in the brightly lit elevator on the way up to Luke's family's loft in Tribeca's distinguished Elmer Building. Formerly a warehouse for Elmer's glue, the Elmer still smelled vaguely of glue despite its polished granite, chrome surfaces, and Armani-clad doorman. But the fumes had nothing to do with Blair and Serena's uncontrollable giggling.

Serena clapped her gray-cashmere-gloved hands over her freshly glossed mouth, her dark blue eyes huge and bright. She stared meaningfully at Blair's crotch and crossed her ankles, which were all zipped up into a pair of taupe, knee-high, pointy-toed biker boots, care of Miu Miu.

Vroom, vroom.

"Stop it!" Blair squealed gleefully. "At least I'm wearing a longer skirt." Not that fourteen inches could actually be categorized as long. The skirt of her mauve distressed-felt Marc Jacobs pinafore barely covered her thighs. "And stockings."

"That's because you're chicken," Serena declared, pulling up the hem of her brown plaid Burberry coat to reveal her ever-tanned bare knees. Her purple velvet Marni tunic clung to the tops of her upper thighs a good eighteen inches above her boots. Tonight they had decided to experiment with a new look and a new purple, brown, and black color scheme. They were also experimenting with going commando.

It was Serena's idea, of course. Blair had only agreed because she never allowed Serena to think she was bolder or more creative or crazier than she was. Anything Serena would do, Blair could do too, though she'd insisted on wearing sheer black stockings, to at least give the illusion that all her bits were covered, and for warmth's sake. Serena had taken it to the extreme, wearing her shortest dress, which was actually meant to be worn over pants, and nothing else. The idea was that if anyone noticed they weren't wearing underwear, they were looking too hard, and were thus demoted to asshole status. It was also a practical joke on Nate. Making him blush was a constant source of entertainment and excitement. Today was Valentine's Day, and this was their funny Valentine to Nate, complete with temporary red heart tattoos on their butt cheeks.

Oh my!

"Do you have to pee or something?" Nate asked Serena, causing the girls to erupt into a fresh round of snorts and giggles.

The elevator arrived at the tenth floor and opened directly into the loft, which was paved with black and white marble tiles and vibrated with the sound of souped-up old James Brown songs. A curly-haired brunette L'École girl was dancing on the twenty-foot-long polished chrome coffee table, her long legs spread into the sort of stripper stance that comes naturally to slutty French girls. In the open kitchen Luke poured something electric green out of a red Miele blender into crystal tumblers full of ice.

"We're not wearing any underwear!" Serena squeaked loudly as she brushed past Nate and threw her coat down on the pile of coats on the floor in the oversize entryway. She wasn't flirting exactly, just telling the truth.

Likely story.

"I thought we weren't supposed to tell," Blair snapped, flinging her new camel hair Max Mara trench in the general direction of the coat pile with genuine irritation. It was fine for Nate to find out on his own when they were alone, ripping each other's clothes off, but she hadn't exactly planned on advertising the fact that she'd gone out without her Hanros. How embarrassing.

"I'm not wearing any either," a tall girl with shoulder-length dark hair highlighted in shades of python and fox confided in a husky voice from across the entryway. Her Chanel Jet–painted toenails peeked out from beneath the hem of a long black halter dress. Her cleavage was so wide and so deep she probably could have carried a Yorkshire terrier in it quite comfortably. Blair, Serena, and Nate stared at her, each experiencing their own cocktail of resentment, envy, and desire. The girl put her hands on her hips and pouted her dark red lips at Nate. "Remember me?"

"Hey L'Wren," he barely mumbled. He'd wanted to sound a lot more surprised so Blair and Serena wouldn't think he'd only wanted to come to the party to see L'Wren, but seeing her ridiculously hot body made him forget himself. All he had to do was untie that knot at the back of her neck and her dress would fall off and then she'd be naked. Oh boy.

Blair grabbed Serena's elbow and dug her nails into it. *Who the fuck was L'Wren?*

"Come on, Natie, let's go get a drink," Serena commanded

briskly. Those green cocktails Luke was making looked yummy. Her plan was to prop herself up on one of those high-backed leather bar stools at the kitchen counter and drink enough of them not to care anymore who saw her butt.

Among other things.

"Actually, I've prepared something special for you in Lukie's room, *Natie*." L'Wren raised her barely there black eyebrows and held out her hand. "Come check it out."

Nate followed her dutifully down the hall, leaving Blair and Serena behind.

Pant, pant, pant.

"What the fuck?" Blair muttered furiously. Nate was hers, whether he knew it yet or not. How could he possibly already know some slutty girl named L'Wren whom she'd never even laid eyes on before? She tugged down her dress and stomped into the kitchen. "What is that anyway?" she demanded, pointing at the green liquid in the blender on the counter.

Luke grinned. He loved it when pretty girls showed up at his house. It made him feel like a complete success. "Try mine," he offered, holding a crystal tumbler to Blair's lips.

She swallowed half of the green concoction, took a breath, and then finished off the rest. It tasted like Lysol but she didn't give a fuck. "Will you make us some?" she asked, wiping her mouth. Kati and Isabel Coates were on the other side of the room, chain-smoking next to the open window. She stood on her tiptoes and waved to them just as Chuck Bass knelt down behind her, presumably to fetch more ice from the Sub-Zero's ice drawer.

"I thought you were a nice girl," he commented, chucking an ice cube up her skirt. "Are those tattoos?"

Blair glared angrily down at him. Chuck's family and her family lived only four blocks apart and had been friends for generations. He was a complete dick, but there was no escaping him. Of course Chuck was destined to be the first to discover that she wasn't wearing any underwear under her stockings. He'd eagerly tell the universe and then it would be over. That's how it was with lame gossip, Chuck's favorite kind.

"Loser," Serena declared definitively, tossing back her neon green drink. It tasted like Fresca mixed with turpentine and fresh mint. Excellent for the digestion. She grabbed two more and motioned for Blair to follow her. They'd get wasted and smoke cigarettes and Serena would finally tell her all about how her parents wanted her to go to boarding school in the fall. Blair was going to freak, but at least she'd freak less with all this green stuff in her system. What was it anyway—absinthe? Serena lined up the two drinks on the deep windowsill that had been planted with green grass. Then she unsnapped her Fendi button mushroom clutch and retrieved a fresh pack of Parliaments, the only cigarettes she could smoke that didn't give her a sore throat. She popped one between her lips and twiddled another between her fingers, waiting for Blair to finish her ice fight with Chuck so they could talk about more serious matters.

But then Blair's favorite song of the moment came on—that stupid Christmas ensemble rap song with Beyoncé and Jay-Z and all those other rappers. Blair grabbed Chuck's hips and started dancing with him. Serena stubbed out her cigarette and knocked back her second green drink. Discussing the scary future wasn't exactly her idea of fun anyway. Dancing pantyless with a groper like Chuck would be much less stressful.

And that's why she gets invited to all the best parties.

n learns to inhale, among other things

"At first I thought maybe you wouldn't remember me," L'Wren murmured before shoving the bottom half of her face into a pink frosted-glass bong. She sat crosslegged on the floor, flicking her yellow Bic to light the bong and inhaling deeply as the bong water bubbled and churned. Throwing her head back, she paused to enjoy the hit before exhaling a thin stream of gray smoke. "But you seem like the type of boy who'd want to finish what he started," she added, her voice cracking.

She passed the bong and the lighter to Nate, who placed them clumsily in his lap. He'd been offered joints at parties dozens of times, but he wasn't a smoker, and maybe because he didn't inhale properly, he'd never really felt it. Still, he was willing to humor L'Wren.

In more ways than one.

"This is sweet stuff. A couple of hits and I'm going to be all over you," she gushed. "Pot makes me horny."

What doesn't?

Nate flicked the lighter and attempted a hit. He squeezed his eyes and mouth shut, trying to keep the smoke in as he coughed and sputtered. Jesus. He had no idea what a bong hit felt like—not inhaling was not an option. He exhaled and took another hit, determined not to look like such a putz this time. L'Wren watched him with a little smile on her face like she was so proud of her little pot-smoking prodigy she just wanted to squeeze him and pinch him and kiss him to bits.

Who doesn't?

"So." Nate placed the bong in the space between them, ever so careful not to tip it over onto the organic Caribbean sea kelp flokati rug that covered most of the floor in Luke's room. Inexplicably, the entire bedroom had a sort of modern Caribbean theme, with sand-dune-colored walls, aqua-colored silk roman blinds, and bamboo furniture. Nate giggled softly to himself. What a dumb room.

"So, who were those girls you came in with?" L'Wren demanded, picking up where he'd left off. She reached up to adjust the ties on her dress, pushing her chest out and almost knocking the bong over with her boobs.

Girls? What girls?

Nate shrugged. "Just some friends." He grinned slyly at L'Wren's chest, his whole body buzzing. "Let's take your dress off," he added, like it was the most logical suggestion he'd ever made.

L'Wren grabbed the bong and took a long hit. She held the smoke in her mouth and then leaned toward Nate, grabbing the back of his neck and pressing her lips against his. A wave of pot smoke entered his esophagus along with her warm, slippery tongue. *Awesome,* Nate thought stonedly to himself. *Fucking awesome.*

He untied her dress and it fell to the floor, knocking over

the bong and getting it and the floor all stinky and wet. She'd lied—she *was* wearing underwear, but it was so tiny it was barely there.

"See what you've been missing?" L'Wren whispered, unbuttoning his shirt. Outside the room a girl squealed and something scattered noisily on the tiled floor. Nate giggled again as L'Wren kissed him. Man, was this fun. It almost didn't matter what girl he was with. At least not when he was so very stoned and when her body was as hot as L'Wren's. There was nothing better right now than holding this sexy, nearly naked girl who probably didn't even know his last name or that he'd sucked his thumb and had a lisp until he was seven. It didn't matter that he couldn't even remember what college L'Wren went to or why she'd messed with the spelling of her name.

Or that he probably wouldn't remember any of this tomorrow?

bald as a fish out of water

Vanessa already hated the party before she even stepped out of the blindingly bright elevator. What sort of assholes played Christmas-themed rap at a party—any party, especially one in February? Fuckers. She could barely muster the strength to grace them with her nearly bald presence.

Tossing her black-wool-lined waxed canvas military jacket on top of the pile of designer coats in the massive front hall, she stomped into the kitchen and ran a cup of warm water from the tap. Her nose was running and she was getting a cold. She certainly wasn't interested in drinking that disgusting neon green shit everyone was tossing back. She preferred black tea but when pressed would drink plain warm tap water.

"Awesome haircut!" Serena van der Woodsen squealed, flinging her über-blondness in Vanessa's general direction. Maybe it was her imagination, but the air around Serena always seemed to smell like honeysuckle and the girl herself seemed to float a fraction of an inch off the ground, even when she was wearing the most impossible-to-walk-in Jimmy Choos. Vanessa stood patiently sipping her water while Serena fondled her head. "I loved your hair so much. I mean, who has natural black hair *that* healthy and shiny? But this is totally beyond cool. You are so brave," Serena gushed, hugging her.

Vanessa dumped the rest of her water into the sink. She liked Serena more than she liked Blair. Serena seemed less calculatedly fashionable, more effortless somehow, which was probably why the other girls in their class—no, the whole school—resented her so much. Still, it was impossible to have a conversation with someone who knew perfectly well how blond and tall and pretty she was but who pretended to be just like everyone else. "Do you mind if I take your picture?" Vanessa demanded, holding her Nikon in front of her face.

Serena pouted her full, lavender-glossed lips like a pro. "Mais non." She laughed an inebriated laugh and did a little twirl, flipping up the hem of her tiny purple velvet dress and exposing the bottoms of her bare, red-heart-embellished ass cheeks.

Happy Valentine's Day!

Blair Waldorf shimmied over to join her friend. "You really do have a perfectly shaped head," she gushed drunkenly as Vanessa snapped away. The two girls grabbed another pair of neon green beverages off the counter, poured them down their swanlike throats, then turned and flipped up their skirts simultaneously so Vanessa could take a super-special shot. Although neither of them would ever admit it out loud, the only reason they were drinking so much and acting so completely obnoxious was because Nate was ignoring them. He was far too busy with L'Wren, who didn't even love him like Blair and Serena did. She was just using him, and he was using her.

Not a bad deal, actually.

Vanessa felt like the stunt double for a photographer on a

Playboy shoot. "Assholes in Paradise" had taken on a whole new meaning. She personally would rather die than bare her ass to the camera, but there was something riveting about her beautiful classmates' total confidence. They were a superior breed, so flawless they seemed to have nothing to hide.

Not even wobbly bum fat.

"Work it, ladies!" a guy with shaving cream commercial good looks and a creepy smile shouted at them from across the room.

"Did I hire you?" a geeky-looking boy with Mick Jagger lips and overgrown reddish brown hair whispered wetly in Vanessa's ear. "Are you the dude from *Vanity Fair*?" He shoved a green drink at her, barely missing her camera.

Another horrible rap song came on, this one by Diddy or Daddy or whatever the fuck his name was—the guy who used dog fur on the clothes in his fashion line.

Nice.

"Hey, I love this song!" Blair grabbed Vanessa's arm. "Come on, dance with us!"

Vanessa hated rap and she hated dancing. Wiggling her hips around to repetitive beats just wasn't her thing. And the boy with the mouth had just called her "dude."

"You know you want to." Serena breathed alcoholic fumes into her face, waggling her perfectly groomed blond eyebrows like she was making an offer Vanessa positively could not refuse.

Vanessa had to leave right away, or at least get some air. A red EXIT sign flashed over a chrome door with a porthole window that seemed to lead somewhere. And just maybe that somewhere had a hot tub and a view of the Hudson River, and everyone at the party was too drunk and stupid to have discovered it yet.

"Just going to grab a few scenic shots," she mumbled and strode over to the EXIT door. She pushed it open and let it slam closed behind her.

"Fuck!" she gasped as the frigid outside air nearly froze her ears off. She leaned her shoulder into the chrome door, thinking she'd just go back inside, grab her coat, and head for the elevator. But the door didn't budge. She was locked out without a cell phone, wearing only a thin black T-shirt and black jeans, on a fire escape that hung ten floors above a dark lot between the backs of two converted warehouse buildings. No hot tub. No friends inside.

And no hair to keep her warm, poor thing.

in one door and out the other

Dan was terrified that he was going to arrive at the party, wouldn't know a soul, and would be asked to leave right in front of Serena van der Woodsen, who from then on would think him a pathetic loser. He'd decided to walk all the way to Tribeca from the Upper West Side, thinking a brisk stroll in the cool night air would give him a boost of confidence. By the time he'd arrived and had stepped onto the glaringly bright elevator, his wasted, overcaffeinated body was rigid with cold, and his shaggy light brown hair was pasted to his forehead with nervous sweat. The doors slid closed and the floor beneath his feet began to rise. Soon the elevator would open right onto the living room of some guy named Luke Goodred's loft, and Serena would be right there in front of him, staring at his dripping cold sweat.

As if she didn't have better things to do than stand outside the elevator?

The doors opened. The black and white tiled floor was throbbing with daft rap music. A gigantic messy pile of coats lay in his way. Dan kept his coat on for armor and kept his eyes on the black and white floor tiles as he skulked carefully toward the source of the music. Luke Goodred's apartment was a massive black, white, and green loftlike space with gigantic rectangular windows, an open kitchen, and a polished chrome coffee table that was at least a mile long. A group of girls were dancing on the table with neon green drinks in their hands. They shimmied their hips and smiled at one another like they'd all just heard the best secret. Dan patted his pockets and pretended to be looking for his keys as he continued to scan the room for Serena. There were two senior guys from his school, smoking by the windows with two curly-haired French-looking girls in matching dark red lipstick. There was Chuck the Fuck, wearing a black pin-striped double-breasted blazer over a crisp white shirt, pressed dark blue jeans, and brown leather loafers without socks, looking like the poster boy for everything Dan hated and could never be. And dancing with Chuck was Serena and that pretty, dark-haired friend of hers. Their gorgeous heads were thrown back and their pantyless butt cheeks shimmered below super-short purple hems. Dan's hands began to shake and he averted his eyes. He was in way over his head.

"Humphrey! My savior!" Chuck roared across the room when he spotted Dan. "I got a freaking one hundred on my math paper. Dude, I've never even gotten a ninety, let alone a one hundred! I'm sitting next to you every fucking day!"

Dan felt like he was hearing Chuck's assault through a wall. As hard as he tried not to stare at her, everything he saw, heard, tasted was Serena. Until Chuck lurched at him and smacked him in the head.

"Dude, are you high or something? I go out of my way to be nice to you and you don't even look at me?"

Dan blinked, a silly smile on his lips. He'd never seen Serena dance before. Her long, lithe body undulated to the music in a slinky but gawky sort of way, like she was a young Thorough-bred that hadn't yet figured out how to use its perfectly formed limbs. Her striking but shorter brunette friend was more manic and more calculated. Serena's gigantic blue eyes were closed, as if her body and the music were having some kind of wonderful conversation.

Tantric beats—a rhythm or a sickness.
What's come over me?
What's to become of me?

Every time Dan laid eyes on her, lines of poetry traversed his consciousness, begging to be written down.

"Jesus. You want me to call 911?" Chuck shouted, spitting all over Dan's eyelids. Serena opened her eyes and glanced at Dan, who had become an instant spectacle because of Chuck's performance.

Does she recognize me? Does she know she's been to my house? Does she know I'm the one who wrote her that poem? Does she know how much I think about her?

Hopefully not!

Dan waved shyly at her, his fingers numb with the realization that he was finally making contact—it was finally happening. But what to do next? Introduce himself? Just stand there, staring? Ask her to dance? Projectile vomit and leave, hopefully not in that order?

"I know what you need." Chuck grabbed Dan's legs and hoisted him over one shoulder. He was pretty strong from lifting weights while he watched porn instead of doing his homework. Dan tried to wriggle away, but Chuck was way stronger than he was, and he refused to put up too much of a fight and make a dick of himself in front of Serena. Instead, he allowed himself to be carried like a bag of laundry across the front hall and out the door marked EXIT.

The door slammed behind Chuck's laughing back and the frigid air hit Dan's lungs, nearly choking him. "Asshole," he exclaimed, fruitlessly slamming his body against the locked door.

"At least you've got a fucking coat," croaked someone beside him.

Dan swung around to find a pale, almost bald girl wearing a skimpy black T-shirt, black jeans, and combat boots squatting on the rails of the fire escape, her bare, not-too-skinny arms wrapped around her shivering frame.

Instinctively he pulled off his black wool army-issue duffel coat and coaxed it around the girl's shoulders. She stood up, easing her arms into the sleeves and zipping it up. Dan noticed they were the same height. "Perfect fit," she told him gratefully, holding out her hand. "I'm Vanessa Abrams by the way. Happy Valentine's Day." She shook Dan's still-sweaty hand firmly with her pale, freezing one. There was something solid and reassuring about her big dark brown eyes, her round, pale, makeup-free face, and her shaved head. She was like the antithesis of Serena van der Woodsen. So atypically feminine and ugly she was almost beautiful.

Is that supposed to be a compliment?

"Dan Humphrey," he introduced himself. "Don't ask me why I'm here. I don't even know the guy having this party." He patted his navy blue corduroy pockets, as if searching for cigarettes, even though he didn't smoke. It just seemed like the thing to do.

"So why *are* you here?" Vanessa asked curiously. The party was full of jerks, she'd gotten locked out, and her coat, which she'd been wearing all winter, was still inside. But here was this scruffy, lost-looking boy with wide light brown eyes like a baby deer's caught in headlights. He was wearing navy blue corduroys that looked so new his mom must have bought them for him at the Gap that morning. But he was clearly not an asshole—they were all still inside. She frowned, realizing she'd already forgotten his name. Doug? Brad? Ned? She sucked with names. By the time someone told her their name, she'd already forgotten it.

Dan wasn't about to admit that he'd come to the party because of Serena even though she didn't even know he existed, or that Chuck Bass had thrown him out the exit door just for fun. But what was she doing out there in the cold? Had she come to the party for some equally pathetic reason? How fortuitous to meet another outcast at a party such as this! Or perhaps this girl didn't really exist. Maybe she'd been conjured by his wild, poetic imagination, a ghostly fairy godmother, come to steer his doomed existence back onto a more sensible course than the one he was about to take tonight.

Vanessa walked to the edge of the fire escape and peered at the metal ladder that ran down to the fire escape below. "Think we can scale it, Slick?" she wondered aloud.

Dan shrugged. He'd rather try that than humiliate himself by banging on the door long enough and loud enough for someone like Serena to finally let him in. Plus, he really didn't want to go back inside.

He led the way, taking it slowly down the nine sets of ladders. They climbed without talking, concentrating on the rather terrifying task at hand. The bottom of the last ladder loomed eight feet above the dark sidewalk. Dan closed his eyes and jumped. The landing hurt his knees, but he was okay. He looked up, prepared to sweet-talk Vanessa down, but she just dropped off the bottom rung and staggered into him, grabbing his elbows as she regained her balance. Nope, she was no ghost.

"Whoops. Sorry, Pete," she laughed, letting go. She stamped her combat boots and smacked the traces of rust from her palms. "Actually, that was sort of fun."

Dan smiled, the realization creeping over him that it *had* been sort of fun. He never did anything with anybody other than Jenny or his Riverside Prep friend Zeke, who didn't count because (a) Dan had known Zeke since kindergarten and hadn't really chosen him as a friend—Zeke had just sort of adopted him—and (b) Zeke had grown up to be completely socially unacceptable. Playing Spider-Man with this Vanessa girl was way better than getting humiliated by Chuck Bass in front of Serena van der Woodsen anyway.

The brick hulls of warehouses turned luxury apartment buildings loomed on either side of them. A lone cab lingered at the corner and then sped away. Vestry Street was dead quiet and almost scarily dark. It was so cold, all the sane people were inside, curled up under blankets, drinking chamomile tea.

But we all know that S-A-N-E = B-O-R-I-N-G.

"You don't smoke, do you?" Dan asked, patting his pockets again.

Vanessa shook her head. "Sorry, Charlie."

"I don't either." Dan wondered if she'd actually forgotten his name or if she was just being funny. She had a crooked, wise-assed sense of humor, he could already tell. "But I think I might start."

"Come on, Sam," Vanessa slung her arm through his. "I'll buy you some."

Something tells me this is the beginning of a beautiful friendship.

once upon a friday night

A shy girl with no close friends save her big brother, who was out at a party she couldn't go to because she was just a lowly seventh grader, can do very little on a Friday night except watch movies, read, or take a bubble bath. As usual, Jenny poured almost an entire bottle of Mr. Bubble into the bath and ran the tap until the hot water had run out and huge puddles splashed onto the cracked white tile when she got in. The bubbles were so plentiful she couldn't see herself, which was just how she liked it. She lay back in the warm water, resting her head with its damp mass of dark brown curls on the ridiculous red inflatable lips bath cushion her mother had left behind all those years ago.

"Jennifer? Get out here—I'm trying a new deviled egg recipe and I want you to taste it!" Rufus bellowed from the kitchen. One of the reasons Jenny had chosen to take a nice hot bath was that her father was experimenting with a blowtorch and boiled eggs while he cantered around the kitchen to some boisterous Italian opera. "Hurry!" he shouted, as if it were a true emergency.

"Dad, I'm in the bathtub!" she yelled back. "Thinking!" she added, hoping that would shut him up.

"Forget it," her father replied from just outside the chipped, white-painted bathroom door. He opened it a crack and shoved his hand in, brandishing something on his palm. "I'm not looking. Just try it and tell me what you think."

Jenny sighed. "Can't it wait?"

Rufus stretched his blind arm out as far as it could go. "Nope. It can't."

She leaned over the side of the tub and reached for the thing in his hand, already sure that it was going to be disgusting. Half a hard-boiled egg, its skin marbled with black veins and filled with something that looked like crunchy peanut butter mixed with yellow dog poop weighed heavily in her palm. Oddly, it smelled like Cracker Jacks.

"I added some almonds, but then I decided the nuts should be caramelized, so I threw in a cup of sugar and some sherry and torched the hell out of it. I thought it'd taste better, you know, flambéed with candied nuts," Rufus's voice echoed outside the door. His approach to food was not unlike his approach to fashion: inventive and utterly appalling.

Jenny stared down at the sad little half of an egg. "But Dad, don't you see? It's not a deviled egg anymore. It's just . . . *gross.*"

"I bet you haven't tasted it yet, though. Come on. Taste it, taste it!"

Jenny sniffed the egg again and then tossed it into the little trash can under the sink. She sank her head back into the red lips pillow and closed her eyes again. "Mmmm. Yum. Wow. Actually, Dad, do you think I could bring some of these to school tomorrow so I can give them out to my teachers? I bet I'd get A's in everything if I told them that's what I got to eat every night for dinner."

"Forget it," Rufus muttered before retreating to the kitchen.

Jenny opened her eyes again to dispense more hot water into the tub and was dismayed to discover that the bubbles had already almost completely evaporated. There it was—her pale, concave chest with those two little pink things that looked more like mouse eyes in a Beatrix Potter illustration than boobs. Even Marx, the Humphreys' overweight black cat, had bigger boobs than she did, and he was a boy. Maybe she should just get used to it. She was doomed. Or maybe not. According to the literature she'd received with the breast enhancement supplements from noknockers.com that had arrived this afternoon care of FedEx, she might feel like nothing was happening for a while. Then one day she might measure herself and find she'd increased by at least a quarter of an inch. Say that happened twice a month. She'd be a B cup by spring! She might even be able to wear a normal bra or even a bikini in a real women's size rather than a child's size ten.

Anxious to measure her progress, Jenny sprang out of the tub and wrapped her unnecessarily thick bubble gum pink fuzzy cotton chenille robe around herself. She padded down the hall to her bedroom, closed the door, and slid her desk chair in front of it. Then she bent down and pulled aside her pale pink dust ruffle to retrieve the white cardboard box beneath her bed. Inside was a giant white plastic canister decorated with an illustration of a redheaded woman with perfect cleavage. Jenny unscrewed the top, tapped two of the organic supplements out onto her palm, and swallowed them dry. Then she unwound the white, neatly coiled paper measuring tape that had come tucked inside the box beside the canister. Pushing down the shoulders of the pink chenille robe so that it hung down from her small hips like a gargantuan fuzzy pink tutu, she wound the tape around her back and over those two pink mouse eyes. She was careful not to pull too tightly and reduce the chance of a tiny incremental increase since the last time she'd measured herself, which happened to be this morning.

"Thirty-one and an eighth," she said aloud. She checked the tape again. Was it twisted? Nope. Thirty-one and an eighth. This morning she'd measured at exactly thirty-one. She'd only taken one dose. Was it possible that the supplements had already started to work? She hurried over to her dresser and pulled out the thing that made her blush with embarrassment and guilt every time she touched it. The powder blue cotton Hanro jog bra had been sort of hanging out of the only accessible crack in Serena's locker when Jenny had needed to shove in Dan's poem yesterday. She'd tugged on the bra, and it had fallen out. The locker had been locked, so instead of just leaving the bra on the floor in the hall, Jenny had replaced it with the poem and stuffed it into her bag. What else was she supposed to do, drag Serena out of French class and tell her she had her *bra?* She'd return it eventually.

Maybe.

The tag inside it read 34B. Not too big, not too small, just perfect. Jenny pulled it on over her head and pushed her arms through the holes. The soft light blue cups sagged so badly she looked like a little girl playing dress-up with Mommy's things. Still, there was something reassuring about wearing the bra. Maybe, just maybe, if she kept on taking the supplements, she'd fit into it. Maybe one day she wouldn't be a tiny mouse of a girl stuck at home on a Friday night with her crazy dad eating flambéed eggs with candied almonds. Maybe one day she'd be the girl wearing the bra, the girl every boy wanted and every girl wanted to be. Just like Serena.

Wouldn't that be something?

snow falling on cheaters

"Where's Nate?" Blair slurred drunkenly into Serena's ear. The two girls were seated back-to-back in the middle of the polished chrome coffee table, sharing a cigarette. Around them revelers lay sprawled on the floor or furniture, their hair matted with sweat from dancing or puking, their lip gloss smeared. Justin Timberlake was singing in slow motion over the sound system, or at least it seemed that way. Of course Blair knew perfectly well that Nate was indisposed at the moment because he was busy getting devirginized by that horrible megaslut L'Wren, but she needed him—*now*. "I want him to take me home."

"Me too," Serena agreed. "My butt's cold." She couldn't wait to put on a pair of big comfy cotton underwear and crawl into bed.

With Nate.

"Yes, where *is* Nathaniel?" Chuck chimed in, from the floor. He'd been staring up the girls' skirts all night, just waiting for one of them to get drunk enough to fall into his lap so he could molest her.

"Do you think he and that girl are really . . . ?" Blair's voice trailed off. The idea of Nate with anyone but her made her feel like she was going to be sick.

Serena shrugged her shoulders sadly. How could the boy she loved so dearly be so careless and insensitive? Didn't he know that she lay in bed every night imagining how it would be—them together—like an Eternity perfume ad, only better? They even looked alike—sort of. Didn't he get it?

Chuck suddenly leapt to his feet. "You know what this calls for?"

Both girls shook their heads. Chuck's ideas were usually terrible.

"Bundle!" he yelled grabbing their hands. He yanked them forward, racing toward the closed door of Luke's bedroom. And without even pausing to knock or give warning, he burst in, setting free a pungent cloud of pot smoke.

Nate and L'Wren were lying on the sea kelp flokati rug, she in a tiny black lace thong and he in his royal blue boxers, smiling up at the ceiling in what could only be complete postcoital bliss.

Well, at least *they* were wearing underwear.

"Bundle!" Chuck shouted again, nonsensically, as he hurled himself on top of them. It was as if he were re-creating a scene from some dumb college frat movie he'd loved but no one else had ever seen.

Serena and Blair clung to each other in the doorway, staring at L'Wren's fake-looking bare boobs. They were balloon-round and tan. Even her nipples appeared to be tan. They glared at Nate's gorgeous, naked, muscular chest. *How could he?* they wondered simultaneously. With that fake-boobed slut in the skanky black Victoria's Secret thong!?

"Natie?" Serena whimpered, a little too tragically. "Blair's feeling bad. We need to go home."

Dutifully, Nate sat up. He rubbed his half-closed green eyes and grinned down at his bare knees. Stoned as he was, getting dressed seemed a monumental task. "Just a minute," he murmured, his tongue leaden. Next to him on the floor, Chuck tickled L'Wren's bare feet and she cackled merrily, loving it. Nate didn't get it. L'Wren seemed to get hornier and hornier the more they smoked, but he could hardly do more than kiss her a few times before going into a pot-induced trance wherein he expounded in a monotone voice much like his father's on how cars should run on pot instead of gas and then there'd be no global warming and everyone would be happy. He hadn't even gotten close to losing his virginity.

Wonder why—global warming is so sexy.

He staggered to his feet and pulled on his gray T-shirt, backward. "Your coat's in the hall," Blair reminded him, all motherly. She took his hand, bending down to retrieve his white Stan Smith tennis shoes from underneath L'Wren's bare calf.

L'Wren sat up. With Chuck in her lap, his back pressed against her voluminous bare breasts and a huge gleaming-toothed grin on his weirdly handsome face, she began to reload her pink bong. "'Bye, Natie," she called out teasingly.

Serena led the way, hauling their coats out of the stack and tumbling into the elevator. "That party sucked," she declared, even though she'd kind of had fun.

Nate fumbled with the toggles on his navy blue cashmere duffel coat. "I missed you guys," he admitted pathetically.

Both girls stared at him, their hearts melting. How did he manage to be so infuriatingly adorable and such a fucking asshole at the same time? They felt especially stupid for going to the party without underwear. They'd spent the whole evening feeling horribly exposed and unsanitary, and Nate hadn't even noticed. The doors rolled open onto the lobby and Serena wrapped her arms around Blair in drunken solidarity. "Just fetch us a cab, love," she told Nate in an imposing British accent.

The cab headed east on Houston, past the Angelika Film Center, where the three of them had seen their first too-dirty-to-be-rated movie together when they were eleven, having begged a pair of bohemian-looking gray-haired women who were holding hands to take them in, pretending they were their adopted triplets. The film had been *Last Tango in Paris,* starring Marlon Brando and Maria Schneider, playing in revival. All the characters in it did was hang out in some apartment in Paris, having sex in weird positions that were totally embarrassing. It was so filthy they'd left early. Their two mommies had been totally into it, though.

Now they were on the FDR Drive headed uptown. On their right, the lights of the Williamsburg Bridge twinkled like Christmas. On their left, the hulking buildings of the NYU Medical Center cut off their view of the Empire State Building, which for the last week had been lit up red for Valentine's Day. Across the river the famous red sign for Silver Cup Studios glowed promisingly as a light snow began to fall. Tiny white flakes danced in the yellow beam of the taxi's headlights.

The driver flicked on his windshield wipers. Serena rested her cheek on Nate's shoulder and stroked Blair's head, which was in her lap. "I don't want to go away," she whispered aloud.

Nate rubbed his jaw against Serena's smooth golden hairline

while he held Blair's small, warm hand. They were so great, his girls. He felt nice. Warm and nice. And stoned.

Yup.

Obviously Blair wanted to avoid her house at all costs, and Nate's parents were probably still awake, having just returned home from some interminably long opera. Serena's parents were at the family's country estate up in Ridgefield, Connecticut, for a weekend of antiquing, so it went without saying that they would all sleep at her house. Blair had to be carried inside the building. She wasn't asleep, but she refused to walk. Serena tucked Blair under the covers, and shuffled into her big Old New York bathroom. The bathroom window was open just a crack, and snow had collected on the sill and spilled over onto the white hexagonal floor tile where it melted instantly. Serena pulled on a flimsy white camisole and a pair of red flannel boxer shorts stolen from Nate years ago.

When she returned to the bedroom, Nate was lying next to a sleeping Blair on top of the white eyelet bedspread, blinking up at the white eyelet canopy overhead as if deciphering the constellations. Serena climbed up next to him and lay down, reluctant to get under the covers and add a layer of separation between her body and his. Instead, she wound her long legs around him and pressed her face into his chest.

"Happy Valentine's Day," she whispered, ever so softly.

They lay like that for a minute, wide awake. Suddenly Nate felt more turned on than he ever had in his life. Why *now*? Was it some sort of delayed reaction to getting stoned with L'Wren? Instead of getting the munchies he was getting the hornies? Actually, he was starving. But he could stave off hunger if Serena would just roll on top of him and kiss him.

"Nate?" Serena was still drunk and felt relaxed and daring. Nate was right there and she was right here. It just felt like the most obvious thing in the world. "I know this might be weird but—" She lifted her head and looked down at him smiling expectantly up at her. Then she didn't say anything more, she just did it. She kissed him.

Blair was only inches away, breathing deeply, but they couldn't stop kissing. Nate wasn't even thinking about Blair. All he knew was how good it felt to kiss the warm, familiar, incredible girl in his arms. Serena had wanted to kiss Nate for so long, doing it for real was an entire-body experience. She opened her eyes, watching him kiss her in a tipsy haze. *This is crazy*, she tried to tell herself, still kissing.

"I could just kiss you *forever*," she murmured softly, her lips brushing his. Nate opened his eyes and smiled ecstatically back at her, and her heart exploded into a thousand glittering stars. She kissed him again, more fervently this time. *I love you, Nate!* Her thoughts were so loud she was sure they'd wake Blair, but maybe Blair would understand. After all, they were best friends. And Blair's crush on Nate was just a flirty, childish thing, not real, grown-up love. Not love like this. Not kisses like this.

Finally they dozed off, holding each other, their lips cracked and parched from so much kissing. The snow was wetter now, almost rain. Early morning light crept through the white eyelet curtains, and buses splattered noisily through the slush on Fifth Avenue. But the three friends slept on, breathing softly into one another's hair, their limbs entwined.

So very innocent—or not.

topics ◀ *previous*   *next* ▶   *post a question*   *reply*

Disclaimer: All the real names of places, people, and events have been altered or abbreviated to protect the innocent. Namely, me.

hey people!

going commando

There's something we need to discuss badly. It's about this underwear-optional thing that seems to be taking over the city, the country, the Earth, and possibly even the universe. Hello aliens on Mars, I'll show you mine if you show me yours! The parts we all used to keep safely inside our undergarments were often called "privates" in the old days because it's simply not polite to put them on display. Perfect strangers really don't need to see said parts, not even while we're clambering out of a taxi, and certainly not while we're dining in restaurants or eating lunch in the school cafeteria.

As far as the term *commando* is concerned, the expression may have something to do with the lack of laundry facilities whilst at war. I'm all for showing off and being brave. Audacity is a good thing. But the truth is, we're not at war: we have maids to do our laundry, and piles of clean, pretty cotton and lace Hanky Panky and Cosabella panties to choose from. So let's keep them on—at least in public.

sightings

C wearing a pearly white perma-grin while canoodling with an older-looking, dark-haired girl wearing only a woolly sea grass rug in a town car on their way to the **Tribeca Star Hotel** where I happen to know his family keeps a penthouse suite. **D** and **V** guzzling Irish coffees in the **Ear Inn**, an intimate dive bar in the West Village well known for serving minors and allowing people to smoke after hours. I know—'tis ever so shocking but ever so handy. **B**, with her head out the window of a taxi on East Eighty-sixth Street, breathing the not-so-fresh air. Tossed back one too many, did we? **S** and **N** carrying **B** into **S**'s apartment building opposite the **Met**. Morning's almost over and not one of the three has come out . . . yet. **V** holding **D**'s hair back while closely inspecting a gutter outside the aforementioned dive bar. How nice—for them. A little advice: it's best not to smoke at all, but if and when you try it for the first time, don't chain-smoke an entire unfiltered pack or you too will wind up tossing your cookies and Irish creams.

a new addition

Well, well, it seems I'm not the only one who can't keep her mouth shut. You've been deluging me with e-mails jam-packed with the latest updates and juicy tidbits of things so stupid I just have to share, so I've decided to include a smattering of your letters in each missive. Enjoy, my pets.

your e-mail

Q:
yo gossipgrl,
u rock. k?
—bug'n

A:
dr bug'n,
k
—gg

Q:
Dearest Gossip Girl,
you don't know how long i've been like planning to start my own Web site or blog or whatever and now you did it and i can't but

I just wanted to tell you how amazing you are because i totally know everyone you're talking about because they're totally me and my friends and sometimes we act stupid but we're all really smart we're just really competitive and sometimes it makes me sad that we can't just all get along and say what we think to our faces you know?

—candyc

Dearest candyc,

I do know. I also know that you and your friends really aren't the people I'm writing about but it's okay if you want to believe you are. I'm sure your problems are quite valid and I do sympathize. I hope I meet your expectations as far as this page is concerned, but please don't let my efforts prevent you from writing something of your own. You have a voice, so by all means use it. But first, a word of advice: take a deep breath, drink a glass of Sancerre, and use some punctuation. It may seem old-fashioned, but your friends will admire you for it.

—GG

Hey GG,

Where do you get off being such a ho, dishing out trash about people that's just lies and pretending you did not make this shit up.

—sucka

Dear sucka,

And where do you get off calling me a liar? Were your friends lying when they called you sucka? Who's the sucka now?

—GG

And now I'm off to take a long hot milk-and-honey bath, get a French pedicure, buy a pretty frock, eat a tiny piece of Payard chocolate, break down and eat a very large piece of Payard chocolate, do something about my eyebrows, and buy an exquisite pair of Louboutin eelskin boots. I'm sure I'll run into one or two of you on Madison and you can tell me anything I might have missed—as if I ever miss anything? Later on you can crawl under your favorite cashmere throw with a bag of Cheetos and a flute of Cristal and read all about it right here. Who has time to make up stories when the truth is so much more interesting?

More soon. Ta ta!

You know you love me,

gossip girl

v can't wash d out of what's left of her hair

Dan. It wasn't the best name in the world. She would have preferred it if he insisted on going by Daniel. Dashiell would have been much more exciting. Then he would have been Dash for short, which was just plain sexy. Dan. Who would have ever thought she'd like a boy named Dan? Dan was so boring, like John or Bob or Brad. But here it was seven o'clock on a Sunday morning and she was wide awake, thinking about *Dan.*

He was so cute when he puked. His skinny body kind of writhed in disgust while he hacked away. She'd tried to warn him that smoking cigarettes was like sucking on a car's exhaust pipe and that his body was going to reject all that carbon monoxide, especially combined with the caffeine and whatever the fuck it was they put in Irish coffee—alcoholic Junior Mints? But Dan wouldn't listen to her. He was stubborn and seriously naïve, but so smart. Hello? Did anyone else she knew quote Goethe and Proust and Joyce without even trying? Clearly he was born in the wrong century. And so damned adorable with his pale skin, shaggy colorless hair, dumpy cords, and his soulful light brown eyes. She just wanted to carry him around in her bag so she could take him out and play with him whenever she wanted.

Woof, woof!

Vanessa pulled out the Ear Inn matchbook with the word *Dan* and his number written on it in her orderly, all-caps handwriting. Before she could talk herself out of it, she grabbed the phone from the windowsill behind her bed and dialed. Outside it was snowing and raining at the same time, and the smell of wet sugar from the sugar factory nearby permeated the air. The radiator behind Vanessa's head coughed and sputtered in its attempt to overheat the tiny apartment.

"Jesus Christ, hello?" a gruff voice answered.

Her heartbeat sped up. Dan's dad? What the fuck should she say? "Oh, hello. This is Vanessa Abrams calling for Dan. I know it's early—"

"Is it? I don't wear a watch," the voice boomed. She could hear the rustle of papers and the clinking of glasses. "I just sleep when I'm tired. Wait, who'd you say this was?"

"Vanessa," she told him again. "Dan and I met last night." She blushed as she said this, realizing it sounded like she and Dan had fooled around or something. She folded her legs over each other proprietarily, even though she was wearing gray longjohn bottoms and was underneath her white down comforter all by herself.

"Finally!" the voice growled. "You have no idea how long this infatuation has gone on for. He's been impossible, mooning over you. But you sound like a wonderful girl. A little too girly for my taste, but I'm sure you've got a noggin underneath all those fancypants clothes."

Vanessa sat up, confused. "Is this Dan Humphrey's residence?"

"Yes, I'm his father, Rufus. So when can you come over for dinner? I have so many new recipes and I'm dying to try them out on someone who isn't completely biased!"

She tried to picture what Dan's apartment might be like. His dad obviously liked to cook, so it probably smelled like garlic and marinara sauce and baking bread all the time. The whole place was probably wall-to-wall bookshelves, stocked with the classics. There were probably lots of big comfy sofas for reading and good natural light and a dog or two. And flowers—flowers and books all over the place. She glanced around at her own plain white room with its hard futon on the floor and nothing on the walls. "That sounds really nice."

"You know, Dan doesn't get out much, so it's lucky you two finally met. He's a good kid, but he's got confidence issues. Not to generalize, but with a charming, beautiful girl like you on his arm, maybe he'll come out of his shell a little."

Vanessa was blushing again. Would talking to Dan's father always be this embarrassing? She rubbed her free hand over her freshly shaven scalp. "Okay. Well, please tell Dan that his friend Vanessa called."

"Okay, Dan's friend Vanessa," Mr. Humphrey repeated mockingly. "Now go give yourself another egg yolk facial, or whatever it is you girls do."

Vanessa hung up and hugged her long-john-covered knees to her chest. So Dan had already talked about her at home! Had he spent the rest of the night thinking about her the way she had about him? Her digital camera lay on the floor next to the futon. She picked up the camera and scanned through some of last night's pictures. There was Serena dancing, traces of her bare, tattooed butt cheeks just grazing the edge of the frame.

With that curtain of blond hair falling halfway down her back and her tan, endless legs, she was so perfect and stunning she looked almost fake. Then there was Dan, shivering in the cold beneath a Tribeca street lamp, his bony fingers wrapped miserably around an unfiltered Camel as he smiled shyly at the lens. She bent her head and carefully kissed the image, not embarrassed in the least.

And she claims she doesn't need a boyfriend.

there were three in the bed and the little one said, "what the *$#@?"

Blair blinked up at the white eyelet canopy looming above her. She'd been dreaming about kissing Nate on a beach somewhere in the Mediterranean, and it had felt so real she could actually smell the Bain de Soleil tanning oil and taste the sea salt in her mouth.

Or maybe that was just cotton mouth from last night's drinking and smoking binge.

She turned her leaden head. Nate's cheek was on Serena's chest. His gray T-shirt was off and he looked totally . . . blissful. Serena was wearing a skimpy white camisole and was hugging Nate's head tight. Blair bolted upright and kicked away the covers, simultaneously removing them from their cozy cuddle sandwich and revealing their long legs, which were all atangle.

"I know you do that, Serena, because you do it to me when I sleep over at your house," she remarked loudly. "Maybe you should just, like, get a teddy bear or something."

Serena's enormous blue eyes opened and she blinked her dark lashes at Blair. Nate's wavy golden brown hair was practically in her mouth as he mumbled, "What time is it?"

"I don't know. Ten, eleven." Blair swung her leg out and kung-fu kicked Nate in the ribs. "Will you get up already?"

His eyes flew open and he sat partially up, looking startled. Rays of unrelenting white winter light blazed through the large plate-glass window. "Jesus," he murmured, letting his head fall back onto the sumptuous goose-down pillow. "Blair, you really know how to wake up a guy. I should have you wake me up every morning."

That's the idea.

Blair stared down at him, so adorable now that he was lying on the pillow and not Serena's perky 34Bs. She cuddled up to his Serena-free side and put his lacrosse-calloused hand over her face, talking into it the way she'd done a thousand times before. "We have to do something really excellent this summer, you guys," she announced emphatically. No way did she want to hang out with her insane family this summer, witnessing her father sneaking around and her mother getting fatter and fatter, especially when there was no school and she could actually escape to someplace far, far away.

Like the Mediterranean?

"Summer," Serena mused aloud. No school. Sunny days filled with kisses. Skinny-dipping. Nate. "I can't wait." She slipped her hand over Nate's wrist and squeezed his free hand. He squeezed back, and she kicked her feet happily against the mattress, silently screaming with the thrill of it. This was just the beginning, the beginning of her and Nate.

Nate held the two girls, feeling happily confused. He remembered kissing Serena last night, and he remembered kissing L'Wren too. Both had felt nice. He remembered feeling super stoned, which also kind of rocked. He loved holding

Blair's face in his hand like he was doing right now. He loved the way her tiny bones felt beneath his palm and the way her soft lips brushed against his fingers. Girls were all so great. Girls rocked. Man, was he lucky.

"Hey Nate. Why don't we spend the summer at your aunt's in France?" Blair rattled on. "Doesn't she live in, like, Provence or something? We could probably even get AP French credit for it."

"No way," Nate responded quickly. "She's even more of a prima donna than my mom. We could stay there, but we'd be her slaves. We'd have to, like, bring her lunch in bed and drive her dogs into town to get them groomed or take her to her plastic surgery appointments."

Blair thought this sounded sort of romantic. She and Nate could be Nate's aunt's live-in couple. They'd help around the house and make love on the porch in the evenings while his aunt was asleep, recovering from one of her many surgeries. And Serena could sleep in the guest house with the dogs. She'd always liked animals.

Oh, she'd love that.

"Then maybe we could go sailing on your boat instead," Serena suggested.

Even better, Blair mused.

And Serena could sleep where—in the dinghy?

Nate and his dad were building a sailing yacht together at the Archibalds' compound on Mt. Desert Island. They'd designed it themselves and had already gotten a good start on the hull this fall before the weather turned. Nate removed his hand from Blair's face. "We've barely started building it yet. It's not going to be ready for at least a year."

Blair hopped off the bed, grabbed Serena's MacBook from off her desk, and carried it back to bed. She opened it and Googled "fabulous European retreat." Of course everything that came up was totally pornographic. *Fabulous nudist retreat! Nude poolside dining! Nude maid service! All inclusive!*

Sign me up!

Nate sat up and grabbed the laptop away from her, intending to look at a traditional travel Web site like Lonely Planet. Reflexively, he checked his e-mail first, where a message from lwren@knowes.com with the subject "to be continued . . ." beckoned from the "unread" list. Nate glanced at Blair and then Serena, and then, feeling particularly studly and bold, he opened the e-mail.

From: lwren@knowes.com
To: narchibald@stjudes.edu
Date: Saturday, February 15, 8:45AM
Subject: to be continued . . .

Dear Natie,
You are très adorable, but I think I got
you a little too wasted—we never finished
what we started, *again*! Lucky you, we're
gonna have a third chance. Next weekend
there's this debutante cotillion at the
St. Claire Hotel. It's sooo not me, but
my mom and my older sister did it so
I have to. Anyway, I need a handsome
escort from an "acceptable" family,
which is where you come in. We can start
downstairs at the cotillion and then
go up to my hotel suite. How does that
sound? I'm taking the train back to
UVA tonight to work on a boring paper.
Missing you already.

You know you love me,
—L'Wren

Nate glanced away from the screen, only to find Serena and Blair reading L'Wren's e-mail over his shoulder.

Serena scowled. "So, are you going?" she challenged, folding her arms over her tiny white camisole. Her long, pale blond hair was matted on one side and black mascara smudges ringed her eyes. She looked like Edie Sedgwick, Andy Warhol's skinny, drugged-out muse, on a good day.

Blair snickered wickedly and grabbed the laptop. She clicked on the reply button and speedily typed, U R SO HOT. LUV UR HOT TITS. —N

She hit "send" before Nate even had a chance to read what she'd written. "Yeah, he's going," she announced triumphantly. "Sucka."

"Hey!" Nate snatched the laptop back and hit the "sent mail" button so he could read Blair's reply. "Christ," he muttered in dismay. Blair was such a bitchy little troublemaker sometimes.

Isn't that what we all—including him—love about her?

Serena wasn't completely sure *what* was going on. Nate and Blair seemed to be bantering with each other just as flirtatiously as ever, and Nate had just gotten a steamy invitation from that tramp with the impossible name. Where exactly did that leave her? Hadn't something kind of *big* happened between them last night?

"Nate," she ventured, "can I talk to you for a minute, um, in the bathroom?"

Blair stood up on the bed and bounced up and down. She was still wearing her purple Marc Jacobs pinafore from last night and no underwear. Oops! She sat back down again. "Hello? If you guys have something to talk about I'd like to hear it."

"It's just . . . um . . ." Serena couldn't wait to tell her best friend about kissing Nate, but she sort of wanted to talk to him first, in private. Mostly she just wanted to make sure that he was as excited about all this as she was. Then they needed to decide how to handle Blair's reaction, which was bound to be spectacular.

In an ugly sort of way.

Nate hadn't said anything in a while. He was pissed at Blair for sending that e-mail to L'Wren, and though he wanted to kiss Serena some more—he really did—he didn't want to do it in the bathroom with Blair peeking at them through the keyhole. Instead, he slid off the bed and put on his pants, then his shoes.

"Where are you going?" Blair demanded, scooting back under the covers. She'd have to borrow some underwear from Serena. And keep it, of course.

"Home," he responded flatly. And maybe he'd stop off at Charlie Dern's house on the way. Charlie's older brother was in Costa Rica for his junior year abroad and was constantly sending Charlie pot hidden inside local artifacts packed in coffee beans. Now that Nate knew how awesome it felt to be thoroughly baked, he wanted to try it again.

"Fine," Blair told him huffily and strode over to Serena's giant antique chest of drawers to look for a pair of underwear.

"Call me later," Serena called out weakly as her bedroom door swung shut behind him. Was he really leaving without so much as a hug or a goodbye kiss?

"He doesn't get it," Blair observed, rifling through Serena's messy drawers.

"Get what?" Serena pulled the thick down comforter up to her chin, trying to decide whether to be happy, angry, or sad. She wanted to sleep all day and wake up to Nate's sweet, apologetic kiss. The poem someone had left in her locker was lying on the floor, peeking out from beneath the white eyelet dust ruffle. *Pretend that you know me. That we're in love.* As far as she knew, Nate had never written a poem in his life. Or maybe he *had* written it, she thought, perking up.

"Nothing." Blair snatched up a pair of white cotton Petit Bateau underwear with red polka dots and took them into the bathroom with her.

Serena remained under the covers, gearing up to tell her best friend all about last night and going to boarding school—everything. She wouldn't like it—at least not at first—but Serena needed advice, and Blair was her best friend.

And if you can't burst your best friend's bubble, then whose bubble can you burst?

our bodies, ourselves

"Jennifer!" Rufus Humphrey bellowed from his office that morning, waking Dan. "What in hell is noknockers.com?"

Dan's sleepy brown eyes slid open. His lips were stuck to his old Calvin & Hobbes pillowcase with a dried mix of vomit-scented drool and Aquafresh. He vaguely remembered being put in a taxi by that shaven-headed girl, Vanessa, with a twenty-dollar bill and a nearly empty pack of unfiltered Camels. She was nice. And cool. He was pretty sure he'd had kind of a good time, except for the vomiting-Irish-coffee-into-the-gutter part right before he got into the cab.

Ouch.

"Jennifer? Will you please explain how you possibly could have donated nearly three hundred dollars of my money to a charity in Tennessee by the name of noknockers? What is it? Some crackpot organization that helps underdeveloped young women find Jesus? Jennifer—are you listening to me?"

Dan drew up the covers and pulled a pillow over his face, gagging on the cigarette stench of his hands. If only he'd had a chance to speak to Serena last night. Just a hello would have been amazing. Instead he'd become a smoker. He pressed the pillow against his closed eyes. And Serena would forever remember him as the geek who showed up at the party and got thrown out the fire door by Chuck Bass, never to be seen or heard from again.

Jenny lay on her back beneath her light pink chenille Pottery Barn Kids bedspread, feeling her chest. "It's just a place I got some underwear from, okay, Dad?" she shouted, hoping to shut him up. They were a family of shouters, so it wasn't the shouting that bothered her. It was the idea of talking about boobs with her dad, which obviously was not going to happen, ever. Her chest had definitely changed overnight though. There were *lumps*— actual palpable apricot-size lumps! She threw back the covers and leapt out of bed, scattering sheets of paper covered with art for Constance Billard's hymnal contest that she'd labored over until late last night. She grabbed the noknockers measuring tape and wound it around herself once more, careful not to twist it. The tape read exactly 32 inches. Jenny yanked her thin cotton Hello Kitty nightgown down so there were absolutely no wrinkles and measured herself again. Definitely 32. It was a *miracle*. Still, the instructions from noknockers said that it was very difficult to measure oneself and suggested that a friend or family member could give a more accurate reading.

"Dan!" Jenny shrieked. "Quick, get in here!"

Dan threw the pillow off his face and yawned noisily. Jesus, was it against the law to sleep in on a Saturday anymore? He should have slept over at that girl Vanessa's house. She said she lived with her big sister who stayed up really late at night playing in her band. They probably slept until sunset in complete peace. Not that sleeping over at Vanessa's house had been an option.

And not that he'd actually considered it in his drunken stupor or anything.

But is he considering it now?

"Dan?" Jenny shouted again. "Are you alive?"

Dan staggered to his feet and shuffled miserably out of his room and down the hall with its creaking, scuffed parquet floor and chipped white paint. Jenny's door was open just a crack. "Okay, so I'm here," he announced, pushing it open.

Jenny was standing in front of the full-length mirror on the back of her closet door, wearing her favorite old pink Hello Kitty nightgown. She cocked her head. "Notice anything different?"

Dan squinted. "You got a haircut?"

She rolled her eyes. "No, stupid, I grew!" She cupped her chest and gave it a good squeeze. Then she grabbed the measuring tape and handed it to him. "Will you just measure me to make sure? It's supposed to be more accurate if someone else does it." She held her arms out like airplane wings.

Dan glanced down at the white laminated paper measuring tape embellished with tiny illustrations of bras with smiley faces on the cups. "You want me to measure you?"

"Don't be embarrassed. I mean, I'm the one who should be embarrassed," she explained, flustered by his hesitation. "Please just do it and get it over with already?"

Dan averted his eyes as best he could as he wound the tape around his sister's upper torso. He reminded himself that Jenny didn't have a mom to help her with such things, otherwise she'd have asked her. *I'm all she has*, he told himself importantly. The tape stuck to his clammy, hungover, cigarette-stained fingers.

"Not too tight," she reminded him, holding the tape securely over her front as he wound it around her back. "But don't do it too loose either." She stood up straight.

"Um, it looks like thirty-two inches. Maybe like a hair more."

A hair *more*? Jenny yanked the tape away and jumped up and down, skipping rope with it. "I'm a thirty-two!" she cried exuberantly. "A thirty-two!" That didn't mean she could quite fill an A cup yet, but almost. Soon.

The scattered sheets of paper on the floor caught Dan's eye and he bent down to take a closer look. Serena's navy blue eyes stared knowingly up at him, her luxurious blond hair spilling over the folds of a filmy white gown. The words *Hark! The Herald Angels Sing* were printed in bold calligraphy beneath her bare, pink, perfect feet, and her downy white wings were spread wide, as if she were about to take flight.

Wings?

He picked up one of the sketches and held it to his chest. "Can I keep this?" he asked without thinking about how perverted, messed up, or deranged he might sound.

"No, it's mine, you freak," Jenny snapped, slipping her arms into her enormous, hairy pink bathrobe. What Dan might do with that drawing in the privacy of his room was too gross to consider. "Drop it."

Reluctantly, he let the page flutter to the floor. He folded his arms and stared down at it. Serena. *Serena, Serena, Serena.* "Well, when the hymnals get printed I'm going to make you steal one for me."

Jenny came over and gazed down at the drawings with him. "You think I could win? I mean, I'm only a seventh grader and there are, like, seniors who are way better artists than I am."

Dan rolled his eyes. Jenny had never grasped how truly gifted an artist she was. Ever since she could hold a pencil, she'd drawn the most incredibly accurate portraits of everyone in the family. Once, she'd gotten in trouble for sketching her school headmistress, Mrs. McLean, during assembly. But when Mrs. M had seen how precise and lifelike the drawing was, down to the headmistress's weirdly square head, she'd forgiven her. Now the portrait was framed and hanging on the wall in Mrs. M's office, much to Jenny's chagrin.

"I *know* you're going to win," Dan told her confidently. He was about to give her a nice, big-brotherly hug when he realized that Jenny had her hands inside her bathrobe and was feeling her chest again, really giving the ol' hooters a good going-over this time.

Nice.

"I'm going to go now." He loved his little sister, he did, but he wasn't really into watching her develop right before his very eyes, no matter how motherless she was.

Just wait till she takes him shopping for her first real bra.

what's love got to do with it?

Serena put her silver MacBook back on her desk, smothering the four shiny boarding school catalogs her mother had left there with a note written in her looping script: *You know Daddy and your brother would be thrilled if you chose Hanover.* As if Serena could even *think* about boarding school now that she and Nate had kissed. She clasped the remote in her hand and flicked through the channels, looking for something absorbing to while away the minutes while Blair took her interminable shower.

"Go back!" Blair shouted from the bathroom. The door flew open, releasing a cloud of steam, and she leapt onto the bed, fully dressed, her dark hair dripping. She tossed her soggy white bath towel onto the desk, further obscuring the boarding school catalogs. "That was *Some Like It Hot.* I'd recognize Marilyn's voice anywhere."

Because it's so like her own?

Both girls stared silently at the movie. Marilyn Monroe was kissing the suave, fast-talking guy who was no good for her.

"Isn't it great how all they do is kiss in these old movies? It's like, kissing really means something," Serena observed wistfully.

"Like, how romantic to say to a guy you really love, 'Let's just kiss.'" She smiled to herself, savoring her secret for a moment until she released it and it was a secret no more. Onscreen, Marilyn and Mr. Suave were looking longingly into each other's eyes. She licked her lips in preparation for her confession.

"Do you ever wonder what it would be like to kiss Nate?" Blair blurted out. She couldn't watch anybody kiss without thinking about Nate.

Serena sucked in her breath. Her whole body felt like it had been thrust under the broiler. "Um . . . Actually I—"

"I do, sometimes." Blair's thin, expressive lips curved into a shy little smile. She sighed and hugged her knees to her chest, feeling a little more sure of herself now that she was clean and wearing underwear. "Actually, I think about it *all the time*." She turned her head, resting her cheek on her knees. "I know I'm always acting bitchy around him and flirting, and you always tease me about having a crush on him. But the truth is, it's not just a crush. I'm totally, completely in love with Nate. I've been in love with him *forever*. And I've just gotten to this point where if I can't be *with* him, I'm going to *die*."

Serena shrank back into the fluffy down pillows on her bed and stared at her oldest and dearest friend in speechless disbelief. The whole room was fuzzy, and Marilyn Monroe's voice seemed to be miles away.

"I know you think it's gross because he's like almost a brother or whatever. But I can't help it. I just love him so much." Blair rocked her body back and forth. "I even daydream about us getting married," she admitted.

Serena swallowed the enormous lump in her throat. How could she say anything about kissing Nate last night and being in love with Nate herself when Blair was talking about marrying him? If only she'd said something right when they'd first woken up. *Nate and I are in love,* she imagined herself saying while Nate was still lying next to her, and her cheeks burned. She stuck her thumb in her mouth and began gnawing on her perfectly manicured thumbnail. She'd never been a nail-biter, but this seemed like a good time to start.

"And now he's with that tacky bitch L'Wren," Blair whined. "You know she went to boarding school? I hate boarding school girls. They pretend to be all hippie and crunchy and laid back, but really they're just assholes. And did you notice she spells her name *L* apostrophe *W-R-E-N*? That's just so retarded. Anyway, you've got to help me."

Serena blinked her huge blue eyes. She could feel a hangover coming on, and it wasn't pretty. "Of course," she offered, pressing her trembling knuckles into her temples. "What do you want me to do?"

"So you know how I answered that bitch's e-mail and basically told her Nate would escort her to her cheesy debutante ball?" Blair bit her lower lip anxiously and wound her dark hair into a tight, wet bun. "I'm such an idiot. I don't know why I did that. He can't go. We've got to stop him. And then I have to tell him . . . you know . . . that I'm in love with him."

Goosebumps stood out on Serena's arms every time Blair said those words. "Don't worry," she responded reassuringly, feeling like a traitor and a martyr all at the same time. "We'll figure something out." She combed her long, elegant fingers through her tangled pale blond tresses. Of course Nate had no intention of escorting L'Wren to the cotillion—not when he was in love with *her*—but she knew Blair liked the idea that she was competing with L'Wren for Nate's affection, and she didn't have the heart to correct her.

Blair imagined Serena dressed up in a tuxedo and ponytail while she pretended to be Blair's escort for the debutante ball. Serena would slip something into L'Wren's champagne and then Blair would whisk Nate away in one of those horse-drawn carriages, galloping all the way to a suite in the Tribeca Star or some equally sumptuous downtown hotel.

How very *Some Like It Hot*.

She threw her arms around Serena and buried her face in her best friend's mane of blond, nicely conditioned hair. "I just love him so much," she gushed, relieved that the information was finally out and that she could talk about it with Serena, her loyal ally.

Serena patted Blair's back, her eyes on the flat-screen TV. Marilyn and her two cross-dressing male cohorts were on a train, traveling to Miami. Even though they were wearing dresses, makeup, and jewelry, the guys were so obviously guys, Marilyn was pretty dumb not to notice.

"You know what we should do this summer?" she mused aloud, desperate to change the subject. "Get Eurail passes and take the train all around Europe, getting off wherever looks cool. My brother did it last summer, remember? He got really skinny and tan? It would be so romantic," she continued enthusiastically, letting go of Blair to see if she was listening.

"That's perfect! My aunt's getting married in Scotland in August, so I have to be there anyway." Blair's bright blue eyes were all aglow. "Nate and I could share one of those little sleeping compartments! We'll travel all over, ordering room service and never getting off the train. And maybe you could meet a boy too," she added generously for Serena's benefit.

Thanks. Thanks a lot.

Serena nodded energetically. She'd always been a natural actress. "Not one—ten! A hundred! I'll go boy crazy!" She stood up on the bed and bounced up and down.

Blair giggled. "You're such a slut."

Serena kept on bouncing as the terrible seed she'd planted took root and began to spread like some wild, poisonous weed. She still hadn't told Blair about her parents wanting to send her to boarding school next year, and she hadn't told her about kissing Nate. Each time her feet made contact with the bed she felt weighed down by dread. She'd lied to Blair. She was a horrible friend. Then she was airborne again, elated. Nate had kissed her! They were in love! Then once more as her feet touched the covers—oh, how could she? Blair giggled merrily, watching her bounce, oblivious to the gap that had already formed between them like a crack in the sidewalk. Serena squeezed her eyes shut, still bouncing. How was it possible to feel so happy, excited, and in love and at the same time so heartbroken, sorry, confused, and scared?

It's called life, babycakes. Get used to it.

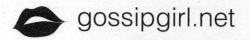 gossipgirl.net

Disclaimer: All the real names of places, people, and events have been altered or abbreviated to protect the innocent. Namely, me.

hey people!

It occurs to me that many of you tuning in don't live anywhere near this fine city and may not have had a chance to visit. Allow me to paint a more vivid picture of my modest little neighborhood, the sixty-karat diamond of Manhattan. Almost all of us live within the same twenty-block radius from East Sixty-eighth Street to East Eighty-eighth Street, from Fifth Avenue to Park Avenue. We see each other in the deli when we're buying cinnamon Trident and Parliaments. We sip cappuccinos together on the Met steps, we share platters of fries at Jackson Hole or cast sympathetic glares at our moms during brunch at Payard. So where do we go when we don't want our parents or our friends' parents to see us? The park, of course, as in Central Park.

The guides on those scary-looking red double-decker tourist buses that tool around the city might try to tell you that New York City is full of parks, but for us there is only one. It might seem a bit odd that we frequent the park so much in our neatly pleated uniforms and highly sought-after shoes, but it truly is our home away from home. The ducks in the reservoir know us by name. The homeless guys wink at us. The rocks have worn spots where we've sat for hours, basking in the sun. And since our parents *would never dream* of stepping out of their shiny black town cars to venture into the park and have no inkling that it would occur to us to go there, they have no idea what we do while we're sitting on those beloved rocks. Which is basically all the things we can't do at home. Of course, our parents are out late or are away half the time, but we need s*omewhere* to go when they're home. Thank goodness for Sheep Meadow. Bethesda Fountain. The statue of Romeo and Juliet. The zoo. Our penthouses and town houses may be beautiful, and our country houses and beach houses even more so, but Central Park is the place we'll remember when we remember growing up.

sightings

N in our beloved park's Sheep Meadow with his **St. Jude's** lax buddies, getting a lesson in the art of buying a dime bag. Looks like someone has a new hobby. **B** at a freaky costume shop in NoHo trying on a doorman suit. Already getting ready for Halloween? **S** getting her ends trimmed at **Bumble and bumble** on Fifty-sixth Street, looking incredibly bummed. Cheer up, sugarplum, spring is just around the corner. **J** walking up Broadway, stopping in front of every freshly Windexed shop-window to admire the latest developments. You know how the song goes: "all it takes is a rake and a hoe and a piece of fertile ground." **D** in the poetry section of the **Strand** bookstore in the Village, reading Keats just for kicks. Soon he'll start dressing in kneesocks and puffy white shirts with ruffles and contract consumption, just for effect. **V**, stalking him with her digital camera. She'd be scary if it wasn't so cute that she's in love. **C** doing his own little runway show complete with white patent leather monogrammed car coat in front of the Italian embassy. Was he modeling for Italian *Vogue* or is he thinking of emigrating?

your e-mail

Dear GG,
I have to go to a debutante ball with this girl because she asked me and I like her but (a) I don't know how to dance to anything but ska; (b) I refuse to wear a tux; (c) I have a pierced tongue that I'm pretty sure she doesn't know about; and (d) I don't know why I said yes.
—ahole

A: Dear ahole,

I didn't call you that, you did. All I can say is, she asked you for a reason and I bet there are all sorts of things you don't know about her either. For instance, she probably has way more piercings than you do, and other things you'd be horrified to discover. So why not discover them?

—GG

Q: Dear Gossip Girl,

I can't believe you're here and I'm here and oh my God life is so crazy. You know how we were all dancing at that party last weekend and I totally barfed all over the radiator? Oh my God. My dad had to, like, pay for that. I'm in so much trouble. Anyway, thanks for sending me home in your car—that was really sweet. I love you!

—cara

A: Dear cara,

I'm still recovering from that party myself—glad to hear you're home safe. Just make sure you soak that gorgeous lavender silk Marc Jacobs blouse in a nice warm Woolite bath. I'd hate to see it ruined. Love you too!

—GG

Speaking of sharing the love. I think it's time to get my bum off this rock and walk slowly and enticingly home through that crowd of adorable boys playing soccer just over there. Some of them look familiar. Even if I don't know them, they all know me. Or they will soon.

You know you love me,

gossip girl

From: lwren@knowes.com
To: narchibald@stjudes.edu
Date: Sunday, February 16, 2:45PM
Subject: Re: Re: to be continued . . .

Dear Natie,
Thanx for ur note. I think u know how
hot I think u are. I have like eight bfs
here, but I can't stop thinking about
u. Please scan down for a pic of me in
the silk leopard-print Victoria's Secret
underwear I bought for the cotillion ur
taking me to. Hope you like it! ;)

Missing you tons,
L'Wren

From: <u>bwaldorf@constancebillard.edu</u>
To: <u>svanderwoodsen@constancebillard.edu</u>
Date: Sunday, February 16, 5:17PM
Subject: me and nate

Hey,
I was just thinking, what if you dressed
up like a waiter and I hid under a table
and when no one was looking we tied up
L'Wren's hands and feet with my mom's
old Hermès scarves. Then I'd get Nate to
come under the table with me, and while
you created a distraction we could, like,
crawl out of the ballroom and make a dash
for it. It could work, right?

I'll keep thinking.
—B

hms stoner boy

Nate stood outside the pizzeria on Eightieth and Madison with a bunch of hot French L'École girls, impressing them with his newfound ability to buy pot, roll a joint, and get high in broad daylight. After the snowfall over the weekend, Monday was unseasonably warm, and the L'École girls flaunted their leftover St. Barts tans by tying up the tails of their white button-down school blouses to reveal their flat stomachs and folding over the waists of their gray pleated wool uniforms until they were more like loincloths than skirts.

Yesterday, Nate's St. Jude's School classmates Charlie Dern and Jeremy Scott Tompkinson had introduced Nate to Mitchell, the pale, alarmingly skinny pizza guy who sold slices and baggies full of premium Thai stick cannabis to whoever knew enough to order "two slices of Sicilian with extra oregano."

Aha, the magic password.

Nate felt like a spy, but then again, he was stoned. In fact, he'd decided yesterday that he liked the feeling of being stoned so much—the way it made everything so much more intense and at the same time so much easier to deal with—he planned on being stoned for the rest of his life.

There's aspiration for you.

Yesterday at Charlie's house he'd discovered that three of his classmates had been smoking pot for years. Anthony Avuldsen, the blond, über-preppy surfer-looking guy in his class, had been stealing pot from his dad's special Guatemalan coffee tin since he was ten. Jeremy, the scrawny kid with a late '60s Beatles haircut whose pants were always falling down, had made his own bong in pottery class, fired on the inside and everything, and glazed with a multicolored paisley design that looked extremely trippy after a few hits. And then there was Charlie, whose older brother, Tao, sent him pot all the time. All four boys had really bonded over hits on Jeremy's bong yesterday. It was pretty intense.

One of the L'École girls kissed Nate on both cheeks before leaving, smothering him with her curly black overly hair-sprayed hair.

Merci! Merci! *Mwa! Mwa!*

Nate sucked in a hit and squinted up at the bright yellow sun, basking in it. Oh yeah, it definitely felt great to be young, hot, stoned, and in demand. L'Wren wanted him, these French girls all wanted him, Blair had always sort of wanted him, and Serena definitely wanted him. In fact, he was on his way to pick her up at school right now to find out just how much.

Serena was in a hurry. Her meeting with the dean of admissions from Hanover and her father was starting in ten minutes at the Yale Club on Vanderbilt Avenue, more than fifty blocks away. Madame Rogers had kept her late, giving the entire class a lecture in French on why the conditional perfect was the most important tense, ranting about how no intelligent person could get along without it because it allowed language to have an imagination and inspired French filmmakers to delve into romantic realms that would otherwise have remained unexplored.

Like *Last Tango in Paris*?

When class was finally over, Serena flew out of the great blue doors of the Constance Billard School for Girls, buttoning her raspberry-colored corduroy Agnès B. mini trench coat as she went and waving her hand wildly for a cab headed downtown. She'd been dreading the meeting all day, but if she was late, her dad would probably send her to military school instead of boarding school.

"Hey—wait up!" All of a sudden Nate's adorable golden head and irresistible, glittering green eyes swam in front of her. He leaned in and kissed her right on the mouth.

Hello.

"I thought about you all weekend," he told her, suddenly realizing that he could have been *kissing* her all weekend if he hadn't been getting high with his buddies.

Duh?

"Me too," Serena whispered back, her heart banging wildly against her ribs. Had he come to apologize for leaving her house so abruptly yesterday morning? Had he come to tell her he loved her? She grasped his hand and swung it back and forth between them, her cheeks turning a bright, happy pink. Behind her she could hear the hum of Constance Billard schoolgirls buzzing with gossip.

"Wait, are they a couple, or do they just kiss on the lips when they like meet up or whatever?" Kati Farkas wanted to know as she glossed and reglossed her lips in complete fascination.

"I don't know. She looks pretty flustered to me," observed Isabel Coates with classic accuracy.

"God, he's hot. I'd grab him and rip his clothes off if I were her," Laura Salmon declared.

"Where's Blair?" demanded Rain Hoffstetter.

Thankfully, Blair was at a tennis tutorial at Asphalt Green. Nate pulled the tiny blue glazed sailboat he'd made in art class out of his book bag and handed it to Serena. "I made it for you," he told her shyly, sounding about seven years old.

Serena had spent most of yesterday with Blair, pretending to be excited about Blair and Nate. Now she could barely resist grabbing him and kissing him all over. She took a step toward him and leaned into his muscular chest. He smelled smoky, and Nate-y, and wonderful. "When are we going to tell Blair?" she asked.

Nate buried his nose in her pale, sweet-smelling hair. It hadn't really occurred to him that they'd have to tell anyone anything. After all, they were pretty much together all the time anyway. Now they'd just kiss when they were together, and sooner or later they'd do even more. Girls were like that, though—they had to know things. They had to plan. "You haven't told her?" he responded. "It's not like it has to be a big secret or anything."

Serena stepped back and examined the little clay boat in her hand. Her Constance classmates were huddled so close by, she lowered her voice to keep from being heard. "I didn't tell her because I thought we should do it together." She looked up at Nate hopefully. *As a couple,* she added silently.

Nate grinned boyishly. The most awesome thing about being

stoned was that he could think something completely selfish and irresponsible and then say it out loud and not feel guilty about it. "I'd rather you just told her. I'm not good with stuff like that. And you know Blair."

Serena rolled her eyes as if she understood. Yeah, she sure did know Blair. Blair was going to decapitate her with her perfectly filed fingernails. But eventually all would be forgiven—maybe. "Okay. Well, I'll tell her soon," she promised vaguely. "Anyway, I have to go."

Nate took a step forward and kissed her lightly on the lips. "You look pretty today," he said, wishing now that he wasn't quite so stoned.

Serena giggled and pushed him away. "I'll call you, okay?" she told him quickly before dashing across the street and into a waiting cab. Sitting back in the sticky vinyl passenger seat, she fished the little blue boat out of her coat pocket again. HMS SERENA was etched in the stern, with a tiny red glazed heart next to her name. It was four o'clock, and Fifth Avenue was swarming with uniformed private school girls and their nannies on their way to ballet class or ice-skating at Sky Rink. The cab stopped at the light on the corner of Fifth Avenue and Ninety-third Street. Nate caught up to it and Serena rolled down her window and stuck her head out.

"Hey, Natie. You're not really taking that L'Wren girl to her debutante thing, are you?" she called out.

Nate stuck his hands into the pockets of his khakis. Blair had answered L'Wren's e-mail with that retardedly horny reply, so he was sort of committed now, wasn't he? Besides, when he'd told Charlie, Anthony, and Jeremy about it yesterday, they'd all agreed—*L'Wren's a sure thing, man. Do it with the older girl and get it over with. If you wait around to do it with someone you're in love with, you'll be a thirty-year-old virgin.* Those sounded like wise words to him.

"Yeah. I guess I have to!" he shouted back, like it was going to be a real chore.

Serena sat back down in her seat as the cab turned down Fifth, passing the Cooper-Hewitt Museum, the Guggenheim Museum, and the Metropolitan Museum in a gray blur. Her cell buzzed with another crazy text message from Blair.

WE CLD HIT N IN HS HEAD SO HE PASES OUT & FORGETS TO GO. BT WHAT IF HE GTS AMNESIA & DOESNT KNW WHO I AM? THN MAYB I CLD PRETND WE ALRDDY WER MRRYD!!

Up until now Serena had ignored Blair's crazy schemes, treating them as just that—crazy. Now that she knew Nate was still planning on taking L'Wren to the cotillion, things were different.

He absolutely could not go.

wimbledon can wait

Blair used to fantasize about rolling in the sand in a batik-print string bikini on some exotic beach with her tennis instructor, Duane, who had the most incredible muscles, black wavy hair, gorgeous turquoise-blue eyes, and spoke with an Australian accent. But now that she'd vocalized her infatuation with Nate to Serena, she was over Duane. Her entire raison d'être was Nate, Nate, Nate, and she no longer cared how taut Duane's hamstrings were or whether his hair was black, green, or purple.

Duane wanted to volley with her and work on her footwork, but Blair was so preoccupied with the notion that she needed to come up with a foolproof get-Nate-out-of-L'Wren's-bed-and-into-hers plan that she insisted on working on her serves. That way, each time Duane reloaded the ball machine she could whip out her cell and text another devious plan to Serena.

WE CLD GT HM DRNK & WRP HM UP IN BLANKTS & LCK HM IN A CLOST & NOT LT HM OUT TIL HE PROMISES NOT TO GO.

Duane released the next ball before Blair was ready and it hit her square in the chest.

"Jesus! Fuck you!" she yelled, glaring at him.

Now, now.

On a bench to the right of center court a little Sacred Heart girl who was waiting for her lesson giggled into her fist. She was wearing a short lemon-colored Lacoste tennis dress and had very impressive arm muscles for a girl of no more than eleven. Blair thought the girl looked a lot like herself only a few years ago—so serious about tennis, and not yet into boys. Now things were different. All she thought about was Nate. It was like there was a movie playing in her head at all times, a love story.

She and Nate would finally declare their passion for each other after so many years of denying it, and they'd spend their last few years of high school glued to each other at the lips. She'd spend most nights at his house, but occasionally they'd steal up to her family's summer home in Newport, Rhode Island, when her parents were playing golf in Scotland, and they'd make love on the sofas without even taking off the dustcovers that were put on each winter. Then they'd graduate and head off to Yale, where they both would have applied early, because really, when it came down to it, there wasn't any other college worth applying to. Then Nate would become a lawyer and she would become something worldly, glamorous, and fun that involved wearing amazing clothes and having intelligent conversations at the same time. They'd have the wedding of the century at St. Patrick's Cathedral, move into an incredible Park Avenue apartment, and have sex all the time. This movie was on constant replay in her mind, making it kind of hard to think about anything else. She certainly couldn't practice her serve.

The pocket of her conch shell pink and cream seersucker Lilly Pulitzer tennis skirt vibrated. Blair thwacked a vigorous serve at Duane's head and whipped out her phone. Serena had just texted her back.

WHAT IF WE GET NATE READY 4 BALL. GET HIM RLLY DRUNK. U KISS HIM. HE 4GETS 2 GO 2 BALL?

Blair speedily texted her reply:

COOL! CME OVR L8T 2 PLN? LV U!!

Duane released another ball, which glanced off Blair's shoulder. The next ball bounced directly in front of her and nearly took out an eye. She looked up from her phone. Duane stood on the other side of the court with his hands on his athletic waist, his nice dark eyebrows furrowed with impatience. "If you're serious about the nationals this year, I suggest you put down that phone!" he called out in his hot Australian accent before turning to fuss with his ball machine.

Blair had plotting to do, and Duane's little performance with the tennis balls was totally annoying. After all, she was the one paying him. He could wait while she texted highly important messages. Or he could go fuck himself. She shrugged her shoulders by way of reply, walked over to the little Sacred Heart girl, and handed the girl her tennis racket. "I think I just got my period. Please put this in my locker and tell Duane I went home," she instructed, casually strolling toward the exit.

Nice backhand.

s channels all the best leading ladies

Serena's cream-colored lace-patterned Wolford tights itched, and her dad was driving her crazy with his endless questions.

"Tell me, Serena's quite creative. It occurred to me that she should act. I can't recall—does Hanover have a decent acting program? I was a debate team man myself."

William van der Woodsen was tall and handsome, with dark blue eyes like his daughter's, blondish gray hair, and an affinity for silk cravats instead of ties. He was the epitome of dapper, and more than once Serena had witnessed women, from young stewardesses to matronly school administrators, swoon in his presence. He crossed his long, squash-playing legs. "I think she'd be quite an asset to any theater program, don't you?"

Serena felt her cell phone buzz in her satin-lined coat pocket. Reflexively she glanced at it and read Blair's text. Leaning forward so that her hands were obscured by the coffee table, she typed back a hasty reply.

Hanover's dean of admissions turned out to be a middle-aged woman named Candice Kaplan who looked like she tried very hard to be cool. Her boyishly cropped hair was dyed a dark amber color and she was wearing a pretty pink angora Chanel suit and black patent leather Manolo pumps. Actually, she *was* sort of cool.

"I played Lady Macbeth in our senior production," Dean Kaplan gushed in her alluring, velvety voice. "We got such good reviews, we toured Europe for the summer." She winked conspiratorially at Serena and pushed her pink hexagonal glasses up on her long, bony nose. A gigantic platinum-and-sapphire engagement ring glittered on the ring finger of her left hand. "I was hoping you would ask me some questions yourself, dear," she said pointedly.

The main lounge of the Yale Club was ballroom size, with floor-to-ceiling navy blue velvet–curtained windows overlooking Grand Central Station. Bow-tied servers whisked in and out of the quietly huddled groups seated in brown leather club chairs, efficiently delivering cocktails and tea and newspapers. It was an excellent choice for a meeting such as this, since there was no chance anyone Serena knew would be anywhere nearby. She took a deep breath, about to deliver the performance of a lifetime.

"I have no idea what I'm good at," she sighed, crossing her arms over her chest and staring down at her brown Marni lace-up boots. "I've traveled all over the world and had private tutors in French, Latin, and world history. I play tennis, field hockey, soccer. I swim, I read, I write. I suck at math, and yeah, I've done some acting. But when I think about the future, I'm like, maybe I'll just be . . ." Her voice trailed off dramatically as she pulled her gorgeous mane of blond hair up on top of her head and pouted her pink-glossed lips. Then she let her hair cascade messily down over her well-defined shoulders. "A hair stylist?

An actress? Who knows? I'll probably learn how to do lots of things, but I won't do anything very well."

Serena didn't know exactly who she was channeling—Liz Taylor as a child prodigy mixed with a little Lindsay Lohan?—but she could tell it was working. Candice took off her glasses and scrutinized Serena, as if noticing for the first time that Serena might be a Thoroughbred, an exquisite specimen of a human being with perfect conformation, but also a stupid, spoiled brat.

"I mean, I'm only fifteen. How am I supposed to know anything?" Serena added, glancing at her father. He took a great big swig of Scotch and uncrossed and recrossed his long, graceful legs. She could tell he could barely resist taking her over his knee and spanking her. *Sorry, Daddy,* she told him silently, *but I can't go now. I just can't.*

"Well, you've certainly got the looks to do anything you set your mind to," Dean Kaplan observed, the corners of her fuchsia-lipsticked mouth turned down with displeasure. She cleared her throat and swiftly pushed her glasses up on her nose. "But you're applying late, your grades are only fair, and your practice SAT scores leave a lot to be desired. Your brother, Erik, is an absolute treasure at Hanover—what a skier!—but I'm afraid that's not quite enough to get you in at such a late date." She pursed her lips. "Serena, you need to prove to me that you really want to go."

Serena stared wordlessly down at her boots. *I don't, I don't, I don't want to go!*

Dean Kaplan stood up and held out her hand to Mr. van der Woodsen. "We'll review her application as soon as we receive it, but I'm sorry to say I can't make any promises. Thank you for the tea."

Serena leapt to her feet and shook the dean's hand, smiling stupidly. As soon as Dean Kaplan had left, Mr. van der Woodsen sat down again, straightened his hunter green silk cravat, and swirled his Scotch around in its crystal tumbler, looking chagrined. "I missed a board meeting for this," he noted bitterly. He glanced up at his daughter, his blue eyes cold with hurt. "If you don't want to go to boarding school, why didn't you just say so?"

Serena chewed on her thumbnail, feeling totally ashamed. Her father had always been so quietly supportive of her, appearing out of nowhere at all her pageants and school plays when she'd always assumed he had no idea what she was up to. She smiled to herself, remembering the time in fourth grade when she'd lost five teeth in one week and was playing the second-oldest daughter in *The Sound of Music*. Her tongue kept popping out of the gap in her mouth so that she could barely talk, let alone yodel.

High on a hill was a lonely goatherd. Lay odl, lay odl lay hee hoo!!

But she finished the performance, her face hot and red and her eyes wet with embarrassed tears. Afterwards her father presented her with a huge bouquet of Japanese daisies from Takashimaya and whisked her away to Serendipity for a gigantic peppermint chip sundae, even though both ice cream and restaurants full of screaming children gave him the chills.

She gazed hopefully across the cocktail table at him. He might be disappointed, but he was her father, and she knew he only wanted her to be happy. "I don't want to go, Daddy," she told him, her great big eyes shiny and blue. "I don't want to go to boarding school."

Mr. van der Woodsen set his drink on the table and opened

up his arms. She rushed into them, sitting on his lap as she sniffled into his perfectly tailored white collar, feeling like that gap-toothed nine-year-old again. She loved the way her father smelled—like well-oiled leather, fresh limes, and Scotch. "It's all right," he soothed, patting her back. "If you don't want to, you certainly don't have to."

Serena sighed happily and played with one of his gold sport coat buttons. She couldn't wait to tell Nate she was staying. There was nothing now to keep them apart. Her cell phone buzzed where she'd left it on the seat of her leather armchair, and she lunged for it as though it were a life preserver. *Natie?* No, just another text from Blair.

Oh, her.

I NEED SOME FANCY UNDERWR FOR U KNW WHO. BARNEYS L8R?

Serena tossed her phone into her quilted black Balenciaga bag and slipped her arms into her raspberry-colored coat. She was tired of lying. Of course she didn't want Nate to go to that ball with L'Wren What's-her-face, but she also didn't want to read any more texts about Blair needing sexy underwear for him. Blair was her best friend. It was time to tell her the truth so they could stop this charade and get on with planning the summer and finding Blair a perfect boyfriend of her own. Sure, she'd be a little miffed, but when Serena told her how amazing-looking the boys in Holland were, she'd get over it.

Sure she would.

"that's one f—ed up little prince," said the caterpillar to the butterfly

"Hey Jenny, listen to this." Dan took a drag from his fourth unfiltered Camel that day and cleared his throat. *"You have hair like the color of gold. Think how wonderful that will be when you have tamed me! The grain, which is also golden, will bring me back the thought of you. And I shall love to listen to the wind in the wheat. . . ."* He stopped reading and looked up at his sister, who was lying on her stomach in the middle of their dusty living room, drawing on a sketch pad with fat sticks of charcoal. "It's like the kind of thing I want to say, I'm just too embarrassed. But in a poem it's different. It's like everything's a metaphor, and even if you're really saying what you mean, there's nothing to be embarrassed about, because it's the poem talking. Get it?"

Jenny stared at her brother for a second and then went back to smudging the lashes on her charcoal angel's eyes. She had no clue what Dan was talking about, but she knew it made him feel better to rattle on in this way, so she didn't say anything. She and Dan were alike in that way. In public they appeared shy. At home you could not shut them up.

"That's from *The Little Prince,* by Antoine de Saint-Exupéry. He's French. This is a translation." Dan took another puff of his cigarette and paged through the slim secondhand hardcover book with its delicate black-and-white illustrations. He'd been smoking on a regular basis, cultivating his image as an angst-ridden poet. So far their dad hadn't said anything about it, but it took him a long time to notice things. "It looks like a children's book, but it's really this profound existential work. And it's really romantic too—he falls in love with this rose, who he knows he can't really have a love affair with. But he loves her—he can't help how much he loves her."

Jenny was barely listening. Obviously everything Dan said was in some way related to his obsession with Serena. Yesterday she'd noticed that some of her angel drawings were missing from her portfolio. She stormed into his room and found them Blu-Tacked to the wall. His shamelessness was pathetic.

"I'm proud of your work," he'd told her defensively when she pointed out that he'd taken them without asking.

Right.

Jenny let him keep the drawings, although she was a little concerned that her big brother was turning into a psychopath who talked to himself and had delusions that one day Serena would just appear in their kitchen and ask him out.

If only.

Dan continued to read. Mr. Sohn, his history teacher at Riverside Prep, had assigned *The Little Prince* to illustrate what creative people were doing and thinking during the Nazi regime. Mr. Sohn was cool. He liked to demonstrate whenever he could that you didn't have to be a boring lawyer or bond trader when you got older. He tried to introduce role models like this

Antoine de Saint-Exupéry guy, who was a naval pilot and also this incredible philosopher-writer-illustrator. He sounded so dashing—even his name was dashing.

"Antoine de Saint-Exupéry." Dan recited the name aloud, rolling it off his tongue with a dramatic French accent.

Jenny looked up from her drawing again. "You need friends."

"That's where I come in," a girl's hoarse voice rang out from the hallway. Rufus appeared in the doorway of the living room wearing electric orange Adidas track pants and a faded red-and-green-plaid flannel button-down shirt. It hurt Dan's eyes to look at him.

"I just came back from buying saffron for my squid-ink paella and I found this rather sweet bald girl in the lobby," he told Dan with a goofy wink. "She's not a blonde, but I asked her to stay for dinner anyway."

Dan closed his book and stood up. "Vanessa?"

Rufus stood to one side to allow Vanessa to enter the room. "Hi," she greeted Dan, and then glanced at Jenny. "Hi." She didn't know why she'd come without calling or anything. She'd just been thinking about him so much, and she suspected that Rufus had forgotten to give Dan her message since he hadn't called her back. Maybe he was just super shy.

All the more reason to be super aggressive.

"I must endure the presence of two or three caterpillars if I wish to become acquainted with the butterflies," Rufus quoted, pointing at Dan's book.

So that's where he got it, Vanessa thought to herself. Dad was a literature buff.

Jenny sat up and crossed her legs. She was still wearing her pleated navy blue wool Constance uniform but had taken off her boring white polo shirt in favor of a black tube top that showed off her new boobs marvelously. Her wildly curly dark hair tickled her bare shoulders so that she looked like some sort of prepubescent Medusa. "Hey, you go to my school," she observed perkily. "You're a sophomore. Do you know Serena?"

Vanessa sat down on the floor in front of Jenny with her back to Dan, who was still seated on the worn brown leather sofa. "Maybe you can tell me," she began in a confidential tone, "why everyone is so obsessed with Serena."

Rufus stood his ground in the doorway. Silently Dan prayed that his dad wouldn't say anything embarrassing about how Serena was basically all Dan and Jenny talked about. It was kind of strange for any of them to be talking about some poor innocent girl who lived across town and had no idea they even existed.

Kind of.

"She's perfect," Jenny finally answered earnestly as she selected a fresh stick of charcoal.

Vanessa rolled her eyes and Rufus excused himself to work on his paella. "Okay, now it's time to change the subject," Vanessa declared, tugging her maroon polyblend uniform skirt down over her pale, shapeless knees, which were very definitely not her best asset. She pointed at Jenny's charcoal drawings. "What's all this?"

Jenny bit her lip. She knew Vanessa was sort of an artist herself. Her creepy, depressing black-and-white photographs of people on the subway had been on exhibit in the hallway outside the science labs all winter. "I'm entering that hymnal design contest. You know the one Mrs. M put up notices about? It's supposed to only be for upper school girls, but Ms. Monet kind of made me enter. I don't know. It's good practice, I guess."

Vanessa pulled one of the drawings closer and studied it. Jenny had that uncanny ability to be neat with charcoal. Her lines were so precise it was as if she were copying something. "You'll win," Vanessa assured her. "You'll totally win."

Jenny liked her at once. She'd noticed her before and had always been a little scared of her, especially now that she was bald. But she wasn't scary, she was just . . . confident. And she had good boobs. Not huge, but definitely there. Jenny stuck her chest out and looked down at herself, checking for signs of cleavage.

"That's really not a good look," Vanessa observed. "Tube tops should be illegal."

"Thank you," Dan agreed, squeezing his pale, knobby knees together. It was weird the way Vanessa had come over unexpectedly and then spent the whole time talking to his sister. But he was grateful she hadn't noticed that he was sitting there in only his white Fruit of the Loom boxer shorts, which is what he always wore when he was doing homework.

"I'm kind of conducting an experiment, on my . . . chest," Jenny explained, tugging up on the tube top. "I'm taking these supplements, and every day when I come home I put on this tube top and measure myself. It's really working. I've already gone from a no cup to almost an A cup, and this is only day four."

"Jesus." Dan shielded his face with his hands.

"Quiet over there, Captain Underpants," Vanessa snapped, and then giggled to herself. All the time she'd been sitting there, she'd been aware of Dan's presence behind her. It made her feel giddy and careless and electric. "Jenny," she said a little more seriously, "you're what—twelve, thirteen?"

Jenny nodded. "I'm in seventh grade."

"Do you think I could see what's in the supplements you've been taking?"

Jenny hurried away to fetch the canister of supplements hidden beneath the Target Shabby Chic pink dust ruffle on her bed. She couldn't believe she'd told Vanessa about her breast enhancement pills, but it was kind of nice to share. Perhaps the bald-headed, black-Doc-Martens-wearing sophomore was the solution to her gaping no-mother, no-big-sister void.

"I'm not through with you," Vanessa informed Dan while they waited for Jenny to return. "Your dad told me on the way up here in the elevator that you write poems. I'm starting this arts magazine at Constance and you should see some of the crap people are turning in. If your poems are any good, I want to publish them."

Dan's face turned beet red. All of his poems were about Serena.

"Here they are." Jenny dashed back into the room and handed over the big white plastic canister.

Vanessa turned it over and read the label out loud. "'Yams, fenugreek, macca root, barley, ginseng, biotin, sea kelp, gelatin.' Sounds pretty healthy, although I have no idea what macca root is." She unscrewed the lid and sniffed the supplements. "They even smell good for you." She screwed the lid back on and handed back the canister. "I don't think those things are doing you any harm. The ingredients sound pretty much like what my crazy sister eats every night for dinner. She's macrobiotic. But my theory is, your boobs will keep on growing without these things. Believe me, by the end of seventh grade I went from totally flat to looking like this. She lifted up her black T-shirt to reveal her sturdy 36Bs encased in a plain black cotton bra made by Playtex for Kmart. "I know they're not huge, but I'm pretty sure they're still growing."

Behind her she could practically hear the sweat dripping off Dan's palms. God, he was cute.

Dan didn't want Vanessa to leave, but he wished they could talk about something else, and that Marx the cat or someone would cause some sort of ruckus so he could dash into his room, put some pants on, burn his black notebook, tear down the angel pictures on his wall, and kill the smell of whatever Rufus was currently cooking up in the kitchen. The air smelled like spicy earwax.

Jenny frowned down at the large container of supplements. "So you think I should stop taking them? The directions say full results won't occur until you've taken them for at least three months."

Vanessa stared at her, realizing now how serious Jenny was about growing boobs. Obviously she'd given it a lot of thought and done a fair amount of research. "I think you should stop taking them for a week, but keep measuring yourself. If you keep growing, you'll know it's you, not the pills. Believe me, our bodies are capable of some crazy shit."

Dan shifted uncomfortably on the sofa. He really didn't want to hear about his sister's chest anymore. "Are we finished with this discussion yet?" he demanded rudely.

Jenny wasn't so sure. "I'll think about it," she agreed tentatively and carried the supplements back to her room. She didn't like being told what to do by someone she barely knew, but Vanessa had planted the seed of doubt. After all, in some of their family pictures her mom really did have quite a nice rack.

Maybe if she just waited for Mother Nature to do her thing, she'd grow an even bigger one.

"Okay, naked man." Vanessa whipped around and slapped Dan's bare thigh. "Show me your stuff."

Blushing fiercely, Dan fished around in his backpack and reluctantly handed over his notebook. If they were going to be friends, her reading his poems was inevitable. So was her finding out about his obsession with Serena. His lameness would also become apparent, but that was inevitable too.

Vanessa held the black leather book in her lap and thumbed through the pages. It was the ones after Valentine's Day she was interested in. After they'd met.

AV?

> *Say*
> *California, never been there*
> *Does anyone smoke in California?*
> *Are they clean, pure, do they kiss with tongues?*
> *Do they wear black like you?*
> *Do you know me?*
> *I think you do.*
> *We only just met but*
> *I suspect you know a lot about*
> *What's lurking beneath*
> *This rock.*
> *Hey, Black Widow,*
> *Bite me.*

Vanessa read the entire poem through twice, feeling almost completely positive that the poem was about her. It was even sort of *shaped* like her. *Do they wear black like you?* Eager for more, she turned the page.

> *Turn around bright eyes*
> *I know that's*
> *Some kind of dumb '80s shit song*
> *But it suits you*
> *I can even picture*
> *You in a fishnet '80s shirt*
> *Your blond hair all freaky*
> *Sitting on my bed*
> *Polishing my toes*
> *And chewing gum*
> *Blow a big bubble*
> *Chew me up and spit me out*

So she didn't have blond hair, but maybe Dan had *imagined* she'd had blond hair before she'd shaved it.

A shaved head does leave a lot up to the imagination.

She flipped back to the previous poem, which she liked the best. "Do you think I could publish these? I wouldn't use your name, since it's supposed to just be for Constance students. I could just call you Anonymous. I'll make you famous," she promised with a sly smile.

Dan slowly grinned back. Vanessa was basically offering him a surefire way of getting his message out to Serena. She would read the poems and gradually it would dawn on her that they were all written for her. Then Jenny would let it slip that Anonymous was actually her dashingly handsome poet of a big brother, and their dreamy love affair would commence.

"Dinner!" Rufus bellowed from the kitchen.

"I'll make copies and give them to Jenny to take to school." Dan took the notebook back from Vanessa and stood up. "You can stay for dinner. I just have to warn you, my dad's cooking is totally insane. Usually Jenny and I just pretend to eat, and then we have donuts or something later."

Vanessa beamed happily back at him. The Humphreys' apartment wasn't as bookishly elegant as she'd thought it would be. Of course there were lots of books, but they were stacked on the floor in dusty piles and there wasn't a vase of flowers in sight. The place probably hadn't been cleaned in at least ten years. Still, she'd fallen in love with the whole family, especially Dan. She was pretty sure she could eat anything if it meant she could sit next to him, watching the adorable way his hands shook as he wrestled with his steak.

Or his flambéed eggs with candied nuts and ham.

b is for binge and p is for purge

The oak-paneled elevator doors rolled open onto the Waldorfs'
foyer. Blocking Blair's path was a small Burberry signature
plaid doggie carrier from which emanated a plaintive mewing
sound. Blair tossed her navy blue cashmere knee-length TSE
cardigan over the handlebars of her brother Tyler's silver Razor
scooter and bent down to examine the doggie carrier. A tiny
blue-gray kitten stared at her from inside with hopeful ice blue
eyes.

"You're okay, little kitty," Blair assured it. She unzipped
the carrier to retrieve the kitten and cradled it in her arms. A
piece of her father's gold-and-cream-striped Crane's statio-
nery was folded inside the carrier. She pulled it out and tore
open the note, reading it as the kitten kneaded its paws into
her palm.

My darling Blair Bear,
As you know, your mom and I have been growing apart. It
probably comes as no surprise that I've decided to move out. I
know this will be difficult, and so I'm giving you this gorgeous

*Russian Blue kitten to provide some solace. He's a boy and
very gentle. Hug him and think of me.*

I love you, my Bear. Call soon.

—Dad

Blair reread the note, squeezing the little kitten so hard it
squirmed to get away. *It probably comes as no surprise . . . ?* What
the frigging fuck?! Sure, her family had never been that great
with sharing what was on their minds, but her father had just up
and *left*? Moved out, like it was no big deal, ditching his respon-
sibility to his family, his children, his firstborn? Had her mother
even noticed he was gone?

Blair was tempted to throw the little kitten against the wall,
but his tiny gray body was so furry and innocent, she couldn't.
His fur was softer than her mother's mink coat, like a newborn
baby mink. She held him up in front of her face and pressed
her nose against his fuzzy gray forehead. "My tiny lost little
Kitty Minky," she crooned dramatically and carried him down
the hall to her bedroom. Pretty soon her bed was going to be
slightly crowded, what with Nate sleeping over all the time, but
until then there might be room for a small kitten. She made him
comfortable on her rose-colored silk pillows, stroking him with
a trembling index finger. She was angry as hell at her father,
and so sad she felt like throwing her bedroom furniture out the
window.

"Dad gave me a pretty cool present," she heard Tyler's ten-
year-old choirboy voice call out from her doorway. "What'd you
get?"

Blair nodded her chin at Kitty Minky, which was what she'd
decided to call the kitten. He'd curled up in a tiny gray ball

and was purring contentedly. Tyler jumped up on the bed and pushed the kitten over on its side, vigorously rubbing its little pink tummy and startling the poor thing half to death. "He gave me this vinyl record collection and this awesome vintage Zenith turntable. The whole collection used to belong to this famous DJ who's in prison or something. Anyway, it's rad."

Tyler was practically hyperventilating he was so excited. He wanted to be a famous DJ himself one day, and he spent a lot of time in his room, cultivating his nerd status by playing Xbox and listening to Led Zeppelin on a pair of gigantic headphones like one of the Little Einsteins on crack. Still, there was something impossibly sad about how excited he sounded, like he was trying his darnedest not to cry and was acting overly chipper instead. It made Blair so angry she felt like she was going to explode. Fuck her fucking fucked-up family.

She scooped up Kitty Minky in her arms and pressed him tenderly against her chest. "Is Mom home?"

Tyler shrugged and violently kicked Blair's Sigerson Morrison gold flats across the room just for the hell of it. "Shopping," he replied. "Dad took her favorite champagne glasses," he added. "The Baccalaureate ones."

"Baccarat," Blair corrected him. The two siblings exchanged glances, half sympathetic, half challenging, but neither one was willing to pour their heart out to the other. Blair hugged her new kitten even tighter to her chest. Tyler got up and snatched a piece of Doublemint gum from the pack on her desk. He popped it into his mouth and dropped the wrapper on the floor.

"Get out, pig," Blair ordered, just as she'd done a thousand times before. No, there would be no tears. Not until she closed the door behind her brother. And put the cat down, and—

She dashed into her bathroom, knelt down in front of the gleaming white porcelain toilet, and stuck her middle finger down her throat until she gagged. Tears streamed down her face as she hacked up the iceberg lettuce and lemon yogurt she'd eaten with Serena in the lunchroom at Constance, the croissant and hot chocolate she'd had for breakfast with her parents, the cheese omelet and pommes frites Myrtle had made for her and Tyler last night for dinner, and every other meal she'd ever eaten in her life. It was as though there was something terrible inside her and she had to get it out, be free of it. And even though the vomiting part was ugly and disgusting and painful and shameful, she felt immediately better. She really did.

The bathroom door stood open. From the end of her bed Kitty Minky watched her with wide, curious eyes. His soft gray ears twitched forward and back, as if he were trying to understand what she was doing on her knees in front of the toilet. Then the bedroom door swung open and Serena breezed in, looking flushed and happy and ready to go shopping. She stopped and stared at Blair.

"What are you doing?"

Blair stood up, quickly flushed the toilet, and splashed cold water on her face. Then she smeared some Colgate onto her finger, scraped it across her teeth and tongue and rinsed it out with a mouthful of cold water. There, all better. She walked back to the bed and scooped Kitty Minky up in her arms.

"My father moved out," she explained, holding the kitten out to her friend in order to distract her from what she had just seen.

Serena examined the gray fur ball, holding it delicately in her long, slender hands. In the cab up to Blair's she'd gotten all fired up to tell her about kissing Nate; about how she'd thought her parents were making her go to boarding school, but now, thank goodness, they weren't; and about how sorry she was for not saying anything about any of this before. They could still have fun keeping Nate from going to the cotillion with L'Wren, only Blair wouldn't be hooking up with him, because he and Serena were already together. Serena couldn't wait to see Nate and tell him the good news, and kiss him, and kiss him, and kiss him. . . .

But now this. Blair's father had moved out. He'd given her a kitten by way of apology, and Blair had just made herself sick because of it. Serena nuzzled her face into Kitty Minky's soft, warm fur. Even if she wasn't going to boarding school anymore, her acting days had only just begun. She'd just have to keep pretending she wanted to help Blair hook up with Nate, when she had absolutely no intention of doing any such thing. Nate was hers; he was already spoken for.

And just exactly when was she planning to break this special news?

She put Kitty Minky carefully down on the bed. Then she linked arms with Blair. "Come on. It's the week after Valentine's Day. I think some of the stuff at Barneys may even be on sale."

As if either of them ever bought anything on sale.

Blair stuffed her feet into a pair of black velvet Tod's loafers and spritzed her face with the nearest Evian water atomizer. Her father had taken her to her first *Nutcracker* and helped her pick out her first pair of Manolo Blahniks, but she had better things to do now than mope. If she was ever finally going to take her clothes off with Nate, she'd need some decent lingerie for the occasion.

And there's no better cure for the blues than Barneys.

stoned dudes can read between the lines

Nate was up in his wing of the Archibald town house, sharing hits with Jeremy, Anthony, and Charlie on the new blue Lucite bong he'd just bought at a head shop on East Fourteenth Street. The windows were open to let out the smoke, and the boys sat huddled together in a tight circle around the bong like Boy Scouts around a campfire.

"Dude, in like two days you're gonna be El Capitán!" Jeremy observed. He handed Nate the blue test tube–like contraption, banged his fists against his chest and snorted through his nostrils like a horny male gorilla. Nate's friends acted like they'd been having sex with older girls since third grade, but the truth was they were all total virgins, vicariously enjoying the thrill of Nate's upcoming tryst with L'Wren.

Nate grinned into the opening at the top of his new bong. It was six inches longer than Jeremy's homemade one and got him thoroughly baked after only half a hit. Even without his friends' encouragement, Nate was feeling totally stoked. He couldn't wait to finally have sex. It was this huge rite of passage that every boy fantasized about, and it was about to happen to him.

He stood up and grabbed his graphite iMac off his desk. "She sends me these horny e-mails every day," he bragged, powering the laptop on and clicking open his inbox. Sure enough, a new message from L'Wren topped the list.

From: lwren@knowes.com
To: narchibald@stjudes.edu
Subject: thinking of u
Date: Wednesday, February 19, 4:18PM

Natie Baby,
Only two more days until I am untying
your bow tie and throwing your boxers out
the window. Get ready to have an amazing
time with a girl who knows what she's
doing, because you know what they say—
practice makes perfect!!

I'm glad it's you and you're gonna be way
glad it's me. ;)

—L'Wren

The other three boys tittered and blew smoke rings as Nate read the message out loud to them. Then he clicked on the message below it.

From: svanderwoodsen@constancebillard.edu
To: narchibald@stjudes.edu
Subject: us
Date: Wednesday, February 19, 3:05PM

Hey Natie,
Just wanted you to know that I still
haven't told Blair because I really
don't think I should. I guess maybe I'm
chicken, but I think she's having a
hard time with her family right now and
I don't want to get her upset? Can we
just sort of pretend nothing is going
on for a while until things aren't so
crazy?

You know I love you,
—S

"See? That's what I'm fucking talking about!" Jeremy Scott Tompkinson crowed, pointing at the screen as he read over Nate's shoulder. He thrust the bong into Nate's hands and read the message out loud to the others while Nate took another wincing hit.

"'Just sort of pretend nothing is going on'?" Jeremy repeated with a disdainful roll of his bloodshot hazel eyes. "Serena's the bomb and all that, but she's leading you down the yellow brick road to no-dickville," he expounded with stoned intensity. "College girl's already got her clothes off. You just gotta turn up and blam!—your virginity is part of your rosy-cheeked childhood."

He pounded on his chest with his fists again. "El Capitán, remember? El fucking *Capitán*!"

Nate took a second consecutive hit, his head spinning with lack of oxygen and an overdose of tetrahydrocannabinol. He wasn't sure what Serena meant about Blair, but then he realized that he hadn't even seen Blair since the morning after that party on Valentine's Day. Maybe she hadn't been hanging out because things were going badly with her family and she didn't really feel like talking about it?

Or maybe he was just too stoned to notice that nearly a whole week had gone by without them talking.

Nate ran his hands through his wavy golden brown hair. If Blair's family was having real problems, that was bad. And it was sweet that Serena didn't want to spill the applecart or tip the can of beans, or whatever the hell the expression was. He'd remember when he wasn't so stoned. But none of that meant that he shouldn't go ahead and lose his virginity to L'Wren, right?

Charlie shrugged his shoulders. "Serena's pretty hot though," he put in, grabbing the bong away from Nate.

"She's a goddamned goddess," Anthony agreed. "But I bet she'll stay a virgin until she's, like, sixty-nine. Sixty-nine—ha!—get it? Then she'll become a nun. Girls that gorgeous never get laid."

Is that a fact?

Nate took the bong back and stared into it, not taking another hit or anything, just holding it because it was his and he liked it. The water inside was a blue-gray color, almost black. He didn't really like talking about girls with his friends. It just made him want to be with the girls they were talking about.

Girls smelled good and they made him feel good. He really liked them a lot.

Sigh. Despite his shortcomings, we like him a lot, too.

Nate's Nokia jingled and vibrated in his pocket and he dragged it out with rubbery fingers that felt like they belonged to someone else. The word *Blair* loomed on the phone's tiny screen.

"She bangs," he answered, and then giggled. Damn it to all fuck, was he ever stoned.

"Natie?" Blair responded in her best, breathily flirtatious, childishly querulous Marilyn Monroe voice. "Guess where I am?"

"Whuzzat?" he slurred. He could barely speak.

"In the dressing room at Bergdorf's. Naked," she taunted.

"Yup!" Nate replied happily. He could picture it. A whole dressing room full of naked girls. "That's what I'm talking about!"

"Anyway, Serena and I want to, like, get you ready for the debutante thing, okay? Like help you tie your bow tie and do your hair? We bumped into Chuck picking up his tux. He's escorting some girl to the cotillion too, and he told us he's totally having a pre-party in the Basses' suite at the Tribeca Star! So does that sound good? We'll get you ready at Chuck's party? It'll be fun!"

Blair's voice sounded a lot like the adults' voices on those old *Peanuts* cartoons—"wa wa wa"—but Nate got the gist of what she was saying. They wanted to dress him for the party and get him all ready, kind of like those teaser mares the breeders used on those horse farms down in Kentucky. He'd visited a Thoroughbred farm on a trip to see the Kentucky Derby with his dad and had watched one of Secretariat's great-granddaughters get bred. First the farm dude surrounded the stallion with mares in heat so he got all turned on. Then they just led the horny stallion up behind Secretariat's great-granddaughter and—she bangs! Nate giggled into the phone.

"Natie?"

"Yup. S'all good," he stammered. "See y'then," he added before hanging up. Then he yawned and stretched his arms overhead, feeling particularly studly and male. He stood up, placed his new bong carefully on his desk, and belched. "Anyone know anything about condoms?"

His three friends rolled around on the floor, cackling and pounding one another with pot-weakened fists.

"Field trip!" Charlie shouted.

"To Duane fucking Reade!" Anthony chimed in.

"El Capitán!" Jeremy roared hoarsely.

"She bangs," Nate giggled again, cracking himself up.

Boys are so dumb. The sad part is, the dumber they are, the more we love them.

Disclaimer: All the real names of places, people, and events have been altered or abbreviated to protect the innocent. Namely, me.

hey people!

the deb

In case you don't actually know what a debutante is or why these things still exist even though we're living in modern times and most of us girls are counting on going to college and having careers and wearing more suits—beautifully tailored, exquisitely cool suits—than poofy taffeta gowns, I'm going to give you the lowdown.

According to *Webster's* dictionary: *debutante (n.)—a girl or woman making a debut, especially into high society.*

It's all about our parents wanting to feel like they've created something as pure-blooded as a racehorse and as chaste as a saint, when all the debs really do is get terrifically drunk before, after, and during the ball, and swap escorts. And just like any other fancy function, it's all about the *before-* and *after-*parties. This year the ominipresent **C** hosts both at his family's penthouse suite at the Tribeca Star Hotel. The idea is to bring your outfit and get dressed at the pre-party, go to the ball, then return to the suite with your escort or someone else's, and get *un*dressed. As **C** is constantly reminding us, the hot tub is *always* hot.

And in case you're ever worried about what to wear to occasions such as these, don't be. Give it a few days and you'll come home from school to find your bedroom absolutely filled with couture gowns from every designer featured in next month's *W* magazine. At least, *I* will. That is, when I make my debut, or "come out," as it is more often called. If I come out. Come out, come out, wherever you are! Never mind. Anyway, the best of us are not quite there yet—give us a few years. Like fine wine, we get better with age.

sightings

S and **B** outfitting themselves with white satin and black lace in **Barneys, Bergdorf's,** and **Bendel's** lingerie departments. If **La Perla** puts an embargo on shipping their underwear to the U.S., these girls will remain well stocked for years to come. Guess they feel the same way I do: the dress is important, but what you wear *under* the dress is crucial. **V** taking pictures of people kissing in the street. Feeling sort of romantic, is she? **D** browsing in the bra department with his sister, **J**, in Bloomingdale's. That boy deserves a gold medal. **C** bellying up to the bar at the **Tribeca Star** while he interviewed debs to escort to the cotillion next week. Isn't it usually the other way around? Of course, none of the debs spoke English, and one of them had tusks for teeth, but all of them were bona fide princesses from faraway lands. As always, he will have his pick of the litter. Some things never change. **B**'s mother at **Baccarat**, ordering crystal like a new bride. From there she moved on to **Gucci**, **Dior**, and **ABC Carpet & Home**. Funny, those are all the places where her husband has charge accounts. It's nice she's found a healthy way to vent.

your e-mail

 Dear GG,
I'm so excited to be a debutante, but my escort is such a loser. How can I ditch him?
—prdmary

A: Dear prdmary,

An escort is just that, an escort. He takes you to the ball, you dance with him once, and then you dance with everyone else and oh-so-casually lose track of him. There are no rules that your escort has to escort you home.

—GG

Q: Dear GG,

I've been really sad lately. Give me something to look forward to. And don't say summer's just around the corner, because that will depress me even more.

—bleu

A: Dear bleu,

I'm sure your birthday must be coming up sometime in the next twelve months. Zip up your pointiest Jimmy Choo boots, grab a cab to Madison Avenue, and don't stop stuffing shopping bags with frivolous goodies until you start feeling happy again.

—GG

Time to get dressed, people.

You know you love me,

gossip girl

s and b create the ultimate distraction

The Basses' suite at the Tribeca Star was big enough to live in. It was the perfect party pad—sleek and modern with tasteful taupe velvet sofas, cherrywood paneling, cream-colored carpets, a king-size bed, two huge plasma-screen TVs, and a generous wet bar. The main attraction was the oversize hot tub, situated in a sort of anteroom between the master bedroom and the bathroom behind a giant sliding frosted glass door. Usually, the door was left open so that revelers could rotate freely between the couch, the bed, the bar, and the hot tub carrying magnums of champagne, their damp bodies wrapped loosely in the hotel's signature white Egyptian cotton Frette towels.

It was six o'clock on Friday night, the night Nate was to escort L'Wren Knowes to the debutante ball; the night Nate had planned to finally lose his virginity and become a man; the night Serena and Blair had been planning all week.

They arrived at the suite early. Serena brought half her parents' liquor cabinet and a carton of Gauloises with her. Blair had Fresh Direct deliver oysters, Godiva chocolate-dipped strawberries, caviar, and salty Triscuits. The idea was to ply Nate with aphrodisiacs, alcohol, and a general aura of seduction, causing him to become so distracted he'd forget all about L'Wren, the cotillion, and his first time.

Those had better be some strong aphrodisiacs!

Chuck's date for the ball was the twenty-year-old Italian contessa Donatella Juliet de la Varga, heiress to the Varga olive oil fortune. The contessa was strikingly beautiful, with hip-length amber-colored hair, dove gray eyes, flawless olive skin, endless legs, and the curvy 34 x 24 x 34 bust-waist-hips ratio of a Victoria's Secret model. To Chuck's complete and utter joy, the contessa was so used to going topless at beaches throughout Europe, she thought nothing of walking around the suite with her top off, asking for advice on which of her two pairs of exquisite gold Prada heels she should wear to the cotillion. Sadly, her English was so limited she could only communicate by saying "okay," "cute!" and "is hot, no?" which made her sound slightly retarded, but added to her allure.

It's hard to be jealous of anyone, however beautiful, who can only say three things.

"Having a bake sale, girls?" Chuck asked when he noticed Blair and Serena setting up shop at the round glass coffee table. They'd borrowed a few of the cut-crystal Baccarat ashtrays stacked on top of the wet bar and had filled them with an array of offerings, from Gauloises to lime wedges.

A bowl of cigarettes anyone? Olives? An oyster?

"Cute!" the tall, mostly naked foreign girl trailing Chuck exclaimed, pointing at the neatly arranged items on the coffee table.

Chuck snaked his arm around the contessa's bare, curvy waist. She was wearing white lacy boy shorts, a pair of gold metallic peep-toe pumps, and nothing else. Her round, navel orange–size boobs were tan and robust, like they'd spent more time in the sunshine and fresh air than her perfectly sculptured face, which was pale in comparison.

Where exactly are these beaches she frequents?

"But my darlings, you forgot condoms," Chuck joked like the horny jackass that he was. "Don't worry, I'm sure there are some lying around." Actually, there were—cases of them, in the cabinet under the bathroom sink. It was gross. Who could get through that many condoms before they passed their sell-by date? But Chuck's parents—although they'd never actually engaged their son in a conversation about safe-sex practices—were adamant that the hotel's cleaning staff keep the bathroom cabinet well stocked. That was de rigueur with families such as the Basses, the Waldorfs, and the van der Woodsens: anything to avoid a scandal.

Better safe than sorry, right?

The contessa reached for an oyster, and Blair slapped her hand away. "Those are for my boyfriend," she hissed, ogling the Italian contessa's perfectly shaped, tan breasts despite herself.

Serena stared at her best friend. *Boyfriend?* She tugged anxiously on the narrow gold Cartier tank watch on her wrist. Tonight was going to be trickier than she'd thought.

She'd been in denial about it all week, telling herself tales such as, *Blair will get drunk anyway and pass out, and then he'll be mine, all mine. . . . I'll just confront Blair and tell her that the last thing she needs right now is Nate. What she really needs is therapy.* The truth was, all she really had to do was kiss Nate herself the minute he walked in the door. He'd forget about L'Wren and carry her in his arms to a hotel suite of their own. Blair would get over it eventually. She might be dangerously angry for a while, but they could just hide out in their suite drinking champagne and snuggling until it was safe to come out.

Blair brandished a Triscuit with a few crumbs of caviar on it. "Here," she offered the Italian exhibitionist generously. "I like your shoes."

"Okay," the contessa replied, munching her Triscuit. She raised one Prada-adorned foot in the air and waggled her sparkling burgundy-colored toes. "Is hot, no?"

Blair and Serena both nodded. Serena, dressed in a black Diane von Furstenberg wrap dress and black Lanvin ballet flats, her hair pulled back in a ponytail, felt plain in comparison. Blair had dressed more carefully and was wearing her favorite charcoal gray Calvin Klein silk jersey T-shirt dress that looked boring on the hanger but hugged her tennis-toned body in all the right places. Still, her boobs had never been nor probably ever would be as tan and robust as Donatella's.

"Is hot," the girls repeated, nodding appreciatively at her fantastic shoes. She really was pretty hot. Chuck didn't deserve her.

Serena stared at Donatella's lovely naked breasts as she munched a Triscuit and contemplated her next move. Then Nate stumbled into the suite, carrying a black Bergdorf's suit bag and looking completely adorable in a baked, wide-eyed sort of way. Serena knew at once that she couldn't go through with Blair's charade. She wasn't a selfish girl by nature, but Nate was already hers and she wanted him. She wanted him all to herself.

"Natie!" she exclaimed, dashing over to help him with his things. "You look nervous. Come on, have a cocktail. It's going to be fun, you'll see."

Nate's eyes were huge and emerald green. Serena was so damned gorgeous. Why the hell was he going to that fancy debutante dance when he could just stay here and kiss her all night? Then Blair was at his side, looking clean and beautiful, and wielding a raw oyster on the end of a gleaming silver fork.

"Eat it, Natie," she cooed. "They're really cold and slippery."

A few feet away some gorgeous girl with big, tanned breasts, wearing only a pair of lacy white underwear, was bent over a cut glass bowl filled with cigarettes. Behind her, steam rose up from the hot tub, which was overflowing with scantily clad girls and boys drinking directly out of a giant bottle of Dom Pérignon. Luckily, Nate had gotten superbly stoned with his new blue bong before he arrived. He felt like he'd just walked into a full-on orgy.

"Come on." Serena and Blair each took one of his hands and pulled him toward the couch. "You know you love us."

Blair's cell phone chimed and twitched in its place on the glass coffee table. She grabbed it, hoping it was Sephora on Broadway in SoHo calling to tell her they'd restocked her favorite Hermès cologne, Eau d'Orange Verte, and were sending some over to her right now. She'd sampled every cologne they carried, and that was the one she'd chosen for Nate—fresh and masculine, yet supremely edible. She was going to spray it all over his chest and then kiss it off.

"Hello? This is Blair Waldorf," she answered in a businesslike tone.

"Blair Bear? It's your dad."

She almost hung up immediately, but the truth was, she missed her dad. She missed seeing him and hearing his reasonable, lawyerly voice. She sat down on a velvety taupe sofa and stuffed a raw oyster into her mouth. "Thanks so much for my kitten, Dad." Her voice was small and little girl–like. "He's the cutest."

"I knew you *had* to have him," her father replied, but he sounded distracted, like he had more serious things than kittens on his mind. "Bear, I don't know what your plans are tonight, but I'd really like you to meet my new partner, and we're staying right here at the Carlyle. You could walk over."

Blair rolled her eyes and glanced over at Nate. He looked so cute the way he was dipping his strawberries into his champagne and licking them off. She couldn't wait to dip *him* in champagne and lick him off.

"I'm actually pretty busy tonight, Dad," she sang into the phone. "Why do you want me to meet some boring lawyer guy you work with anyway? I mean, don't you guys have, like, a case to work on or something?" She knew she sounded spoiled and obnoxious, but she'd inherited her sassiness from him and she really did have a lot better things to do tonight than meet one of his stuffy colleagues.

Her father chuckled. "Actually, Giles and I don't work together. We met at a wine tasting at Bouley. He's my new partner, meaning we're *together*. We're a couple."

Blair clutched the phone to her ear. A *couple*? Her father had been having a "what's my bouquet" conversation with someone named Giles when she'd overheard him in his dressing room? Her father was *gay*? He was leaving her mother and his own flesh and blood for some French loser named Giles, and he was staying with Giles in a hotel only a few blocks from their home? It was too unfathomable to digest, especially with a stomach full of vodka and raw oysters.

Across the coffee table Nate dug into the pockets of his Brooks Brothers khakis and pulled out handfuls of condoms. One of the glass ashtrays was empty now, and he filled it up with an assortment of the colorfully wrapped prophylactics that he'd obviously brought to use later on, with L'Wren. Blair's father preferred Frenchmen and her beloved was about to have sex with a pushy older slut. Blair snatched up her glass of Stoli on the rocks and poured it down her throat.

"Sorry, Daddy," she managed to gasp. "Maybe some other time." Then she threw her phone across the room and bolted past the crowded hot tub, headed for the super-private toilet room located deep inside the stark white bathroom, and locked the door behind her.

Serena lit a Gauloise and followed Blair, abandoning a severely stoned Nate, who was feasting on oversize chocolate-dipped strawberries while building a tower of colorful condoms and staring at Donatella's boobs. She could hear her friend retching on the other side of the door. She knocked softly. "Blair? Are you all right?"

Blair coughed, staggered to her feet, and flushed the toilet. "He's gay," she gasped. Then she fell to her knees and retched into the white porcelain bowl all over again.

"Who? Nate?" Of course Serena thought Blair was talking about Nate. He was the only person on her mind, forever and always.

Rising unsteadily to her feet, Blair flushed the toilet again and opened the door. She walked out into the main bathroom, wiped her mouth on her sleeve, and yanked open the cabinet underneath the sink. Trojan. Durex. The shiny, brightly colored packages with their bold brand names screamed at her like a lurid chorus. But behind the cartons of condoms was a bottle of green minty Scope. She grabbed it and took a giant swig, swirling it around before spitting noisily into the sink. "No." Serena could be such an idiot sometimes. "My *dad*. My dad is gay. He even has a boyfriend. Some French fucker."

Serena stared at her. "But—"

"He just called me. He wanted me to come meet him and his 'partner' at their hotel." She clutched her stomach again, her face as green as the Scope she was holding in her hands. Jesus. Jesus fucking Christ.

"Oh, Blair." Serena's delicately clefted chin trembled. Her navy blue eyes grew shiny, and two big fat tears rolled down each lovely cheek. Blair's life was a disaster. But that wasn't why she was crying. She was crying because now that Blair had found out this extra-special bit of news about her father, there was no way Serena could take Nate away from her.

Could she?

one day little j woke up and she wasn't so little anymore

"I am the master, I am the king. You lie at my feet! You ululate when you hear my name!!" Zeke Freedman roared as he gesticulated wildly with his Nintendo joystick. Zeke had been Dan's best and only friend since kindergarten. Back then, they had been the smallest boys in the class and were more proficient in reading than wrestling, and so they had bonded in their classroom's library corner. Zeke was still a kindergartner in a lot of ways. After doing the reading for their sophomore Africa and the Middle East class last night, he had become obsessed with the word *ululate* and was now trying to use it in almost every sentence.

"And I'll urinate on your feet, dickweed," Dan shot back as his lanky dreadlocked player onscreen made a perfect jump shot.

"Oh, man," Zeke whined, hauling his gigantic gray wide-wale corduroys up over his woman-hips. In the past five years Zeke had grown from the second-smallest boy in the class to the largest. His shoulders were massive and sloping, his hips resembled those of a woman pregnant with her third set of triplets, his waist was undefined, his chin was doughy—even his dark, curly hair was big. It wasn't that he ate too much or didn't exercise, he was just "genetically awkward," as Dan liked to remind him, in a playful, best-friend sort of way. "Next game my cheerleaders are gonna ululate so loud, you're gonna get so distracted you won't know where my shit is coming from!" Zeke proclaimed, fervently tapping the buttons on his joystick to restart the game.

Down the hall in her room, Jenny plugged her ears with her fingers. It was bad enough that she was the only girl in the house—did she have to spend another lonely Friday night at home listening to boys talk about urinating on each other? She slammed the door and unbuttoned her shirt, dropping it on the floor where she stood. Then she unfastened her cream-colored satin Maidenform 32A bra, which had been cutting into her all day, leaving angry red welts on the tops of her shoulders. She threw it into her trash can and pulled open her underwear drawer, carefully removing Serena's powder blue jog bra. "34B," the tag beckoned to her excitingly. Sewn onto the bra's outer hem with tiny, perfectly formed white thread x's was a small rectangular white label with the name SERENA VAN DER WOODSEN printed on it in looping red script. Without a mother or a maid to sew name tags into their clothes, Jenny and Dan had lost a lot of clothes over the years.

Hence the need to steal other people's things?

Jenny slung her underdeveloped arms through the armholes and pulled the bra on over her head. Last time she'd tried it on it had just sort of fallen loosely down over her rib cage, the way things do when they're ten sizes too big. This time, the bra got stuck above her new boobs. She yanked it down, amazed to find that she filled it almost completely.

"Dan!" she shouted, throwing open her door. Without

thinking about what she was doing, she sprinted down the hall, her new boobs bouncing softly against their cottony encasement. "It fits!" She slid into the study in her sock feet, wearing only the powder blue jog bra and the pair of red-heart Nick & Nora pajama bottoms her Dad had given her last year for Valentine's Day.

"Yowza!" Zeke exclaimed, his big, curly dark hair looking bigger than ever. And then he ululated. Or at least tried to.

"What the fuck, Jen?" Dan shook his head at her, annoyed. She knew Zeke was there. What was she trying to prove?

Jenny's cheeks turned pink, but she stood her ground. "I just wanted to tell you that you-know-who's you-know-what almost fits me. See?" She pointed to her nicely swollen chest.

How discreet.

Then she spotted Dan's beaten-up cell phone on the worn brown leather sofa and lunged for it.

"Hey," he cried, attempting to rescue it. Zeke ululated again, and Dan realized he'd lost the game.

Jenny crouched protectively on the linty Oriental rug as she began to punch the phone's buttons. "I'm just calling Vanessa to tell her—"

"No!" Dan shrieked, diving floorward to tackle her. He and Zeke were supposed to be hanging out, and Zeke didn't even know Vanessa existed. Dan didn't want to have to explain his and Vanessa's relationship, because he honestly didn't quite know *how* to explain it. Jenny rolled onto her back, still holding the phone, and kicked him roughly away. Dan flew across the room like one of those disposable bad guys in a James Bond movie.

Even a tiny girl's legs can be surprisingly powerful. It's all that ballet we're forced to take in elementary school.

"Hey Vanessa, it's Jenny." She spoke quickly into the phone. "You know, Dan's sister?" Obviously Vanessa didn't say much because Jenny immediately blurted out her news. "Guess what? They grew! So I totally won't take the pills anymore. I'm stopping today. I mean, I'm already at the size I wanted so I guess it's time to stop. Anyway, I just thought you should know. Oh, and Dan wants to talk to you," she added, tossing the phone to her disgruntled brother.

He glared menacingly at his little sister and put the phone to his ear. "Hi," he greeted her in a tiny voice. His face was flushed and his hands were all sweaty. He swallowed nervously. "How are you?" She didn't say anything. "Hello?"

Zeke stopped mid-ululation. "Who's *Vanessa*?" he asked loudly. "Dan's got a girlfriend! Dan's got a girlfriend! Who is she? One of Jenny's classmates?"

"Hello?" Dan repeated, his face hot.

"Shush!" Jenny scolded Zeke. She kicked him in the foot. "Please?"

"Hello?" Dan asked for the third time. Vanessa must have hung up on him. Or maybe she was never there in the first place. Jenny could be sneaky like that.

"Dan's got a girlfriend!" Zeke cried and ululated again. "Oh, and by the way, you lost another game."

Dan sat on the leather sofa, glaring at life in general.

Now who's feeling genetically awkward?

s scores with two girls in one night!

"Remember cuddles in the kitchen. . . ."

Nate listened to his favorite Arctic Monkeys song with a devilish grin plastered across his face. Damn, was this going to be a good night. Already he was at a party with a mostly naked gorgeous Italian countess and his two best friends, who were looking particularly hot themselves. Pretty soon he'd be all decked out in his Armani tux, ready to meet L'Wren, who was just about the horniest girl he'd ever met in his life. Of course, her parents would be at the cotillion, and he'd have to dance and make stupid polite conversation with some of the debs and their escorts. But as soon as they'd gotten through all the formalities, they'd be up in L'Wren's hotel suite, doing it.

He checked his watch. Five after seven. Time to start getting ready if he was going to be at the St. Claire Hotel in Midtown by eight. He glanced around the crowded suite in semi-stoned confusion. Kati Farkas and Isabel Coates were trying on Chuck's father's Hermès ties, wearing nothing but bras and jeans. When did they get so *mature*? Nate wondered, ogling them. Did Serena and Blair look like that in just their bras? Weren't they supposed to be helping him get ready—giving him dancing school pointers and rubbing aftershave on his temples? Where *were* they, anyway?

Donatella perched on the edge of the glass coffee table and spread a lump of black beluga caviar on a Triscuit. She took a tiny bite and then offered Nate the rest. "Okay?" she asked with a bright smile.

He took the Triscuit and devoured it, wondering if she was retarded or just foreign. "Have you seen my friends? The two pretty girls who were sitting here before? They were wearing clothes," he added helpfully.

Donatella's gray eyes lit up enthusiastically. "Cute!" She turned and pointed through the steam drifting from the hot tub.

The suite was crowded and noisy, and someone had turned up the latest cheesy Justin Timberlake dance song on the Bose sound system, but a series of hysterical giggles penetrated the din. The little hairs on Nate's lacrosse-toned arms stood on end. He'd recognize that sound anywhere. It was a sound that made more than just his hair stand on end.

Yikes!

Listening to Serena laugh was like being tickled. It gave him shivers and an adrenaline rush. It made him see stars and lose coordination. It made him feel like he had to go to the bathroom, which was exactly where he was going right now. Not the toilet part of the bathroom, the hot tub part of the bathroom—the source of the sound.

"Hello?" Nate called cautiously through the steam. More giggles, combined with the humming gurgle of the hot tub's jets. Bare pink skin glistened wetly beneath the surface of the churning water. "Who's in there, anyway?" He took a step closer.

Two slick heads popped up out of the bubbles, one fair and one dark.

"It's just us, Natie," Blair called out. She smoothed her chestnut brown hair back against her head so that it was shampoo-commercial perfect. Her still-tan-from-Christmas-in-St.-Barts arms were crossed over her chest in a totally lame attempt to hide the fact that she was completely naked. "I was feeling yucky, so I decided to take a Jacuzzi," she explained, glossing over the more painful details of her absurdly depressing home life.

"Hot tubs are my favorite," Serena chimed in. She leaned her damp blond head back on the marble tile, exposing her long, perfect neck, among other things. "From now on, I'm conducting all my affairs from underwater."

Nate sat down on the edge of the tub, soaking his khakis. Jesus, Serena was so damned gorgeous. It made him unspeakably horny just to look at her. Strangely, he was hoping his night with L'Wren would cure him of this problem. If he had sex with L'Wren and sort of got it out of his system, maybe he wouldn't think about Serena so much—at least not in such a horny way. After all, he was in love with her, and it seemed sort of wrong to feel that jacked up about a girl you were so in love with, especially when she was your best friend.

Like that makes any sense?

"Aren't you guys supposed to be helping me get ready?" he demanded, glancing at his watch. He was already late. It was only a matter of how late. L'Wren didn't seem like the type of girl who'd be that forgiving, either, especially not when she had a hidden agenda. "You know I'm ass at bow ties," he added, wincing at how stupid he sounded. Lately his friends had been using the word *ass* all the time, but whenever he said it, he thought he sounded like a weiner.

Yup.

Serena giggled again, sending Nate's entire body into a frenzy. If he didn't get to that cotillion and lose his virginity ASAP, he was going to freaking lose his mind. "I better go," he muttered, standing up.

"No!" Blair's heart was racing. She was naked and Nate was *right there,* looking stoned and a little tipsy and totally overwhelmed, but also so ridiculously cute that she just wanted to grab him and pull him into the water. He couldn't leave. She absolutely could not allow him to leave. Tonight was supposed to be their night, and no way was Nate going to hook up with that slutty bitch who would totally ruin him forever. She shot Serena a "help me, do something!" glance and jabbed her friend's shapely gluteus maximus with her carefully exfoliated heel.

Serena kicked her back. She wanted Nate to hop into the tub with them just as much as Blair did. "Natie?" she cooed. "You have to change into your tux anyway. Why don't you just get in, and then we'll help you get dressed."

Nate shrugged. He could never say no to Serena, especially not when she was so naked in a bathtub built for two, or three, or four or five. "All right. But just for a minute." He tugged off his gray T-shirt and threw it on the floor. "Close your eyes."

Both girls pretended to close their eyes, barely staying conscious as he removed his pants, his silly sherbet orange boxer shorts, and finally his socks. Oh, oh, *oh!*

Then, just as quickly, the boxers were back on. "I can't do this. I'm late. I have to go. Will you guys please just, like, put some robes on or something and help me?" Nate pleaded.

Aw.

Serena and Blair had to pinch themselves to keep from squealing at his utter adorableness. "We *are* helping you," Blair insisted firmly. "Get in."

"Would it help if you knew we weren't at all threatening?" Serena asked coyly, cocking a perfectly plucked pale eyebrow. She grabbed Blair and kissed her right on the lips, using her tongue and everything. "See?" she said, pulling away. "We're lesbians." Underwater Blair stomped on her foot and elbowed her in the side, but Serena kept on smiling at Nate, daring him to get in.

Of course now he had to, because something ridiculous was happening inside his orange boxers, and the only place to hide it or kill it was under the bubbles in 103-degree water. "Cover your eyes again, with your hands. And no peeking, you jerks," he told them angrily, even though he was anything but angry. How the fuck could they do this to him? Serena especially. Fuck the party. Fuck L'Wren. He was going to hook up with Serena again tonight. And this time they weren't just going to kiss, he was pretty damned sure of it. He loved her, and he was pretty damned sure she loved him back, and there was absolutely nothing wrong with getting together with someone you loved and trusted. It had to be way better than any one-night thing with some college chick.

He jumped in with a huge warm splash and all his worries left him. "Hello, ladies," he greeted them goofily. "I mean, hello, friendly lesbians."

Blair giggled and swam a little closer to him. Her whole body felt so electric she was worried she'd get a shock. "I'm not really a lesbian," she declared boldly. "I just like kissing. I'll kiss anyone. Especially my friends."

Serena could feel her own hands drifting through the warm water toward Nate's body, reaching for him. He was hers, her Natie, and she couldn't wait to kiss him again. And again. And again.

"I don't want you to go to that dance with that girl," Serena heard Blair murmur bravely. Serena dropped her hands and forced them behind her back. Blair looked so hopeful, and her life was just so shitty right now. She deserved to have a moment alone with Nate. After a few minutes, he'd sweetly reject her, come find Serena, sweep her up in his arms, and carry her off to spend a blissfully romantic night together. The first of many.

"Maybe I won't go," Nate replied, edging toward Serena.

That's right, Serena coaxed silently as Nate drifted in her direction. He was grinning at her in that irresistibly cocky way of his, and it was all she could do to keep from hurling herself at him. Then Blair giggled giddily and flicked water at Nate's head, and Serena was once more reminded of her mission. "I've changed my mind," she announced, placing her hands firmly on the side of the tub. "I do like boys."

Nate chuckled and slipped his arm around her bare waist, pulling her toward him. Of course she liked boys. She liked him. She loved him.

Serena squeezed her eyes shut and forced herself to wriggle and splash out of his grasp. "Actually, I've always really wanted to kiss *Chuck,*" she lied, pulling herself up and out of the tub. She grabbed a white terry-cloth Tribeca Star Frette robe from off a chrome hook and wrapped it tightly around her body. "This should be fun," she added glibly and traipsed off to find Chuck, whom she'd have to kiss now to give her lie some authenticity.

Chuck and Donatella were standing by the door of the suite, feeding each other one last Stoli-dipped oyster before leaving for the cotillion. They were both dressed now—rather exquisitely, too—she in a cream-colored 1940s Old Hollywood–style Prada cap-sleeved gown embellished with pearls and a white ermine shrug, and he in a sleek black Armani tux with tails and a white bow tie. They looked like actors about to walk down the aisle for the first take of their big wedding scene.

"Kiss me," Serena commanded Chuck urgently. She stood on tiptoe, shut her eyes tight, and pulled his handsome but still repulsive face toward hers. "Quickly."

"I'm all over it!" he exclaimed loudly, lunging at her with his big, hungry mouth. Serena kept her eyes closed, her head swimming with the strong scent of Chuck's Égoiste cologne. It felt like he was gobbling her whole.

"Cute!" Donatella exclaimed, clapping her hands in delight.

Serena managed to tear herself away from Chuck and wiped her mouth thoroughly on the sleeve of her robe.

Blech.

"Your turn!" Chuck cried ecstatically and grabbed Donatella, delivering another one of his famous, head-eating kisses. Donatella giggled and then whirled around, her white silk gown fanning out around her ankles as she grasped Serena's shoulders and kissed her on the mouth just for good measure. She tasted like olives and kissed way better than Chuck could ever hope to.

"Cute!" she exclaimed again as Serena wiped her mouth on her other sleeve. Obviously Donatella thought this was some sort of American pre-party custom—a kiss orgy.

Or maybe she really was retarded.

d really sort of maybe does have a girlfriend

"Are you getting that?" Jenny yelled at Dan from her room when the downstairs buzzer rang for the second time. They weren't expecting anyone, but their dad, Rufus, had gone downtown to a poetry slam with some of his communist Beat poet cronies. Maybe he'd drunk too much absinthe and had come home early to sleep it off, losing his keys in the process. Jenny was busy trying on bras and shirts and dresses and admiring her budding boobs. She needed an entirely new, more womanly wardrobe—clothes with V-necks and scoop necks and buttons to unbutton and show off her cleavage. Not that she really wanted anyone else to look at it—she just liked looking at it herself. She wanted to be able to go to the bathroom in the middle of math class, see her reflection in the mirror over the sink, and say, "Hello, cleavage! Where have you been all my life?"

Rest assured, she won't be the only one saying hello.

The bell rang again. "Dan?" Jenny shouted again. She opened her door wearing a child's size ten pink-and-purple vertical-striped Speedo one-piece that was so tight and revealing on top it looked like more like a bustier than a bathing suit, and stomped angrily down the hall to see who it was.

Dan was in the study, busy writing another poem in his black leather-bound notebook. Zeke had left soon after Jenny's embarrassing announcement that her chest was finally a size 54X or whatever. Since then, Dan had been busy cutting out one of Jenny's blond paper angels and pasting it on the inside cover of his notebook while he mused on a new metaphor. He thought about how angels had wings and were therefore more like birds than people. The only birds he was really familiar with were pigeons, and the pigeons he knew were always taking baths in puddles or water fountains. What if Serena were a pigeon and flew up to his window, but he couldn't open the window and let her in because he had been caught like a lobster and was being boiled alive in a big pot?

Okay, Crazy. Whatever you say.

I can't breathe with this lid on
Let a little air in
Dip your wing
Take a bath
Get in
I'm turning red
It's not your fault
I'm so red

"Hi honey, I'm home."

Dan looked up from his latest masterpiece. Vanessa stood in the doorway wearing black fishnet kneesocks, black wool Bermuda shorts, a black peacoat, and her black combat boots. Her pale cheeks were pink with cold and her big brown eyes were bright with amusement. Dan had only seen her twice before, and he'd thought she was unique-looking. Not ugly, but not beautiful either. Right now, though, she looked perfectly fresh and amazing, like she'd just been unwrapped from cellophane—the coolest, most original girl ever invented. Jenny hovered behind her wearing a little kid's Speedo swimsuit that was ten times too small. Her curly dark hair was pulled into a tight ponytail, as if to make her chest more pronounced. Like he hadn't seen enough of it already?

Vanessa unbuttoned her peacoat and threw it down on the worn leather sofa next to Dan. "Whatcha writing? Anything I need to see?"

He closed the book and held it protectively against his chest. "I'm still working on it."

She shrugged her shoulders, knowing she'd get him to show it to her eventually. Dan was looking at her funny. "Did you miss me?" she asked hopefully. It was all she could do to keep from jumping into his lap and planting a big fat kiss on those thin blue-pink lips of his.

Dan didn't say anything, but his face turned as red as the lobster in his poem.

Vanessa glanced at Jenny. "If you need bigger tops or whatever, I can loan you some. I can even take you shopping." She felt sorry for Jenny, growing up in a house full of weird, awkward men who dressed badly. Not that Dan's clothes were too awful—they just looked like they'd been thrown from the washing machine into a drawer without ever being folded properly.

As long as he stays away from his dad's red stretch pants he'll be fine.

Jenny looked skeptically at Vanessa's all-black outfit and closely shorn hair. Thanks, but no thanks. "That's okay. Dad said I could borrow the credit card tomorrow. He gave me a three-hundred-dollar limit, which isn't great, but I guess it's fair. I mean, whatever I buy now probably won't even fit in the fall. I'm still growing."

Yes, we know.

"Okay," Vanessa responded. "But why don't you put something else on now and toss that bathing suit in the Goodwill pile? It's hurting us just as much as it's hurting you," she added gently.

Jenny blushed and trotted down the hall, loving the way her new boobs bounced. Vanessa was nice. She was glad she'd let her in. If only Dan wasn't such a loser. He'd probably say something really dumb now and Vanessa would run from the apartment screaming, when what he really ought to do was just kiss her.

So young, and yet so wise.

"Sorry I didn't say anything on the phone," Vanessa apologized, still standing in the doorway. "I can get pretty testy sometimes. I'm better in person," she added, feeling slightly embarrassed. It was pretty obvious that she liked him. He must have figured it out by now.

"You *are* better in person. Did you get another haircut or something?" Dan faltered. What he meant to say was, she looked prettier than when he'd seen her a few days ago, but he couldn't exactly say that, could he? What were they supposed to be talking about anyway?

Vanessa shrugged and shook her head. Then she went over to the sofa, pushed her coat out of the way, and sat down. The Humphreys' apartment reminded her of her parents' house in

Vermont, the house she'd grown up in. It was full of shit, like everyone was afraid to throw anything away. Used tissues that had missed the trash can collected on the floor. Decks of playing cards with missing cards were stacked on the bookshelves. A dusty red Radio Flyer wagon was parked in the corner of the living room, a relic of Jenny and Dan's childhood.

Dan was still clutching the black leather-bound book. She touched it with her fingertips. "Can I?"

He hugged the notebook even closer to his chest. The more Vanessa read, the more transparent he became. It was scary, letting someone read the crazy stuff that poured out of his mind, unchecked. Even scarier still was the notion that she wanted to publish his ravings for everyone to read—including Serena.

"Only if you let me see some of your pictures first," he bargained.

"Fine," Vanessa agreed. She dug around in her coat pocket and retrieved her Nikon digital camera. "I'm not even sure what's on here." The camera beeped on and she scooted closer to Dan so he could see the pictures on the tiny screen.

This was nice, he realized, loosening his hold on the little black book. It was nice to hang out with a cool girl on a Friday night. His father wasn't even home. They could get drunk if they wanted to. Watch R-rated movies. Do normal teenagery things. *Was* this what normal people did? He couldn't even remember what he normally did on Friday nights. Sometimes he and Jenny played Scrabble.

Good times.

Vanessa clicked through the photos in her camera's memory. "Hold on. My sister would kill me if she knew I showed you these." She shielded the screen and skipped over some pretty risqué shots of Ruby taking a bath with Tofu. When she reached the series of gum-on-the-sidewalk shots, she handed the camera back to Dan.

"Nice," he observed. It was sort of heartening to know that Vanessa could spend that much time photographing a wad of spat-out gum. It was almost worse than writing a poem from the point of view of a lobster being boiled alive.

Almost.

"It looks like something from inside you, doesn't it? You know that pink color that you see when they're doing operations on like, *ER*?" she observed, admiring her own handiwork.

Dan looked up from the camera. Sometimes Vanessa said things that sounded exactly like something he might have said himself. He liked it, but it was also a little freaky.

"What?" she demanded, trying not to sound hopeful. Was Dan about to kiss her?

"Nothing." Dan turned back to the camera. The next series of pictures were the ones Blair had taken of Vanessa getting her head shaved at the barber. "Wow, your hair was really long before. Weren't you nervous?" It was hard to imagine her with all that luxurious-looking shiny black hair. It was also hard to imagine why she'd want to shave it all off.

"Nah." Vanessa admired the picture of herself smiling devilishly at her own reflection in the barbershop mirror while the barber shaved a swath of hair off the back of her scalp. She looked pretty cool, even if she did say so herself. Dan hit the right-hand arrow key with his thumb and a picture of Serena with her back to the camera, her bare butt cheeks just peeking out from beneath a barely-there purple velvet minidress, appeared on the screen. She glanced over her shoulder, grinning knowingly. Printed on each curvaceous pale pink butt cheek was a perfect rosy red heart.

"Oh!" Dan exclaimed. His hands began to shake, and he dropped the camera on the faded Oriental carpet.

Vanessa retrieved it, turned it off, and tossed it back in her bag. "Sorry, that one was sort of pornographic too." She frowned. "I guess I'm kind of a pervert. I never realized."

Dan stared blankly back at her, wondering if he could send her on some sort of time-consuming errand so he could scan through the rest of her pictures and see if there were any more of Serena. He didn't care how perverted it was, he had to see them.

Hey, since they're both self-proclaimed perverts, why not look at the pictures *together* and have a pervert party?

"Do you want to order a pizza? I think my dad even has some beer in the fridge." He fumbled in his pockets and lit a cigarette with trembling fingers. It had only been a week, but he was already hooked. Of course he knew it was bad for him, but that was the most alluring part of it. If he wanted to be a poet like Keats or Kerouac, he had to die early. His dad even let him smoke in his room. "You make your own choices, you pay the consequences," Rufus had told him dismissively.

If only more parents were equally dismissive.

Vanessa shrugged her shoulders. "Sure, pizza is good. I don't drink beer, it tastes like snot." She waited for him to get up and get the pizza menu or bring her a glass of water, but he just sat there, puffing furiously on his cigarette, looking adorably forlorn.

"The menus are in the kitchen," he lied. Dan and Jenny had the number for the pizza place memorized. Rufus distrusted takeout, saying it was "full of rat poop and cockroach feelers," and usually threw out all the menus that appeared under the front door. "Try the drawer to the right of the sink," Dan suggested, knowing that was the drawer where Rufus threw all the recipes he clipped out of newspapers and magazines, plus all the gizmos he used to tie up his unruly hair. The drawer was absolutely loaded with crap.

Vanessa glared critically at him for a moment. Was Dan one of those guys who seemed enlightened but was really living in the dark ages, expecting the females to do everything in the way of preparing food and keeping house? Or maybe he just wasn't supposed to smoke in the kitchen. She got up to look for the menu. "I'll be right back," she told him, snatching his black leather-bound notebook from off his lap and tucking it under her arm. If the pizza place kept her on hold, at least she'd have something to read.

"No, please d—" Dan began to protest. Then he remembered he was about to steal Vanessa's camera out of her bag and hopefully download some of the pictures of Serena stored inside it onto his computer, although he wasn't sure he had the capacity to be that sneaky. "I like pepperoni," he said instead.

"Gotcha." Vanessa flipped open the notebook as she walked down the hall to the kitchen. Pasted inside the cover was one of the blond angels Jenny had drawn for the hymnal contest. Vanessa continued to turn the pages. Supporting his sister, that was nice, she guessed.

Guess again.

a kiss is just a kiss—at least, that's the lie we tell ourselves

Blair sat on her hands on one of the hot tub's submerged marble ledges. The jets pummeled her back, causing her whole body to vibrate. Nate sat on the opposite ledge, his damp chin resting listlessly on the side of the tub as he watched Serena kiss Chuck and then Donatella. What the fuck was going on? Serena could be such a tease. Or maybe he'd been totally wrong and she wasn't as into him as he thought she was.

But maybe all was not lost. He was still going to the cotillion with L'Wren. The loss of his virginity was imminent. This was a good thing. The idea that he was going to have sex with Serena instead of L'Wren had been just a momentary blunder caused by too much THC in the marijuana. *El Capitán. El Capitán!* He raised his head. "I'm late," he told Blair urgently. "I have to go."

Blair knew this was her cue. She blinked the steam out of her fierce blue eyes, steeling herself for the most important role she'd played thus far in the movie that was her life. Her mother was fat and pathetic. Her father was selfish and gay. Her little brother was destined for loserdom. Basically, her life had been a colossal waste of time—until now. Nate was right there in front of her. *Carpe diem.* Now was her chance to seize the day.

Among other things worth seizing.

Nate lunged for one of the white plush towels folded neatly on the heated metal shelving unit standing just out of reach of the tub. "Damn."

Blair sprang out of the tub and gathered up two towels. She wrapped one around her body and then handed one to Nate.

He got out, trying to act as cool as possible, and wrapped the towel tightly around his middle. "Thanks," he smiled down at her appreciatively and shook the water out of his hair. "Damn, I'm so late."

"I don't want you to go, Nate," Blair murmured again, her voice quavering but insistent. Water dripped off the ends of her long dark hair and onto her bare shoulders, causing her to shiver.

Nate's glittering green eyes seemed to brighten even more as he looked at her, as if he were noticing her for the first time. Blair looked up at him, feeling like she was going to be sick again, but this time in a good way. "What if we—" she began, wishing her heart wasn't beating quite so loudly, so she could hear herself think. "What if we just—" She stopped and licked her shapely lips. Nate's almond-shaped eyes and perfectly sculpted face seemed to be the only things of color in the room. God, how she loved him. "Why don't we just kiss?" she finished quickly.

Nate frowned. Blair wanted him to kiss her—*now*, when he was about to leave to meet a very hot older girl and hopefully have sex with her? Now, when he'd just been rejected by Serena? How could he kiss Blair when they'd known each other since preschool? She used to leave little lumpy Play-Doh hearts in his shoes when he took them off during nap time. He cinched his towel a little tighter. Actually, it made perfect sense. Blair had always had a crush on him, and she was one of his best friends. She was pretty and funny and smart, and she probably knew him better than he knew himself. She was such a perfectionist, but she'd always accepted him, with all his faults.

Serena had left because she *didn't* want to kiss him. But Blair did, and he loved Blair too. He'd never thought about kissing her until now, but why not? Maybe he'd had the wrong girl all along. Maybe he'd just lusted after Serena and thought it was love, when really it was Blair he loved all along. Even the way she said "Let's just kiss" was pretty romantic. She wasn't all hot and bothered. She didn't want to writhe around naked in the hot tub like L'Wren would have. She just wanted to keep their towels on and kiss, which made him feel sort of mature and cool.

Nate took a step forward. Blair looked up at him expectantly, her lips parted. He wrapped his arms around her as he'd done so many times before, and it wasn't awkward or tense—it was totally familiar. He ducked his head down and kissed her, as he'd also done so many times before, but this time he kissed her on her nice peach-colored lips, not her cheek. The kiss was long and sweet, and she was sort of exploring his mouth with her quick, warm tongue in a way that made him smile when he was kissing her. He held her a little tighter. Yeah, kissing Blair was all right.

She pulled away and pressed her cheek into his bare chest. "I love you, Nate," she whispered quietly into his damp skin. "I've always loved you." Blair's entire body felt like wax after it had melted and then cooled. She was rubbery, pliable.

Nate tucked his hands under her wet hair and pulled her

head away from his chest so he could kiss her again. Blair was so cute and dramatic, it made him feel like he was acting in some big cheesy romance movie. Guess he'd have to forget the cotillion and hooking up with L'Wren. He couldn't leave now, not when there was all this kissing to do. Blair's lips tasted like Triscuits and vodka. They tasted nice. And she wasn't going anywhere. He could kiss her all night if he wanted to, because he wasn't going anywhere either. Knowing that made him feel satisfied and happy and psyched to kiss her even more.

Across the suite, through the steam, Serena watched their dark, wet heads come together and stay together. It really was romantic—the way their pristine white towels were wrapped so neatly around their bodies, the tender way Nate was holding Blair's head. Serena's vision began to blur and hot tears slid down her cheeks. Angry with herself for standing there gaping like an idiot, she grabbed her discarded clothes and her raspberry-colored coat from off the floor and hurried out of the suite to change in one of the hotel's lobby restrooms. She couldn't bear to watch any more.

And this is only the beginning.

don't believe everything you read

Dear noknockers.com,
I just want to thank you for making an affordable product that actually works. I started taking the supplements one week ago and I went from not even an A cup to a whole B cup! I'm only twelve and a half, and I was totally flat before. I feel so much better about myself now, and I can actually wear clothes that I like, like bikinis and V-necks, with no drooping parts in the front! I think I even walk differently now. Anyway, thanks for listening. You're the best!!

Sincerely,
Jennifer Humphrey
P.S. See below for pictures of my transformation!

While Jenny was next door in her room, uploading pictures from her pink Hello Kitty digital camera of herself wearing her black tube top at various stages of growth to share with the digital universe, Dan sat at his desk in front of his computer and frantically whizzed through Vanessa's morbid pictures until he came to the one of Serena and her bare butt cheeks. He clicked "Download" and then moved on to the picture of Serena and her pretty, dark-haired friend. Serena's smile was even better in that one—more otherworldly and cunning. He could always crop the other girl out. He clicked download again.

"Jesus fucking Christ!" Vanessa's voice echoed down the hall from the kitchen. There was a clattering sound as various objects dropped out of Rufus's special drawer and skittered across the linoleum. Hastily Dan clicked through the fifty-odd other photos on the camera. There were lots of pictures of pigeons, puddles, people sleeping on benches, assorted garbage, and Vanessa's sister, Ruby, but no more of Serena. He yanked the cord out of the camera and hurried back to the study.

"Screw the pizza menu, I can't even find a fucking cup in this kitchen," Vanessa called down the hall from the kitchen, her voice brassy with annoyance. "Are you done smoking? Think you could maybe help me find this fucker since it's your house, not mine?"

Dan grinned at Vanessa's total lack of falsehood. She wasn't trying to impress anyone. She wasn't flirting, or pretending to be bored, or up-talking. She just wanted to order a pizza. He felt bad for sneaking her camera behind her back, but she'd never have to know about it, and it was for a good cause.

The I Worship Serena van der Woodsen Lameness Fund?

"Coming!" he shouted as he tossed the camera back into

Vanessa's black waxed canvas rucksack. He hurried down the hall to the kitchen to find her seated at the cracked Formica kitchen table, busily reading one of his latest poems, her cheeks flushed with delight.

> *I'm turning red*
> *It's not your fault*
> *I'm so red*

Oh, yes it is, Vanessa thought to herself, thrilled with the notion that Dan blushed when he thought about her, just like she blushed when she thought about him.

"That one's not finished yet," he explained awkwardly as he reread the poem over her shoulder, his hands trembling with embarrassment. He still wanted to add a few lines, something about how Cupid had wings so he was a bird too. Cupid was a pigeon? No, that was ridiculous. But it seemed necessary to invoke Cupid when he was discussing Serena as a pigeon/angel.

Okay, freak/genius.

"Just give it to me when it's ready. I figure I'll publish a series of five or six of your poems in the magazine. People are going to be so impressed with Anonymous when it comes out, it'll be a fuckfest, with everyone trying to figure out who she is." She slapped the book closed. "Hey, what happened to our pizza?"

Dan took his notebook back and tucked it protectively under his arm. "646-555-PEEZA," he recited mechanically.

Vanessa stood up, a full two inches taller than him. She poked him hard in his skinny stomach, all of a sudden grateful that she'd never had a brother. Boys were idiots. "Thanks,

Stormfield. I'll take extra cheese and onions." She bit her lip, wondering if she and Dan were going to be doing any kissing later. "Actually no onions. Just cheese. *Please*," she added hastily. "And some ginger ale."

Two hours later, a wasted half pepperoni, half extra cheese pizza, two cans of ginger ale, and four empty bottles of Amstel Light lay on the floor of the Humphreys' study. *The Late Show* flickered dumbly on the old Philips TV screen, but neither Vanessa nor Dan was really watching it. They sat on the floor with their backs propped up against the ancient brown leather sofa, their shoulders touching. Vanessa wondered if Dan had drunk enough beer now that he wouldn't have a seizure if she kissed him. She was pretty sure it would be a first kiss for both of them. He certainly acted like someone who'd never been kissed, and she knew she definitely hadn't.

Dan had been watching Vanessa out of the corner of his eye for a while. Her big brown eyes were really pretty, and her lips were really red. Or maybe her lips were having some sort of allergic reaction to the pepperoni, which she kept stealing off his slices. Vanessa was no Serena, but he still couldn't help wondering what it would feel like to kiss her. Then he felt perverted for even thinking about it. Just because she was a girl didn't mean she was a sex object, Jenny's voice scolded him. His little feminist sister who desperately wanted tits.

He stretched his legs out and yawned, sort of nudging Vanessa in the process. She giggled and kicked him back. Then she just sort of grabbed him and pulled his face toward hers until their lips were touching. It was just a little wet kiss that tasted like pepperoni; no tongue.

Dan's brain flickered off and on, like a TV set in an electrical storm. A pigeon flapped by his face and he thought he smelled the perfume from the sample Jenny dabbed on her wrists and ankles after she took a bath. She claimed it was the same perfume Serena wore: Cristalle. Then the TV set in his head went off for good.

Vanessa stared at Dan where he lay sprawled out on the floor in front of her. He appeared to be unconscious. She seized his shoulders and shook him gently. "Dan? Are you alive? Do I need to call 911?"

His eyes fluttered open. "Cristalle," he murmured with a bad French accent.

"You're scaring me," she whispered. A strand of drool clung to his pale cheek. She wiped it away with her stub-nailed thumb. "Say something normal. Who wrote *Jude the Obscure*?"

"Thomas Hardy," he responded automatically.

She relaxed her grip on his shoulders. Of course the boy she was falling for had to be the most immature person alive. A mere kiss sent him reeling. Maybe she was moving too fast. Maybe he needed a month or two of just sitting on the sofa feeling the electricity between their thighs and taking walks and breathing in the sultry spring air. Then finally he'd pounce on her, unable to resist.

"I think you need to stop smoking so much," she advised, helping him stagger to his feet. She led him down the hall to his bedroom. "And drink more water instead of instant coffee and beer."

The room was dark and soothing. Dan climbed into bed like a good boy. He'd always been a lightweight, but to faint like that—come on, how *embarrassing*. He took the glass of water Vanessa handed him and drank it slowly. His hands were shaking. Maybe it wasn't the beer. Maybe it was all the excitement of downloading those pictures of Serena.

Or the excitement of knowing he could look at them any time he wanted?

"You go to sleep." Vanessa took the empty glass and patted his hand. "I'm going home." She hesitated, not daring to kiss him again, not even on the cheek, for fear of sending him into cardiac arrest. Instead, she tiptoed out of the room and softly closed the door. Dan was so fragile, he was exactly like one of those sickly poets from England who died in their twenties because life was too full of beauty and tragedy for them to bear. He was probably more romantic than she was, more romantic than any girl.

And that kind of made her love him even more.

even though he's not a cat person

"Want to meet my new kitten?" Blair took Nate's hand and pulled him down the hall to her bedroom. They hadn't even talked in the car on the way home from the Tribeca Star. They hadn't talked much all night. They'd just been kissing—in the steamy hot tub, in their comfy white robes, on the crowded sofa while they shared one last cocktail, and then in the cab on the way home. It was as if they couldn't get enough of each other. They just wanted to kiss and kiss. Like they'd been craving something for years but hadn't known what it was and now finally they'd found it.

Yum.

A small gray cat with creepy blue eyes lay curled up on Blair's bed.

"There you are," Blair greeted the kitten tenderly and picked him up, cradling him in her arms. "He's a Russian Blue." She handed the kitten to Nate. "Kitty Minky, this is your daddy."

Nate wasn't an animal person, and he definitely wasn't anybody's daddy. "Hey," he greeted the cat gruffly. "What's up?"

Kitty Minky kneaded his claws into his hand and Nate released him onto the floor.

"Careful!" Blair cried out sharply. She scooped the cat up again. "He's just a baby."

"Sorry." Nate stuck his hands in his pockets, feeling a little self-conscious. He'd been in Blair's room a thousand times, but her mom and brother were home and he just felt . . . weird. He'd wanted to finally do it tonight, but he didn't know if he could do it with that cat watching. Or in the bed he used to play hide-and-seek under all the time when he was little. He walked over to her white flat-screen TV and flicked it on. "Want to watch a movie or something?"

God, was he adorable. "No. Come here." Instead of waiting for him to go over to her, Blair pounced, yanking his belt out of his pants and whipping it across the room. She giggled. "I know we just got dressed, but . . ." Then she kissed him, reminding him of why he was there.

Okay, now he didn't feel so weird. He picked her up and carried her over to the bed. Then he let the cat out of the room.

Meow-meow, no watchie. Bye-bye.

He went back to the bed and took off his heathered gray T-shirt. Blair followed his movements with a little smile on her lips. "I love you, Nate," she whispered, blushing.

Nate stared down at her, wondering what to say. Not that he didn't love her. Of course he loved her. She was Blair. He just wasn't ready to get all . . . boyfriendy about it. Right now he just wanted to take her dress off. He grabbed the hem and began to tug it up. Up, up, up and over her head. Damn, dresses were great. Just one big piece of material over the head and blam!— she was practically naked.

Blair's underwear was the kind that makes girls look *more* naked. Dirty-magazine underwear, with lacy stuff on it. He was afraid to touch it. Instead, he lay down next to her and sort of stroked her arm, her shoulder, her neck. She propped her head up on her hand and smiled at him.

"Nate?"

"Hmm," he responded, his green eyes closed. Her skin was soft, her hair silky.

"You didn't say anything. I said I loved you, and you didn't say anything." She waited expectantly.

Nate opened his eyes. She wasn't going to let him get away with it. "I love you too," he responded automatically. "I thought you knew."

Blair was not a religious person, not really, but she was having a religious experience. Nate was a god, her god, and he'd blessed her with his love.

Oh, lordy!

"You can kiss me now, you idiot," she commanded, grabbing his golden head. They kissed for a while, happily, hungrily. Then she pushed his head away again. "I'm not ready to have sex," she declared simply. "We *will* have sex soon," she promised, her face serious. "When I'm ready."

Best not to keep anyone guessing. Just say it like it is.

Nate liked that she was being honest with him. Girls could be so confusing. Like Serena—she was totally confusing. Blair was not confusing. Her honesty felt almost generous. "Okay. I can wait."

She grabbed his head again, wishing she could eat it. God, God, God, he was so cute, cute, cute! She kissed him hard, getting really into it. And he got into it right back.

"Girls, would you like some cookies?" Eleanor Waldorf's sing-songy voice echoed from outside the door. She opened it just a crack. "And I have truffles from La Maison du Chocolat!"

Blair threw a pillow at the door. "Go away, Mom."

Eleanor poked her head into the room. "Oh!" she exclaimed when she saw Nate lying on top of her almost-naked daughter with his shirt off. "Hello, Nathaniel. That's fine. Don't mind me. I'm leaving." She quickly closed the door.

"Sorry." Nate pulled away and hung his head and torso off the bed, feeling for his shirt on the floor. This was too weird. He could come back when there was no one home.

"Stop it. You're not leaving." Blair grabbed his hair, practically scalping him. "You know my mom. She takes too much Xanax. She won't even remember this in the morning. Even if she does, she doesn't care. She's probably on the phone with Crane's right now, ordering our wedding invitations." She blushed, then kissed Nate's neck just below his earlobe. "Not that we're getting married or anything." Meanwhile, in the movie playing in her mind, she could hear the wedding march, see her amazing white strapless Vera Wang wedding gown, picture Nate waiting at the altar in his Thomas Wylde tux, his green eyes glittering with tears as he marveled at how beautiful she was.

Let's not get carried away.

Nate settled back down on the bed again. "So, I know we aren't going to do it, but can you take that thing off?" he asked, pointing at her intimidating ivory satin and black French lace La Perla bra.

Blair blushed again and scooted under the rose-colored silk bedspread. She wriggled around like a fish and then extracted the bra, flinging it against her closet door. "Like that?" she asked coyly, her dark, neatly plucked eyebrows raised.

Nate scooted under the covers after her. Her skin was so soft, like the chamois cloths he used to polish the hull of his sailboat. It was so nice being with Blair. He couldn't help feeling surprised by how nice it was. He was pretty sure she was the one he was meant to be with all along.

"Just like that," he murmured, kissing her.

"I love you, Nate," Blair whispered again.

This time he'd do it right. He propped himself up and looked into her hopeful, familiar blue eyes. "I love you, too, Blair."

She bangs!

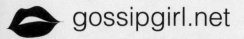
gossipgirl.net

Disclaimer: All the real names of places, people, and events have been altered or abbreviated to protect the innocent. Namely, me.

hey people!

It's barely midnight, and just like Cinderella I'm home, dry and snug and out of my mauve patent-leather Louboutin stilettos, which are ruined for good from the snow. Call me Granny Sensible, but from now until the first day of seventy-degree weather I'm wearing my furry leopard-print slippers, inside and out. Now that I'm warm and comfortable we can discuss this intriguing evening's festivities.

a ball's a ball—but there's nothing like a pre-party

Debutantes among us, you came out tonight and now you're out for good. I hate to say it, though—the ball was a complete snooze. Except for the part when that gorgeous Italian countess took her dress off. Apparently there's a whole nudist faction of the Italian aristocracy—who knew? And then there was the part when that very angry debutante with the dubious name got on the table and shouted expletives at her missing escort. That was great, the highlight of the whole razzle-dazzle. But most of the excitement was happening downtown at the Tribeca Star Hotel. . . .

sightings

S skulking around the hotel lobby wrapped in a white **Tribeca Star**–issue bathrobe. Has she started a new trend—suite-hopping? **B**'s father, picking up the keys to a suite in the **Carlyle Hotel** accompanied by a guy so handsome anyone would want to elope with him, male or female. **B** and **N** all cutesy, tumbling into the back of a taxi and tumbling out again, together, outside her building on the corner of **Seventy-second and Fifth**. **C** in the lobby of **S**'s building on **Eighty-third and Fifth**, getting turned away by the white-haired night doorman. What's with that? You'd think he'd have put that gorgeous nude Italian countess on a private jet to **Las Vegas** and married her by now. And later, **S**, shivering while she smoked alone on the **Met** steps, a ghostly martyr in a Patagonia fleece and baggy jeans. I'd like to say she looked tragic, but the traffic on **Fifth Avenue** was almost at a standstill because of her, so she couldn't have looked *too* bad. **V** riding the midnight **L train** back to **Williamsburg**, snapping pictures of the gross drunk guy peeing on himself as he lay sleeping on the seats across from her. She seemed to find it very amusing. That girl is twisted.

fyi

This may be extremely obvious to most, but if you are going to post pictures of yourself on the Internet, especially quasi-revealing pictures of your physical attributes, it's probably not a good idea to give out your full name. Just a warning. I know who you are now—everyone does. And this isn't the last you're going to hear about it. Those pictures are going to reach the far corners of the earth, and come summer, you'll be getting fan mail from jerks in Bora-Bora. Don't say I didn't warn you.

your e-mail

Dear GG,
I think I'm in love. No, dammit. I know I am. And I let her go. I got on the wrong bus. She thinks I'm with someone else. Damn. Love stinks.
—CBreft

A: Dear CBreft,

It's never too late to say "I love you." Bring her two dozen long-stemmed roses and dark chocolate truffles and a black-and-white milkshake and she'll forget all about the other girl.

—GG

Q: Dearest Gossip Girl,

I know my daughter has a boy in her room tonight and I'm not sure what to do about it. They have known each other forever, but they are so young. Should I offer to bring them some warm milk and profiteroles and then tell him to go home?

—hypermom

A: Dear hypermom,

You are sweet to worry, but it's probably okay to leave them alone. If you have always been this sweet and concerned, your daughter probably has a good head on her shoulders and the boy is probably quite respectable if she decided to bring him home. You should feel lucky they're not out doing something naughty. It's nice they're home. Go to bed. You can make them breakfast in the morning. French toast from Balthazar is always a hit. Sweet dreams.

—GG

Q: Dear GG,

I am taxi driver to stars. Give me call sometime.

—zip

A: Dear zip,

Thanks for the tip, but I prefer my town car.

—GG

not the last word

Something tells me this isn't the last we're going to hear about tonight. Some of us are alone, some us are not, and, as Scarlett O'Hara once said, tomorrow is another day. If there's anything to report, you know where to find me, and I certainly know how to find you.

You know you love me,

gossip girl

look what the tooth fairy dragged in

Serena lay on top of her white eyelet bedspread, fully dressed in her favorite pair of TSE charcoal-colored cashmere leggings and a black cashmere J.Crew V-neck. It was Saturday morning. She'd been asleep for part of the night but had woken up at five a.m. to take a bath and give herself a milk facial and never made it back to sleep. It must have been eight o'clock or maybe even nine by now, she wasn't sure. It had stopped snowing, and sunlight filtered into the room through her white eyelet curtains, which were shut tight.

With a listless hand she reached for the little silver Tiffany box on her antique mahogany bedside table. The lid was monogrammed with her initials: *SvdW*. She pulled it off and examined the inside of the box, which was lined with Tiffany's signature light blue velvet. Six tiny teeth were clustered together on the velvet, a little brown around the edges—her baby teeth. Why were there only six, Nate always wanted to know. There were two incisors, two top teeth, and two bottom teeth. Where were the molars? Where were the rest? Serena always told him that the others had fallen out while she was eating chocolate mousse cake at his eighth birthday party and she'd swallowed them all at once, but they both knew that wasn't the truth. It was a mystery.

She dumped the teeth out of the box and held them in her hand. They felt sort of gross, like the bones of roadkill, something she wasn't supposed to touch. She returned them to the box and closed the lid, keeping it balanced on her tummy. Her body felt tired, so tired she could have slept for days, but she was afraid to close her eyes and see Blair and Nate kissing again. It was something she'd never forget.

"Miss Serena?" The van der Woodsens' Brazilian housekeeper, Deidre, knocked lightly on the door. "There is a Mr. Chuck Bass here. He has *presents*," she added teasingly, like Serena would be totally overjoyed to see Mr. Chuck Bass so early on a Saturday morning.

"Uh-oh," Serena muttered, stuffing her feet into her old black sheepskin Ugg slippers. She padded over to the door and opened it a crack. "Hey Deidre, is he, like, in the house? Or is he waiting down in the lobby?" she asked, hoping the maid could tell the doorman to send Chuck away.

"I'm right here," Chuck's loud voice responded grandly. He appeared in front of the door brandishing a bouquet of smelly white lilies and a gigantic venti frozen mocha-choco-frappi drink topped with Reddi Whip in a clear plastic trough-size cup from Starbucks. "Good morning, darling." He kissed her cheek and stepped into her bedroom like this was their regular Saturday morning routine. Deidre swished down the hall in her gray-and-white maid's uniform, shooting Serena an amused backward glance with her soft brown eyes as if to say, "What a charmer!"

Serena didn't hate a lot of things, but she despised overly

sweet frozen Starbucks beverages, and the overpowering scent of lilies had always repulsed her. As did Chuck's manly cologne, his wet-looking hair, and his huge, shiny white teeth. She wondered fleetingly if Chuck had ever had baby teeth. It was hard to imagine him with baby anything.

"Hi, Chuck," she greeted him tiredly. She took the coffee and put the lilies on her desk. She wanted to toss them out the window, but thought that might be rude. "You're up early. Where's Donatella?"

She noticed that he was still wearing his coat and tails, and he still looked nice, in a deodorant-commercial sort of way. All of a sudden he was kneeling in front of her, holding her limp hands.

"All night I was awake, watching your building. Watching your lights go on and off. The night doorman wouldn't let me in. He wouldn't even ring up." He stopped, as if that was all he needed to say.

Serena frowned. She had the feeling she was missing something. "Where's Donatella?" she repeated stupidly. "You guys looked so . . . good together."

Chuck rolled his eyes as though Donatella de la Varga and her perfectly round naked breasts were so yesterday. "She was a baby. A total virgin. It turns out she's betrothed to some Swiss prince, and he has it in writing that she has to be a virgin on their wedding night, which is in, like, two months. Her dad was watching her like a hawk the whole time. Maybe he wasn't even her dad. I'm pretty sure he had a gun. Kind of ruined my plans. Anyway, it doesn't matter." Chuck held her hands a little tighter. "When you kissed me last night, I knew. You're the one I love."

Serena stared down at him, the corners of her perfectly

shaped mouth twitching. He couldn't possibly be serious. "Did Blair put you up to this?" she demanded suspiciously. Blair loved pranks. And she was completely unaware that she'd broken Serena's heart last night. She was very apt to pull a prank.

Chuck frowned. "No. She was a little busy last night." He did something disgusting with his hands, sliding his right index finger in and out of an O-shaped hole he'd made with his left index finger and thumb. "With Nate," he added for good measure.

The gesture felt like a kick in the stomach. Serena grimaced and clutched her throat. "I don't mean to hurt your feelings, Chuck," she told him quietly, "but I need you to go now." She tugged urgently on his hands, trying to pull him to a standing position.

Chuck stood up and grasped her cashmere-swathed upper arms. He was about to swallow her face in one of his overwhelming wet, gulping kisses, but Serena stepped back, yanking her arms out of his hands. "Please," she pleaded.

He stood there, glaring at her. This was not what he'd expected. Obviously, he thought her kiss last night had been some kind of open invitation. "You're supposed to be so slutty," he growled. "Or do you only do it with girls?"

Serena decided not to answer that question. "'Bye, Chuck." She picked up the phone, thinking he'd be more likely to leave if she was busy doing something else. She pushed a few buttons at random.

"I'll call you," he told her breezily, and flapped his hand in her direction before leaving.

Please don't.

The phone rang in Serena's anxious hand.

"Hey!" It was Blair, sounding so excited she was practically screaming. "We did it!"

Serena flopped dizzily down on her bed. She felt wrung out or waterlogged. What was she supposed to say—congratulations? At least Blair was happy now and not leaning over the toilet, miserably puking her guts up.

"Is he still there?" Serena whispered hoarsely.

"Yes," Blair whispered giddily back. "He's sleeping."

Serena closed her eyes as tears spilled out of them uncontrollably. "Oh."

"Don't forget to call that travel agent with our itinerary for our trip this summer," Blair reminded her bossily. "Tell him we don't care about hiking in the Alps or the Appian Way or whatever. I don't hike. I just want to spend as much time on the train as possible, in my *couchette*, with Nate."

"Okay," Serena sobbed breathlessly. "I'll call you later," she added hurriedly and hung up. She remained seated on the edge of her bed, staring at her cheery pink-and-blue rose-patterned needlepoint rug while the tears coursed down her cheeks and into her lap. So complete was her misery, she might have sat there for a minute or ten minutes or forty-five, she didn't know.

Finally she wiped her tears and went over to her desk. She shoved aside the forgotten pile of boarding school catalogs and flipped open her Latin textbook. *Amo, amas, amat.* In her entire life she'd never done homework on a Saturday morning. But since her two best friends were now otherwise engaged—with each other—maybe this was her chance to become a model student, devote her spare time to charity, perfect her backhand.

Rehabilitate her broken heart.

something is amiss in the state of denmark

HAMLET: Lady, shall I lie in your lap?
OPHELIA: No, my lord.
HAMLET: I mean, my head upon your lap?
OPHELIA: Ay, my lord.
HAMLET: Did you think I meant country matters?

Dan stared at the same faded page of his Shakespeare anthology, the words crossing his frame of reference and then skittering away without any hope of comprehension. He'd read *Hamlet* before and marveled at it, but today he could not concentrate. *Laundry,* he decided, apropos of nothing. He'd do his laundry and then go back to homework. He pushed away his desk chair and gathered up the dirty clothes strewn across the lint-speckled dirt brown wall-to-wall carpeting on his bedroom floor. Maybe he'd do everyone's laundry. His dad would love that. Anything to keep from staring stupidly at those pictures of Serena van der Woodsen on his computer, or from thinking about the fact that he was pretty sure Vanessa had tried to kiss him last night. Before he fainted, and before she tucked him into bed and went home.

It was pretty obvious that she liked him. You don't drop in unannounced at someone's house and start kissing them if you don't like them—right? He just didn't know what to do about it. He removed the faded Calvin & Hobbes pillowcase from his pillow and stuffed a wad of dirty clothes into it, mostly shirts he didn't even remember wearing and underwear that he'd discreetly kicked under the bed.

Nice.

Dan headed down the narrow dusty hallway to his dad's bedroom. As usual, Rufus was still in bed. He spent Saturday mornings—and every other morning, for that matter—tucked under a scratchy red wool blanket reading newspapers and literary journals, smoking and cursing all the while. Hunger would force him to get up around one, and then he'd venture out to the supermarket to shop for the day's culinary adventure. It was after one now, but Rufus had been out late last night in the East Village with his anarchist writer friends, so he was sleeping in.

"Dad?" Dan called from outside the bedroom. "Got any laundry you want me to do?"

A muffled grunting and muttering sounded from within and then Rufus opened the door. Last night's purple ponytail elastic was dangling from a few strands of wiry gray hair near his left ear. His gray-and-black beard looked like it had been in a fight. His stomach bulged above the waistband of his light blue Hanes boxer shorts, exposing a bare slab of furry flesh beneath a too-tight black Mets hoodie that Dan suspected was his.

"You're doing laundry?"

"I guess I'm procrastinating." Dan shrugged. "I have a paper to write. *Hamlet*."

Rufus nodded. If there was one thing father and son had in

common, it was their interest in literature. "That shouldn't be too hard. But you've decided to do laundry instead." He sniffed the air suspiciously. *"Something is rotten in the state of Denmark,"* he quoted Shakespeare's famous lines, his muddy brown eyes bulging out of his head with toadlike imperiousness.

"Dan has a girlfriend . . . !" Jenny's annoying-little-sister voice singsonged from down the hall. She danced out of her room wearing a denim Diesel zip-up shirtdress strategically unzipped to show off her budding cleavage. She was wearing makeup, and had obviously been dressing up and staring at herself in the mirror since dawn.

"Do not!" Dan swung around and hurled the Spider-Man pillowcase full of laundry at her. His dirty underwear scattered at his sister's feet.

She wrinkled her freckled, turned-up nose. "Hello, uncalled for?"

"Is it the same girl? The hairless one I met from before?" Rufus inquired as he got down on his hands and knees and began patrolling his bedroom for soiled clothing, stashing it under one arm as he went. A lot of the clothes he wore were dry-clean only, but that didn't stop him from washing and wearing them. It was his opinion that the more shrunken and wrinkled clothes became, the more interesting they were to wear. He stood up and handed the unsavory armload to Dan. "Where does she live? We should invite her parents over for dinner."

"No!" both of his children exclaimed at the same time.

"She lives with her sister," Dan added, feeling a little mean for insulting his dad's cooking all the time. "She's macrobiotic. Or something, I forget."

"Are you doing laundry?" Jenny asked eagerly as Dan

continued down the hall past her room. She always got stuck with laundry duty, so it was crucial that she take advantage of her older brother's generosity. "Wait!" She dashed into her closet and gathered up a tidy pile of jeans and T-shirts. No way would she let him handle her underwear.

Dan waited in the doorway. A picture of some girl's perky chest was floating on Jenny's computer screen. The chest was clothed in a sheer nude bra. "Nice," he observed.

Jenny shrugged and handed him her dirty clothes, stuffed into a pink-and-white-striped pillowcase. "I wrote a thank-you letter to the breast supplement company last night and got a bunch of really nice e-mails from other girls." Actually, the e-mails were mostly from guys, but she didn't mention those.

"This girl sent me her picture," she continued, sitting down at her Pottery Barn Kids white "Madeleine" desk. "And here's what she wrote: 'Dear Jennifer, you are so inspiring. I've been complaining my whole life about my flat chest and I'm way older than you. I was taking the supplements for only like a week and I was gonna quit, but ever since you wrote your testimonial I've decided I have to give it some time. Good luck—you deserve it.'" Jenny turned around. "Isn't that so nice?"

Dan shrugged. He couldn't believe how much time some people spent online. He preferred to scribble things on paper, cross them out, and then smoke himself sick while staring furiously at a new blank page.

Hence his fainting problem?

Jenny scrolled quickly over the next e-mail, which was from some crazy guy in Lancaster, Pennsylvania, who'd sent her a picture of his bare ass with the words *New and Improved!* scrawled across it in neon blue marker. Some people were so stupid.

"Anyway, I'm going out soon to this bra store I read about online where they fit you better than anywhere else and they have bras from all over the world. I really need bigger ones now, and this place sounds cool. It's in the Village. Want to come?"

Shop for bras with his sister, or stay home, smoking and drinking coffee and contemplating his status in the universe? It was a tough one.

"Maybe some other time," he told her kindly.

Dan headed down to the basement with a fistful of quarters and two pillowcases full of dirty clothes. He used to think he was the only kid in the world who had to do his own laundry. Certainly he was the only boy in his class who did. So it was actually pretty comforting to have met someone who did her own laundry too. And Vanessa was a diva of coolness. He'd just always thought that if he were to have a girlfriend, she'd be someone else. A certain platinum blond, blue-eyed leggy angel someone else.

Oh, yes? And who might that be?

The thing was, despite the fact that he had been writing poems for her, Serena van der Woodsen honestly didn't know he existed. Vanessa had already been over to his house. She'd seen him vomit. She'd stuck her face in his and kissed him. She was *real*—so real he could still taste the pepperoni grease on her red lips. She liked him, and he'd never really been liked by a girl before. Still, did they *have* to kiss? Even if it never actually happened in real life, it was happening all the time in his mind, in his poems: kissing was reserved for Serena.

Good luck explaining that.

v practices restraint

Vanessa sat cross-legged on her futon mattress with her iMac in her lap, forcing herself to write a boring, friendly e-mail when what she really wanted to do was show up unannounced at Dan's house again, dive under his sad frayed Spider-Man quilt, and ravage his hopelessly pale, spent, and hungover bones. His room had been dark when she helped him into bed the night before, lit only by the flickering blue computer screen. She could just make out more of Jenny's artwork hanging crookedly from the walls. Who could not love such a devoted brother? He was the sweetest boy alive.

```
Dear Dan,
Hope you are feeling okay today. Just
wanted to thank you for the pepperoni.
We should catch a foreign flick sometime
when you're feeling up to it. Maybe
tomorrow at the Paris? Oh, but you have
that big Hamlet term paper to write. Skip
it. Spring break is in two weeks—let's
```

```
definitely get together then. I promise
not to do anything you're not ready for.
```

Her unmanicured fingers hovered over the gray keyboard. She'd wanted to be encouraging, but what she'd written sounded like she was ready to do all sorts of kinky things. Actually, she was pretty sure she *would* like to do all sorts of kinky things with Dan, but that wan't what she meant. She just wanted him to know that she wasn't going to try and kiss him again. Not when it had made him so nervous he'd fainted. She'd just have to restrain herself and wait for him to kiss *her*.

She erased everything except the first three lines of the e-mail and then added,

```
See you over spring break, maybe. xo —V
P.S. E-mail me those poems immediately
when you finish them!
```

She pressed send and then clicked on the pages of Dan's poems that were already stored in her computer. She scanned through them, lingering on the lines she treasured most. *Do they wear black like you? . . . We only just met but . . . bite me.*

Yes, she would restrain herself. Then, sometime soon, Dan would be in the middle of writing a poem and suddenly realize that he could stand it no more. He'd rush out to Brooklyn, take her in his arms, and kiss her madly, desperately. From then on they would be inseparable. In fifteen years, when Dan won the Pulitzer Prize for poetry and she won an Oscar for her courageous documentary about the detritus of the city, they would leak the news that she had been the muse for his poetry since he first began to write. They would live together in a crazy factory loft building in Williamsburg and create raw, magical master-pieces together until they died in each other's shriveled arms at the age of one hundred and three. Books would be written about them. They'd be famous for their work and for their part-nership in love and art, like Gertrude Stein and Alice B. Toklas or Henry Miller and Anaïs Nin. Together forever.

Sounds like the stuff of poetry. Or fiction.

n knows the magic password

Nate woke up before Blair. He could tell it was late because the cat—Tiger Monkey or whatever the fuck its name was—was sprawled out on the windowsill, soaking up the sun. It had stopped snowing, and every once in a while a big chunk of melting snow would cascade down from the roof of the building and fall to the street below with a pillowy thud.

Nate thought he smelled bacon, and his stomach growled urgently. Beside him, Blair lay sleeping on her side wearing only his heathered gray T-shirt and her ivory satin underwear as she hugged her pillow, her lips curved into a smile. She looked sated and happy, even though they hadn't had sex. She was like an advertisement for sex. Nate slipped out from under the covers, still wearing his khakis. He combed his fingers through his wavy golden brown hair and located a Yale sweatshirt in Blair's closet that would do for now. He'd slept over at her house many times before, in the guest room, on the floor, even in her bed. But she'd always worn pajamas, they'd never so much as kissed, and Serena had always been there. To find Serena missing felt strange. How had it turned out like this? Did Serena have something better to do, someone else to be with? The details were foggy, as if he were remembering them through a cloud of steam, but it was pretty obvious now that he was with Blair.

Quietly, he opened her bedroom door, tiptoed into the hall, and closed the door behind him. Definitely bacon. He padded down the parquet-floored hall in his bare feet, hoping the Waldorfs' cook, Myrtle, would hand him a big heaping plateful, and then he could retire to the library, where he'd watch English Premier League soccer and pig out.

"Is that you, Bear?" Blair's father's courtroom voice rang out. Nate stopped in his tracks. He was pretty sure her father didn't even live there anymore. At least not all the time. "We just dropped in to pick up some things!"

"There's bacon and juice," Mrs. Waldorf added vaguely when Nate appeared in the dining room. Her normally perfect blond bob was smashed in at the back, and her slightly chunky body was wrapped in a quilted black satin floor-length dressing gown that looked like some sort of 1940s ski garment, tied at the waist with a tasseled golden rope. Her feet sparkled in gold sequined evening slippers with spiky gold-plated heels.

Was she trying to win her husband back or scare him away?

Harold Waldorf, Esquire, was crouched in front of the French Imperial buffet, packing crystal goblets into some sort of red velvet–lined carrying case like a thief. Crouched next to him was a dark, sleek-haired, extremely tan younger man wearing a salmon pink dress shirt and a shiny platinum Piaget watch.

Good morning, Rico Suave.

"Blair's still sleeping," Nate announced, a little louder than he'd intended. He pulled out the chair next to Eleanor and sat down, ogling the china platter of crispy bacon in front of him.

Eleanor pushed the platter toward him and used a pair of silver tongs to plunk a few strips on his plate. "It's good," she told him distractedly. Something about the way she wasn't really looking at him or at anything in the room made Nate feel sad. He picked up a piece of bacon and shoved it in his mouth. Man, he loved bacon.

Mr. Waldorf stood up as if noticing Nate for the first time. He walked over to the table and clapped him on the shoulder. "Nathaniel. Long time no see. Just picking up a few things. Glad you stopped by. I think Blair's still sleeping."

Duh?

He took off the pair of white cotton gloves he'd been wearing to handle the crystal. "Just picking up a few things," he said for the third time. His pink-shirted friend smiled at Nate self-consciously. "This is my partner," Mr. Waldorf introduced them. "Giles."

The tan guy stuck out his hand and Nate reached across his plate and shook it. The guy had a very firm handshake, but then he held on and bent down and kissed both of Nate's cheeks. "Charmed," he murmured, gay as gay can be. It suddenly dawned on Nate that Mr. Waldorf didn't mean business partner, he meant partner-partner. Jesus. No wonder Eleanor looked so fucked up. Poor Blair.

"Nate slept over," Eleanor told them, trancelike. She poured more coffee into her cup from the silver decanter on the table. "I saw them last night."

Nate's cheeks flamed, but her tone wasn't accusing. She was simply making it clear that he hadn't just arrived.

As if his rumpled hair and bare feet didn't already make that clear enough?

"I'm just going to grab Bear," Mr. Waldorf announced, zipping up the black leather carrying case. He handed the case to his French boyfriend. "She's dying to meet you."

Nate shoved another piece of bacon into his mouth and quickly wolfed it down. Then he stood up and pushed his chair back. Mr. Waldorf was already on his way out of the dining room. "Please, let her sleep," Nate called after him. Blair's father stopped and turned. "She's been a little stressed out about everything." He gestured at Blair's mother, the black leather carrying case, Giles. "Please, just let her sleep."

Mr. Waldorf shrugged and came back into the room. He picked up his half-empty crystal glass full of freshly squeezed orange juice and finished it off. "If you think she needs the rest," he acquiesced.

Nate picked up another piece of bacon and shoved it into his mouth, whole. Eleanor was looking at him now, her baby blue eyes wide and surprised. It was kind of cool the way he'd just, like, protected Blair from meeting her dad's gay lover. Like she was his little missus and he was looking after her. It made him feel manly and primal, like King Kong. Now, of course, he wanted to go wake up Blair and have loud, crazy gorilla sex.

Easy, Tarzan.

"I'll guess we'll be going, then," Mr. Waldorf addressed his wife. He bent down and gave her a quick stiff peck on the cheek. "We fly to Paris tomorrow, but I'm sure I'll talk to Bear before then. Anyway, tell her I'll be back to take her and Tyler skiing in Sun Valley for spring break, just like always." He glanced at Nate. "You're invited, of course."

Nate half smiled his thanks and bit off another hunk of

226

bacon. Something about Mr. Waldorf's gayness made him feel like a freaking caveman. Like all he could do was grunt and whack things with a club.

And hump the furniture?

Mrs. Waldorf was sitting up very straight. "Have fun in France," she told her husband tonelessly. Nate wondered if she was thinking about what *she* was going to do for spring break while they were skiing. He wanted to invite her along too, as his date, but then that wouldn't make any sense. Still, Mrs. Waldorf was a nice lady. She didn't deserve to look so sad. He stood up, desperate to be out of the room and away from this entire fucked-up situation.

"Good luck, Nathaniel," Mr. Waldorf told him, shaking his hand as though Nate were a business client.

"Thanks," Nate responded. Giles winked at him but Nate didn't wink back. He wasn't ready to get all winky-winky with a guy he'd only just met.

They went out into the hall to get their coats. Mrs. Waldorf was still looking at Nate like she was waiting for him to tell her what to do.

"Have a good day." He walked over and kissed her gently on the cheek. "I'm taking Blair out—" He paused. "To the zoo." He grabbed another piece of bacon and walked briskly out of the dining room and down the long hall to Blair's room. He opened the door. Nothing had changed. She was still hugging her pillow, asleep, with that satisfied grin on her face. Pussy Willow, or whatever the fuck his name was, was still stretched out on the windowsill.

Nate swallowed the rest of his bacon and walked over to the bed, trying to control the gorilla-man within. He bent down and kissed Blair on her smiling pink lips. She opened her eyes and grinned up at him, looking perfectly beautiful and innocent.

"Hi."

"Hi."

"I was actually awake earlier," Blair yawned. "I called Serena. Then I went back to bed."

Nate didn't care about any of this. He just wanted to get Blair out of the house without talking to her sad mother and getting bogged down in a screamfest about her dad's sudden gayness and his weird handling of the crystal. He wanted to get a slice of mushroom pizza and look at the sea lions. And maybe when Blair was in the bathroom or talking to the penguins, he'd take a little walk and smoke the roach that was still in his pocket. He'd been horny and craving pot ever since he got into the hot tub last night, and if he couldn't have one of the things he was craving, at least he could have the other.

"I'm going to sneak you out of the house," he told her, his voice cracking sexily.

Blair was still reeling from the amazing feeling of waking up to Nate kissing her. She felt like Sleeping Beauty when Prince Charming finally comes to wake her up and everything in the kingdom comes alive. He was totally perfect. Her *life* was totally perfect.

"I'm not going anywhere," she insisted, pulling him down on the soft, silk-covered bed. His lips tasted like bacon. "You're supposed to bring me breakfast."

Nate rolled off the side of the bed and swung open Blair's closet door. He grabbed a pair of boot-cut jeans from off the floor, a red sweater hanging on a hanger, and a pair of short, black, kitten-heeled boots that he thought looked sexy but comfortable. Then he opened her dresser drawer and pulled out a pair of plain white underwear and a white cotton bra.

Blair sat up, watching him, the rose-colored bedspread pulled up to her neck. Her gray kitten jumped into her lap, kneading his paws into her thigh in a horny sort of way. Nate tossed the clothes on the bed, scaring the cat away.

"I'm not wearing those." She wrinkled her nose. "Those jeans are queer, and they totally don't go with those boots."

Nate rolled his eyes impatiently. He didn't want to listen to her princessy bullshit. He was just trying to get her out of the house. "Wear whatever you want. I just want to take a walk. Get some air. Buy you a present."

Blair's robin's egg blue eyes opened wide. "A present?" She clapped her hands together like a little girl and grabbed the underwear and the bra, slithering under the covers to change into them. She stood up, wobbling on the mattress as she shoved her feet into the leg holes of the True Religion jeans he'd picked out. Nate had to avert his eyes as she struggled with her sweater, to keep from losing his mind. The sight of her in that innocent-looking white cotton bra was driving him absolutely bonkers.

She was dressed within seconds—even her boots were on. Dashing into the bathroom, she smeared Crest in her mouth with her finger, flipped her head over, and ran her Mason Pearson wooden-handled boar-bristle brush through her hair a few times. Then she spritzed the air with a cloud of Chanel Mademoiselle and walked through it, out of the bathroom, coating her entire person with the scent. "Okay. Ready!"

See how quick and obedient we can be when you say the magic word?

Nate held her hand as they hurried down the hall. "I didn't

even take a shower," Blair muttered under her breath. Not that she cared. She was getting a present. *Present, present, present!*

Nate squeezed her hand. "Me neither. It's okay, we smell like each other. It's nice."

Could he *be* any cuter?

Out in the foyer Nate punched the button for the elevator. "Is that you, Blair?" Eleanor Waldorf's voice trilled from the dining room.

Blair buttoned up her black Searle peacoat, wound her white TSE cashmere scarf around her neck, and stuffed her hands into a pair of gray cashmere gloves. "We're going out for breakfast!" she shouted back as the elevator doors rolled closed behind them.

The elevator descended to the lobby. Nate wrapped his arm around Blair's shoulders, feeling the sort of smug satisfaction one feels when one has saved the day.

Okay, so he's impossibly handsome and a touch conceited, but he wears it so, *so* well.

ugly hearts have feelings too

Tiffany was Nate's idea. They'd watched that Audrey Hepburn movie a thousand times a few weekends ago, and Blair seemed to like it so much. He just wanted her to be happy.

The centuries-old jewelry emporium Tiffany & Co. had resided on the corner of Fifth Avenue and Fifty-seventh Street since 1940. Constructed of gray limestone, with high, square, curtained windows, it looked more like a bank than a jewelry store. A doorman wearing a knee-length navy blue uniform coat with gold buttons, a black patent leather–brimmed cap, and spotless white gloves swung open the glass entrance to the store. "Morning!" he called out cheerfully, tipping his cap.

"Oh, look," Blair cooed, heading straight for the heirloom diamond display. "I love a plain diamond," she added.

As if there were such a thing.

Nate was thinking more along the lines of a Tiffany blue pen, or a little red Swarovski crystal cupid paperweight. The pen would be totally useful, and the cupid would make a really good paperweight for all of Blair's . . . papers.

An overeager salesman with a tiny black mustache had already produced a pair of diamond earrings for Blair to try on. They were platinum chandelier earrings, dripping with princess-cut diamonds, and cost about as much as Nate's dad's Aston Martin.

"Oh!" Blair gasped, loving the way the diamonds sparkled in the sunlight blasting through the store's oversize windows.

"They look wonderful with your beautiful blue eyes," the salesman cooed, working it.

Nate shot the guy an annoyed glance. He was fifteen years old and yeah, maybe he wore nice clothes and had a nice life and a beautiful girlfriend, but did he really look like someone who could buy those earrings with his dad's credit card and get away with it? They were the kind of earrings movie stars borrow to wear to the Oscars. Not buy. Borrow.

This whole ordeal was kind of killing Nate's mood. He'd never been into shopping. All he really wanted was to smoke a big fatty and then maybe grab a big greasy burger at Jackson Hole, even though he knew Blair hated it there because it made her hair smell like onion rings.

"Those are pretty," was all he said. He leaned against the display case, his back to the salesman, arms folded across his chest.

Blair giggled, admiring herself in the gold mirror the salesman was holding up. She knew Nate's patience was already waning and that she had to find the perfect item to put in one of those pretty little blue Tiffany boxes before he got a craving for pizza or had to pee or whatever and demanded they leave. "I know we're not buying them, I just thought it would be fun to try them on." She plucked the earrings out of her ears and tossed them on top of the glass display case like they were made of plastic. "Come on."

She slipped her arm through Nate's and he dutifully led her across the room to a display of Elsa Peretti signature gold jewelry, Tiffany classics. Blair wrinkled her nose. Boring.

"There." Nate pointed to a small, plain gold heart pendant hanging from a black silk cord. It was simple and elegant and the black cord was actually kind of sexy. He could imagine it dangling from Blair's neck when they did it. It would look cool—a nice contrast—with the white cotton bra she was wearing. "That's it." He signaled the saleslady behind the display case. "That's what I'm getting for you."

Blair tried not to pout. The heart pendant was kind of ugly. Who wanted to wear a black string around their neck? Who would *pay* for a piece of black string to wear around their neck? And the heart itself was lopsided and deformed-looking. But maybe if she strung the heart on a gold chain from some other necklace it might look more normal. She'd accumulated a lot of jewelry in her fifteen years—surely there was *something* in her jewelry box. And it was sweet that Nate wanted to buy her a present at all. It wasn't her birthday. It wasn't even Valentine's Day anymore.

That's the spirit. Never say no to a gift. Plus, there's always regifting. . . .

"Would you like to try it on?" the saleslady asked. She adjusted her thick glasses on her nose and crouched down to unlock the case with shaking hands. She was about a hundred and ten, and her skin and hair looked like they'd been powdered with baby powder. Even her hands were a chalky white. She removed the pendant from the case and held it out to Nate, swinging it in front of his face like a hypnotist. "Would the young gentleman like to do the honors?"

Blair unbuttoned her peacoat and Nate wound the black silk cord around her neck. The small gold heart lay against her chest, pointing straight down into her cleavage. Nate couldn't stop looking at it, a constant reminder of Blair's breasts. It was awesome.

The grandmotherly saleslady shoved a mirror at them, but Blair didn't even glance at it. She could tell by the intense look in Nate's glittering green eyes that he liked it, and even though she would have preferred diamonds, she kind of loved the way he was staring at her chest like he wanted to attack it.

"I'll wear it out," she told the saleslady.

Nate wound his arm around Blair's waist and gave her an adorable squeeze. "Yeah, but can we get one of those little blue boxes and a ribbon anyway?" he asked. "She really likes those boxes."

Blair closed her eyes as her heart caved in just a little. She'd never been into public displays of affection—who wanted to watch other people rub against each other like animals?—but Nate was completely irresistible. She could not keep her hands off him. She threw her arms around his neck, kissing him and licking his face like a puppy. "I love you, I love you, I love you!" she murmured wetly into his ear.

"You know I love you," he murmured back as he paid the woman for the necklace. He felt like some sort of Good Samaritan, rescuing Blair from her crazy family, buying her the heart, making her happy. Not that he wasn't happy too. He was having a ball. But he might have been a fraction happier if he'd smoked that roach in the guest bathroom before they'd left.

"Next stop, the zoo," he announced as the white-gloved doorman pushed open the door for them and they spilled out onto Fifth Avenue. Blair could pet the goats in the petting zoo while he snuck off to "the john" and smoked a doobie on an ice bank next to the polar bear.

Cool.

"Wait!" Blair cried, flinging her arms around Nate's neck one more time. She just had to kiss him in the exact spot where Audrey Hepburn ate a Danish out of a brown paper bag on the sidewalk outside of Tiffany in the opening scene in *Breakfast at Tiffany's*. *This is way better than any cheese Danish,* she thought greedily as she ran her tongue over Nate's perfect teeth. Today a gold heart, in a few years a diamond engagement ring! Suddenly Nate pulled away and took a step back.

"Hey," he called over Blair's shoulder. He wiped his mouth on the sleeve of his blue wool toggle coat, looking slightly sheepish.

Blair whipped around. There was Serena, looking cold and sort of bedraggled and completely gorgeous, like the princess in *The Princess and the Pea* before she stumbles into the castle out of the storm and meets the prince who winds up marrying her.

Not that there were any princes available to marry her in this particular scenario.

Serena darted away from them, about to cross Fifth Avenue, when Nate called out to her again.

"Hey, wait up!"

She stopped and turned, her stunning navy blue eyes wide and startled looking, as if she'd only just noticed them standing there. "Oh, hey," she faltered. "I didn't see you guys."

Likely story.

polar bears and falcons and pigeons, oh my!

The color of the sodden wintry slush piled between the parked cars on Fifth Avenue matched Serena's mood exactly. It was a strange feeling. Usually she was the sunny one, the glass-half-full one, the perker-upper. Today she felt positively bleak. Her efforts to placate herself with reminders that she'd done a very unselfish thing and made her best friend unspeakably happy simply weren't working. The fairy tale of her dreams had been ruthlessly adapted into a film starring different actors, and her part had been written out. The question was, what part would she play next?

The other woman? Just a thought . . .

She'd purposely left her cell phone behind for fear of receiving another one of Blair's stomach-turning I'm-so-*happy* calls. She walked aimlessly, bare hands stuffed into the pockets of her brown plaid Burberry coat, chin tucked into the buttoned-up collar, chilled to the bone because she'd run out of the house without a hat and gloves or even any breakfast. Her baby blue Uggs were soaked through, and the backs of her Earl jeans were dotted with smatterings of slush. She hadn't realized how far she'd walked until she heard a familiar, well-loved voice call out, "Hey, wait up!" and she'd looked up to find her worst nightmare come to life: Blair and Nate, looking like the cutest couple ever, waggling a miniature light blue Tiffany shopping bag, their arms entwined.

Blair looked like she'd had a face-lift by one of those plastic surgeons who really knows what he's doing. She was positively radiant. Nate just looked like Nate. Serena wanted to be angry with him for not showing any signs of remorse, but as soon as she saw his dear, unspeakably handsome face, the anger didn't come. She loved him. It was as simple as that. No matter what happened, she would always love him.

Which kind of made this particular moment all the more awkward.

"Look what Nate got me." Blair hastily unbuttoned her coat and flashed the gold heart at Serena. "Isn't he just the cutest?"

Ouch.

Serena sensed that Blair was absolutely bursting with news and couldn't wait to bombard her when they saw each other at school on Monday. She could already picture the cluster of girls gathered around her at their favorite lunchroom table as Blair pretended not to want to give them a play-by-play of her glorious night with Nate. Kati, Isabel, Rain, and Laura would ply her with questions while a group of ninth graders led by Kathy Reinerson huddled nearby, eavesdropping. Serena would be required to act excited and intrigued, while every word Blair uttered would feel like a punch in the face.

"It's lovely," Serena responded with remote pleasantness, channeling her British ancestors. Like Queen Elizabeth of England,

Serena had been bred and educated to be gracious, not to stamp her foot and pout in the face of adversity.

If only she had a few corgis to cuddle with.

The corner of Fifty-seventh and Fifth was probably the most ill-advised place to try to stand still and hold a conversation in all of Manhattan. Tourists bustled past them, jostling their shopping bags and cursing under their breath in all manner of languages. Normally the three friends would have been walking fast, arm in arm, interrupting one another with the latest gossip or non sequitur. The awkwardness was not lost on Serena.

"So, Natie," she cleverly changed the subject, "whatever happened to that girl you were supposed to escort to the debutante ball?"

"Who?" he responded with genuine cluelessness.

Serena and Blair exchanged glances. Oh, to be young, hot, and thick as a post, at least when it came to girls. Nate was like a hound dog, capable of following only one scent at a time.

"You know, *L'Wren?*" Serena reminded him, pronouncing the girl's idiotic name with humorous precision.

Blair's amused look morphed into a warning glance. She did not want to discuss that slutty college girl on the best day of her life, so would Serena kindly shut the fuck up? "We're going to the zoo," she announced, taking her friend's arm. "You have to come." As soon as she'd said it, though, she realized with a strange sort of queasy meanness that she really didn't want Serena to come at all. When she was with Nate, she wanted him to herself, because now he was hers—*all* hers.

"You know how much you love the polar bear," Nate reminded Serena. It was one of the things he adored about her, the way she talked to the polar bear like it was her long-lost twin.

"I have a date," Serena lied, marveling at herself. A date? With *whom*?

"With Chuck?" Blair asked perkily.

Serena stared at her, horrified. Did Blair actually believe that she'd kissed Chuck last night because she was *into* him?

"I'm meeting my dad for brunch," she informed them. "He wants to discuss my future," she added, shooting Nate a pointed look as if to say, *Remember me? The girl who has a stack of boarding school brochures in her room, put there by her parents, who couldn't wait to get rid of her? The girl who was heartbroken at the thought of going to boarding school because she wouldn't get to see your perfect face every day? The girl who decided to stay in the city to be with you? The girl on the verge of a nervous breakdown right now as we speak?*

Nate grinned back at her blankly. His night with Blair seemed to have erased his memory of any quandaries except when and where he and Blair were going to hook up next and how to score the next dime bag.

Serena glanced at her gold Cartier tank watch. "I'm late," she muttered, elaborating on the lie. "Have a good time, guys," she added, thrusting her long, delicate hand in the air and stepping off the curb to hail a cab. So what if she hadn't brought any money with her. Wasn't that what doormen were for?

Blair and Nate waved brightly to her as the cab performed an illegal U-turn and headed east on Fifty-seventh Street. Serena felt like she was seeing them for the last time, like they were waving goodbye for good. And in a way, maybe they were.

Back in her room, she sat on her bed and stared at the silver-framed photograph propped on her bedside table. Ironically, the frame was from Tiffany. Nate stood between her and Blair with his arms around them beside the pool outside the van der Woodsens' Ridgefield country house. All three wore brightly colored bathing suits and were smiling goofily, like they were in on some big secret.

She stood up and went over to the window, gazing across Fifth Avenue at the Met and Central Park. Outside it had begun to sleet. Wet snow fell lazily downward until it melted on the pavement. A horse and buggy trotted by on Fifth, carrying two passengers snuggled together beneath a gray woolen blanket. Serena could have sworn she recognized Blair's creamy white cashmere scarf, and wasn't that a blue Tiffany bag in her lap? Then something moved atop the Met's white limestone roof, and she looked up at it, squinting. It was a large, elegant brown bird with a hooked beak, perhaps one of those peregrine falcons from the news, the endangered ones. It must have really loved the city to want to stay there all by itself in the sleet with no one to talk to but the pigeons and the squirrels. Or maybe it was waiting for another falcon that had been momentarily led astray by some other pretty bird. The lonely falcon looked like she'd been waiting a long time, and, considering the weather, there was a good chance the other falcon wasn't coming back.

But the stubborn falcon wasn't ready to give him up. All she could do was tuck her head under her wing and wait.

j meets the mother she never had

The Village Bra Shop, located on the corner of Christopher Street and Seventh Avenue, looked like the kind of store that had been around since the 1970s, selling wigs, hairnets, and peds to dotty old ladies. The peach-colored painted brick was cracked and peeling; the store's plain black-and-white sign was so badly faded it was barely legible; and the only window displayed a dusty, shapeless mannequin with cracked green eye shadow wearing a pink raincoat and black rubber rain boots. Her raincoat hid her boobs so completely there wasn't even a suggestion of a bra. Jenny was worried. Where were the bras?

She pushed the door open and stuck her head inside the tiny shop, ready to flee if it looked scary. Immediately facing her were racks and racks of beautifully crafted, impossible-to-find-anywhere-else bras from faraway places like Hungary, Poland, Belgium, France, England, Brazil, and Hong Kong. There were push-ups and gel-lifts and racer-backs and nursing bras, strapless bras, convertible bras, underwire bras, and wire-free bras. The Village Bra Shop was bra heaven.

Jenny stepped all the way inside and rang the little bell at the unmanned desk at the front of the store. A tiny old lady sporting a white bun, huge black-framed glasses, a white lab coat, and lumpy ankles appeared from the back. She looked like Nanny from the animated Disney version of *101 Dalmatians*, which Jenny used to be addicted to.

"Help you?" she demanded in a thick Brooklyn accent. Her head bobbed as she sized Jenny up. A yellow measuring tape dangled from her neck. Jenny could almost see the numbers flashing in the thick lenses of Nanny's specs: 32 x 22 x 27. "I understand. You're growing. I can help," she added before Jenny could explain herself, then swiftly locked the shop's glass door, lowered a black Venetian blind to obscure the view from the street, and yanked her measuring tape down off her shoulders. "Take everything off the top. Arms up like an airplane. Don't worry, no one can see inside. It's very private."

Jenny timidly took off her sweater and her Playtex bra and placed them on top of the metal desk with the bell on it. She closed her eyes and raised her arms up like airplane wings. She was naked in front of a complete stranger inside a store—it seemed crucial to keep her eyes closed to keep from dying of embarrassment.

Nanny wound the measuring tape around her chest. It tickled. Jenny kept her eyes shut tight as Nanny muttered to herself and fished around for a pen on the desk. She measured each of Jenny's boobs individually, from several different angles.

"Thirty-two C," she finally pronounced, tapping Jenny's forearm to indicate that it was okay to put her arms down. She shuffled deep into the store and came back carrying a plain white cotton underwire bra with a plain white satin bow on the front of it. "Doesn't look like much but it's perfect for a growing girl. It will give you nice coverage and keep its shape in the wash." She smiled as she helped Jenny adjust the bra's straps. "From Poland. Very good quality bra."

Jenny waited while Nanny fastened the three hook-and-eye closures. Then she followed her to the back of the store to look at herself in the mirror. Her body looked tiny, and then there was the bra. It didn't push her up or give her extra cleavage—it swallowed her.

There was something very old-fashioned about it, Jenny decided with a disappointed frown. Like it was the first bra ever made. And it made her boobs look like torpedoes. Poland wasn't exactly the epicenter of the fashion industry, either. "It's too big," she complained. After all, it was a *C* cup. She'd been measuring herself every day for the last week and she was no C cup.

"It's really not," Nanny insisted calmly. "In a month you'll be back asking for a bigger one."

Jenny's brown eyes opened wide. But she'd stopped taking the supplements. Her boobs were perfect now. She liked them just the way they were—the same size as Serena van der Woodsen's—give or take a quarter inch. "What do you mean?"

"I said before, you're growing. Probably you'll make it up to a 34 double-D. For a little girl you got a big, healthy chest." Nanny smiled and pointed to her own misshapen boobs, which looked like partially deflated birthday balloons stuffed inside a lab coat. "Just like me."

Jenny crossed her arms over her chest. *A double-D?* Impossible. She'd spent her entire life painfully flat-chested and now this woman was telling her that she was about to become a monster with super-size breasts?

Wonder Boobs to the rescue!

"Put your sweater back on. The lines on that bra are very

nice," Nanny coaxed. She fetched Jenny's sweater for her and eased it carefully over her head, tugging it down and smoothing it out like she was Jenny's mom or something. "Good. See?"

Jenny took a step back and examined her reflection critically. The lines *were* good. Her chest looked perky, but not overly so, and the torpedo effect was somehow diminished by her plain black V-neck sweater. Her boobs looked natural and normal.

Not for long.

"It's comfortable, too. You buy two of these—one white and one nude, in case you wear a white T-shirt or something sheer. You can alternate between the two until you're ready for a bigger size." Nanny fumbled around in a drawer and extracted the nude version of the bra. It looked like strap-on prosthetic buttocks for a person with weirdly beige skin.

Not exactly what we dream of when we dream of lingerie.

"Cash or charge?"

Jenny paid for the bras with her father's Discover card, still dazed by what Nanny had said about her growing chest. She was a boob professional—she would know. The bras were expensive, seventy-five dollars each. Was she destined to spend all her allowance and half her salary when she was an adult and had a career as a graphic artist on bras alone? Would this have happened if she hadn't taken those stupid supplements from noknockers.com? Had the supplements somehow overstimulated the growth hormone in her mammary glands? The words of one of her male online admirers flashed in her mind. *When I look at your chest in your black tube top I see my future and you're in it, girl.* Was she destined for a life of icky come-ons from complete strangers?

Well, at least she won't be lonely.

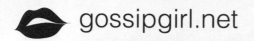

gossipgirl.net

topics ◀ *previous*   *next* ▶   *post a question*   *reply*

Disclaimer: All the real names of places, people, and events have been altered or abbreviated to protect the innocent. Namely, me.

hey people!

the wedding of the year

Okay, so they're not married—yet. They didn't buy a ring and she didn't get fitted for the dress. But they did buy jewelry—at Tiffany, no less. And where did these two people who two days ago were just friends *not* kiss and fondle each other in a very public way all week? They were like emperor penguins, doing that "I've found my partner for life" dance, all over the entire city. I wouldn't be surprised if they had to stop in at the ER at Lenox Hill Hospital to have their lips surgically separated just so they could go to school tomorrow. And you know what? I sort of hate happy couples. It's like, we love that you've found each other, but sometimes it's more polite to be happy in private, so people don't have to watch you being all cutesy and boring. Think of it this way: if you leave more up to our imaginations, we might be kinder to you when we talk about you, which we are bound to do.

At least, *I* am. I simply cannot keep my mouth shut! And neither can some of you.

your e-mail

Dear GG,
I am a guy and probably not the best judge, but if you really think a girl is hot and you, like, bring her all sorts of shit, and basically

make it clear that you want her, and she tells you to leave, does that mean she's really into you and she's just playing hard to get so you'll want her even more?
—callme

A: Dear callme,
No.
—GG

Q: Dear GG,
I've been with the same guy since we were twelve. Now it's 4 years later and he's like, what's the deal? R u ever gonna give it up? Maybe it's different 4 grls. I dunno. Maybe I should just take the plunge.
—virg

A: Dear virg,
I will address this in more detail below, but just because you have been together for a long time doesn't mean you owe him anything. If you are fine with how things are, then he should be too, or you can tell him to stick it. If you want, *I'll* tell him to stick it—where it *hurts*.
—GG

Q: Dear GG,
I just think that when a guy is supposed to be your escort at a very important event, he should at least have the decency to show up. Some guys should just be castrated, don't you think?
—bitr

A: Dear bitr,
No.
—GG

the right time to do it

For whatever reason, some of my fans have decided that I'm their mom, and keep popping the "do you think I'm ready?" question in their mail. Let's just get this straight: I am not your mom. I'm not even close to being old enough to be your mom. But even your mom can't tell you what to do. You are your own best judge. And the best advice I can give is, if you have even the slightest doubt, if you're even thinking of asking yourself or me or anyone else if you're really ready, you're probably not ready. Trust yourself, and if you can't do that, trust me. I know everything.

sightings

N and **B** in **Tiffany & Co.**, being cute and annoying. **N** and **B** in the **Central Park Zoo**, teaching the sea lions how to kiss and being even cuter and more annoying. **N** and **B** in a horse-drawn carriage, being cute and annoying all over the place. **N** and **B** feeding each other strawberry ice cream. Will they please just get a room? Oops—I guess they already did! **S** reading the Travel section of the *New York Times* alone in the **Three Guys coffee shop** on **Madison**. Planning her getaway? **C** in the **Hallmark** store on **Madison**, demanding that they paste his head shot onto the front of a half-price V-Day card and messenger the card to a certain Upper East Side address. Wonder who the lucky girl Is? **B**'s dad at a wine tasting in **Provence**. **B**'s dad hitting on a shoe salesman in the **Prada** boutique in **Paris**. **B**'s dad testing new mattresses at a bedding store in **Nice**. **B**'s dad sitting on the lap of a tractor operator at a vineyard in a little village outside **Cannes**. *Zut alors,* that fellow sure does get around!

revenge of the spurned

A certain college freshman whom a lot of our guy friends know way better than you think has decided to leave school and move to Italy. It seems she befriended a certain Italian countess at the same deb ball where both debs were dissed by their escorts. They decided to start a secret society in Florence, the tenets of which will involve nudism and no boys! Sounds a little like a certain island off the coast of Greece beginning with the letter *L*. I'm sure the weather's lovely there this time of year.

speaking of lovely weather . . .

Spring break is less than two weeks away, and what with all the slush and sleet and subzero temperatures, it's about time. Some of us—including yours truly—will spend our vacation wisely, sunning ourselves in the latest Missoni string bikinis on remote Caribbean beaches. The more foolhardy among you will be doing more athletic things like skiing or scuba diving or playing soccer. I promise to soak up some extra rays for you. And please use some SPF 15 on your faces—the raccoon tan you get from wearing ski goggles or a diving mask is simply not a good look. Whatever you do, enjoy yourself. You absolutely deserve it.

I'm off to soak in a nice hot milk bath surrounded by my favorite bath toys: a bottle of chilled Veuve Cliquot and a box of Godiva dark chocolate truffles. Why don't you do the same, pronto.

You know you love me,

Air Mail - Par Avion - March 4

Hi Bearita,

We are staying in the most adorable B&B, but we've already fallen in love with a gorgeous château in the next village that needs some serious TLC. I've decided to retire early and settle here. It's a dream come true. And guess what?—it has a vineyard! I'll have my own wine, and you'll be the first to sample it, ma petite chardonnay. I miss you loads, but we'll see each other v. soon in Sun Valley. I'll meet you at the lodge in twelve days, and please bring that hunky boyfriend of yours (he is your bf now, yes? Do tell!!), and Serena of course. Enclosed are three first-class tickets.

The shopping over here is beyond fantastic. Don't worry, I can't leave a boutique without buying something pour toi, Bear.

Love you to pieces,

Dad

check out their sweet suite

"Those two bags go in here," Blair instructed the strapping, tan Sun Valley Lodge porter. She indicated her black quilted leather Louis Vuitton travel valise and Nate's red nylon Burton snowboarding bag. The porter removed a wooden luggage rack from the closet, unfolded it at the end of the king-size California bed, and gently placed Blair's valise on top of it. Blair pointed at Serena's silver Tumi duffel. "That one goes next door."

Nate came out of the suite's beige marble–tiled bathroom wearing only a pair of red-and-royal-blue paisley board shorts. His chest and arms were muscled from playing lacrosse and still bore the remnants of a tan from Christmas sailing in the Virgin Islands. Smoke oozed out of the bathroom where he'd just enjoyed a wee joint from the stash he'd hidden inside a knotted sock at the bottom of his snowboarding bag.

"I'm going for a swim. Want to come?" He grinned widely at Blair and she threw herself at him with the total abandon of someone on vacation at the same resort where Marilyn Monroe had flirted with Ernest Hemingway. The gold Tiffany pendant he'd given her banged between her breasts in the deep plunge of her black Loro Piana V-neck sweater. He gazed down at it with stoned adoration.

"I have to wait for my dad," Blair breathed, kissing him fiercely. The room's beige-and-black décor and heavy tan canvas curtains were unexpectedly ugly, but as long as she was in Nate's arms she didn't care. "We're going to have so much fun!"

Nate held her small, foxlike face in his hands and kissed her back. He couldn't wait until that night. Hotel beds were so comfortable, and there were no weird reminders of childhood or parents. No pets, or photographs, or teddy bears, or eavesdropping moms. Just him and Blair and that big bed. Awesome.

Serena stood in the suite's adjoining junior bedroom in front of the oversize windows, watching the skiers in the distance as they crisscrossed the snowy slopes of Baldy Mountain like colorful insects. The porter came in and placed her silver duffel bag on the wooden luggage rack at the foot of the lone double bed. She didn't mind having a room all to herself. She'd just have to sleep with the television on to drown out the sound of Blair and Nate, giggling and talking in baby voices to each other like they were doing right now.

She didn't even know why she'd come, except that she always went to Sun Valley with Blair for spring break. Plus, Blair was going to be with her dad for the first time since he'd run away to France with his boyfriend. If she was going to start acting weird and making herself sick all over the place, Serena wanted to be there.

Masochist.

"We got six inches of powder last night," the porter informed her with the dorky hell-yeah enthusiasm of a true ski bum.

Serena whirled around, the skirt of her gray cashmere pleated

Marc Jacobs tunic fanning out around the thighs of her skinny black True Religion jeans. The porter was actually pretty cute. Thick coppery brown hair poked out from beneath the dark green Dartmouth cap he was wearing to accessorize his boring brown Sun Valley Lodge sweater with the queer golden sun embroidered on the chest. His turquoise blue eyes sparkled, and his surfer dude–handsome face was dotted with freckles. He was about twenty-two, and had probably graduated from Dartmouth last year. Still, he didn't seem the least bit embarrassed about being a porter.

Although his parents were probably slightly disappointed.

Serena cocked her magnificent blond head. She might be able to tolerate this vacation if she had some sort of distraction in the form of an older boy. Maybe Nate would see her with this other guy and become unspeakably jealous. He'd spend the rest of their holiday trying to make it up to her. After all, Blair really did need to spend some quality time with her dad.

That's the spirit!

"Are you working all day? Could you take me skiing?" she asked boldly. She took a step toward him and held out her hand. "I'm Serena."

The porter smiled broadly and stretched out a tan, competent hand. "Love to," he agreed, closing his ski-pole-calloused hand around hers. "I'm Fenner. I don't get off till two, but that'll give you a little time to settle in, and we can definitely catch some powder runs before the lifts close. I know where to find the untracked stuff."

Serena just stood there smiling nervously. She'd never really spoken to a strange guy like this before. His name—Fenner— was sort of odd, but he seemed like a nice guy. "I'll meet you in the lobby at two," she agreed, hoping she wouldn't wind up naked and freezing to death on an abandoned cliffside.

"Serena? Who are you talking to in there?" Blair's blissed-out voice rang out from the other room.

Fenner tipped the brim of his green Dartmouth cap and strode out of the suite. "Later," he called, closing the door behind him.

Serena padded warily into Blair and Nate's portion of the suite, half expecting to find them writhing naked on the bed. "Nate went for a swim," Blair announced. Her suitcase lay empty on the wooden luggage stand. She'd already unpacked into the lodge's sturdy beech armoire and generous cedar closet. Four pairs of ballet flats, three pairs of knee-high boots, and two pairs of cozy tan Uggs stood at the ready on the closet floor.

Not that she planned to venture out much.

Blair prodded Nate's red duffel bag. "Do you think it would be weird if I unpacked for him?"

Serena considered the bag. She'd never used the drawers in any hotel she'd ever stayed in. She was a live-out-of-her-suitcase kind of gal. "I don't know." She shrugged her shoulders. "He's *your*—" She was about to say the word *boyfriend,* but she couldn't bring herself to utter it. Nate wasn't Blair's yet, because Serena wasn't ready to give him up.

The phone beside the bed rang loudly and both girls jumped. "Hello?" Blair answered with a sexy purr, undoubtedly thinking it was Nate. Serena watched her friend's body stiffen. "Fine," she said coldly and hung up the phone. She grabbed the cellophane-wrapped box of Lindt chocolate truffles from the minibar and tore it open. "Dad's on his way up." She popped an entire truffle into her mouth. "With his boyfriend."

Serena noticed that her friend's cheeks were totally ashen. "Are you okay?" she asked, carefully removing the box of truffles from Blair's grasp. If she was going to hurl, one truffle was enough. "Do you want some water?"

Someone rapped on the door with a fist. "Bear?"

Blair wobbled on her mint green sheepskin Kors platform slippers. "Just a minute!" she gasped, clutching her stomach. Then she bolted for the bathroom and slammed the door.

"Blair Bear? We're here!" Mr. Waldorf called out once more.

Serena ventured forward to open the door. "Hi!" she chirped enthusiastically. "Blair's just in the bathroom." Mr. Waldorf looked younger and tanner and gayer than she'd ever seen him look before, wearing a tight buttery yellow turtleneck, white wool pants, and brown Italian loafers with no socks. Beside him stood a dark, handsome, neatly dressed man with combed-back black hair wearing a gray cashmere suit, a crisp white shirt, and what looked like a platinum man's engagement ring, studded with sapphires. Blair's little brother, Tyler, lurked behind them in the hallway wearing a pair of giant white Bose headphones, a sleeveless black Duran Duran T-shirt, and freshly creased brown leather pants. He looked pretty gay himself.

"Hello, gorgeous," Mr. Waldorf greeted Serena, kissing her on both cheeks. "I'd like you to meet my partner, Giles." He hugged her one last time and then turned to his sleekly turned-out friend. "This is Serena, part of our family."

Serena blushed with the corniness of it. No sound emitted from the bathroom. What had happened to Blair? Had she fallen in? Fainted?

Giles kissed her graciously on both cheeks. "But you are so

beautiful," he enthused in a luscious French accent, squeezing her hands in his and flashing a brilliant white smile.

Serena giggled. Giles looked like he'd spent his entire life basking in the Mediterranean sun, shopping for beautiful clothes, and drinking wine. He smelled like lemon verbena. And that voice! He was très charmant. No wonder Mr. Waldorf had decided he was gay.

Blair's dad glanced into the closet and grinned at the vast array of clothes and shoes. "I'm glad to see you girls have settled in. Blair?" He rapped his knuckles on the bathroom door. "You're not *canoodling* with that boyfriend of yours in there, are you?"

It takes a canoodler to know one.

Serena was about to improvise an elaborate lie about why Nate's suitcase was in this room—the room she was supposed to be sharing with Blair—and her suitcase was in Nate's room, when Blair stepped out of the bathroom. She looked fresh and sparkling, as if she'd just had a makeover. "Hello, Father," she greeted them haughtily, filling the room with the minty alcoholic odor of mouthwash. "How's France?"

"France is fabulous, darling." Mr. Waldorf swooped her up in a tight hug and then let go. He put his arm around his handsome boyfriend. "Bear, this is Giles, the wonderful man I've been telling you about."

Blair hesitated. There was no risk of her vomiting all over Giles's handsome gray cashmere suit, because she'd vomited up everything in her stomach already. "Hello," she managed curtly as her father's overly cologned gay lover kissed each of her pale cheeks. Tyler slouched in the doorway in his ridiculous trying-desperately-to-look-like-Jim-Morrison-from-the-Doors leather pants, bopping his head up and down to his own loser beat.

"Harold, you did not tell me these girls would be so beautiful," Giles observed. "They are like movie stars." He pointed at Blair's outrageous green sheepskin platform slippers and flared his tidy French nostrils. "Cute *sleepers!*"

Blair smiled despite herself. Okay, so he was nice. So what? Did her father have to wear yellow turtlenecks now that he was gay? Did his boyfriend have to wear sparkly man jewelry?

"Now where is that adorable Nate?" Mr. Waldorf asked, peering into the bathroom as if Nate might be hiding in there amongst the complimentary Clarins toiletries.

"His muscles were sore. He needed a swim," Blair announced, hoping to shock them with the implication that she and Nate had been having wild and crazy sex ever since they arrived.

Mr. Waldorf winked conspiratorially at Serena, as if they'd secretly shared their opinions about what a superb couple Nate and Blair made. "Well, as soon as he gets back, why don't we all go out skiing together? There are simply *buckets* of fresh powder, and I can't wait to try out my new Rossis."

Blair couldn't believe her father had just said the words *simply buckets* with a straight face. "Nate's muscles are sore," she repeated with a whine. "And I'm tired." She didn't really care about skiing. All she wanted to do was roll around on that big hotel bed with Nate, wearing the shimmery red Hanky Panky boy shorts and matching bralette she'd bought at Bendel's only yesterday.

Serena couldn't wait to get out of this suffocating love den. "I'm meeting this guy I met in the lobby at two. He works here. He knows all the good runs. We could all ski together."

Blair stared at her friend, impressed. She certainly didn't waste any time.

"Just a minute. You've got something important to do first." Mr. Waldorf dashed out into the hall and retrieved two giant shopping bags loaded with shoe boxes and various items wrapped in black and white tissue paper. "Presents for all!" he cried, like a camped-up, yellow turtleneck–wearing Santa. He plunked the shopping bags down on the bed.

Blair had wanted to be aloof and standoffish to let her father know just how mad at him she was for dumping his family and running off to France with his new jewelry-wearing boyfriend. Instead, she clapped her hands together, unable to control her excitement. "Oh, Daddy!"

Mr. Waldorf blew her a kiss and ushered Giles and Tyler out of the room. "See you at two!"

Blair reached inside the first bag and found something large wrapped in white tissue paper with the famous black double-*C* Chanel logo on it. She tore the tissue paper away greedily. The new Jaguar Cub hobo bag! The waiting list for the bag at the Chanel store on Madison was at least ten pages long.

Maybe having a gay dad won't be quite so bad after all.

swimsuit weather is just around the corner

"I'm looking for something more along the lines of a working farm. Somewhere she can learn to make cheese, harvest her own vegetables, skin a goat," Rufus told the director of the annual Ninety-second Street Y Summer Camp Fair. Rufus was concerned that Jenny was spending her entire spring break analyzing her rapidly developing figure in the mirror and perfecting her calligraphy. In order to avoid a repeat over the summer, he'd dragged her to the fair. What better place to hone life's necessary skills like cheese making and goat skinning than at summer camp?

What about a camp for champagne drinking and shopping? Burp!

Jenny clutched her father's arm as she took in her surroundings. The Y's gym was crowded with tables bearing summer camp leaflets and testimonials from previous campers. Camp directors aired films exhibiting their camp's offerings as parents and their charges wandered around the room, looking as dazed and overwhelmed as she felt.

The camp fair director flipped through her clipboard. She

wore a khaki-colored safari dress, thick clear plastic glasses, flesh-colored knee-highs, and beige orthopedic shoes. Her hair was cut in a thick gray pageboy and her skin was doughy. She looked like she'd been doing her job a long time. "Lake Quinnipiac has goats, but the concentration there is on swimming."

"No!" Jenny practically shouted. The way her boobs were growing she'd be a double-F by summer. No way was she going swimming in public. "No swimming. What about an art camp?" Or perhaps there was a slimming camp for girls with giant breasts?

We must, we must, we must decrease our busts!

The director flipped through the pages in her clipboard again. "The Rhode Island School of Design has a wonderful camp." She peered at Jenny over her dorky thick plastic glasses. "You have to be fourteen," she added with a frown, obviously unable to determine the age of this tiny girl with a baby face and the chest of a stripper.

At least she'll never get carded.

Rufus was already distracted by a table covered with rocks. "Come on." He grabbed Jenny by the elbow and dragged her over. "What's this?" he demanded of the woman seated behind the table. She wore a confusing brown-and-blue wool poncho that looked like it had been knit by left-handed two-year-olds. Her frizzy hair hung in two graying waist-length braids. On her feet were the type of woven leather sandals sold by street peddlers in Mexico.

"Rock people," she explained, even though the rocks were just plain rocks. "I'm Cindi Bridgehutter. And this is what we do at Camp Bridgehutter—make people out of rocks."

Jenny stared at the woman, who was obviously insane. She

tugged on her father's too-tight Ben & Jerry's purple tie-dyed T-shirt. Maybe summer camp wasn't such a good idea after all. But Rufus stood his ground, already smitten with Camp Bridgehutter and its Rapunzel-haired founder.

"Dad," Jenny whined under her breath. Behind her two tall, skinny blond girls in skimpy white tennis dresses were registering for a tennis camp on Lake Placid. Jenny couldn't imagine her boobs bouncing around inside a tennis dress. Nope, tennis was out too.

"Of course that's just a metaphor. I'm an artist. It's an arts camp," Cindi Bridgehutter elaborated gaily. Her teeth were vaguely blue, and Jenny wondered if maybe she'd done too many weird drugs in her twenties or worn braces as an adult. Or maybe it was a rare gum disease.

Rock peoplitis?

"Aha! An arts camp!" Rufus crowed. "Sign her up!"

"*Dad!*" Jenny protested. Didn't he even want to know where the camp was? And what about goats? Five minutes ago he was adamant that she learn to skin a goat.

"We're based in my hometown of Wooten, Pennsylvania, near a lovely lake. Of course we have all the usual camp offerings like swimming, archery, and tennis, but they're optional. Our campers are encouraged to work on their craft. Our mission is to bring out the rock person within," Ms. Bridgehutter expounded, tugging on her braids for emphasis. "Every camper creates their own mounds. It's a wonderful thing each summer to watch the mounds grow."

Haven't a certain person's mounds grown quite enough?

"The rock person within!" Rufus sounded thrilled.

Actually, the camp didn't sound so bad. Jenny liked that

swimming was optional. She didn't know what was meant by "mounds," but she hoped it was another metaphor. "I do calligraphy," she ventured shyly. "And portraits. I entered the hymnal contest at school."

Ms. Bridgehutter flashed her blue teeth in a freaky Cat-in-the-Hat-like smile. She clearly had no idea what Jenny was talking about. Rufus was already filling in Jenny's name, address, and birthday on an admissions form. "I'll need a deposit check to secure her spot," the camp's director told him greedily.

Jenny glanced over at the next table, where a perky redheaded girl in a cheerleading outfit was showing off her latest cheer to the director of a cheerleading camp in Princeton, New Jersey.

"Give me an S-U-M-M-E-R! What's that spell? Summer! Go summer! Summertime!!"

There were long lines to sign up for both the cheerleading camp and the tennis camp. Across the gym a TV showed a girl riding a horse around an impressive course of jumps. The line for that camp was even longer. No one was signing up for Camp Bridgehutter. No one.

Um. Wonder why.

Jenny turned back to the table where her father was furiously filling out forms. Beneath one of the rock people was a photograph of a boy carving a face out of wood. He had wild, dark hair and fantastic arm muscles. "Oh, are there boys there?" she asked the blue-toothed camp director eagerly. She'd never even gone to school with boys, let alone sleepaway camp.

Boys, boys, boys!

"The ratio of boys to girls is three to one," Ms. Brigehutter explained. "Girls are all signing up for horseback riding and soccer camps these days." She handed Jenny an egg-size rock and flashed her blue teeth again. "I'm sure you'll have lots of inspiration."

Jenny turned the rock over and over in her hands as her father finished filling out the forms. Three boys to every girl. With those sorts of numbers, who wouldn't want to find the rock person within?

Give me an S-U-M-M-E-R! What does that spell? *Boys!*

the hills are alive with the sound of s's beating heart

"Oops! Sorry!" Blair cried as she crashed into the three large men in front of her in the lift line. Even though she'd never tried it before, she'd insisted on snowboarding instead of skiing, so that she and Nate would be the same. She'd been skiing since she was four. How hard could it be?

"Bear, ride with us!" Her father grabbed the elbow of her white Bogner ski jacket and yanked her back into line as he was about to board the triple chairlift beside Giles. Blair hopped awkwardly up and down on one foot, clutching her father until she was seated securely on the lift's padded chair.

"She's nuts," Fenner observed. "There are no easy runs up there. She should be on Dollar Mountain, taking lessons."

Serena pushed her silvery poles into the snow as they advanced in the line. Then it was their turn to board the chair. Fenner was on her left, and she guessed Tyler would ride up with them, but then—*whoosh!*—Nate scooted in on her right on his nifty neon green Burton board.

"Hey," he greeted them breathlessly. "Sorry I'm late." The lift eased up behind them and swept them off their feet. Serena was wearing a navy blue Patagonia parka the same color as her eyes. Her blond hair spilled out from beneath a white hand-knit earflap hat, and her hands were bundled into a pair of gigantic black mittens. Next to her was a tall guy wearing a very professional-looking black North Face powder suit and orange goggles with no hat. "Hey, you're the guy from the hotel," Nate observed.

Fenner introduced himself. "Serena asked me to show her some untracked snow," he said, grinning at her. The chairlift rose up on its cable until their skis skimmed the treetops. The sky was blue, the mountain was crisp and white, and the air smelled like Christmas, even though it was March.

Nate tapped Serena's skis with his snowboard. "I never see you anymore," he told her accusingly.

"Well, I'm still here," she responded quietly. Their thighs and shoulders were touching, and Serena could feel the whole Nate side of her vibrate with a familiar, warm hum. Could he feel it? Was he humming too?

Actually he *was* humming, but that was because he'd smoked a joint before and after he'd gone swimming. Nate turned and looked at her and she looked back. His glittering green eyes were bloodshot from the pot and swimming in the lodge's over-chlorinated pool. Her dark blue eyes were big and hopeful. "Hi," he greeted her.

"Hi," Serena replied, wondering if they would survive if she pulled him off the lift with her. It was at least a seventy-foot drop, but she was dying to kidnap him and tunnel way down deep in the snow so they could kiss in private. Deep down, he was dying to kiss her too. Wasn't he? *Jump!* She wanted to scream. *Jump!*

Emergency rooms are anything *but* private.

"I'm thinking of going out for ski patrol next year," Fenner told them, whacking his long skis together in a noisy display of skierly cool. "My dad's into it. He wanted me to go to medical school, but ski patrol is like being a doctor on skis, except all you need to know is first aid and CPR."

Dude, medical school is *so* yesterday.

"Cool," Nate responded, tearing his eyes away from Serena. Up ahead he heard Blair shriek as she attempted to dismount from the chair. That was one of the hardest things about snowboarding; it had taken him a year to get it right. The chairlift halted abruptly. Obviously Blair had wiped out.

Serena shifted uncomfortably in her seat. Fenner was even more good-looking in his black North Face ski clothes, but he was a little too old for her, and a little too much of a snow geek. "I totally *love* those red ski patrol uniforms," she gushed lamely, her attempt at girlish flirtation falling flat.

The chairlift started moving again. Nate lifted the toe of his snowboard, preparing to dismount. Just below the off ramp, Blair sat in a giggling, snow-covered heap. Her father and his French boyfriend stood over her looking like slalom racers for the Gay French Olympics in their matching black Bogner stretch suits.

"Natie!" Blair cried, waving her pink-mittened hands overhead. Nate dismounted from the chair and coasted effortlessly over to her. "My necklace broke," she told him, holding up the torn rope of black silk.

Maybe it's a sign, Serena thought, appalled by her meanness.

"I still have the heart, though," Blair explained, rising to her knees and patting her parka pocket. "The chairlift guy put in it here for me."

Nate pulled off his gloves and tucked the black silk rope into his own pocket. Then he coaxed Blair to her feet and strapped her free foot onto the back of her snowboard. He grasped her hands and put them on his waist. "Hold on to me," he instructed competently. "I'll get you down."

Serena stared after them as Nate led Blair out into the easiest section of the run. *I'm still here!* she shouted at them silently. Then Fenner blew by her, shredding the snow with his long racing skis. "Torque it!" he called over his shoulder like the snow-bum geek that he was. Blair's dad and Giles started down after him, making concise little figure-eight turns with their matching red Rossignol skis. Serena wiped her nose on her mitten, lifted her head, and sucked in a gulp of cold mountain air. She'd wanted Nate to be jealous of her and Fenner, but she couldn't exactly flirt with Fenner when she only had eyes for Nate.

"What's up, gorgeous?" A studly-looking snowboarder in an army fatigue print Burton snowsuit skidded by, flashing her a cocky smile. Serena watched him disappear down the slope and into the trees. Then she kicked up her skis and let out a loud, giddy whoop as she catapulted down the hill. The powder was fresh and she was surrounded by gorgeous boys on snowboards. She wasn't about to let a broken heart ruin her vacation.

There's something they don't teach you in private school, you have to be born to it: the art of the rally.

v plays hard to get

danhum: i thought we were gonna do stuff over spring break. my friends are all away.

hairlesskat: what friends?

danhum: ok my 1 friend. I already filled up that notebook with poems. I'm bored.

hairlesskat: my whole mag is ur poems and my pics bc the girls in my school are hopeless

danhum: my sister goes to yr school.

hairlesskat: shes not hopeless—her art is in it

danhum: so do you want to see a movie?

hairlesskat: I prefer films to movies. Warhol Sucked opens at the Film Forum next Thursday

hairlesskat: hello?

danhum: ok i guess, if you can't make it before then.

hairlesskat: im worth the wait

danhum: huh?

hairlesskat: nevermind

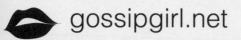
gossipgirl.net

Disclaimer: All the real names of places, people, and events have been altered or abbreviated to protect the innocent. Namely, me.

hey people!

greetings from paradise

I write to you from an undisclosed location, beneath a palm tree, the barely there breeze wafting over my perfectly tanned, barely bikinied form. It has occurred to me that I needn't ever return. I can do what I do best—write this column—from anywhere. And I do so hate the idea of ever wearing clothes again. There is the problem of missing the final, important years of high school, and college would be out of the question, but I'm sure in ten years or so some wise Ivy League institution will bequeath me an honorary degree after being amused and informed by the wisdom of my words for so long. There is one small problem, though: I miss you all terribly. And if I'm not where you are, I honestly don't have much to write about. Still, you've been ever so good about keeping me informed. . . .

your e-mail

Dear Gossip Girl,
So my family has a condo in Sun Valley and it's right behind the lodge. You can see the heated outdoor pool from my bedroom. I'm not a stalker, but, I'm sorry, I watched that boy you call N do the backstroke for an hour smoking this huge joint. These other girls started showing up at the pool because he was there. His girlfriend had better watch it, because we are all crazy about him.
—skibetty

A: Dear skibetty,

Yes. And the thing that makes him even more delightful is that he has no idea how completely smitten we all are.

—GG

Q: Dear GG,

Okay, so first of all I'm a guy, so it's kind of embarrassing for me to be talking to you. But I figure, if you can't help me, who can? I saw this girl's picture on the Internet and I think she's really cute and I want to meet her, but I don't want her to know I know who she is, because I don't think she meant to, like, put herself out there. You know?

—bud

A: Dear bud,

It's hard for me to tell how creepy you are or aren't without meeting you, but I will venture to say that if you saw this girl's picture on the Internet, she did indeed mean to "put herself out there"— it's just a matter of how far. With her best interests in mind, I'd like to suggest that you leave your meeting in person up to fate. Got it? Good.

—GG

Q: Dear GG,

I was getting to be friends with this girl and now she's kind of acting like we're online dating or something. No, that's not it . . . but she's being weird. I know she likes me, but I just want to be friends with her and hang out. Do things have to be so complicated?

—insomniac

A: Dear insomniac,

She likes you, but you "just want to hang out." I believe you've answered your own question.

—GG

sightings

B and **N** in the mountaintop lunch spot in **Sun Valley** with their ski boots off, playing footsie under the table. **S** flirting with a tall blond male ski instructor in the line for chili dogs. You know what they say: if you can't beat 'em, join 'em. **B**'s dad and his French boy toy, also playing footsie under the table. **B**'s little brother, **T**, surrounded by admiring eleven-year-old girls as he skipped lunch to catch a few more runs wearing only a black Led Zeppelin T-shirt and brown leather pants care of **Hermès, Paris**. Another stud in the making? **C** in **Rome**, slathered in extra-virgin olive oil and sunbathing topless on the steps of the **Coliseum**. Is he trying to lure back his extra-virgin Italian countess? You know what they say—when in Rome . . . **K** and **I** skidding down the slopes in **Stowe**, trying desperately to make a fashion statement while freezing their little tushies off in denim short shorts and black legwarmers. Sorry dears, but **Vermont** and **Sun Valley** just do not compare. **D** at the main branch of the **Public Library** on **Forty-second and Fifth** in the Romantics section. Aw. And finally, yours truly, glorious as usual in the latest white Eres bikini, lying prone on a white sand beach, lazily tap-tap-tapping the keys of my laptop. . . .

campari is not as harmless as it looks

My cure-all for too many days sipping too many bottles of champagne has always been a nice tall Campari and soda with a fresh wedge of lime. However, the reason I lie here, quite unable to swim or read or disengage myself from my batik-print chaise lounge, is that four or five Campari and sodas will quite do you in. Campari, after all, is alcohol. And I thought it was a bitter sort of cherry syrup. Hiccup! Oh well, live and learn. Or maybe I should say, live *well* and learn.

Enjoy the rest of your holiday, darlings. Whether you're on the slopes or in the surf, I want to see every one of you dressed in a to-die-for tan when we return.

You know you love me,

gossip girl

her heart's on his sleeve and he's wrapped around her little finger

"Ow, ow, ow, ow, ow!" Blair howled as Nate eased her black Ellesse ski pants down over her snowboard-sore calves. He'd warned her that snowboarding used a different set of muscles and a different skill set than skiing, but as usual Blair had refused to listen. Now she was paying the price. Yesterday she'd collapsed in a heap after dinner. This morning she'd barely been able to walk, but she'd insisted that Nate give her another snowboarding lesson on the baby run while Serena skied with her father and Giles. Nate pulled off her white cashmere turtleneck and rubbed her bare arms.

Sounds like she's really suffering.

"Want me to run you a bath?" he offered.

Blair lay back on the bed, her pain forgotten. He'd already cured her. "Just kiss it better, please," she directed.

He walked over and closed the door between their room and Serena's. Serena seemed to be having a blast hopping moguls with Blair's dad and his boyfriend. All the more time to finally do it with Blair. She lay on the bed in her black underwear and a ridiculously see-through black mesh undershirt that was supposed to be some sort of high-tech self-wicking polypropylene undergarment but was actually pretty fucking sexy. Nate took off his snow pants and then his shirt. His heart was beating fast.

"You were so patient with me today," Blair observed. She propped herself up on her elbows to look at him. The brown-and-gold floral bedspread was totally heinous, but she looked hot on it anyway. "I love you, Nate."

Nate sat down on the end of the bed. "I love you too, Blair." His heart was beating even faster now. This was it, he was sure of it. When they'd first gotten together Blair had said they would have sex "later." Well, it was later now. It was time. He bent down and kissed her on the shoulder.

Blair grabbed his head and pulled him down on top of her. Her own hotel room with the boy of her dreams—the movie that was her life just kept getting better and better! She smiled up at Nate and almost said, *Let's pretend we just got married and we're on our honeymoon,* but then she remembered that not everyone was as crazy as she was. "Just kiss me," she whispered instead.

Nate kissed her— all over. It was a good thing he'd had such a long day of skiing and swimming and getting high, because if he'd been slightly less tired, he'd have had trouble containing himself. "I don't think I want to just kiss you anymore," he told her as he smoothed her long dark hair away from her face. "I want to do something else."

On the other side of the door the sounds of a TV roared noisily. Then there was a series of thumps and bumps. Serena appeared to be back and rearranging the furniture. Was she with that Fenner dude? Nate wondered fleetingly. It was cool how easily Serena met people and made friends. He traced his finger across Blair's collarbone and down her arm.

She giggled ticklishly and propped herself up on her elbow, then kissed Nate's temple. He was such a boy. Obviously he was dying to have sex, but she just wasn't ready yet. "I know you want to. I want to too," she murmured sympathetically. "But we have to wait." She kissed his cheek. "Until this summer." She kissed his lips and smiled coyly. "On the train." They'd spend the day in Paris, ambling the side streets around Nôtre-Dame and drinking rosé in romantic cafés. When night fell they'd board the train at the Gare du Nord. As it eased out of the station and across the city, they'd lock their couchette, strip off their clothes, feed each other champagne-dipped strawberries, and make wild, passionate love until the train had reached the oceanside.

Nate suspected that he was supposed to be as excited by this as Blair seemed to be, but waiting until summer sounded like the worst idea he'd ever heard. He flopped back on the ugly, scratchy bedspread. "Dad said he 'wasn't too keen on the idea of me traveling alone with two young girls,'" he admitted, quoting him nearly verbatim but not exactly telling Blair everything. The truth was, he was pretty sure his hard-ass navy captain father had done one of his extremely sporadic "routine checks" of his room just before Nate left for Sun Valley, and had possibly found his bong. Not that his clueless father would know what the bong was for, but it had probably aroused some suspicion. "He might not let me go."

Blair pressed her cheek against his smooth, bare chest, closing her eyes and grinning as she breathed in his wonderful Nateness. Then she walked her fingers up his belly, spiderlike. "Since when have our parents ever not let us do what we wanted?"

Nate laughed halfheartedly. "I just love you, that's all." Losing their virginity together on a train sounded pretty damn

274

uncomfortable. There wouldn't be any room to spread out or try different positions. And the pillows would probably suck. Couldn't they just do it now? What difference could a couple of months make?

Blair slapped his stomach playfully and sat up. "I have a present for you. Actually, the present is from France. My dad brought it." She didn't tell him that she had embellished the gift with her own ingenious touch using the lodge's mini sewing kit. She got up, went over to the walk-in closet, and took out the carefully rewrapped parcel. "It's from Courrèges," she gushed, handing it to him. "In Paris."

Nate sat up and tore the white tissue paper away from the squishy package, unsheathing a thick and luxurious moss green cashmere V-neck sweater.

Blair snatched the sweater up and held it against his bare chest. She couldn't wait for him to try it on so she could rip it off of him again. "Try it on, try it on," she urged.

Nate slipped his arms into the sleeves and pulled the sweater on over his head. It was soft and felt nice against his skin. It was going to be one of his favorites—he could tell. "It's great. Thanks."

The moss green hue of the sweater made his eyes look even greener, and the bare V of his tan chest made Blair want to scream. She was dying to tell him that she had sewn the gold heart he'd bought her at Tiffany into the inside of one of the sweater's sleeves so that he would always be wearing her heart on his sleeve. But Nate would only want to cut the heart out and make her wear it again. She liked it better where it was, hidden against his adorable skin. She kissed his neck and nuzzled her face into his wonderful, cashmere-coated chest.

Nate played with a lock of her shiny chestnut-colored hair, loving the soft, cozy feel of the sweater. "Hey, where's the heart I gave you?" he asked suddenly, as if reading her mind.

Blair lifted her head. "In a safe place." She kissed him on the lips—long and slow—partly to make him forget the question and partly because he looked so delicious wearing the sweater, she just couldn't resist.

"I love you, Blair," he murmured, tugging up on her black mesh undershirt.

Her heart on his sleeve, indeed.

s comes of age in the wrinkle room

After that first day of skiing, Fenner had invited Serena out with his other ski bum friends, but she had turned him down. She preferred solitude or the reassuring company of Blair's father and his nice gay lover over pretending to flirt with a boy she wasn't even remotely interested in. While Nate and Blair fooled around on the other side of the door, she tried to watch *Cocktail*—the worst Tom Cruise movie ever made—but had to turn away when the people in Tom's hideously crowded bar started to recite terrible poetry and everyone in the bar hooted and clapped like it was the most kick-ass, profound stuff they'd ever heard. She turned the TV off and tried to unpack her clothes into the lodge's bureau drawers. She washed her hair and blow-dried it. She filed her nails. She turned the TV back on and tried to watch *Marie Antoinette* starring Kirsten Dunst, but the story was so thin she quickly grew bored. Every few minutes a sultry giggle or an amused chuckle emanated from the next room. Marie Antoinette wasn't getting any action from King Louis, but it sounded like Blair and Nate were getting plenty.

Finally, when she could stand it no longer, she threw on a

black merino cardigan and her favorite pair of beat-up black Chanel flats and hastily left the room. On the second floor of the lodge was the famous bar and late-night dance lounge, popular with the over-sixty set, that the lodge staff had nicknamed the Wrinkle Room. Serena sat down at the bar, feeling young and conspicuous. Older couples crowded the dance floor, gingerly holding each other as they waltzed and tangoed to the medley of Frank Sinatra songs belted out by the tuxedoed, mustachioed piano player.

Come fly with me, come fly, come fly away. . . .

"I'd like a shot of Absolut, please," Serena told the frail, thousand-year-old bartender. "And a Coke." The bartender poured her the Coke but not the shot. His body looked totally decrepit, but his mind must have been working fine. Clearly she was too young for him to even card.

Serena was grateful he allowed her to stay. The lounge was lit by candlelight, and through the windows she could see a light snow begin to fall. The snow appeared to be made of gold. A couple swept by her place at the bar. They were the best dancers of the bunch, and the best dressed. He was silver-haired and dapper in a hunter green velvet evening jacket and tuxedo pants. She was elegant in a pewter-colored silk gown, her white hair done up in a neat French twist. They danced gracefully and eas-ily, as if they'd practiced for such a long time that the steps were second nature. Their eyes never strayed from each other's faces, and they were both smiling, like they were the luckiest couple alive.

It was difficult not to see herself and Nate in them. Half a century after their romance had begun, they would celebrate by dancing here. If things were entirely different, that is. Now it seemed a lot more likely that Nate and Blair would be the ones to do the dancing. How could he have changed partners so easily and guiltlessly, without batting a single one of his perfect golden brown eyelashes? How could he forget how they'd kissed in her warm bed that cold February night? And kissed, and kissed . . .

She lit a cigarette, letting the smoke trail away into the candlelight. If only she could give Nate up to Blair wholly and completely and stop thinking about kissing him. But she couldn't. Even if it was all in her head, he was still just a little bit hers. One thing was certain: she wouldn't torture herself again by traveling with them this summer. After this drink she would e-mail the agent in charge of arranging their summer train trip to tell him there would only be two travelers this summer, not three. No way was she going to sit in romantic French cafés with Blair and Nate while they fondled each other beneath the table and called each other pet names like Gummy Bear and Noodle. No way was she going to listen to them having loud, giggly sex in their romantic couchette while she sat alone in *her* couchette, knitting misshapen sweaters or doing the crossword in French, which had never been her best subject. She'd find something else to do this summer, like help her mother prune the rose-bushes up in Ridgefield, learn to juggle, perfect her breaststroke, meet another boy.

As if there could ever be another boy.

Serena's well-defined shoulders slumped and she leaned heavily on the dark wooden bar. Salty tears seeped out of her sad navy blue eyes and slid down her cheeks. She suddenly felt older and more tired than any of the other patrons in the lounge. She pushed her Coke away and was about to slip off her lonely bar stool when the bartender set a shot glass down in front of her. He poured out a shot of Absolut. The piano player belted out another tune.

It had to be you, wonderful you, it had to be you. . . .

Serena steeled herself, tipped her head back, and did the shot. She'd never done a shot before, but she'd always been bolder when she was alone.

Looks like this might be the dawn of a bold new era.

v catches d with his pants on

It was the last Thursday of spring break. Vanessa had finally freed up her schedule enough to bring a DVD over to Dan's house along with some sushi and a bottle of sake, care of Ruby. Vanessa had always thought sushi was sort of romantic, the way everything was so neat and bite-size. You could feed each other without making too much of a mess. You barely even needed a napkin. Not that she and Dan were in the feeding-each-other stages just yet, especially not when she'd barely spoken to him in weeks. But maybe by the end of the evening . . .

Never underestimate the power of sake.

Dan had been looking forward to tonight all week because with Zeke away in Florida he was dying of boredom and loneliness and had even contemplated writing a novel. The thing was, the only thing he could think of to write about was a bored, lonely fifteen-year-old loser, and no one would want to read about that. Thankfully, Vanessa had arrived to relieve him of his navel-gazing. They sat on the floor of the study with their backs against the worn brown leather sofa. He stuck in the DVD and pressed play. A Japanese couple rode the subway, looking tired and greasy. They were Japanese but they were speaking Spanish. "Where are the subtitles?" Dan wondered aloud. "Am I supposed to understand what they're saying?"

Ruby had recommended the movie *Mystery Train*, which she claimed was the best film ever made, and was all about lost souls finding each other. Vanessa thought that sounded just right. She'd searched for almost an hour and finally found it in the Imports section of the tiny, dirty video rental place down the street from their apartment. Now she knew why. "It's in Spanish," she observed. Ruby hadn't told her it was a foreign film. Then she noticed that the actor's lips were moving differently from the sound. Elvis appeared and his lips were definitely moving in English but his voice came out sounding like Julio Iglesias's. "It's dubbed," she realized, feeling rather stupid.

"That's okay, I can read lips." Dan opened the bag of sushi and began to carefully lay out the containers on the coffee table. He poured sake into two plastic cups, his hands shaking as usual. He handed a cup to Vanessa. She looked just the same as she had when he'd seen her last. Her head was shaved close and she was dressed entirely in black. It was kind of reassuring.

Vanessa watched the way Dan's hands shook as he attempted to pick up a California roll with his chopsticks. She poured more sake into his cup. Maybe it was a good thing the movie was practically unwatchable. He seemed pretty nervous, and she was pretty sure she knew why. He wanted her to kiss him again, but he was terrified he was going to black out again. The way he tortured himself was so damned irresistible. It was all she could do to keep from jumping his pale, skinny bones.

Dan lit a cigarette, getting into the movie despite the fact that he couldn't understand it most of the time. He liked that all the people in it seemed to be up doing stuff when everyone else was asleep. He'd been having some trouble sleeping himself lately. Maybe it was the cigarettes.

Or the instant coffee he drank all day?

He finished his sake and poured himself some more. The little bottle was almost empty. "Dad's out," he observed. "But he opened some Chianti before he left. Should I get it?"

Vanessa nodded encouragingly. The drunker Dan got the more likely he was to let his guard down and kiss her.

Or faint again. Or throw up.

"This movie reminds me of Kerouac," Dan told her, coming back with a liter bottle of red wine with a picture of a black bull on the label. "My dad would love it. *Whither goest thou, America, in thy shiny car in the night?*" he quoted, puffing out his skinny chest like a jackass.

Here was one of the things Vanessa liked most about him, one of the things that set him apart: he could drop a literary quote without even pausing to think about it. He was a boy out of times past. Her scruffy little Shakespeare. Her bard. Oh, she was glad she'd come. And glad he had more wine.

Soon Dan had finished off the Chianti too, and half a pack of Camels. His head was woozy and the room seemed set on a tilt. It didn't matter anymore that he couldn't really understand the movie. Then the room dipped and tilted at an even sharper angle. He felt like he was on a ride at Hershey Park in Pennsylvania, where his dad had taken him and Jenny that one time. *Whoa, easy does it.* He slumped against Vanessa and put his arm around her for support.

"Hey," she laughed, turning to face him. Her mouth was so close to his cheek she could smell his smoky skin, the wine on his warm breath. She noticed for the first time that the tips of his eyelashes were strawberry blond, the same color as the fuzz on his upper lip. It was all she could do to keep from kissing him again. She wanted him to make the move. Any time now . . .

"Oof," Dan grunted. "I think I need to lie down." He grasped her thigh as he attempted to heave himself up onto the leather sofa.

Little electric pulses ran up and down Vanessa's leg. "Here." She knelt beside him and helped him up. "I'll get you some water," she offered, trying not to sound disappointed. "You little wuss."

She fetched the water, and then on impulse pulled out her camera. Dan's head was thrown to the side at an uncomfortable angle and his eyelids were open just a crack so that she could see the whites. His hands were pressed into a praying position between his knees. He looked half dead. Vanessa snapped the picture. Then, just to be funny and mean and to remind him that she had witnessed his demise and still had a sense of humor about it, she decided to upload the picture on Dan's computer. She'd leave it open for him to stumble upon when he woke up in the morning.

The desk lamp was on in his room and the computer hummed. Cracked mugs half full of cold coffee littered the desk, and an old Coke can held the traces of Dan's new cigarette obsession. The room smelled stale and the brown paper bag colored shag carpet was filled with lint. Vanessa loved it. It was just so . . . Dan.

She hooked up her camera, jiggled the mouse, and clicked around until she found a folder called Dan's Pictures. Opening the folder, she scrolled absently through the files, and was about to download her own silly photo when she came upon two files called "serenavday1" and "serenavday2." She clicked on the first one, and the picture she'd taken of Serena looking cockily back at the camera while she flashed her bare, heart-tattooed butt cheeks loomed large on the screen. Vanessa stared at the photo. The lines from Dan's poem—one of her favorites—appeared in her mind:

> *Your blond hair all freaky*
> *Sitting on my bed*
> *Polishing my toes*

Dan's leather-bound poetry journal lay on the desk beside the computer monitor. She flipped it open to Jenny's illustration of a blond angel that Dan had pasted on the inside cover. The angel had the same dark blue eyes, the same seductive "you know you love me" smile as Serena in the photo. Vanessa whirled around in Dan's swivel chair. More of Jenny's illustrations were pasted on the wall. There were five of them in total. Each of the five was of an angel in flight, her long golden hair trailing out between her widespread wings, her head haloed and lovely. She could've have been any blond angel, except for her navy blue Constance Billard uniform, her dark blue eyes, and the gold *S* pendant around her neck.

More lines from Dan's poems streaked through her mind

> *Do you know me?*
> *I think you do*

But she hadn't known him, she'd just thought she had. Dan wasn't just a doting brother, she realized now. These weren't angels. They were all likenesses of Serena. He was so obsessed with her gorgeous blond classmate that he'd stolen her pictures and pasted reminders of her all over his cracked, cream-colored wall. Dan Humphrey, the object of her undying affection, was a Serena-stalking freak.

Vanessa tossed the leather-bound journal on the desk, stomped back into the study, and glared at Dan's sleeping form. He looked like a little boy, his eyelids ticking, drool pooling in the corners of his mouth. She spun around and tiptoed into the kitchen, hunting around in the cupboards until she found a saucepan. Then she filled it with water and tiptoed back to the living room. Dan was snoring softly now, one arm dangling over the side of the couch. Vanessa set the saucepan on the floor, lifted his arm, and carefully lowered his hand into the tepid water. She stood up and slipped on her black PVC rain jacket, leaving him to his own demise.

The sound of her Doc Martens reverberating noisily on the dusty hardwood floor followed by the slam of the front door startled Dan awake. He hadn't meant to fall asleep—he just needed to rest until the room righted itself again.

"Hey . . . Vanessa?" he called out, sitting up. He looked down at his pants. They were soaked. He'd wet himself like a three-year-old. And his hand was wet too. He swung his legs to the floor, knocking over the saucepan of water. The scent of wet, stale cigarette smoke emanated from the musty Persian rug, making him gag. "Christ," he muttered, staggering toward the door. He shuffled soggily down the hall to his room. Vanessa's wildly gorgeous picture of Serena and her bare butt cheeks swam gaudily in front of him on his computer screen. Oh. *Oh!*

"What's going on?" Jenny poked her head into his room. "Ew!" she cried, pointing at his soaked crotch. "Gross!"

"Fuck off," Dan told her miserably. He flicked off the power to his computer monitor before Jenny could see what was on it. Vanessa must hate him. He hated himself.

"I just saw Vanessa leave." Jenny stepped into his room wearing a pair of pink Powerpuff Girls baby-doll pajama shorts and a tiny red J.Crew bikini top, her curly dark hair brushed into two tight pigtails. "She's so weird. Have you guys kissed yet? I think she really likes you."

Dan stared at his sister in disbelief. Vanessa had made him pee on himself. Even if she'd liked him before, she didn't like him very much anymore.

"I have to change," he sighed miserably, hunting on the floor for a semi-clean pair of cords.

And clearly it's not just his clothes that need changing.

the mean reds vs. the blues

After nine grueling but glorious days of skiing, their last morning in Sun Valley had arrived. Nate felt guilty about not getting more runs in while he was there, so he'd woken up early and hit the slopes. Blair threw open the door to Serena's room and crawled into bed with her. "*Breakfast at Tiffany's* is on," she announced, pressing "select" on the cable remote and grabbing the room service menu from off the bedside table. The lodge had the best Belgian waffles she'd ever tasted. Belgian waffles and *Breakfast at Tiffany's*. What better way to end a perfect vacation?

Well, there is *one* other thing that might make it even more special.

Serena opened a dark blue eye and peeked at Blair through a curtain of thick blond hair. She reached for the clay boat Nate had made for her with HMS *Serena* and the little red heart inscribed on it and tucked it farther under her pillow. Each night she fell asleep with the boat in her hand, holding it against her heart like a good-luck charm and remembering the night she and Nate had kissed. She knew it was vaguely psychotic, but

Nate had made the boat for her as a token of his . . . love. Hadn't he?

Or maybe he just thought it would make a good paper-weight.

Blair's cheeks were glowing from skiing in the sun during the day and fooling around with Nate all night. She looked pretty and annoyingly happy. Serena sat up and shoved her hair out of her face. "I need coffee. A whole pot." She'd spent the last four nights doing shots and watching the old people dance in the Wrinkle Room, and she was constantly hungover.

"The blues are because you're getting fat and maybe it's been raining too long. You're just sad, that's all," Audrey Hepburn as Holly Golightly said onscreen. *"The mean reds are horrible. Suddenly you're afraid, and you don't know what you're afraid of."*

Serena didn't know which she had, the blues or the mean reds. Maybe a little bit of both.

Blair picked up the phone and ordered nearly everything on the menu. Waffles. Rare steak with béarnaise sauce. Bagels and lox. An American cheese omelet. A chocolate milk shake. "I can't decide what I want," she explained. Maybe it was the mountain air, but she'd been starving ever since she arrived.

The two girls sat propped up on Serena's down pillows, watching the now-familiar film. Room service came and Blair spread the bountiful feast out on the bedspread. She took a bite of syrupy waffle and then stuffed a ketchup-smeared French fry in her mouth. "I don't know what I'm doing. I want to be skinny, skinny, skinny when we go away this summer." She reached for her chocolate milkshake and took a long slurp. "Europe by train," she murmured dreamily, watching as Audrey played "Moon River" on her mandolin. Maybe she'd learn how to play guitar this summer too. She could serenade Nate, and he'd get so turned on she'd have to wrestle him to the floor of their couchette. "It's going to be so incredibly romantic."

Serena sipped her bitter coffee. Sun streamed through the window. Skiers silently crisscrossed the snowy mountain. *"My huckleberry friend,"* Audrey crooned.

"I can't go to Europe with you guys," she blurted out.

Blair frowned and reached for more fries. "Is this an April Fool's Day joke?"

Serena shook her head. Wasn't April Fool's Day, like, two weeks away? "No, I really can't go."

"Why not?" Blair demanded, stuffing her mouth with fries.

Isn't it obvious? Serena wanted to yell. "My parents just want me to stay home, that's all. And there's this really cool summer acting workshop that's pretty close to our house in Ridgefield. It sounds amazing. Gwyneth did it, before she got famous." She wound her white cloth napkin around her wrist. She knew only vaguely that there was a community theater near her house in Connecticut where Gwyneth Paltrow had once acted in a play when she was younger. When did she become such an elaborate liar?

Blair shoved more fries into her mouth and took a swig of her shake. "Oh, really? You're not going?" she repeated with obvious annoyance. "You're such a flake, Serena, you really are."

"I'm sorry." Serena hung her head. Her lower lip twitched and she bit it, hard. She was afraid that if she started to cry, she might pour her heart out to Blair, and that was the last thing she wanted to do.

Blair grabbed the steak knife and sawed at her steak until the blood ran. Actually, when she thought about it, this was even better. She and Nate would have their couchette on the train all to themselves. They wouldn't have to worry about doing touristy things and entertaining Serena—they could just have sex, constantly, in every country in the EU. How could she even think of having sex when Serena was always hovering nearby? She was glad she'd asked Nate to wait: it was going to be even more perfect this way.

"Never mind," she said airily, forking a piece of steak and shoving it into her mouth. "It's actually fine."

"Really?" Serena blew out her breath. She hated it when Blair was mad at her.

"Really." Blair flashed Serena a fake little smile, the kind of smile she usually reserved for her annoying wannabe classmates like Nicki Button and Rain Hoffstetter. Over the last few days she'd felt a new distance between herself and Serena that she couldn't quite put her finger on. They weren't like sisters anymore. They were more like stepsisters. She glanced down at the pile of food in front of her. It really was a disgusting display. "Can you put this outside, please?" she gasped, dashing for the bathroom.

Serena gathered up the plates and covered them with their silver warming covers. She returned them to the tray and set the tray outside in the hall. She could hear Blair retch in the bathroom, the sucking flush of the toilet, the sound of her gargling. This time she didn't ask Blair if she was okay—she just pulled her silver Tumi duffel bag out of the closet and started to pack. She tossed the little clay boat into the bag, eager to get it home and out of Blair's sight.

But you know what they say. Home is where the heart is.

n tosses and turns in his teeny-tiny twin bed

"Don't forget your towel, sir," the bald guy behind the pristine white gym desk called. He handed Nate a warm white bath towel. "The girls are in the steam room," he added helpfully.

Nate pushed open the heavy door to the locker room. It wasn't the locker room at St. Jude's with its old muddy green-painted locker doors—it was the locker room at the Bridge, his dad's golf club in Bridgehampton. The lockers had teak doors. A freshly laundered white towel and a hand-rolled cigar were placed in each one. Very nice.

A receiving line of his lacrosse team buddies stood waiting for him, wearing their St. Jude's lacrosse team hunter-green-and-white-striped uniforms and carrying their sticks.

"Way to go, man." Jeremy Scott Tompkinson slapped Nate's hand and flashed his wicked stoner grin.

"Fucking awesome, dude," Anthony Avuldsen agreed, holding out his fist for Nate to bang.

"You're the man," Charlie Dern agreed. He shook Nate's hand, placing a fat, neatly rolled joint in his palm as he did so.

"It's an honor to have a player like you on my team." Coach Michaels reached out and gave Nate a burly bear hug.

The team disappeared into the ether and Nate fired up the joint. Smoking it was like eating the most amazing hot fudge sundae he'd ever tasted. He took one last hit and then took off his khakis and polo shirt and boxer shorts and wrapped the white towel the clerk had given him around his waist. He put his clothes in an empty locker. He wasn't wearing any shoes.

The glass door of the steam room was all fogged up. He pulled it open and stepped inside.

"Hey Natie," a girl's voice greeted him.

Nate moved through the steam in the direction of the voice. Suddenly he felt arms around his neck and the girl was kissing him. It was so unbelievably fantastic. Just kissing her was the most amazing sensation he'd ever experienced. It was like this total natural high, and he could have kept on kissing her forever. The girl's hair looked brown but it was wet and she felt ribbier than Blair, and taller. She smelled like Blair's perfume, though, and she kissed like Blair—eager, ravenous, hyperactive.

"You know you love me," the girl murmured in his ear, and her voice sounded exactly like Serena's voice on her voice-mail greeting.

"Let's do it," Nate told her. "I really want to do it with you."

"Nate, darling? Are you all right?"

Nate woke with a start and sat up. His tartan plaid flannel sheets were soaked with sweat. His parents' heads peered in at him through the open bedroom door. They looked tan and dapper. His mother wore a diamond comb in her hair and a mink stole around her neck. His dad was holding a glass of Scotch.

"You were talking in your sleep," his mother told him in her aristocratic French accent. "Quite loudly."

Nate rubbed his eyes and checked his bed for girls. Was he still dreaming? "You guys are back?" he asked, dazed. While he was in

Sun Valley his parents had gone to St. Barts. Or maybe Barcelona. He couldn't remember.

His father cleared his throat and swirled the ice around in his Scotch. "As a matter of fact, we got back yesterday. We've been at the opera. The first installment of Wagner's Ring Cycle began tonight. How was the skiing?"

"Skiing was good," Nate responded automatically, even though he hadn't really done much skiing. He rubbed his eyes some more, hoping his room didn't smell like pot. He didn't think it did, although the green sweater Blair had given him reeked, and it was draped over his desk chair, not four feet from the door.

"Go back to sleep, darling," his mother commanded with a knowing smile.

Nate flopped down on the pillows and closed his eyes, trying to ease back into the same dream again. All he could see in his sleepy mind's eye were the faces of the two girls he loved more than anyone in world, his two best friends. *"You know you love us,"* they whispered, loud and clear.

It would probably be safer to dream about someone else.

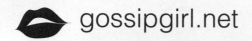
topics ◄ *previous*   **next** ▶   *post a question*   **reply**

hey people!

april showers bring may flowers, but what does june bring?

Cute skirts, flip-flops, and shirtless boys! It truly baffles me why school doesn't end in May. How on earth are we supposed to pay attention in class when it's ninety degrees outside? Spring was a blur of electrical storms and exams and the occasional, totally irresponsible let's-trash-the-penthouse-while-the-parents-are-at-the-Cannes-Film-Festival rage. But now the windows are open, birds are singing, bees are buzzing, and the park is humming with boys playing Frisbee with nary a shirt in sight. And yet we have to wear our hot, itchy school uniforms and *closed-toe shoes* for two more weeks, sweating over our geometry textbooks while we daydream about the summer. It's funny—some girls I know get so worked up about their summer plans. All I want to do is dangle my feet in the pool. Of course, I'm very particular about which pool, and who I'm going to dangle with. Some of you are absolutely *dying* to dangle with me. See come-on below.

your e-mail

Dearest GG,
I have been watching you. Well, not watching, but reading and rereading your every word. I'm pretty sure you're my soul mate. I want to send you my picture. I want to send you my soul. I

really dig you. And tonight I'll dream about you, just like I do every night.

—smittn

 Dear smittn,

I'm truly flattered, but my soul mate doesn't have time to read and reread girlish prattle. Not that anything I write is actually prattle, but it's definitely girlish. No, my soul mate is out stalking lions and scouting for watering holes. You can send me your picture, but I'd rather you didn't and kept on dreaming about me.

—GG

Dear GG,

Simple question. What do you do when you're mad at someone, but you also like them a lot?

—boots

Dear boots,

That is not a simple question. All I can't think of to say is, yell at them until they get it, or give them the silent treatment. They'll come around eventually. Hopefully. Good luck!

—GG

sightings

V at a karaoke bar on **Orchard Street** singing "Crimson and Clover" with her big sister. It's about time she let her hair down. Wait, she doesn't have any hair. **D** playing hoops in **Riverside Park** with his desperately-in-need-of-a-*Queer-Eye*-makeover friend. Well, at least he still has one friend. **S** in the **Central Park Zoo**, talking to the polar bear. At least *she* still has one friend. **B** and **N** shopping for his summer clothes at **Brooks Brothers** on **Fifth**. If she really wants to help him, she should take him somewhere else. He's sixteen years old—time to branch out and wear something other than Bermuda shorts and pastel polos. Actually, scratch that—we love him just the way he is.

the girls of *rancor*

Looks like our favorite shaven-headed friend has been busy, busy, busy outsmarting us all by putting out her first issue of a very sleek, very cool new arts magazine. It's just a girl's school publication, but it's impossible not to walk down Madison Avenue without spotting at least one person reading it. Most of the photographs are pretty damn gross. Hello? Who honestly wants to look at pictures of spat-out gum and dead pigeons? The biggest draw by far are the poems by Anonymous. They're totally freaky, a little sad, and kind of sexy. There's something in them for everyone. Best of all, they're written *by* a girl, *about* a girl. Which leads me to . . .

so close and yet so far away

Has anyone noticed how a certain threesome has turned into a two-some plus a stray? The Terrific Three are now just a boring lovey-dovey couple and a blonde who walks a few feet apart from them, if she's walking with them at all. Hmm, just a thought, but could a certain gorgeous blonde *be* Anonymous? Maybe that girl-on-girl kiss a few of us spied her and a certain glossy brunette sharing in a steamy hot tub in a certain hotel suite way back on Valentine's Day really *meant* something—to her. Whee! All the more fodder for my favorite pastime. No, not *that* pastime, you gutterhogs. I meant *gossip* of course!

Oops, it's lunchtime. Gotta slather on that Guerlain SPF 4 ultrabronzing tanning oil and hit the roof. And you thought the roof gym at school was for dodgeball.

Let's see who can get the best tan by the time school gets out. And no cheating with that fake-tan crap. I know a real tan when I see one. On your marks, ready, set—go!

You know you love me,

gossip girl

b has mail

From: narchibald@stjudes.edu
To: bwaldorf@constancebillard.edu
Date: Thursday, June 1 11:50AM
Subject: Bad news

Hey,
I know I'm already late for lunchtime lax
practice but I wanted to get this to you so
you can make new plans or whatever. I know
you're going to be pissed but I kind of let
it slip to my dad that it was just going
to be the two of us this summer and he went
apeshit. I think he's seriously becoming
more of an uptight prick in his old age.
Bottom line is, I can't go to Europe this
summer. Basically my dad wants me around to
help finish building our boat up in Maine.
It'll be cool once it's done, and I promise
to take you out on it. I'm really sorry,
but I promise to make it up to you v. soon.

—N

what the ladies-who-lunch talk about during lunch

"Wait your turn, girls," Mrs. Wiley, the wide-nostriled lunch proctor instructed the semi-orderly queue of uniformed Constance Billard girls lined up at the entrance to the cafeteria, orange plastic trays in hand. "There are plenty of fish sticks to go around. Watch out for the little ones."

Constance Billard parents had been complaining about the uninspired school lunches for years, and the school was determined to improve on its standard fare of cold roast beef and powdered mash potatoes. The first step was to hire a lunch proctor whose job was to monitor how much the girls ate, what their preferences were, and what sorts of foods they brought from home to supplement the disgusting school lunch. During the upcoming summer, the administration had promised to refurbish the cafeteria, and in the fall it would offer a deluxe salad bar and smoothie center, with offerings garnered from Mrs. Wiley's observations. Not that she'd garnered anything awe-inspiring. Who wouldn't prefer braised carrot sticks in pesto, sourdough baguettes, and green-tea yogurt to scary gray meat loaf and canned string beans? If the students and parents were satisfied with the new menu, Mrs. Wiley would take her nostrils to another malnourished school.

And she would be sorely missed. Not.

Blair and Serena stood in line for the salad bar, remaining oddly silent. Blair was in a foul mood. She'd received Nate's horrendous e-mail only moments before—and to think, all morning she'd been in a blissed-out pre-summer trance, gloriously reviewing every momentous event since she and Nate had kissed that first night in Chuck's suite. How thrilled she'd felt to wake up the next morning to him kissing her. Tiffany. Watching the sea lion feeding at the zoo. The hour-long carriage ride in the snow, fooling around the whole time beneath a scratchy woolen blanket. Giving Nate the moss green sweater with the gold heart sewn into it. Promising to finally do it with him this summer on the train as it left Paris. Now they weren't even going to Europe anymore.

The girls placed modest piles of iceberg lettuce on their plates, ladling a dollop of bleu cheese dressing next to it before moving along to the dessert area, where they each selected a Dannon nonfat lemon yogurt. This was the "diet plate" they'd invented in fifth grade and had been eating ever since. Serena followed Blair over to their favorite table, in front of a full wall of mirrors. As usual, Serena sat facing the mirror and Blair sat with her back to it. Blair couldn't look at herself and eat at the same time.

Serena twirled her spoon around in her yogurt, wondering why Blair looked so glum. Had she done badly on her AP French test? Had she and Nate had a fight? she couldn't help but wonder hopefully. Across the lunchroom Rain, Laura, Kati, and Isabel were getting their trays and lining up. Now was Serena's chance for a private conversation before they were bombarded. Blair stirred her coffee with exaggerated annoyance, spilling half of it onto her tray.

"Are you okay?" Serena asked tentatively. She unbuttoned the top button of her white Peter Pan–collared short-sleeved Tocca blouse and then buttoned it again.

The small, crowded cafeteria was teeming with chattering girls, but an almost imperceptible hush seemed to fall over them when Serena uttered this question. Without actually moving, the room full of girls bent their ears toward the two pretty sophomores speaking in low voices at their special table near the mirrored wall, and their mindless chatter morphed into ruthless gossip.

"You know those poems by Anonymous? Serena is Anonymous. She's totally in love with Blair. It's really sad," a bed-wetting eighth-grader named Susie Wexler declared.

"They're so beautiful," sighed a freshman with Coke bottle glasses.

"Serena had a nose job," countered her frizzy-haired classmate. "My dad's a podiatrist—I should know."

"I heard Blair and Nate are getting married. I heard someone saw him looking at engagement rings in Tiffany this weekend. Oh my God, do you think she's pregnant?" a tragically stubby-legged senior wondered gleefully.

"But I thought I heard she was a lesbian," another senior remarked. "Didn't she write all those lesbian poems by Anonymous?"

Blair touched the spot in the middle of her chest where the gold heart pendant used to fall. Even if it was ugly, maybe she should have strung it on a gold chain from another necklace and resigned herself to wearing it until Nate gave her something better. At least the necklace meant something—that she and Nate were a couple, that they were in love, that he was hers. Even if they couldn't be together this summer, at least she could have had that. She dunked a piece of lettuce in bleu cheese dressing and stuffed it into her mouth.

"Actually, I'm not okay. Thanks to you, Nate can't go to Europe with me this summer," she informed Serena icily. She snatched up her plastic fork and used it to scratch the back of her neck. The lace-edged turquoise-colored cami she'd chosen to wear to school today was totally out of uniform, and the lace was itchy as hell.

Serena contemplated her own reflection in the mirror. She was afraid that if she didn't watch herself, the glimmer in her navy blue eyes might actually reveal that she was pleased. "But that's terrible." She shook her head and shifted her gaze to Blair's darkly pissed-off glare.

Blair stabbed at her yogurt with her spoon. "His dad won't let him. He wants Nate to help him build that stupid boat way up in Maine. It's your fault. If the three of us were going, his dad would have been fine with it." She let out a loud, irritated sigh and flung her yogurty spoon down on the orange plastic tray. "Nate and I were supposed to finally have sex on the train as it pulled out of Paris. I bought beautiful underwear. I even bought an exact replica of the sunglasses Audrey wears in the first scene in *Breakfast at Tiffany's*. Now I'm going to have to spend half the summer up in Newport playing boring tennis with my flaming father and his fake-tan, barely-speaks-English boyfriend, and the other half with my idiotic mother in boring fucking Scotland for my crazy aunt's second fucking wedding to the same guy."

Just then Rain, Laura, Kati, and Isabel swooped in and sat down at their table. "Aren't you going to finish your dressing?" Kati asked, dipping her pinky nail into Serena's bleu cheese. "They ran out. I had to get ranch—gross." She pulled her straight, shoulder-length strawberry blond hair up into a bun on top of her head and then let it cascade dramatically onto her shoulders. Kati had very pretty hair. Too bad she was so dumb.

At least she has something going for her.

Isabel glanced from Blair to Serena. Blair looked like she wanted to chop Serena's head off with her plastic knife, and Serena was staring into her yogurt like she was mind-melding with the live cultures inside it. *Nate and I were supposed to finally have sex on the train as it pulled out of Paris.* All this time she'd thought they'd been having sex all over the place, but they were both still virgins. She could scarcely believe it.

Believe it, baby.

"Did we, like, interrupt something?" Isabel demanded sagely. She was wearing a bright purple cowl neck sweater, a color only someone with her confidence and flawless dark complexion could get away with. She had a genius IQ, but she preferred to apply it to the science of choosing a new shade of highlights for her hair or finding the identical dress to the one Kate Bosworth had worn at the Costume Institute gala, rather than say, AP Chemistry.

Well, if given a choice, which would you choose?

Serena heaved a huge, shuddering sigh. She couldn't wait for school to be over. And maybe the summer apart from each other was just what they needed. They'd have a nice, relaxing vacation and then come back in the fall and start afresh. Maybe Blair would meet a hot tennis player in Newport and decide

Nate wasn't so special after all. Maybe she and Blair would miss each other so much they'd make a pact never to be mean to each other again. Maybe Nate would remember that he was in love with *her*, not Blair. Blair could be very convincing, but with a little distance Nate might realize it was Serena he missed, not Blair.

Anything's possible.

"I'm sorry, Blair," Serena ventured, looking hopefully up at her friend.

Blair thrust her tray away with such force that it teetered precariously on the edge of the table. She stood up, her whole body trembling. "Sorry isn't good enough." Leaving her full tray for Mrs. Wiley to freak out about, she stalked out of the lunchroom to the nurse's office, where she'd use the private bathroom to heave up her lunch, then complain of cramps and get the heavy-duty prescription-strength Motrin, her favorite.

The other girls waited for Serena to say something, but she didn't, or wouldn't. Instead, she picked up her tray and Blair's and carried them back to the kitchen to be cleared off and cleaned. The lunchroom was buzzing now, with news of their fight.

"See what happens when you kiss your best friend?" Isabel joked cuttingly. "It always ends in tears."

"I wonder if Nate has anything to do with this," Laura Salmon offered. "Their fight, I mean."

Whatever gave her that idea?

Gossip about Serena and Blair leaked from one table to the next until it had completely infected the room like a bad case of strep throat. Finally it hit Jenny's seventh-grade-loner table, near the faculty bathroom.

"Serena's not Anonymous," Jenny mumbled aloud to herself as she peeled her third nectarine. She had started an all-fruit fast in hopes that it would stunt the growth of her boobs. She was wearing the tan version of her Polish bra today and was feeling particularly conspicuous, because, as the proprietor of the Village Bra Shop had predicted, it was already too tight. She'd always attributed her lack of friends to the fact that she was shy and quiet in school; now Jenny blamed her boobs. Her classmates had no idea that if they'd deigned to speak to her, she could have told them exactly who Anonymous was.

Serena was on her way out of the cafeteria when she noticed Vanessa Abrams with her shaved head, sitting by herself and reading her magazine over a cup of black tea. The cover of *Rancor* bore a photograph of a piece of spat-out gum on the sidewalk. It looked like a piece of meat someone had dropped on their way home from the butcher.

On a whim, Serena plunked down in the seat across from her shaven-headed classmate. "I love your magazine," she said with genuine admiration.

Vanessa cocked her head defiantly. It hadn't escaped her notice that Ms. Perfect and Ms. Bitchy had just had a big fight. Was Ms. Perfect already looking for a new friend?

"Especially those poems by Anonymous." Serena giggled and leaned forward. "Someone left me an anonymous love poem in my locker once. I think it was the same person."

Vanessa glared at her perfect blond classmate with her big brown eyes. She knew it was wrong to hate someone she hardly even knew, but she couldn't help it. It was all too clear now that the only reason Dan had allowed her to use his poems in *Rancor* was because he was sure Serena would read them. How could she have been so dumb when she was usually so smart?

When we're in lust, we just don't think straight.

"Congratulations." Vanessa flipped the magazine closed and stood up abruptly. "I hope you'll be very happy together."

From across the cafeteria Jenny watched Serena watch Vanessa leave. She looked so alarmingly sad, Jenny wished she could do something to console her. But Serena van der Woodsen was Serena van der Woodsen, the girl every boy wanted and every girl wanted to be. Jenny was pretty sure she'd think of some way to console herself.

She always does.

d can't lose this loving feeling

Dan had jogged through Central Park and over to Constance from Riverside Prep on West End Avenue and now he was dying. Sweat poured from his face and seeped into his collar. He was shaking and red-faced and looked like he needed to go to the hospital. It was a hot and breezeless day. He lit a cigarette and sucked on it desperately. There . . . much better. He still felt awful, but a better, more intriguing kind of awful. Now all he had to do was think of something nice to say to Vanessa so she wouldn't hate him anymore. Too bad the only thing he could think of to say was, "You're nice. I like you," which sounded like a marriage proposal from somebody who'd been living in a windowless basement all his life, eating cockroaches.

At least it would be a step in the right direction.

With its flawless red brick façade, billowing American flag, and great blue doors, Constance Billard was much more imposing than Riverside Prep. Even the teachers looked more intimidating, with their crisp linen suits, pointy shoes, perfectly coiffed hair, and steely makeup. No wonder Vanessa hated school. She must have felt like the ugly duckling in this place.

Dan lit another cigarette, tossing his old one discreetly beside the front tire of the parked gray town car he was leaning against. The sturdy red brick school building in front of him seemed to shudder with relief as the final bell rang within. Then the great blue doors flew open and a stream of girls wearing Constance's blue and white seersucker summer uniforms poured out. First came the little ones in their white Peter Pan–collared blouses, lugging enormous wheeled backpacks full of lunchboxes, sticker albums, pencil kits, and scrapbooks. Next came the middle schoolers, looking awkward in their braces and glasses, weighed down by their enormous math and Latin textbooks. And finally the upper schoolers began to ooze out more casually, after changing into shorts, halter tops, and flip-flops, turning on their iPods, and applying their one thousandth coat of MAC lip gloss for the day.

Jenny should have been out already, but she often got caught up with a project in the art room, so Dan wasn't surprised she was late. Still, she was supposed to be his cover. If Vanessa refused to talk to him or gave him a hard time, he was counting on pretending he was just there to pick up Jenny.

Finally he spotted Vanessa exiting the great blue doors wearing a cap-sleeved black T-shirt, a super-short, maroon wool Constance winter uniform skirt, and cut-off-at-the-knee black fishnet stockings with her ever-present black Doc Martens. She traipsed down the stairs in that deliberately slow, fuck-all-you-losers-for-rushing way she had of walking and headed straight for him. Her big brown eyes were mild and almost bored-looking, and he could tell she was determined not to let on how mad at him she truly was.

"Been staying dry and secure?" she demanded, pointing at

his black corduroys. "I hear Depend undergarments give a better fit than Pampers."

Nice.

Dan threw his cigarette onto the steaming sidewalk. "It's not my fault you stuck my hand in a bowl of water. What'd you expect?" He wasn't about to mention why she'd stuck his hand in a bowl of water in the first place. How could he explain his tireless obsession with a girl who didn't even know his name?

Vanessa shrugged her shoulders. What did she expect? A lot, actually. She squinted at him. "What's wrong with your face? Have you been exercising or are you just happy to see me?" She cackled at her own joke. "Did you come to finally demand an apology for my little prank, or are you just waiting for your sister?"

Dan smiled, then frowned, suddenly confused. Why *was* he here? "I could say I'm here to pick up Jenny, but I'm not." Words spilled out of his mouth before he could stop them. "I ran all the way here . . . to see you . . . to apologize for being . . . I don't know, a jerk."

Vanessa wanted to hug him, she really did. But hugs were so corny. She just wasn't a hugger.

Aw, go on. Hug him.

Besides, she still wasn't sure what Dan's apology *meant*. Had he burned the illustrations of Serena over his bed? Had he trashed the pictures of Serena's naked butt cheeks? Was he ready to devote himself to her instead? She certainly hoped so, because the meek, apologetic way he was looking at her was pretty fucking cute. She reached out and tweaked one of his rather dangly pink earlobes. "S'okay," she relented. "Maybe you could buy me a seltzer to make it up to me. But I think we should wait for your sister. She has news."

Dan looked up at the red brick schoolhouse. He noticed for the first time that the second-floor windows were decorated with student artwork. He squinted up at them. It wasn't just random student artwork, either. Pasted on the paned windows were the golden-haired angels of Jenny's hymnal illustrations. Serena, Serena, Serena—her face was all over the place.

Dan turned away. He'd be fine if he didn't look at them. Everything would be fine.

"Go blue team, go blue team, go BLUE!!" shouted a group of overinvigorated volleyball players as they piled into a school bus on their way to a game. The second bell rang. Still no Jenny.

"It's sunny," Vanessa observed, shielding her pale face from the light. She'd noticed Dan notice the illustrations in the windows of the auditorium upstairs, noticed how he turned his back on them. Maybe she *could* forgive him; maybe there was hope for him after all.

Dan lit another cigarette, and they waited in almost comfortable silence for Jenny to turn up. Not one of the girls coming out of school spoke to Vanessa. Dan realized she was just as friendless as he, and he was glad he'd come. Vanessa was good enough to be met by a boy after school, and he was good enough to have a girl to meet.

The great blue doors swung open and a tall girl with long, pale blond hair appeared wearing cutoff jeans, a white tank top, and silver flip-flops. She paused in the doorway, watching as a tall, stoned-looking boy in a green-and-white-striped St. Jude's lacrosse T-shirt and his fancily dressed brunette Constance girlfriend climbed into a taxi. The tall blonde hugged her arms to her chest and her whole body seemed to shudder. Then she fished a pair of huge tortoiseshell sunglasses from out of her bag, put them on, and continued west down Ninety-third Street toward the park, alone.

Hold yourself until I get there, then I'll do the holding.
We're flapping like fish on a rock. Come on, flap in and swim!
Catch me. Or better yet, I'll catch you.

Dan wasn't sure about the expression "flap in." It didn't sound right, at least not in his head. "Catch me," he murmured under his breath, like a crazy person.

Vanessa waved her hand in front of his face. "Ground control to Mars. Mars, do you copy?"

Dan hadn't realized he was staring. Actually, he knew he was staring—what he'd forgotten was that Vanessa was standing there with him, watching him stare.

"Sorry," he apologized, still staring. Serena was just turning the corner, her golden angel hair flying out behind her, leaving a trail of tears.

A trail of tears. That's good!

Dan couldn't hide the fact that he'd been staring. He also couldn't hide his desperation. Why, oh why had Serena looked so miserable, sad, and alone? Was she in love with that stoner jock? Hadn't she read the poems? Didn't she know that *he* was the one for her?

Vanessa rolled her eyes in annoyance. Dan was no less over Serena than she was over him. She couldn't say anything, though. It wasn't worth it. He was like an alcoholic or a junkie. He couldn't be cured until he admitted he had a problem.

Or found a better drug.

She was about to kick Dan hard in the shins with her steel-toed boots when Jenny burst out of the great blue doors and threw herself at her brother like an overexcited puppy, bouncing her new boobs against him and chattering hysterically. "I have *so* much to tell you guys! Oh my God. Today has been totally crazy. I think I'm going to have a heart attack!" She grabbed Vanessa's arm. "I won! I totally won the hymnal competition. And it's, like, so unreal, because they liked the angels and all, but what they really liked was my calligraphy. I'm so excited!!" She dove at Dan again, practically knocking him down on the sidewalk. "And oh my God, it's so weird—everyone thinks Serena wrote your poems, you know, the ones by Anonymous? Everyone thinks she's, like, into girls, and her heart's broken because Blair has a boyfriend."

Dan blinked his light brown eyes at her. Who was Blair? Was he that stoned-looking boy he just saw getting into a cab with that pretty brunette? Was Jenny even speaking English?

"Actually, I don't really know exactly what happened, but Serena and her best friend Blair had like, this huge, huge fight in the lunchroom at school. It was really dramatic. Vanessa saw it." Jenny glanced eagerly at Vanessa. "Wasn't it dramatic?"

She pursed her lips. "I prefer foreign films."

Jenny rolled her eyes. "So what are we doing? Where are we going? Are you guys friends again? Are you, like, *going out* now?"

Vanessa tried hard not to blush. "No way. We're way too cool for that."

Dan felt hollow and waterlogged, like driftwood. "It's weird they think she's me," he mused aloud to himself, his feet rooted to the spot. If he stood there long enough, maybe Serena would come back. He could explain that he wrote the poems for her. He'd make her smile again.

"Come on." Vanessa slipped her arm through Jenny's and led her away, leaving Dan behind. He was hopeless—utterly and entirely hopeless. "Let's go find something else to talk about."

As if that were possible.

Disclaimer: All the real names of places, people, and events have been altered or abbreviated to protect the innocent. Namely, me.

hey people!

we did it!

We made it through another school year. Right now you're wearing a Tracey Feith sundress and Tory Burch espadrilles, you're gorgeously bronzed, the city smells like an intoxicating combination of Coppertone and bus exhaust, it's one hundred and ten degrees in the shade, *and you don't have to go to school for almost three months.* I know you already know this—I just can't believe it myself. No more waking up at the crack of dawn's ass, no more itchy uniforms, no more mind-numbing trigonometry homework, no more tortuous hungover jogging around the reservoir in Central Park during P.E., following the gym teacher like lemmings, no more onion-bagel-breath Latin teacher. Summer is all about *you*. A whole eleven weeks to do absolutely everything or absolutely nothing. Or maybe a bit of each.

your e-mail

Dear GG,

So I was sent a picture of this curly-brown-haired girl who's supposed to share my cabin this summer at camp and there's like no way she's twelve. She looks like a stripper, I swear. Maybe she got implants and they made a mistake and put too much

silicone in. If that's true, then I feel sorry for her. But they should have a special camp for people like that, you know?
—bunkgrl

A: Dear bunkgrl,
They actually have a special camp for people like you: it's called Camp Bitchalot. It's totally fun. I should know. I went there.
—GG

Q: Dear GG,
My sister is trying to kill me. Not in an overt way, but she got the worst summer job available to man and she did it to torture me, I'm sure of it. She just started today and she came home stinking like a rotten can of tuna fish. Now our whole place reeks and I can't sleep. I'm a musician, I work late, and sleep is sacred. I wish I could do something to sabotage her job so she'll get fired. Is that so terrible?
—rubadub

A: Dear rubadub,
Sabotage is my middle name.
—GG

Q: Dear GG,
I'm going away tomorrow for the summer. I'm not going to see my girlfriend for more than two months, and I want to give her a going-away present, if you know what I mean. I'm kind of new at this whole thing, so any suggestions would be appreciated.
—salur

A: Dear salur,
You cutie. It's so nice that you'd ask little ol' me for advice. I think that if you are somewhere comfortable, the candles are

lit, there's soft music playing, and you say sweet things, that's all good. But she's the one who's gonna decide if it's gonna happen—not me, and not you. Got it?
—GG

sightings

N in **Tiffany & Co.** *alone*. Looking for something special for that special someone so she'll forget you totally ruined her summer plans? **S** sitting on the floor at the **Corner Bookstore** on **Ninety-third and Madison**, voraciously rereading *The Age of Innocence*, that famous New York story about a woman spurned by society. Books like that are so much more meaningful the second time around. **D** on a broken green bench in the divider in the middle of Broadway at Ninety-sixth, chain-smoking. Please don't tell me *that's* what he plans to do all summer. **B** in **Barneys**, buying up the whole Lilly Pulitzer tennis collection. **N** in **Central Park** later, smoking up with a tiny light blue **Tiffany** bag slung around his wrist. It might take more than a couple hits to recuperate from spending a fortune on something that fits into a tiny velvet box. I know it hurts, but in no time at all she'll be kissing it better. . . .

the truth about summer

We talk about it all year long: summer romance, lazing in the sun, sleeping late, no shoes. But the truth is, those very last weeks in August, we start getting antsy. We want to wear our knee-high Miu Miu boots and shop for coats again; we can't wait to be back on the steps of the Met sipping cappuccinos and describing the particulars of our summers *in detail*. Because even though we're about to have the best summer ever—we *will*, you'll see!—there'll always be that nagging feeling that we're missing something.

Never fear, GG is here. I may be on vacation, hiding behind my new gigantic tortoiseshell Chanel shades and floppy Philip Treacy straw hat, but that doesn't mean I can keep my mouth shut. I promise to fill you in on anything and everything worth talking about.

See you at the beach!

You know you love me,

gossip girl

b only comes in one color

It was the Monday after the last day of school and the air was heavy with humidity and the promise of a hot and heady summer. Nate's red duffel bag was packed. Tonight was the last night before Blair left for Newport and he headed up to Maine. This was the night he'd been waiting for, their big summer send-off—the night he and Blair were finally going to do it. Nate had everything ready: Diptyque musk candles, thirty of his favorite songs playing continuously from his iPod Sound-Dock, a chilled bottle of Dom Pérignon he'd stolen from his father's wet bar, and a package of Chips Ahoy cookies—Blair's favorite. The housekeeper had the day off, so he'd even made his bed all by himself. And he'd bought Blair another present from Tiffany.

As if he needed to score more points.

"Since the summer got all messed up and you don't wear the heart anymore," Nate said, pressing the little robin's egg blue Tiffany box into Blair's hand.

She tore the lid off the box and snapped open the black velvet ring box. Inside was a delicate brushed gold band set with a gorgeous deep red ruby. It was the most beautiful ring she'd ever seen. She shoved it onto the ring finger of her left hand and threw her arms around Nate's neck. In the movie that was her life, he'd just asked her to marry him, and the answer was yes, oh, yes. Definitely—*yes!*

Cue straitjacket.

"I'm not mad at you anymore," she told him in a sultry whisper. She was so glad she'd found another use for that ugly Elsa Peretti gold heart pendant. The ruby ring was so much better.

Nate grinned eagerly down at her, his emerald green eyes glittering. His parents were at the last installment of Wagner's Ring Cycle. All that was left to do now was get naked.

And now that it was summer, there really wasn't much to take off.

Blair's neatly plucked eyebrows arched expectantly. "Are you about to get all romantic on me?" she demanded, loving it.

Nate ran his hands through her dark, luxurious hair. "Let's do it," he murmured, trying not to sound anxious. "I really want to do it with you." Somehow the words were so familiar, he felt like he'd said them before. Or maybe he'd just thought about saying them so much it only felt that way.

Blair eased her hands underneath his plain gray T-shirt. "I know, Natie. Me too."

His whole body felt prickly with excitement. It was about to happen. It was about to happen. Oh, goody, goody, goody!

Steady, boy.

He pulled her in close and covered her bare shoulders, neck, and collarbone with kisses. Then he tugged the straps down on her yellow Issa palm leaf print sundress. No bra, just Blair.

She took a step back and pressed her freshly manicured palms against his smooth, wonderfully lacrosse-toned chest. "But I've been thinking about it a lot," she told him firmly. "And I think we should wait until August, when I come back from my aunt's wedding in Scotland."

Nate's roving hands ceased their roving. What the hell was she talking about? In Sun Valley she'd said summer; well, it was summer now. He was through with waiting. "But—" he started to say. Just then a Beck song came on the SoundDock. Nate had stopped liking Beck when he found out he was a Scientologist.

"Think about it. We'll miss each other like crazy all summer. We'll be, like, imagining what it's like to finally be together. And then, when I'm finally back, we'll do it, and then we'll totally stay together *forever*," Blair explained, like she was decoding the meaning of life.

That would be the meaning of life according to Blair.

"But—"

She dug her fingernails ever so gently into the skin on Nate's chest. "It's what I want," Blair insisted, indicating that the discussion was over. She slipped her hands up to his shoulders and down his arms, easing them out of the sleeves of his gray T-shirt. "That doesn't mean we can't still kiss."

Nate tugged his T-shirt out of her hands and walked over to the open window. His bedroom was on the top floor of his family's town house, and the window he was looking out of faced the back. Three stories below, his mother's coveted Venus de Milo fountain gurgled in the garden. Fireflies flitted in the still night air. Music and laughter echoed out of a distant open window.

She comes in colors everywhere,
She combs her hair,
She's like a rainbow

The song reminded him of Serena. In his mind Blair was just one color—red—but Serena really was like a rainbow. She didn't comb her hair much, though; she didn't have to.

He and Serena e-mailed every once in a while, but they rarely saw each other anymore. She might already have gone up to Ridgefield—Nate wasn't sure. Apparently the tryouts for some play she wanted to be in were starting tomorrow. Serena suddenly seemed so busy. Or maybe it was he who was busy.

Having a girlfriend can be pretty time-consuming.

"I have to take a shower," he mumbled to Blair and turned away. He slammed the bathroom door closed and turned the cold water on full blast. Then he opened the bottom drawer of the marble-topped vanity and retrieved his emergency stash: four slim little joints in an Altoids can. He fished his silver Zippo lighter out of his pocket and lit one. Normally he didn't smoke in Blair's presence, but he'd abstained all afternoon because he'd thought they were finally going to do it. This waiting thing was driving him apeshit. What exactly was the point of being together if they couldn't be *together*?

Boys.

As soon as Nate closed the bathroom door, Blair yanked open the bottom drawer of the antique mahogany armoire he'd inherited from his dead French grandfather. She upended the drawer, searching through the piles of wool and cashmere for the moss green cashmere V-neck sweater she'd given him in Sun Valley. She found the sweater and yanked the sleeves inside out.

There it was, the gold heart, still there. She put it to her lips and kissed it. Nate might be sore with her now for making him wait, but he was still wearing her heart on his sleeve—still hers for better or for worse. When they finally did it, it would be so amazingly perfect he'd forget all about being mad. It would be totally worth the wait—she'd make sure of it.

She carefully refolded the sweater and tucked it into his red duffel bag. Maine was pretty far north. Surely Nate would need something to wear on those chilly nights without her. She righted the drawer and put the other sweaters back as neatly as she could. Pot smoke seeped out from beneath the bathroom door. *You know you love me,* Blair scrawled with a dark green Sharpie across a piece of blank printer paper. She propped the note up against one of the wooden model sailboats on Nate's desk, grabbed her white Celine seashell clutch and left. *Absence makes the heart grow fonder,* she reminded herself.

If she's lucky.

s is lucky to have a brother who can't read her mind

"So, I just finished reading *Franny and Zooey*, by J. D. Salinger," Erik van der Woodsen informed his sister as their Metro-North train ambled out of Grand Central and down the long dark tunnel leading out of the city. "He's the guy who wrote *The Catcher in the Rye*. You've read that, right?" Erik eagle-eyed her with navy blue eyes just as dark and huge as her own. His wavy pale blond hair skimmed his gray Brown T-shirt–clad shoulders. Nearly everyone who met them assumed they were twins.

Serena nodded as she fished in her orange canvas Coach beach tote for some cherry-flavored ChapStick. She was barely listening. She couldn't believe she was headed to Ridgefield to spend another summer with her family. It was just so weird. And so depressing.

"Well, anyway, this book wasn't nearly as good. Actually, it was really boring. There's all this stuff about religion that I totally didn't expect. Anyway, you really remind me of the girl in the book, Franny. I mean, you really remind me of her right now. She's, like, totally depressed, and her brother Zooey tries to help her snap out of it. He's kind of this wise-ass fag actor, but it's nice that he cares."

Serena was seated between the window and Erik. The train rolled out of the tunnel and eased above ground near 125th Street. "I'm not depressed," she told the depressing-looking high-rise apartment buildings rising up beside her. "I'm—" She stopped short and closed her ChapStick-slick mouth. If she said anything more, she'd burst into tears. Instead she let her head fall away from the window, onto Erik's familiar, muscular shoulder, and allowed him to stroke her hair. "I'm just glad to be leaving," she sighed, shutting her eyes tight to hold back the tears.

"And I'm just glad we get to hang out this summer." Erik would be working at the Ridgefield Polo Club serving drinks in the open-air clubhouse next to the polo field. He was only seventeen, but somehow he'd landed the most coveted summer bartending job in Connecticut. Serena had a feeling she wouldn't see much of him once he befriended all the polo players and found a few pretty equestriennes to hit on.

Nate might have been the love of her life, but Erik was her knight in shining armor. The first time she'd ever gotten her period the family was sailing in the Greek Islands. Serena was too embarrassed to tell her mom, so Erik dove overboard, swam to the nearest village, and swam back with Stayfree maxi pads in a plastic bag tied to his head. Every Christmas since they were babies they'd snuck downstairs in the house in Ridgefield in the middle of the night on Christmas Eve, unwrapped their presents, and then rewrapped them again. They'd driven the family's Mercedes station wagon into a ditch and left it there, claiming they had no idea how it got there. They'd stayed up till dawn almost every summer night, talking and talking, pretending to be great philosophers. If Serena was going to be sad with anyone, she would choose Erik. He knew her better than anyone else. But she still couldn't bring herself to tell him what was really wrong. They had to spend the whole summer together, after all, and she couldn't bear the thought of him hovering over her and worrying about her when all he really wanted to do was drink beer and listen to music by the pool with his boarding school friends.

Selfless as always, but wasn't it her selflessness that got her into this mess in the first place?

She replaced the cap on her ChapStick and shoved it back into her bag. The little clay boat Nate had made for her toppled against her knuckles. As the train sped through the Bronx, she reached for it and held on. It was pathetic, she knew.

But it was all she had.

fish heads, fish heads, roly-poly fish heads

"Gimme summa dose porgies. Two ninety-five a pound? Dat's a bargain, right? Gimme a pounda dose and some crab claws. Make it a dozen."

Vanessa scooped up the dead fish bodies with her latex-gloved hand and slapped them down on a fresh piece of waxed paper. There was something supremely satisfying about working at her local Williamsburg fish shop. The shop was called Brok, which wasn't even a word, at least not in English. It stank of raw fish. There was fish blood in the black laces of her Doc Martens. People looked at her funny when she waited on them, as if to say, *What's a shaven-headed all-black-wearing sixteen-year-old girl like you doing in a place like this?* She didn't know a cod from a sturgeon, but the shop was super-duper air-conditioned, she worked nine-hour shifts, and she loved the gritty intensity of chopping up raw fish bodies with a cleaver. She even got to wear a hairnet over her shaved head. She'd bought a black one, so her head kind of looked like a giant big toe in a black fishnet stocking.

How lovely.

Vanessa was the only employee who actually spoke English. Her boss was Russian and all her coworkers were old Chinese men. They would joke around with her and point at her head like it was the funniest thing in the world, but she'd just point at their heads and laugh back. Fish was the universal language. When she needed help discerning the difference between Chilean sea bass and red snapper, Vanessa would point to the waxy labeled place mats with pictures of live fish on them decorating the walls, and her Chinese friends would point out the steaks and filets she was looking for inside the glass case. They taught her how to scale and slice a Dover sole. She got to cut heads off and squeeze out guts. It was awesome.

"Hey stinky." Ruby came into the shop as the porgy-and-crab-claw guy was leaving. "I told my drummer I'd bring him some scallops. You'll give them to me free, right?" Ruby was wearing her favorite pair of purple leather pants and a black T-shirt with the sleeves cut off that read B ^^s across the front. She always got a lot of stares when she wore that shirt.

Which was exactly the point.

Vanessa glanced behind her at Hon, her white-haired Chinese fish shop friend. Then she pointed at her sister's pants and covered her mouth, pretending to giggle, like they were the most ridiculous pants she'd ever seen. Ruby glared at her. "At least I don't stink of raw tuna vaginas."

Good one.

Vanessa stuffed a handful of scallops into a clear plastic bag and tied a knot in the top of the bag. They looked like water-logged earlobes. She handed the bag to Ruby. "No charge."

"Nice presentation." Ruby dangled the bag in front of her. "Could you at least give me a brown paper bag so I don't get arrested for chopping up my children or something?" She squinted her glassy dark brown eyes at her sister. "You have the demeanor of someone who's broken up with her boyfriend and has decided to get all stinky in case he comes calling. Like you're trying to make yourself as repulsive as possible." She cocked her head, the shiny ends of her black chin-length bob just brushed her shoulder. "Only problem is, there was no boyfriend to break up with."

"I just like it here," Vanessa explained tersely and handed her sister a white waxed paper sack. Something about the bag of scallops reminded her of Dan. She hadn't seen him since he came to her school to apologize more than a month ago. Of course she still thought about him all the time, but she wasn't about to waste her time on somebody who was in love with Serena van der fucking Woodsen. Part of the reason she'd gotten the Brok job in the first place was because it was a job Serena would never take in a million years. The other reason she'd taken the job was that if for any totally random reason Dan turned up in Williamsburg looking for her, he'd run screaming once he caught a whiff of her. Then she'd have the last laugh.

At least, that's the stinking lie she's telling herself.

She watched her sister squeeze the clear plastic bag full of raw scallops into the white paper sack. The thing about Dan was, he really did have cute earlobes, and his poems were really quite good.

And the thing about fish shops is, they're really quite poetic.

down and out in malariaville

Camp Bridgehutter in Wooten, Pennsylvania, turned out to have a pretty nifty art program. Campers were encouraged to roll themselves in paint, make clay molds of their fellow campers' bodies, and weave clothing for each other. All of the art was hands-on, meaning paintbrushes, pencil sharpeners, scissors, and potter's wheels were strictly forbidden. Campers were supposed to "use their raw materials" to make their art, meaning they had to use their own bodies or things they found in the woods to smear on the paint, mold the clay, or cut the wool.

Let's hope they allow toilet paper.

Jenny liked paintbrushes and scissors and pencil sharpeners. She didn't want to use a rock to cut a goddamned piece of paper or an ant-infested stick to mix her paint. She'd been at camp for nearly two weeks and she could safely say she hated it. The entire campus reeked of rancid organic crunchy peanut butter. Her cabin was damp. The shower had spiders. Her mattress smelled like pee and squeaked like crazy. Some of her art teachers were okay, but it was hard to get excited about chiseling wood with a rock. And her boobs refused to stop growing.

Her father had sent her a care package full of marshmallows and Cadbury chocolate and Hostess cupcakes on the second day of camp because he already missed her so much, but she'd thrown it out, for fear that all that fat and sugar would only make her boobs grow even bigger. And for fear that the mean girls in her cabin would be even meaner.

"She looks like she *drank* the stuff they put in breast implants," Rachel Werner told her best friend and cabinmate, Jill Dube, in a loud whisper. Rachel and Jill were from Delaware and this was their second year at Camp Bridgehutter. They'd requested tiny cabin 5, nicknamed Malariaville because of all the mosquitoes, for themselves. But the camp had run out of room and had been forced to stick Jenny in there with them. Rachel had curly blond hair down to her waist that she liked to show off by dangling it off the side of the top bunk, blocking Jenny's reading light. Jill wore her straight brown hair in a ponytail every day and gave herself a pedicure every single night. She'd brought seven bottles of nail polish to camp along with a very comprehensive Bliss Spa pedicure kit.

It is crucial to keep one's toenails trimmed and buffed when one is scouring the woods for useful rocks and twigs.

"You mean silicone?" Jill offered helpfully.

Rachel snickered. "Yeah. She looks like she drank it and her boobs just totally inflated."

Today it was raining, so Jenny and her bunkmates were stuck in their cabin for the rest of the two-hour lunch period until weaving class began. Jenny had been weaving a set of four green-and-yellow hemp napkins. She couldn't wait to send them to her dad—he'd be so proud. Jenny lay on the bottom bunk pretending to ignore the nasty whispering above her head while she read *The Age of Innocence* by Edith Wharton, one of the books on the Constance Billard eighth-grade summer reading list. Poor Countess Olenska was totally ostracized by everybody in New York simply because she was beautiful and wanted to have a little fun after leaving her mean old husband back in Europe. *Well, good for her,* Jenny thought, wondering briefly what size bra Countess Olenska would wear if she lived in modern times.

She slapped at herself while she read, killing three mosquitoes as they gang-raped her calf. The mosquitoes at Camp Bridgehutter were rabid and ravenous. They went up your nose and feasted on the flesh between your fingers. She scratched miserably at an old bite on her knee, smearing blood all over the place. It was safe to say Serena van der Woodsen never went to Camp Bridgehutter. Jenny would have noticed the scars. Right now Serena was probably stretched out in the sand on some pristine white beach in southern France wearing only a pair of Gucci bikini bottoms and her Chanel sunglasses.

Rain fell in torrents outside the cabin. Every time Jenny glanced out the window at her wet, densely forested surroundings she yearned for the noisy brick, limestone, and asphalt surroundings of home. She could hardly fall sleep to the persistent *cheep-cheep* of crickets. Give her a police siren any day. The cabin's screen door banged open and a lanky, soaking wet, redheaded, freckle-faced boy Jenny had seen around the camp poked his head in.

"Hey." The boy greeted her like she was the only one there, even though Rachel was lying in the bunk above Jenny, and Jill was in the other top bunk. Jenny could feel them peering curiously down from above. "I'm Matt. You're Jennifer Humphrey, right?" He was wearing fatigue-print swim trunks and nothing else. His body was skinny, sunburnt, and mosquito-bitten.

Jenny nodded, blushing at the sight of his bare, rain-spattered ribs. How did he know her name? She was afraid to say anything that Rachel and Jill might make fun of later, and afraid to move in case her boobs did something embarrassing all on their own. At the beginning of June she'd upped her bra size to a 32D, but she'd stuck with the Polish bras because they provided the most coverage.

It sounds like she needs it.

"I just wanted to say hi," Matt told her. His nose was small and pointy like a doll's and he was absolutely covered with freckles. His eyes were light blue, and his teeth were small and straight. He was kind of gangly and goofy-looking, but what boy her age wasn't?

"Hi," Jenny squeaked. She waited for him to say something else, but he just raised his hand in salute and the screen door slammed shut behind him as he dashed out into the rainy Pennsylvania woods once more.

"Hail, Camp Big Hooters, hail!" Rachel and Jill sang from above, cackling hilariously as they had done so many times before.

If Serena were there, she would have thought of something clever to say, but Jenny just held her book open in front of her face, her cheeks aflame and her mind racing. Matt was cute and seemed super nice. Maybe she was turning into the type of girl who would have more guy friends than girl friends. She and Dan had always gotten along, so that would make sense. Girls seemed to hate her now before she even opened her mouth. Guys were more understanding.

Hmm. Wonder why?

d's already found it

"Just have a read through that pile there and tell me if you think any of it is worth saving," Dan's father had instructed earlier that morning as he indicated the heap of yellowing manuscripts and newspapers beneath and surrounding the desk in the small, cluttered office just off his bedroom. Dan almost wished he'd gone to sleepaway camp like his sister instead of offering to work for his dad. He'd had the very stupid and unrealistic idea that sometime this summer Serena would bump into him accidentally, find out that *he* was the author of all those wonderful love poems written by Anonymous, and fall madly in love with him.

But of course, like most Upper East Siders with any sense, Serena had fled the unbearable city heat for the country. The proof of her whereabouts was in the Styles section of today's *New York Times*, which happened to be lying right in front of Dan on his father's scratched metal desk. *Serena van der Woodsen, 15, daughter of Lillian and William van der Woodsen, at the 64th annual Ridgefield Polo Club Classic,* the caption read beneath a photograph of her wearing a white eyelet sundress and yellow lace-up espadrilles, her pale blond hair spilling carelessly over her perfect, tan shoulders.

Dan slid open his dad's desk drawer and removed a pair of scissors. Careful not to fray the edges, he began to cut out Serena's picture and the caption beneath. Then he stopped himself. What kind of self-respecting person collects images of a girl he's never even spoken to? Next thing he knew he'd be getting a tattoo that said "Serena Forever" on his chest and eating cat food straight out the can.

At least he'd be getting a balanced meal.

He shut his eyes, ripped the entire page of the newspaper out, crumpled it up in his fist, and tossed it into his dad's metal wastepaper basket, where it landed with a hollow pong. Then he grabbed a stack of papers from off the floor and began sorting through them. Rufus was possibly the most disorganized person on the planet. His papers were like his hairstyles and outfits—totally insane. There were doctors' bills, crossword puzzles, a random word written in pencil on a scrap of paper, essays in Russian printed on colored paper, and weird typewritten paragraphs of quasi-inspirational, quasi-profound thoughts that could only have been written by Rufus himself.

> Brautigan's *In Watermelon Sugar* was
> not the acid-inspired ramblings of a
> madman. The man was more poet than
> Whitman, barring *Song of Myself*.
> Aspire to Brautigan and produce
> Whitman. Originality is key.

Rufus appeared in the doorway while Dan was still reading. "Find anything?" he asked hopefully.

Dan looked up from the creased, coffee-stained piece of paper. His father was wearing a dapper-looking pair of brown tweed britches circa 1917, paired with a stained orange Lacoste turtleneck with the sleeves cut off, and a pair of white perforated leather Dansko clogs. The little green alligator perched over his left nipple had come partially unsewn, so it looked like it was swimming for its life. Rufus's wild and wiry gray hair was braided and tied with the red-and-white string from the box of cookies he'd bought at the Italian bakery that morning. He looked like Paul Revere on mushrooms.

As featured in the July issue of *Men's Vogue*. Not.

"What exactly am I looking for?" Dan thought he was supposed to just throw his dad's old shit out so he could find his way around his office again and maybe write something worth saving for once.

"*It!*" Rufus bellowed at him, his nostrils flaring so widely that Dan could see his forest of gray-black nose hair. "You're supposed to find the nugget, the *thing*."

Dan had no idea what his father was talking about. "Nugget?" he repeated. The word sounded vaguely pornographic, like "the family jewels," a euphemism for balls.

Like any guy needs help finding those?

Rufus yanked on his earlobes and ran his hands over his distended belly. "Lookit, kid, I want to write the novel, but I don't have time to get all inspired again. I'm too old for that." He waved his bare, flabby arms around in the air. "This office is full of inspiration. I've been getting inspired for years! I hired you to find the source, that kernel of inspiration that's going to set off the whole fireworks show. Got it?" His bloodshot, muddy brown eyes bulged with excitement.

Dan lit a Camel and finished off his mug of cold instant coffee, feeling suddenly depressed. His father's office had one tiny window that faced West End Avenue but was completely blocked by the noisy air conditioner. Most days Rufus stayed in his office with the door closed, smoking and typing on an old typewriter, emerging only to cook or shop for one of his heinous concoctions. He wore mismatched clothes bought at the Salvation Army or found on the street. Some of his anarchist friends slept on benches in Riverside Park simply because they refused to conform. He supported Dan and Jenny with the royalties from his own father's book, the biography of some obscure Russian painter, which Rufus had managed to translate into English.

"You shouldn't smoke," Rufus told him, fishing one of Dan's cigarettes out of the pack and lighting it for himself. "It fries your brain."

Never mind the lungs.

Still, smoking with his dad while having a literary discussion was pretty mature. Dan felt sort of cool, like he was already in college. "How do you know when you've found it, though?" he asked, blowing a thin stream of smoke up at the cracked white ceiling. He stuck his thumb into the bottom of his empty coffee mug and dabbed at the grounds.

"It speaks to you," Rufus explained, throwing back his head and blowing a series of huge, obnoxious smoke rings. "You just see it and think there must be more. It's not done. So it's your job to flip the burger and finish it."

Dan licked his thumb and frowned. Only his dad would compare the creative process to flipping burgers.

Rufus stubbed his cigarette out on the wooden sole of one

of his clogs and flicked the butt into the trash can. "I gotta get out there and find some cardamom." He held out his hand for Dan to slap. "Just shout when you find it. I'm counting on you, kid."

As soon as his father had gone, Dan fished the wadded-up page from the Styles section out of the wastepaper basket. He unfolded it and laid it out on the desk, smoothing the wrinkles out with the flat of his hand and flicking away any remnants of his father's cigarette ash. There she was again in her white eyelet sundress, smiling up at the camera with those sad, seductive navy blue eyes. Dan didn't need to sort through piles of useless crap to find his nugget. He'd already found it.

Yes, but it's what we *do* with our nuggets and our family jewels that makes all the difference.

if only the captain would jump ship

"What you've got to be sure of, son, is that there are no gaps. We want her tight. Tight as can be," Captain Archibald told Nate as they crawled around on their hands and knees hammering planks into the deck of the eighty-foot cruising yacht they were building together. The boat would be named the *Charlotte*, after the captain's grand dame of New York society mother, Nate's grandmother, and one day Nate planned to sail it around the world. He could already imagine motoring out of the harbor there on Mt. Desert Island, hoisting the sails, and sailing off into the blue—just him and the enormous stash of pot he'd Ziploc into individual waterproof baggies for the journey. Enough to last at least six months.

Speaking of pot, it was the last week in June and hot as hell, especially for Maine. Nate was worried about his plants. He'd started a mini garden of his own, out behind the boat barn—ten little marijuana plants with seeds he'd bought online from Thailand. The little seedlings had been thriving since he planted them two weeks ago, but the direct sun and ninety-degree heat were bound to take their toll day after day, especially when Nate could only sneak out to water them in the middle of the night, after his parents were in bed or went out to a party. Even if they never amounted to anything, it was kind of fun to watch them sprout and grow leaves. He was proud of them.

Okay, Peter Rabbit, just watch out for Mr. MacGregor.

Nate crawled over to a spot his dad had missed and whacked the nail into the plank until the head disappeared. The carcass of the *Charlotte* was set up on four huge wooden sawhorses just outside the barn, five hundred feet from the beach. Building the boat had been awesome so far—good, old-fashioned manual labor—as long as his dad didn't try to talk to him too much.

And as long as he smoked a big fatty behind the boat barn before getting to work.

Captain Archibald was a totally anal perfectionist, so even if Nate was high all the time, it wasn't like he could fuck anything up. The wood guy had cut each piece to size and basically built the hull for them. All Nate had to do was nail the nails in, apply the sealant, and give the boat good karma. He was all about positive vibes these days. Positive vibes and sex. All he had to do was stay positive, build the boat, get through the summer, and soon enough he'd be having sex with Blair. Waiting sucked, but soon he'd be waiting no more.

Waves crashed on the beach and seagulls screeched overhead. The air smelled like cranberries and salt. On the other side of the thicket of birch trees that hid the outbuildings from view loomed the Archibalds' white colonial mansion with its twenty gabled windows and cheerful red shutters. The lush green lawn was fringed with exquisitely landscaped flower beds and rolled downhill like a magnificent green carpet a quarter of a mile to the churling gray sea.

"So tell me, son," Nate's father began in his authoritative captain-of-the-ship voice as he lay down on his taut stomach, squinting at the rough-hewn bow of the boat to see if it was level. "Tell me about the girls in your life. How's that lovely van der Woodsen girl, Serena? And the other one, the lawyer's daughter. What's her name?"

"Blair." Nate picked up a plank and crawled starboard with it hoping to get out of hearing range. To his dismay, his father crawled right after him.

"Get it straight," he ordered, hovering directly over Nate's tanned, bare back. "If we screw this up, we'll have to scrap the whole project."

No pressure or anything, though.

Captain Archibald handed his son a level, then thought better of it and grabbed the plank out of Nate's hands so he could adjust it himself. "I know you like to pretend those girls are just your friends. But my guess is there's a little more to it than that."

How insightful.

Nate sat back on his haunches and watched his dad fuss over the five-foot piece of wood. Captain Archibald was wearing gray flannel suit pants and a light blue button-down J. Press shirt, tucked in, with a white undershirt underneath it, and Top-Siders. It was his standard casual uniform, but Nate didn't see how he could bear it in the heat.

"Blair is my girlfriend," he clarified, blushing slightly as he said it. "And Serena is my . . ." His voice trailed off.

"Mistress?" Captain Archibald offered helpfully. He sat up, an amused twinkle shining in his dark green eyes. With his thinning fair hair and regal deportment he probably would have been kind of a handsome dude if he hadn't been such a hard-ass.

"She's my friend," Nate clarified firmly. "Blair's really smart," he added, surprising himself. "She wants to go to Yale." It felt nice complimenting Blair like that. It made him feel like a good boyfriend.

His father handed him a hammer. "Gently but firmly," he instructed. "If you hit it too hard you can damage the integrity of the timber."

Yes, sir, HMS *Cocksucker*, sir!

Nate banged in a few more nails while his father looked on. He was tempted to fuck up just so his dad would kick him off the project and he could spend the rest of the summer on the beach getting baked. But he really did love to sail and he wanted the boat to get built.

"Make sure you don't distract her too much," the Captain advised, reaching for another plank. "She'll need to be at the top of her game to get into Yale."

Nate sat cross-legged on the partially built deck, rubbing his sore, muscled arms. He shook his head as his dad continued to work. Something about what his dad had just said implied that Nate himself would never be good enough for Yale. He was just a distraction, like a sunny day or a bumblebee. His dad would never understand how he calmed Blair down and distracted her when she was upset about her parents. How he brought her Ben & Jerry's vanilla ice cream or Chips Ahoy after tennis so she'd eat more. He chucked the hammer overboard and into the scrappy sea grass. "I'm taking ten, Dad. You want anything?"

Bong hit? Doobie?

rapunzel, rapunzel, let down your hair

Blair knew it was slightly immature, but she'd spent the last month at her dad's Newport, Rhode Island, estate watching the sailboats go by in the bay, daydreaming about having sex with Nate, and playing dress-up. Every item in her mother's wardrobe that had been worn more than twice or was too small was stored in a cedar closet outside Blair's bedroom, so the dress-up costumes were limitless. Her father was supposed to have the clothes shipped back to the city as part of the divorce settlement, since he would be keeping the Newport house, but they were a long way from settling, so the clothes remained for Blair to play with.

There was Eleanor's wedding dress, a beaded ivory strapless Carolina Herrera gown sealed in a giant clear cellophane bag, and the purple velvet suit Eleanor had tailored just for her at the Yves Saint Laurent boutique in Paris when she was still a size 2. And the shoes—rows and rows of shoes from every designer imaginable, especially Prada, which had always been Eleanor's favorite. Stilettos, wedges, sandals, and slides—they were all a size and a half too large for Blair, but still fine for dress-up.

This sweltering July afternoon Blair's father and his flaming French hunk, Jacques or Jean or whatever the fuck his name was, were out playing doubles with another gay couple they'd met at a club in town the night before. Blair carried the nail scissors she used to trim Kitty Minky's claws into her mom's closet and began to slice open the cellophane bag containing her mom's Carolina Herrera wedding gown. She knew she really shouldn't, but her mom wouldn't know it was her. She'd just assume that Harold and his gay friends had dressed up in her clothes and had a gay old *Paris Is Burning* time.

And then her lawyers could ask for yet *another* million.

"Keep your head out of the bag, silly," Blair warned Kitty Minky, gently shoving the gray kitten away so he wouldn't asphyxiate himself. The pretty half-grown Russian Blue cat amused himself by jumping into one of Eleanor's Gucci bamboo-handled handbags and playing peekaboo.

Blair slipped the gown off its padded white satin hanger and let her lime green seersucker J.Crew sundress fall to the floor. Then she stepped into the wedding gown and zipped it up. Amazingly, it was an almost perfect fit. Impossible as it was for her to imagine, seventeen years ago her lumpy, freaky mom had nearly the same figure she did.

Incredible what nearly two decades on antidepressants can do to a person.

A pair of gold Prada evening sandals with four-inch heels beckoned. Blair slipped her bare feet into them and clip-clopped back down the hall to her enormous bedroom. She examined her reflection in the mirror. Was this the dress she would wear when she married Nate? She'd have diamonds, of course, and a big elaborate hairstyle like Marie Antoinette. She wrinkled her nose critically and turned away from the mirror. Strapless had never been her thing, and how could she resist shopping for a new dress for her very own wedding?

Her four-story Victorian dollhouse stood on its wooden dais in front of a series of dormer windows with deep window seats, their cushions upholstered in pink pinstripes. The dollhouse had been made especially for Blair, modeled after the Newport house itself. The largest bedroom on the fourth floor of the dollhouse was an exact replica of her own bedroom, down to the rose-colored satin lampshades and the large circular wool rug adorned with pink peonies in full bloom. Instead of people, mice made of gray rabbit fur and dressed in exquisite satin clothes inhabited the dollhouse. On a recent antiquing expedition her father had even found a little gray rabbit-fur cat. It slept on the tiny dollhouse version of Blair's brass bed, a rabbit-fur miniature of Kitty Minky.

Blair picked up the mother mouse, dressed in a dorky floral-patterned Laura Ashley dress and a white lace apron, and sat her on the toilet in the bathroom downstairs. Then she put the father mouse, who was wearing a red velvet smoking jacket and tuxedo pants, in the claw-foot bathtub in the master bathroom. Next, she set the butler mouse, who was fat and bloated and had a huge red nose, on top of the father mouse. Finally, she chucked the little-brother mouse, a white midget sporting denim overalls and a red wool cap, onto her real live bed for Kitty Minky to bat around and chew on. Torturing her dollhouse mice was one of Blair's favorite pastimes.

And it's oh so therapeutic.

She reached for her cell and dialed Nate's number, perching daintily on a window seat as she waited for him to pick up.

Outside the windows, her father's dramatic hilltop lawn rolled greenly down to the sea. Sailboats bobbed in the waves, looking tiny enough for her dollhouse mice. Off to the left was the clay tennis court. Her father and his French "partner," probably still hungover from last night's gay rave, were being totally creamed by their middle-aged-mom neighbors.

Blair should have felt guilty for being inside on such a beautiful summer day, but for the remainder of the summer she was intent on cultivating the persona of a beautiful maiden locked in her ivory tower—until the day she finally had sex with Nate. And part of that image was to flirt with him mercilessly over the phone.

"Hey." Nate finally answered, sounding slightly out of it. "I was just thinking about you," he added sweetly.

Blair wanted to tell him she was wearing her mom's wedding dress and totally thinking about their wedding night but she didn't want him to think she was insane.

As if he didn't already know that by now.

"Only five more weeks," she whispered. "I can't wait to be naked with you," she added teasingly. She lifted her gold-sandaled feet up off the floor and smoothed out the folds in her white silk taffeta gown.

"Me neither," Nate agreed. "I think about it all the time."

Understatement of the month.

Blair shook her head, her long, wavy chestnut-colored hair fanning out over her bare shoulders. She felt exactly like Rapunzel, trapped in her impossibly high tower and waiting for the dashing prince. She stood up and adjusted the butler mouse so that his swollen red nose was sticking directly into the crotch of the father mouse's tuxedo pants. "Oh, Nate. I miss you so much."

Nate didn't say anything. She could tell he was probably thinking they could have done it way back in Sun Valley, or before they both left for the summer. But he was going to be glad she'd made him wait—she'd make sure of it.

"How's your boat?" she asked, changing the subject. "Are you naming her after me?"

"We named her *Charlotte*."

Blair's hackles rose. She stuck her chest out to keep the strapless wedding dress from falling down. Who the fuck was *Charlotte*?

Just when you think you know everything about each other . . .

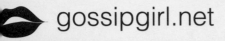
topics ◀ *previous* *next* ▶ *post a question* *reply*

Disclaimer: All the real names of places, people, and events have been altered or abbreviated to protect the innocent. Namely, me.

hey people!

a midsummer's night's scheme

Summer's halfway over, but I've been thinking: if I got everyone on this glorious beach with me here to sign a petition to start school the *month* after Labor Day instead of the *week* after, maybe the mayor could pass a new law. It's only the city that matters. Sorry, people, but we city folk just need more R & R. It's all that time pounding the pavement, hailing cabs, waiting for tables at La Goulue, fighting over the last size 0 Marc Jacobs peacoat at Barneys. Life is stressful, and summer is just too damned short. I know I said once that by this time we might start missing one another. Well, I'm sorry, I really don't miss anyone that much—*yet*.

sightings

V declawing lobsters—yes, lobsters. It has to be the worst summer job ever, but—big surprise—she seems to have found her calling and never stops whistling while she works. **J** buying a noise machine at **Kmart** on the weekly camp excursion to town. Hope she made sure it had a City Sounds setting. Who can sleep to the sound of a babbling brook? **D** "working" hard for his dad down by the boat basin in **Riverside Park** with a pack of Camels, his little black notebook, and a thermos of cold black coffee. Maybe the weird people living in their houseboats will inspire him. **B** playing tennis with her father in Newport wearing a super-fabulous sequined flapper dress. How very **Great Gatsby** of her. **N** purchasing a pair of deerskin gardening gloves at a **Mt. Desert Island** hardware store. Let's hope they're smokeproof. **S** at a local Connecticut dive bar with her fellow actors, dancing on the bar to Lynyrd Skynyrd. We knew she'd pull through—or maybe she's a more talented actress than we thought. **K** and **I** getting thrown out of that trendy no-name club in **East Hampton** for dancing on the bar. Wannabes. **C** traveling all the way to Ridgefield, Connecticut, in his convertible Jag to watch a certain dress rehearsal. Is he still not over her? Me, stalking surfer boys on an unidentified beach in **Montauk**—somebody's got to do it!

your e-mail

Dear GG,
There's this girl at camp who I think is cute but I'm too shy to even talk to her. What should I do?
—quietkd

Dear quietkd,
Just trip over her feet and say sorry. She'll get all blushy, then you'll get all blushy, then she'll introduce herself, and then you'll introduce yourself. Before you know it, you'll be slathering Banana Boat sunblock all over each other and telling your life stories. *J'adore!*
—GG

Dear GG,
I'm turning 16 soon and I feel like something monumental is supposed to happen, but I'm pretty sure it's just going to be another boring summer day.
—bleu

A: Dear bleu,

There is no such thing! You need to wake up; take a cold shower; put on some Chanel No. 5, your most lovely Marni sundress, and your least practical high-heeled sandals; call some friends . . . and then I have one word for you: *partay!*
—GG

no news is good news

I have to say that lately most of you are doing a terrible job as informants. I can only conclude that this means you really *are* having the best summer ever. Well, you'll have to tell me all about it once we're all back. If you ever come back.

Surf's up—time to don my opera glasses and catch the action. Thank goodness it's too warm for wet suits!

You know you love me,

gossip girl

sixteen candles

"Happy birthday to you, happy birthday to you, happy birthday to you, Serena, mon—Jah rule!—happy birthday to you!"

Serena awoke to the tinny plink-plink-plink sound of steel drums and the rumble of planes flying low overhead. She pulled her goose-down pillow over her head and giggled into it. There. Erik had made her smile first thing on her birthday, July 14, Bastille Day, which was most likely what he'd set out to achieve. She rolled out of bed and stuck her head out the open window, giving the steel-drum-playing Rasta dudes a little thrill because she was wearing only a sheer pink tank top and matching underpants. Erik was standing by the pool with some of his boarding school friends wearing a red, green, and yellow tie-dyed bandana on his head. Why her birthday had become some big reggae festival, especially on Bastille Day, she wasn't sure. Erik waved a three-foot-long baguette at her and beckoned her downstairs.

"Get up, lazybones! There's something you have to see!"

Serena pulled on a pair of denim cutoffs and her favorite T-shirt, which happened to be a faded gray St. Jude's T-shirt that she'd borrowed from Nate in seventh grade and never returned.

She padded downstairs and picked up a Granny Smith apple in the kitchen, carrying it out with her to the pool. It was hot and bright. The sensitive skin on her regal nose was already burning.

"Look up!" Erik shouted at her.

Serena took a bite of her apple and tipped her head back. A small plane roared noisily by, leaving a trail of smoke in its wake. Then the smoke began to take shape and Serena realized it was skywriting, like in *The Wizard of Oz*. S-W-E-E-T S-I-X-T-E-E-N! the writing read.

"Mom and Dad felt guilty for being away on such a big day, so they gave me their credit card to spend it on you however I wanted," Erik explained, handing her a frozen royal blue drink with a red cocktail umbrella sticking out of it. "I started riffing on Bastille Day and got kind of into the whole French-Jamaican thing. Then I saw some skywriting down at the polo club the other day and had a total lightbulb moment."

Serena had no idea what he meant by "French Jamaican thing." Erik was wearing yesterday's shorts and nothing else and looked like he'd been up all night, partying. She tipped her head back and looked up at the skywriting again. The letters had swelled and faded so that they were nearly illegible. She tossed her half-eaten apple into the grass and flexed the straw in her drink, gulping half of it in one go. Whatever was in it was very strong and very tasty.

Just the way we like it.

"Your cards and shit are on the table." Erik indicated the glass-topped outdoor table with its festive red sun umbrella. A few of his friends were seated around the table. Corky, Dorian, and Chase? Serena could never remember their names. With their long hair and frayed Brooks Brothers clothes, they were all so interchangeably boarding school.

"Happy birthday." One of the boys stood up and kissed her on the cheek. He wore only a pair of shredded white Adidas soccer shorts and smelled like beer.

"Thanks," Serena muttered, sorting through her birthday mail. Two cards from her parents with checks. Cards from her conscientious aunts and uncles. A card from Blair's mom of all people. And one from Maine. Serena ripped open the plain white envelope and removed a white index card. A tiny green leaf was Scotch-taped to the card. *Happy Birthday* was scrawled beneath the leaf in Nate's surprisingly neat, boyish writing, with a big exclamation point drawn next to the leaf. Serena studied the card. It wasn't just an ordinary leaf, she realized. It was marijuana.

"Hello! Is that what I think it is?" Erik peered over her shoulder at the card. He leaned in and sniffed it. "Nice." He turned to his friends. "My little sister's all grown up," he told them in a mock-weepy voice. Then he swiped the card out of her hands and held up for them to see. "Look at this!"

"Hey." Serena grabbed the card back. "That's mine." She held the card against her chest. "It's not like you could smoke such a tiny leaf anyway," she told him, sounding more pissed off than she'd intended. Erik could be such a dork sometimes. Except for her rehearsals for a small part in the local summer workshop production of *The Age of Innocence*, Serena had spent most of vacation in the company of these idiotic boarding school boys. She missed girls. She missed Blair. But it wasn't like she could just call her up. Or maybe she could, but she wasn't sure what she would say. *The reason*

I've been acting so strange is that I'm madly in love with your boyfriend?

Maybe not.

She carried the card into the house and upstairs, tucking it safely into her underwear drawer. Then she put on her red J.Crew halter-top one-piece and went back downstairs. The guys from the steel band had started up again. They were smiling at her as they played, dreadlocks bouncing in time to the music.

"Good, I see you're ready," Erik observed putting down his frozen blue concoction.

"Ready for what?" Serena sighed a little wearily.

He sprinted up to her with his arms outstretched, snatched her up, and heaved her over his shoulder like a sack of grain. He kept on running toward the pool. "For a swim!" he shouted, jumping into the water and pulling her in with him.

Serena came up laughing and pinched the chlorine out of her nose. God, was he a dork. But it was kind of hard to stay mad at him when he was so determined to make her laugh. After all, it was her goddamned freaking sixteenth birthday and she'd been in absolute doldrums all summer. This was the first day of the rest of her life. It was time to snap out of it.

"You're in so much trouble," she cried and dove down beneath the surface like a porpoise. She yanked up on Erik's dorky yellow-and-black surfboard-print board shorts, giving him the worst wedgie ever. Then she broke the surface again. "Everybody in the pool!" she ordered, like some sort of birthday girl drill sergeant. Corky, Dorian, and Chase stood up and began to tear off their clothes.

That's one way to celebrate.

the real reason for going to sleepaway camp

It was searingly hot, even for the first days of August, and since camp was ending tomorrow anyway, most of the campers were down by the lake cooling off. Too embarrassed to wear a bathing suit in front of her mean cabinmates, Jenny was in the weaving room, threading a strand of raw purple silk through the stays in her weeping-willow-twig loom in a risky attempt to make something more colorful than her collection of lumpy barf-green napkins. She felt like the miller's daughter in *Rumpelstiltskin*, trying to weave straw into gold.

Suddenly someone came up behind her and put his hands over her eyes. It was Matt. At least she was pretty sure it was him, since she hadn't really made eye contact with any other boy the whole time she'd been at camp. "Hey," she giggled nervously. He'd only waved hello to her twice from afar since barging into her cabin more than two weeks ago. Now he was touching her?

"Okay, here's what I want you to do. You've got to stand up very carefully, and we're going to walk like this to my cabin." He kept his hands sealed over her eyes.

It wasn't Matt, Jenny realized, her body rigid. "But—"

"Don't be scared," the boy whispered in a lispy, spitty voice that made Jenny relax just a little. If things got weird she could probably kick Lispy's butt. "Nothing bad's gonna happen. Promise."

Wanting to trust him, she stood up and allowed him to lead her out of the art building. "Come on, it's going to be fun," he murmured spittily in her ear as he pulled her down the path to his cabin. Jenny was pretty sure Matt lived in cabin 12, the last of the boys' woods cabins. Was that where they were headed?

"What's going to be fun?" she demanded, stumbling forward. It was hard to keep her footing when she couldn't see where she was walking and her boobs were bouncing so much it hurt. *Where's he taking me?* she wondered, feeling scared and curious all at the same time.

"You'll see," the boy lisped, adjusting his grip over her eyes. His fingers smelled like bug repellent. Everything at camp smelled like bug repellent or pee or peanut butter.

"Okay, step up. Another step up," he directed, guiding her carefully up the wooden cabin steps. He opened the creaking screen door to the cabin and they stepped inside. Jenny's heart was pounding. Sweat beaded on her upper lip and trickled down the unventilated crevice between her boobs. "Now walk forward one, two, three steps—" He removed his hands from her eyes and gave her a little push between her shoulder blades. Jenny stumbled forward, right into Matt, who was standing in the middle of the cabin, his freckly face so red it was almost purple. He didn't smile at her or anything. He didn't even look at her.

"Whoa," she faltered, regaining her balance. She smiled cautiously up at Matt. "What's going on?" He swallowed nervously, the bump of his Adam's apple bobbing up and down. He looked terrified.

"Go on," Lispy urged. Jenny glanced behind her. He was a year or two older than she, tan and muscular in a sleeveless black Puma T-shirt, with dark hair shaved into a crew cut and a cocky smirk on his face. He actually looked a lot more threatening than he sounded.

"You know you want to," came another boy's voice. She looked up to find two more campers huddled on the top bunk of the bed on the far side of the room. The cabin was four times the size of the one she shared with Rachel and Jill and was decorated with boyish paraphernalia like posters of soccer players and the various archery awards they'd won over the summer. The mattress the two boys were huddled on was made up with black pirate sheets covered with white skulls and crossbones. The idea that one of the boys was so into pirates he had actual pirate sheets almost made Jenny smile.

"Honk, honk," one of the pirate boys croaked, holding up his hands and squeezing his fingers open and shut.

Blushing furiously, Jenny turned back to Matt. Whatever it was Lispy and these other boys were doing, she had a feeling Matt wasn't completely in on it. He took a deep breath, swallowed again, and then ducked down and pressed his dry, chapped lips against hers. Then he reached up and quickly patted her chest with his clumsy freckled fingers.

"Hey!" she cried, taking a step back. "Stop it." Her boobs were so new even to her, the idea of anyone besides the woman from the Village Bra Shop touching them was completely out of the question.

"I'm sorry. I wanted to kiss you," Matt stammered, his

freckly face a tie-dyed mixture of purples and pinks. "But they made me—"

"Lame," one of the pirates jeered.

"He saw your boobs on the Internet," Lispy joined in. "We all did."

Jenny whirled around to glare furiously at him through tear-filled brown eyes. She'd thought Matt might turn out to be nice. She'd thought he might be her first boyfriend. But he was just as big a jerk as Lispy and his pirate friends. Was it fun making her feel so bad? If this was their idea of fun, then she felt sorry for them. They were losers; they'd probably always be losers.

Well, at least she got a first kiss out of it. That's something.

"Have a good rest of the summer, guys," she told them breezily, blinking back the tears and refusing to reveal how angry and humiliated she was. She pushed open the screen door and hurried down the steps of the cabin, letting the door bang shut behind her. She raced down the path through the stinking, mosquito-infested woods. Maybe she *would* be the kind of girl who had more boy-friends than girl-friends, but those boys were so immature they hardly counted as boys.

Get used to it, sweetie—they're all like that. But they get hotter with age, and we become more tolerant.

b engages in phone pda in jfk

Blair stood outside the VIP lounge in the British Airways terminal at JFK with her cell phone pressed to her ear. On either side of her, whole families sat on the floor like homeless people, eating stale bagels and drinking Starbucks. Peasants.

That's what you get for traveling in August.

Come on, Nate. Answer your frigging phone. Blair tapped the toe of her black suede French Sole ballet flat impatiently. Her plane to Glasgow was leaving in less than an hour and she wanted to say goodbye and leave Nate with a little something to keep him thinking about her. She'd worn a gorgeous new black Diane von Furstenberg shirtdress to travel in, thinking she'd sit alone at a table in the VIP lounge, looking mysterious. A cast of handsome admirers would eavesdrop jealously while she smoked and drank dirty martinis and flirted on the phone with Nate. But as soon as she'd arrived, she discovered her phone didn't work in the lounge.

"Hey." Nate suddenly picked up.

"My plane's leaving soon," Blair told him breathily. "Only two more weeks until we see each other again."

"Sweet," he responded.

"I should have asked you meet me here," she added suggestively, as if they could have had sex right there in the middle of the airport. Maybe they would have been arrested for indecent exposure. They might have gotten locked in a jail cell together. They could have had sex all week. But then she'd miss her plane.

Not to mention the wedding.

"I can't wait to kiss you," Nate told her, his voice hoarse from all the pot he'd been smoking. She tried to picture him sprawled out on his single bed in his house in Maine, where she'd actually never been. The picture in her mind was of a ramshackle fishing cabin with screens for windows and a dilapidated wood stove in the corner, but she knew it was a lot nicer than that.

Kind of.

Still, the idea of him lying on a scratchy red wool camping blanket thinking of her in her gorgeous ivory satin and black lace underwear was too delicious to dispel. She smiled into her silver Samsung. Across the terminal a couple held hands while they watched the planes taxi out to their respective runways. On the floor a few feet away a girl with spiky black hair and an eyebrow ring was kissing her gray-haired, tattooed boyfriend. Airports were so sexy.

"You know, Serena always said just kissing was the most romantic thing," Blair murmured. "But that's so boring. I'm definitely ready to go all the way." She twirled the little ruby ring he'd given her around and around on her finger. "When I get back. Like, the *minute* I get back," she giggled.

A gong went off inside the VIP lounge and Eleanor stuck her head out the door. She'd lost thirty pounds since March and wore a black linen Chanel dress, a wide-brimmed black linen hat, and enormous round black Chanel sunglasses—looking every inch the jaded divorcée. "Blair, darling, our flight's leaving in half an hour. We have to get to the gate."

Blair pressed the phone to her lips and kissed it noisily. *Mwa!*

"I love you," she whispered loudly as she followed her mother down the corridor to the awaiting plane. "And next time no more boring kisses."

Long after Blair had signed off, Nate stood in his little weed garden behind the boat barn, looking at the small black phone in his hand. He was baked after smoking the first two joints of his very own homegrown pot. It wasn't the best stuff in the world—it hurt his throat and gave him the shakes. But that thing Blair said about Serena had shaken him up even more. He'd barely seen Serena since they were in Sun Valley together. Even then, they hadn't really hung out. And, as it turned out, it was Serena who was the romantic, the one who talked about kissing. The one who had kissed him first.

"I could just kiss you forever," she'd whispered to him in the dark in her bed on Valentine's Day. Those words were more powerful than anything he'd ever smoked. And the craving he had right now for the sound of her voice, her soft breath on his skin, the honeysuckle scent of her lush blond hair, the way her lips moved against his, the feel of her long, lean body beneath his hands, was stronger than any craving he'd ever had.

Uh-oh.

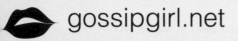
topics ◄ *previous* *next* ► *post a question* *reply*

hey people!

something's fishy

Did anyone see the write-up in *Time Out* about that tiny Russian fish shop in Williamsburg? Apparently it's *the* place to get the freshest fish for grilling in your backyard this summer. As if any of us is doing any grilling. Well, not grilling of that nature. **B** will be doing a bit of grilling when she next sees her boyfriend (see sightings).

belle of the ball

Word in from Connecticut that **S** has been partying up a storm and acting her little tushy off at her summer acting workshop. It's about time she learned the art of distraction: surround yourself with gorgeous boys, play pretty temptresses onstage, and pretend you're not missing a damn thing.

sightings

B getting buffed and polished at the **Vidal Sassoon** salon in Glasgow in preparation for her aunt's wedding. She's got her chastity belt locked, but all that Rhode Island country air has her looking bronzed, fit, and gorgeous. **S** in a black silk bonnet and low-cut golden gown on-stage in the *The Age of Innocence*. **S** at the after-party at the polo club, dancing on tables sans bonnet and gown. **N** installing an automatic watering system behind an old red barn in Maine. What's he growing back there, pumpkins? **K** and **I** wearing their blue and white seersucker school uniforms as cover-ups on the beach in **East Hampton**. Do they really think this is a trend that's going to catch on? Maybe they just miss school. **C** picketing at his local beach in **Bar Harbor** to reverse the no-topless-sunbathing rule. **N** in NYC, buying Molson and everything bagels in his local deli. Hey—summer's not over yet. What's he doing back??

your e-mail

Q: Dear GG,
Have you been to that crazy fish shop in Williamsburg? I swear that bald girl slices a mean filet of sole. She's freaking cute, too.
—crbby

A: Dear crbby,
I guess I'm going to have to make the trip, since no one will stop talking about this.
—GG

Q: Dear GG,
There's this girl, actually a friend's younger sister, who all my friends are talking about. She's gorgeous. Everyone always lies about hooking up with her, but of course I want to hook up with her too. What should I do?
—gdflw

A: Dear gdflw,
Do not pop out of the bushes at her and pretend you don't know who she is. She gets that all the time. If it's meant to be, maybe she'll pop out of the bushes at you!
—GG

All right, people, I'm off to Williamsburg to watch this notorious bald girl slice fish firsthand. It better be as good as everyone says it is, because I do not like to leave the island of Manhattan unless it involves going to the beach. And I better not get lost getting there. You might be wondering what *I'm* doing back in the city. Whither a certain boy goes, I cannot stay away. . . .

Don't worry, we'll save some beluga caviar for you.

You know you love me,

gossip girl

j sure hasn't missed much

Her bus was stuck in stop-and-go traffic all the way home from
Pennsylvania, and her cab from Port Authority was manned by
the slowest driver alive, but just before midnight Jenny unlocked
the door to her family's apartment and tiptoed inside. It was
dark and the windows in the living room were open. The ancient
flax-colored linen curtains wafted pleasantly in the hot summer
breeze. How nice it was to hear the sounds of traffic, to feel the
musty floorboards creak beneath her feet, to smell the homey
smells of cigarettes and coffee and curry powder. The dining
room table was still covered with the remainders of dinner: a
Pyrex lasagna pan containing baked chicken legs, pineapple
slices, whole bananas, and what looked like partially melted
Hershey's kisses. Next to the pan were two mostly empty bottles
of Guinness. A light glowed from the study down the hall and
she could hear the familiar voices of her dad and Dan.

"Hey people," she greeted Dan and her father. They lay on
their tummies on the faded Oriental rug in the study, playing
hangman. Dan wore a white wifebeater, backwards, and cutoff
black corduroys. His shaggy light brown hair was sticking out all

over the place and his eyes were bloodshot. There was a cigarette behind his ear and he was nursing a bottle of Amstel Light.

Rufus wore his favorite red cotton ankle-length nightshirt with the sleeves rolled up. There was lint in his beard. He sat up and held out his arms for a hug. "What's an eight-letter word beginning with *t* with two *o*'s in it?"

Jenny crawled into his lap like a little girl and allowed herself to be smothered in his embrace. "You guys are scary, you know that? I mean, what would happen to you if I never came home?"

They'd eat each other?

Dan pointed at her bare, mosquito-bitten legs. "Jesus."

Jenny shrugged her shoulders. She had already decided to pretend that camp had never happened. "I don't want to talk about it."

Marx, the Humphreys' enormous black cat, strutted up and butted his head against Jenny's hands. Rufus adjusted her on his lap so he could add another letter to his hangman word. So far he had TO_ TO_SE, and his hangman was fully formed.

"I'm allowing feet, hands, and ears," Dan explained, swigging his beer.

"And a face! You promised me a face," Rufus grumbled, frowning at the word. *"Tobnoise. Towpoise?"* he muttered nonsensically.

Up on its roost on the bookshelf the dusty Sony stereo made a clicking sound and one of Rufus's weird arrhythmic jazz CDs came on. "So this is what you guys have been doing all summer?" Jenny demanded.

Dan nodded like it was no big deal. "Pretty much."

"And what about the rest of the human population? Have you

gotten out? Seen anyone?" He shrugged his shoulders and Jenny wished he at least was wearing his shirt the right way around. "So basically you've spent the whole summer being a little Dad-in-training. No offense, Dad. And what about Vanessa?"

Dan shrugged his shoulders again. It was August, hot, and his skin was as pale as a mushroom. Jenny wanted to slap him.

"*Tontoise?*" Rufus muttered idiotically.

She extracted herself from her father's lap and stood up. Was it just her or were all boys retarded? She was tired from the journey and needed to sleep. "Dad, the word's *tortoise*. And Dan, if you don't call Vanessa, I'm going to call her for you, because some people are just nice, and some people are not."

Amen.

Lying under her cool pink sheet on the bed she'd slept on since she was two years old Jenny drifted defiantly to sleep. She'd spend the last three weeks of summer working on the calligraphy for the hymnals, learning breast-toning exercises, and making sure Dan showered every day and got out more. Soon she'd be in eighth grade—which was practically high school—armed with an awe-inspiring chest and the knowledge that most boys really are retarded.

How could she go wrong?

s finds instant cure for the doldrums

Serena sat on a chaise lounge by the pool, watching her mother do laps and painting each one of her toenails a different color. She'd wanted to do the colors of the rainbow, but she was missing some crucial hues like yellow and violet. She settled for one foot in different shades of reds and browns and one foot in different shades of pinks and blacks. Actually, they looked kind of cool. She wouldn't be surprised if she started a trend.

As if everything she'd ever done in her life didn't start a trend?

It was another one of those sweltering mid-August days when the only reasonable thing to do was to stay wet. Her mother was wearing a white-and-black vertical-striped forties-style bathing suit that fit low on the leg and tied at the neck. Serena thought she looked exactly like Katharine Hepburn, at least underwater. She was a strong swimmer, too, slicing through the water with her capable, impeccably manicured hands and kicking rhythmically with her size eleven feet. It was kind of fascinating to watch a person who dressed so well, gave money to all the right charities, had such marvelous parties, and even tended her own roses, do something so basic as go for a swim.

Serena's cell phone whirred and bounced atop the glass outdoor table. Serena saw the word NATE appear on the phone's tiny screen. She snatched it up and flipped it open.

"Natie?" she cried, clutching the phone. Did he know how much she'd thought about him all summer long? Did he realize how much she missed him? How lonely and sad she'd been? "Where are you?"

"I'm here. At home. In the city." He took a deep breath. "Can you come down?"

Serena's whole body trembled. If only she could have beamed herself to Manhattan, she could be standing in front of Nate right now, kissing, and kissing, and kissing him. Not that he necessarily wanted to kiss her. No, she would have to control herself. But she could *pretend*.

She checked her watch. It was 2:45 p.m. There was a train out of Ridgefield every hour at seven minutes past the hour. "Meet me at Grand Central at four thirty-five." She flipped her phone closed and flew into the house to change. Upstairs, she yanked a dress over her head and shoved her feet into a pair of flip-flops. Then she flew down the stairs again. The keys to the family's old Mercedes station wagon were on the kitchen table. She'd drive it to the station, leave the doors unlocked, and leave the keys under the seat. Erik did it all the time.

That was the joy of being a van der Woodsen. Things just worked out.

d has smelled worse

It was a Friday, and Brok was busy as hell. Smelly or not, everyone seemed to want to eat fish when it was hot out. Vanessa doled out softshell crabs, filets of grouper, swordfish steaks, and some new trendy oversize yellow scallops that looked like Twinkies. Her latex-gloved hands were caked in fish guts and her bare calves were spattered with fish blood and unidentified gray slime.

"I'll take six pounds of calamari, and all the clams you got," the next guy in line told her.

Vanessa checked the glass case without looking up. Six pounds of squid? She stood on tiptoe and peered over the top of the high countertop. Smiling at her was the shaggy-haired, goofy-grinned boy of her dreams. "Hey, I know you. You're SpongeBob SquarePants." She turned to Hon and pointed directly at Dan's face, covering her mouth like Dan was absolutely the funniest-looking guy she'd ever seen. Hon just smiled uncomfortably, wary of what was obviously some sort of twisted lover's quarrel.

"Cool job," Dan observed. He'd been watching Vanessa for

a while. She looked supremely self-assured, slapping fish filets down on waxed paper and wrapping them up so professionally. She even knew how to use the cool old cash register. It made him wish he'd spent the summer working in the fish shop with her.

Duh.

"My sister has been sleeping at her friends' house. She can't stand the way I smell." Vanessa began to help the next customer, conscious of how closely Dan was watching her. She paid extra attention to the folds in the waxed paper. It was like making paper airplanes: the neater your folds, the straighter the plane flies. Which had absolutely nothing whatsoever to do with fish.

But we know what she means.

"So I was wondering!" Dan was forced to yell over an older woman's head. The woman had ordered twenty fresh sardines and now she was counting each one to make sure Vanessa hadn't gypped her. "There's this movie at the Angelika I want to see—"

"The Tom Waits one?" Vanessa yelled back, tossing a soft-shell crab at Hon just for fun.

Dan nodded. "You want to go?"

Vanessa considered Dan's face. It hadn't changed. If anything, he was paler now than he'd been in May. And as long as they stuck to Brooklyn and downtown, they'd be at no risk of bumping into Serena van der Woodsen. She took off her apron and tore her gloves off with her teeth. Her shift was over in half an hour. Hon could cover for her. Besides, she was honestly sort of sick of slinging fish. Hell, she might not even come back.

She stepped around the counter and led Dan out of the tiny shop. Outside the sun beat down on the sidewalks, turning everything white. Vanessa shielded her big brown eyes. "You don't mind walking around with me all stinky?"

Dan put his arm around her shoulders and took a good whiff. After years of smelling the impossible odors that emanated from his dad's kitchen, he didn't mind her eau de poisson at all. "You smell like a sushi restaurant." He lit a cigarette and smiled sexily at her without meaning to. "It's nice."

Vanessa totally hated him for being so disarming, but she also still totally loved him. Dan kept his arm around her shoulder as they walked down the street to the subway. She wasn't sure what his arm *meant*, but it was enough for now.

As long as nobody mentions a certain blonde.

s is a sight for sore eyes

Serena hadn't specified where he should meet her, so Nate stood at the end of the platform where her train was supposed to arrive, waiting. He'd been in the city for two days before he'd finally called. He didn't want to be stoned when he talked to her or stoned when he saw her, and it had taken him that long to get it out of his system. Not that he had a clear head. He was shaking all over, partly from withdrawal but mostly because he couldn't wait to see her get off that train and—

There it was, the silver Metro-North train with its thick orangey-red stripe. The headlights eased toward him and then the train stopped with a whoosh. The doors opened and she stepped onto the platform, three cars down, wearing a thin light blue slip dress and pink rubber flip-flops, her pale blond hair hanging nearly to her waist. She spotted him and her face lit up with the most glorious smile. Then she broke into a run, her flip-flops thwacking the ground as she came closer and closer.

He wrapped her in his arms and picked her up, swinging her around like a little kid. "Oh, Natie, you're so strong!" she laughed, and then she leaned in and kissed him right on the lips.

Nate closed his eyes and held her for a second longer before putting her feet back down on the platform. He was pretty sure this was about to be the best day of his summer, or maybe even his life. He was in no hurry. "Let's get a drink in that place upstairs," he told her gruffly, trying to hide the fact that he had just experienced his very first swoon.

"I'm such an idiot," Serena gushed, threading her arm through his. "I didn't bring any money or keys or anything. I had to beg the conductor to let me stay on."

They walked up the marble stairs from the lower level and entered the station's enormous, elegant main terminal. Briefcase-toting commuters in linen summer suits hurried past to catch the trains back to their homes in Westchester and Connecticut. A woman wearing a green-palm-leaf-and-pink-flamingo-print Lilly Pulitzer dress and a gigantic yellow straw hat stood in the center of the terminal examining the train schedules on the board over the quaintly old-fashioned marble and steel Metro-North ticket counter while her white Yorkie nervously circled her pink espadrilled feet. Serena had always loved the gorgeous station with its cool marble corridors, romantic Old New York restaurants and bars, and the vast, sea-green vaulted ceiling decorated with marvelously unexpected gold paintings of the zodiac. Despite the fact that Grand Central was the largest station in the city with trains servicing the whole of New England, it maintained its regal air of competence, just like a good society hostess remained beautifully poised under pressure.

Nate took her hand and led her upstairs to the open-air bar overlooking the main terminal. The bar stools were covered with red velvet and the inside of the station was so airy and timeless, it was hard to believe the sun was blazing outside, raising the temperature to a horrifically humid one hundred degrees.

The seats of their stools were already touching when they sat down, and they didn't bother to move them. "Two dirty martinis, please!" Serena barked at the bartender in a superior voice and then collapsed against Nate's wonderful-smelling chest, giggling. She felt drunk already. What was wrong with her?

Love, baby.

The young bartender looked like David Beckham in a white tux and didn't even card them. Serena sipped her martini without tasting it and stared into Nate's adoring, glittering green eyes. She couldn't tear her eyes away. He looked just like he always looked in a plain white Ralph Lauren polo shirt, khaki Brooks Brothers shorts, and docksiders with no socks, his skin bronzed from working outside all summer and his hair bleached gold by the sun. He was the same—exactly the same Natie she'd dreamt about all summer—but better. He was everything, perfect. She reached out and smoothed down the fine blond hair on his deeply tanned forearm. Then she pulled her hand away, grabbed her martini glass, and gulped her drink. "Aren't you going to tell me about Maine?"

Nate wanted to grab her hand back and put it on his arm again. Touching her was all he could think about. Serena, his girl, his *dream* girl, was right here, right now, sitting so close, her thigh pressed against his, breathing the same air he was, talking to him and stroking his arm. What was to stop him from kissing her again? And kissing her, and kissing her . . . He tossed back his martini and signaled the bartender for another. "We did a lot of work on the boat. One day I'll take you sailing in it," he gasped, finding it hard to talk.

Why talk when they could be kissing?

Her huge blue eyes were like oceans themselves. "Oh, Natie. It's so good to see you," she gushed, her whole body trembling. "I've been so . . . there's just been way too much of me and not enough of . . . *you* this summer."

Nate gulped down most of his second martini. His hands felt all grabby and he wasn't sure he could control them. He just wanted to grab every gorgeous bit of her and hold on. Below them the terminal was milling with people, but it felt like they were the only people in it. Like the entire station had been built for them alone. Their little bar with its pressed-together velvet-covered stools and view of the busy station was pretty damned intimate, but not nearly intimate enough. "Let's go home," he suggested, because he couldn't *not* suggest it.

And he was pretty sure she wouldn't say no.

a nice day for an off-white wedding

The thing about Scotland was it was always fucking freezing, and even though the wedding was on the grounds of Hume Castle, a stately home in Gleneagles near the Queen's country house that had been in the family for over four hundred years, there was deer shit everywhere, and the women were wearing the ugliest fucking hats Blair had ever seen. She knew it was English and everything to wear hats at weddings, but did the hats have to have dead animals on them?

Forty large round tables were scattered across the deer shit–strewn green lawns, with the castle looming ominously behind them like something out of *Scooby-Doo*—haunted and ghost-ridden, with a constant black rain cloud over it and bats in its belfries. Thick ten-foot-high hedges bordered the lawns, shielding the well-heeled guests from the paparazzi and riffraff. The reception tables were covered in creamy linens and decorated with simple sprays of lilac and ferns. A stage had been provided to accommodate the entertainment, headlined by Sting himself. Blair had hoped to see Madonna, but she must have stayed home with her horses and all those kids she kept adopting.

Blair sat shivering at her table, wearing the lilac-colored, puffy-sleeved organza gown with a huge bow in the back that her aunt had had made especially for her by the worst tailor in Scotland and a garland of white roses and baby's breath in her retardedly curled hair. At least the hideous dress went down to her ankles so no one could tell she was wearing black cashmere leggings underneath it, rolled up above her knees.

Forever bucking fashion trends.

Tyler sat next to her in a creased dove gray morning suit with a white rose in the lapel, nursing a bottle of Guinness and giggling to himself. Bald, paunchy, red-nosed Uncle Ray was giving a speech and was plastered as usual. "I just want to thank my wife for marrying me—at least, I *think* we're still married," he began, spilling champagne down the groom's boots.

This was Blair's Aunt Catherine's second wedding to the same man. The groom, Blair's uncle Bruce, was a former keyboard player for Sting. Bruce and Catherine had eloped when they were nineteen and divorced a year later. During their second marriages they'd had children and the usual affairs, but they'd never forgotten their first love. Now well into middle age, they were back together again and ready to give marriage another try.

Amor vincit omnia!

Uncle Bruce had stringy haphazardly bleached blond hair and wore white cowboy boots with his iridescent-lilac-tinted morning suit and shimmering lilac-tinted top hat. Aunt Catherine was dressed like Lady Marian from *Robin Hood* in a dark green corseted satin gown, feathered felt hunting hat, and purple satin cloak. Blair felt like she'd fallen down the rabbit hole into some sort of fucked-up Wonderland. The whole affair made her want to puke.

"And I'm glad Bruce is marrying Catherine again, because if he doesn't, someone else will," Uncle Ray continued sloppily. Tyler was turning blue he was laughing so hard. This was his third or fourth Guinness, so he was bound to throw up anytime now.

"Shut up," Blair hissed at him. Her weird Scottish cousins—ten-year-old Peter, nine-year-old Willie, and eight-year-old Becky, who went to some creepy Catholic boarding school in the country and looked like trained assassins—stared at her blankly with their queer, lashless gray eyes and blond pageboy haircuts. She'd tried to talk to them earlier, but their Scottish accents were so fucking impossible to understand she'd given up.

Everyone applauded as Uncle Ray gave the mic up to Sting, who looked exactly the same as he did in pictures, with spiky blond hair, squintily earnest blue eyes, and a tanned yoga-wiry body stuffed into the tiniest black peg-legged jeans and white T-shirt Blair had ever seen on a man. He looked like a one-hundred-and-ten-year-old Galápagos tortoise in skinny jeans.

"I'd like to dedicate this song to my dear friends Catherine and Bruce!" Sting shouted into the mic. Then he began to strum the first bars of "Every Breath You Take" on his white guitar. To the left of the stage Blair's mother stood swaying back and forth to the music, blitzed out on champagne and wearing a purple-and-gold hoopskirted bridesmaid gown that looked like it had been fashioned by a coked-out fairy godmother. Aunt Catherine and her new husband, Bruce, slow danced on the shit-smeared grass with their bodies pressed together like teenagers at a prom. It was supposed to be romantic, but it made Blair want to strangle someone.

Blair Cornelia Archibald, she doodled on her napkin with her black Lancôme eyeliner. It sounded even better than Blair Cornelia Waldorf. She especially liked the way each word had an *a* and an *i* in it.

> *Eleanor and Harold Waldorf III, Esq.,*
> *proudly invite you to attend*
> *the marriage of their daughter*
> *Blair Cornelia*
> *to*
> *Nathaniel Archibald*
> *on August the seventeenth*
> *at four o'clock*
> *in the St. Claire Hotel's Grand Ballroom.*

The only problem was that first line. If her mom and dad were getting divorced and her dad was living with Giles or Raoul-Pierre or whatever the hell his name was, then surely it couldn't say "Eleanor and Harold Waldorf" on the invitation, could it? Maybe she'd just leave her mother out of it entirely, although that didn't really seem fair.

One thing was certain: she wouldn't be wearing a purple cloak, Nate wouldn't be wearing white cowboy boots, and Sting wouldn't sing.

How about Seal? Bono?

the best way to cool off is to take your clothes off

Like so many of the beautiful prewar town houses and apartment buildings in New York City, the Archibalds' East Eighty-second Street town house was without air-conditioning. Nate's family had never bothered with it because they wanted to preserve the original qualities of the house, and they spent most of the summer at their compound in Maine or away in Europe, anyway. Nate had opened all the windows upstairs in his wing and his parents', but it was still stifling. He grabbed a six-pack of Molson from the fridge and led Serena into the shady sheltered garden out back. A nude marble Venus de Milo fountain was the garden's centerpiece. Water spilled out of the top of her head, cascaded over her placid-looking face, onto her bare shoulders, and down her bare thighs until it pooled at her feet. Nate and Serena perched on the bench his dad had made from slate imported from their property in Maine. A mild breeze wafted through the slim branches of the Japanese cherry trees planted along the tall brick walls surrounding them, doing little to cool them off.

Nate cracked open a beer and handed it to Serena, who took

it eagerly. Her eyelids and cheeks had a sultry, sweaty sheen that was better than makeup. Nate tried not to look at her. He'd been trying not to look at her all the way home in the cab. Instead, he stared out at the tall, colorless buildings on Park Avenue like a tourist. He knew if he had looked at her—really looked—they wouldn't have made it home without taking their clothes off.

But now they were home.

"Christ, it's hot," Nate observed. He took a swig of beer and put the bottle down on the flagstone beneath his feet. Then he tugged up on the hem of his white polo shirt and pulled it off over his head. He tossed it on the ground and flexed his nicely toned back muscles as he picked up his beer again and took another swig.

Serena stared at the smatterings of adorable golden brown freckles that danced across his muscled shoulders. Here she was with Nate, Nate, Nate, *her Natie*, back behind his house where they'd played since they were little kids. She'd tied an imaginary rope around her hands to keep from grabbing him and throwing him down on the flagstones. Nate *wasn't* hers to grab, she reminded herself. But the rope felt so flimsy, she could break it anytime. Of course Nate was hers. He'd always been hers.

"It *is* hot," she giggled, springing to her feet and shimmying toward the Venus de Milo in an attempt to switch channels. She danced right out of her pink flip-flops and climbed into the fountain, getting completely soaked as she perched precariously on Venus's lap. The cold water felt totally amazing, exactly what she needed.

And she looked amazing in it—a real, live, in-the-flesh goddess. Nate stood up, put his beer down on the bench, and dashed into the fountain after her.

"Hi," Serena greeted him, grabbing his arm so he wouldn't slip and crack his skull on the marble. Water beaded on Nate's tanned, perfect chest. They stood there together for several awestruck minutes under the two little burbling streams of cold water, gazing into each other's eyes. Finding themselves together in the fountain behind Nate's house on a hot August afternoon was so predictable yet so surprising, it was like they were acting out a dream and making up the parts they couldn't remember.

Serena tightened her grip on Nate's arm and pulled him toward her. She kissed him softly on the lips and then quickly pulled away, her face flushed. Her light blue slip dress was soaked. Nate's pants were soaked. What were they doing? "Sorry," she apologized, removing a strand of wet pale blond hair from her cheek.

Nate grabbed her hand and laced his fingers through hers. "It's okay. Don't stop. I don't want you to stop." He kissed her perfect cheek, and then her perfect nose, and then her perfect lips, and then her perfect neck, and then her lips again.

And they didn't stop. They kept going, kissing like mad and yanking the rest of each other's clothes off. It was kind of embarrassing to be outside in front of the security cameras, though, and besides, the fountain was kind of small and wet and there was no place to lie down.

"Let's go upstairs," Nate murmured, picking Serena up in his strong arms before she could even answer.

As if in a dream—the most glorious dream she'd ever dreamt—Serena allowed Nate to carry her inside the house and up the elegant, red-carpeted staircase. She was done being a martyr. Nate wanted her and she wanted him. End of story.

Actually, this is just the beginning.

life according to b

Sting had given it up to a band of Scottish folk rockers in white patent leather clogs and black leather pants. The guests were all drunk now, and everyone was dancing, ruining their shoes in deer shit, even Eleanor—*especially* Eleanor. She'd cast off her strappy gold Prada sandals and hiked up her iridescent lilac hoop skirt to boogie down with Sting himself, barefoot.

Watch out, Trudie!

Blair remained at her table with her own private bottle of Cristal champagne, chain-smoking from a pack of cast-off Chesterfields while she continued to direct the movie that was her life, in her head. They'd honeymoon on Nate's boat, which he would rename *Blair*, of course, sailing around Europe and maybe the nice parts of Africa. When they returned home, they'd settle into the classic Park Avenue apartment their parents would have bought for them as a wedding gift, decorated to Blair's specifications in velvet and furs, while they were away. Nate would work for a venture capitalist firm, doing something easy that made lots of money but allowed him to be home by seven so they could have sex and then go out to dinner. Blair would be a lawyer like her father, but her clients would be very few and select and she'd have a giant staff of super-efficient mousy-looking assistants to do absolutely everything for her except go to the bathroom and have sex with Nate.

Speaking of having sex with Nate, why was she sitting here watching her sad, desperate mother attempt to get it on with Sting, of all people, to the most headache-inducing music she'd ever heard in her life, when she could be home with Nate, doing it *right now*?

No comment.

Poor Nate—she couldn't believe she'd abandoned him for this clown show. She yanked her cell phone out of the ridiculous lilac-colored puffball drawstring bag that had come with her nasty puffball dress and searched her contact list for her mother's travel agent. Surely there was a flight leaving this god-forsaken Scottish shithole in the next twenty-four hours. She didn't care if the flight was overbooked. She'd fly the plane herself if she had to. She knew Nate was back in the city, because the maid in Maine had told her so this morning after she'd called his cell seven times and he hadn't picked up. Poor Nate, all alone in his stuffy New York town house, pining for her while he wasted away on a diet of pot and tonic water. She couldn't wait to tell him all about the wedding she'd planned, and the wonderful life they would have together.

No comment.

summer lovin' happened so fast

Nate carried Serena up two flights of stairs to his parents' bedroom. Her dress was in the fountain, a soaking ball of blue silk.
So were his pants and his belt. There wasn't much left to take
off. He settled her gently on top of the golden yellow Italian cotton coverlet and lay down next to her, admiring the glow of her
smooth skin in the rays of late summer sun beaming through
the skylight overhead. Serena turned her head and pressed her
forehead into his. "I could just kiss you forever," she murmured,
her lips brushing his. "But I don't want to just kiss."

They looked into each other's eyes with an excited intensity
that only excited them even more. This was it: the thing neither
of them had ever done before was about to happen, and in the
most perfect way—with each other.

Nate pulled Serena close. "I love you," he said loudly, because
he wanted the whole city to hear it.

"I love *you*," she replied, even louder. Then she erupted into
excited giggles and began tearing his white cotton boxers off
with her long, graceful, overeager fingers, followed by her own
fountain-soaked white underwear. She tossed the soggy under-

garments across the room and they landed on the floor by the door.

Ta-da!

But wait, the condom. Nate rushed away to get one from his room. That awkward, slimy, silly-looking necessity. They'd both played with them before—blown them up like balloons and filled them with water—but they'd never actually used one. Putting it on was like a science experiment in lab class at school, and they wanted to do the experiment absolutely right. Serena tossed the empty wrapper on the floor.

Ready, set, *go!*

How fun, how right, to be doing the scariest thing for a girl to do for the first time with her best friend, the boy she'd loved forever. Her Nate. There was really nothing scary about it. It was exactly the way it was supposed to be.

He brushed his nose against hers. "Are you sure?" he asked quietly, even though he was pretty sure he knew the answer.

"Yes," Serena nodded, pressing her body against his. She'd never been more sure of anything. "Please?" she added with a giggle, because it was pretty obvious that he wanted to too.

So they did it. And the fun part was watching each other's faces, because they both looked so scared and happy and surprised. Serena could not stop laughing. It hurt, it did, but not in the way she'd thought. It was still so much fun, because Nate was so sweet. He didn't want it to hurt, and every time she flinched he just kissed the hurt away. She loved him so much, *hurt* was the wrong word. There were no words for how it felt. It was like getting the present she'd wanted for such a long, long time and finding out it was even better than she'd anticipated. It was amazing. He was amazing.

Nate couldn't believe he got to do this for the first time with the most beautiful girl in the universe. He was damned glad he'd waited, because nothing could top this. He loved Serena so badly it made him feel like he was going to explode. He couldn't stop smiling and laughing and looking at her. It was amazing. She was amazing.

And their bodies were amazing, the way they fit together and knew instinctively what to do. It was like this was somehow preordained. They'd been built for each other, created to be together, like two pieces from a model sailboat.

Click!

They weren't laughing anymore, because there wasn't anything funny. They just held each other, shivering with the thrill of being closer than they'd ever been before, sharing something they didn't know existed, something they'd keep with them forever.

Eventually they dozed off in each other's arms. Nate woke up first. It was nighttime now. The stars had come out in the skylight overhead. Without thinking about what he was doing, he reached for the remote on his dad's bedside table and switched on the TV. It was tuned to the History Channel, and the narrator for a documentary about Moses, who sounded an awful lot like Serena's friend Isabel Coates's dad, said in an incredibly loud voice, *"Moses saw no alternative but to part the Red Sea so that he and his people could cross it."*

Jesus, it was loud. Nate had forgotten his father was practically deaf. He pressed the volume button over and over again to soften it, but Serena's long eyelashes were already fluttering open against his chest. She lifted her head and grinned at him. "You parted my Red Sea!"

They both snorted, erupting into giddy giggles until they were howling with laughter. It was kind of a gross analogy but pretty funny too. They wrestled with each other under the covers, their bodies sleek with sweat. Soon they were kissing, unable to stop, and before they knew it, he was parting her Red Sea once more.

There they go again, making history.

honesty: it's just another word

Blair's greasy-haired cabdriver seemed to think she was a tourist who would want to see the sights upon her arrival in the city. He wound his way from the bottom of the island up, pointing out City Hall, the Stock Exchange, the Guggenheim SoHo, and the Gandhi statue in Union Square. Blair's flight out of Glasgow had been delayed because of fog, the stewardess refused to serve her vodka, and there was nothing decent to eat for ten interminable hours. Now that she was finally on the ground, all she wanted to do was get a hotel room with Nate somewhere, order a huge brunch, and feed each other French toast and mimosas, naked.

"The World Trade Center used to be the tallest, but now it's the Empire State building again," the cab driver informed her, shaking his greasy head sadly.

"Would you please just drive the fucking car up Park Avenue?" Blair screamed through the plastic barrier between them.

Good thing it was bulletproof.

What reason could Nate have for being in town at all other than to prepare for Blair's impending arrival? She imagined him shopping for new Frette sheets, stocking the fridge with Ketel One, and ordering a Rolls to pick her up at the airport. She imagined his elated surprise to find her back already, a whole week early! They'd have a picnic in the park and then he'd whisk her home to his town house and make sweet, passionate love to her on his cozy single bed, exclaiming all the while how much he'd missed her all summer and how depressed he'd been without her.

Uh-huh.

Finally, the cab pulled up in front of the Archibalds' town house on Eighty-second Street and she got out, hauling her Louis Vuitton mini steamer trunk out of the trunk herself and throwing a pile of money at the driver. It was nearly noon on a sunny Saturday, and the rest of the city had been bustling and crowded, but the Upper East Side appeared to be abandoned. Nate's house was still and quiet. The curtains were drawn on the first two floors. But up on the third floor the curtains were open and the windows were up.

Blair pressed the button on the intercom with her thumb, leaning her whole body into it. "Nate? It's me!"

Serena's head was nestled against Nate's bare chest as she daydreamed about the coming school year. She'd spend every waking and sleeping moment that she wasn't in school with him. Or she could kidnap him and stash him under her bed for safekeeping. One thing was certain: she never wanted to be away from Nate again.

Nate was still asleep, dreaming of mermaids. He was stranded on a windless sea on his boat, the *Charlotte*. The glassy water stretched out endlessly before him as he stood on the bow, searching for land. Then a voice began calling his name—"*Nate? Nate?*"—and bubbles burst on the surface of the water. A long, lithe fish shimmied past, its golden head glimmering in the sunlight. Then a dark head popped up out of the water; it was a girl, a mermaid. "*Nate? Nate? Can you hear me, Nate?*"

Blair.

Nate sat up abruptly, his whole body covered in nervous sweat.

"Nate? Are you there?" Blair's voice echoed throughout the house.

Serena was already out of bed, scrambling on the floor for something—anything—to wear. There was her underwear, but fuck, her dress! She tossed Nate's boxers at him and flew into his mother's walk-in closet, scanning the hangers for something remotely wearable. Mrs. Archibald dressed for the opera even when there was no opera. Dior chiffon. De la Renta taffeta. Valentino silk charmeuse with a train. Help! Serena pulled a pair of gray satin Armani cigarette pants down off the hanger and stepped into them. Then she pulled on a cream-colored wool Chanel jacket with crystal buttons. She looked kind of cool, but the wool was itchy and hot and never in a million years would she have worn such an outfit on a Saturday afternoon in August.

Yes, but this wasn't just *any* Saturday afternoon in August.

She started to make the bed, careful to flush the condom wrappers down the toilet. Nate returned from his room, looking normal in a pair of shorts and a T-shirt.

"We could just wait for her to leave," he suggested. His cell phone began to ring. Then the house phone.

"Nate? Wake up, Nate. It's me."

"No, let her in," she told him, tucking her sex-mussed blond hair neatly behind her her ears, as if giving herself the final finishing touch. "I'll go outside and hide our stuff. Bring her out there after you let her in. Tell her that's why we couldn't hear her."

Serena was sort of missing one very big hole in the story—why the hell she was there in the first place—but neither of them said anything about that.

Nate did as he was told. "Hello?" He spoke cautiously into the intercom.

"Nate? What the fuck, Nate. I've been out here for like an hour with my fucking *suitcase*."

"Sorry," Nate mumbled and buzzed her in.

Serena raced downstairs and out into the garden. There were the waterlogged remnants of their clothes, wadded up at the Venus de Milo's feet where they'd left them. She wrung them out, lifted the cover of the Archibalds' gas grill, and stuffed the clothes inside. Then she slid her feet into her pink rubber flip-flops, which looked positively bizarre with the rest of her outfit. Her face was slick with sweat and her heart was beating so fast it hurt. *Calm down,* she told herself. But all at once the source of her distress was right there in the garden with her: Blair, looking very clean and chic in a black linen tunic with cap sleeves, white patent leather lace-up sandals, and her black Audrey Hepburn sunglasses perched on top of her head.

"Hi!" Serena threw herself in Blair's direction, embracing her with a breathless, clumsy hug. "How was your summer? Did your aunt get married okay and everything?"

"My summer sucked." Blair extracted herself from the hug

with pursed lips. "But it looks like you guys have been having fun." She picked up an empty beer bottle and put it down again. "Where are you going, anyway?" she asked, eyeing Serena's outfit curiously.

Serena looked down at her stupid clothes. Her toes were painted all different colors, something she hadn't even remembered doing. "Shopping." she blurted out. "At Bloomingdale's. My feet grew and none of my shoes fit. Erik's taking me to some play tonight and I need shoes." She'd only been to Bloomingdale's once, when she was twelve, but Nate's house was sort of on the way so it was the only store that made sense. "I just stopped in to say hi," she added, explaining away her presence at Nate's house as briefly as possible.

Nate stood a few feet behind Blair with his arms folded across his chest. Serena met his bewildered gaze for a fleeting second and then forced herself to look away.

Blair didn't seem even remotely suspicious. She lit a cigarette and puffed on it dramatically. "You guys would not believe what a freak show my aunt's wedding was. I just had to get the fuck out of there. And Scotland is so medieval. The toilet paper was like burlap." She turned and walked over to Nate. "Our wedding's not going to be anything like that," she told him, slipping her arms around his waist and resting her head on his shoulder. She heaved a huge, exhausted sigh. "My family is so fucked up. I'm just so glad to be home."

Nate patted her chestnut-colored hair, his face twitching with conflicting emotions. Part of him wanted to blurt out that he was in love with Serena, that they were together now, and though he was sorry for hurting Blair's feelings, she'd just have to deal. But part of him still loved Blair too. He loved how unsuspicious she was right now. How she was so caught up in the drama of her life she didn't have time to be petty.

Blair lifted her head and kissed him on the lips, a long, inviting, *remember me?* kiss. And he did remember her. He remembered kissing her for the first time, and he remembered loving her. And he remembered that he couldn't just break up with her right now because he'd hooked up with her best friend, whom he happened to be in love with too. He clasped her small, confident shoulders and kissed her back, oblivious to the pain he was causing.

Serena tore through her thumbnail with her teeth. She could see now that what she and Nate had done last night was so dangerous and explosive and hurtful it was best to pretend that it hadn't happened at all. Blair and Nate were still a couple. He wasn't going to volunteer any information about what had happened last night, and she certainly wasn't going to say anything. She felt like her chest had been cut open with a dull knife and without any anesthesia, and Blair was ripping her heart out with her bare hands. But what could she do? How could she stand by and watch them kiss and be in love all next year? Last spring had been torture enough.

Blair giggled as she zipped up the fly of Nate's white J.Crew bermuda shorts, which he'd overlooked in his haste to get dressed. Serena stood watching, gnawing furiously on her thumbnail. She felt like she'd been in a car wreck and was bleeding internally. It wasn't safe to move. Then it occurred to her that there *was* something she could do after all: she could go to boarding school. Her dad could get her into Hanover—surely he could. Blair and Nate would never have to see her again, and she'd never have to see them. Everyone would be happy.

Sure they would.

"I'm late," she told them, turning away. The longer she stayed, the harder it would be to leave.

"Wait!" Blair cried. She broke away from Nate and rushed over to Serena, throwing her arms around her. "Good luck." She gave her old friend a generous hug. "And have fun."

Serena wished she had the biggest pair of sunglasses ever made to cover up her face, because she felt like it had split in two. Blair thought she was only wishing her luck finding a pair of shoes and fun seeing a play; she didn't realize she had just uttered the equivalent of "have a nice life."

"Thanks," Serena whispered back, her voice cracking as a tsunami of tears welled up in her huge, navy blue eyes. She blinked them away and then looked up to find Nate staring at her, his golden brown eyebrows furrowed in confusion. She wanted to hug him too, but she was afraid that if she touched him she would lose control. Instead, she swallowed a sob, flashed him her famous *you know you love me* smile, and lifted a gorgeous, stubbornly independent hand. "Au revoir."

Adieu.

epilogue

Erik's red Jeep bounced along the twisting local New Hampshire roads on the way to Hanover Academy, threatening to dislodge Serena's trunk from the roof. Serena sat in the passenger seat with her bare feet perched on the black dashboard, wearing a gigantic pair of tortoiseshell Gucci sunglasses. She hadn't spoken since they'd left Manhattan, and she remained silent now. Erik was listening to a Beatles compilation album playing very softly on the car stereo.

I don't know why you say goodbye
I say hello

"Dad's a freaking genius, getting you in the way he did. You didn't even have to write a freaking essay!" Erik declared. He glanced at his sister. "And when we get there you'll probably score the biggest single room on freaking campus, you lucky duck."

Guess who's not feeling so lucky?

Serena remained silent. Over and over in her head, she was

writing e-mails. First there was the one to Blair in which she would confess everything and ask to be forgiven. Then there was the one to Nate, telling him that she couldn't live without him and so would he please ditch Blair and come to Hanover to be with her? Then there was the one in which she set Nate free, telling him that their hookup had been nice and all, but she had a whole future of hookups ahead of her. And then there was the chatty one she wrote to both of them sounding thrilled to be away, and full of funny little details about her fantastic new life at boarding school.

Great food, great friends, good times!

None of these e-mails would ever get sent. As her old nanny Agatha used to say when she was little and would cry at the sight of peas on her plate, "You get what you get and you don't get upset." Blair would have Nate forever, and she would have him for just that one, perfect night.

Her new green metallic Treo was clutched in her white-knuckled hands, where it had been the whole ride up. She flipped it open and snapped a picture of her bare toes on the dashboard. Her toenails were chipped and weather-beaten, but they were still painted all different colors, the way they'd been that night with Nate. She pressed send and e-mailed the picture to him, hoping it would make him laugh. Then she flipped her phone closed and tossed it into her bag. Two big, glistening tears slid down her cheeks.

Hello, hello
I don't know why you say goodbye
I say hello

hey people!

Summer has finally come to an end and school's starting all over again. But our favorite, most fabulous classmate is missing. Everyone who's anyone is talking about why she decided to go to boarding school in the first place. Why would the most popular, beautiful, best-loved girl in the city leave? Of course, some of us know the truth—at least, we think we do. And if we don't know the truth, we have our opinions, and we're always willing to share them.

your e-mail

Hey GG,
I was in a play this summer at a theater-acting workshop near Ridgefield, Connecticut, and there was this girl in it who was, like, a total mess. Like she would go home with every guy in the whole play, including the kind of old director, and I'm pretty sure she was on drugs. When I heard she was going to boarding school I was like, oh, no, bad idea. She needs parents!
—gdgrl

Dear gdgrl,
It's nice of you to worry, but you'd be surprised. Boarding schools have honor codes and rule books. They can be very strict. Of course we all know that rules are meant to be broken. . . .
—GG

Q: Dear GG,

All the girls at my boarding school are talking about this new girl, and basically, we've all decided she's bad news. If she's going to have any friends at all, they're gonna be boys.
—bordgrl

A: Dear bordgrl,

Are you quite sure this is the tactic you want to take? Do you really want the new girl to be best friends with your boyfriend? Wait, this is all starting to sound weirdly familiar.
—GG

sightings

N carrying **B**'s brand-new nickel-plated Balenciaga book bag while he walked her to school—wearing a leash. Just kidding. **V**, **D**, and **J** shopping for new school clothes at vintage stores in **Williamsburg**. Looking forward to another year at the loner table? Sorry, that was mean, but most of the time vintage clothes just look . . . old. **C** handing out his glossy new headshot in front of **L'École**, where all the easy—I mean French—girls go. **K** and **I** getting to **Constance Billard** early on the first day and waiting outside with buttered bagels and cappuccinos for everyone, including the teachers. Guess they simply could not wait till school started! **S** at a table full of adorable boys hanging on her every word in the dining hall at **Hanover Academy**. She can't be suffering too much, right?

questions

Will **B** and **N** stay together? Will they ever seal the deal? And when they do, will she guess that he's been there, done that already?

Will **J**'s chest stop growing? Will she ever meet a nice boy who likes her for her pretty smile? Or will her you-know-whats keep growing so we can't see her smile anymore? For her sake, I sure hope not.

Will **V** ever admit to **D** that she thinks about what he looks like without his crappy old T-shirt on? Wait, what *does* he look like without his crappy old T-shirt on?

Will **D** ever get over **S** and admit that he already has a girlfriend?

Will **S** get over **N**? Will she survive boarding school? Will she thrive at boarding school? Will she ever come back?

Some of you already know the answers—at least, you think you do. If you don't, you know where to find them. I have no plans to stop talking about any of the above.

Until next time.

You know you love me,

gossip girl

Acknowledgments

I am grateful for the opportunity to finally thank everyone who has contributed to the success of *Gossip Girl*. No thanks does justice to the thanks I owe my friend and editor at Little, Brown, Cindy Eagan—*beyond!* You are the ultimate it girl behind each book's triumph, never uttering a doubting word, always 2,000 percent positive, hysterically funny, and just what I needed. To my friend and editor at Alloy Entertainment, Sara Shandler, always so perceptive, sympathetic, secretly cynical, ridiculously funny, and impossible to get off the phone. Thank you to my friend Josh Bank at Alloy Entertainment for being my ally, for making me laugh when I'm grumpy, and for directing my ideas into something that makes sense. We'll always have Last Dog. Thank you to my friend Les Morgenstein at Alloy Entertainment for not treating me like an idiot even when I act like one, and for not hanging up when I cried over the phone all those times. And thank you to everyone else at Little, Brown and Alloy Entertainment over the years for all their behind-the-scenes hard work. I couldn't have done it without you. Thanks ever so much to my agent, Suzanne Gluck, for seeing past the idiot savant and taking me on. Thank you to Liz and Papa, for your love and pride and for being the ultimate guerilla marketers, you made the books bestsellers. Omi, I could never have written this book or any of the others without your love, support, and help, especially with the children. I can't imagine what I did to deserve you. Thank you Erasmo for bringing music into my children's lives. Thank you to my children for really getting that I can like what I do and love them too. And thank you Richard, you know I love you.

Thank you, thank you, thank you to everyone I mentioned and everyone I missed. It has been a wild and wicked ride.

Anna Percy, Cammie Sheppard, and Sam Sharpe ruled the A-LIST. But there are three new princesses in Tinseltown.

THE A-LIST
HOLLYWOOD ROYALTY

Meet the new Hollywood Royalty: Amelie, the not-so-innocent starlet; Myla and Ash, the golden couple; Jacob, the geek turned hottie; and Jojo, the outsider who'll do anything to get on the A-List.

SOME PEOPLE ARE BORN WITH IT.

Turn the page for a sneak peek of this scandulous new novel by *New York Times* bestselling author Zoey Dean.

FAIRY PRUDENESS

Even before the white stretch limo pulled to a stop outside the Nokia Theatre, Amelie Adams could hear the screams of hundreds of fans. She blinked out the tinted windows as the driver slowed to a stop in front of the ruby red carpet. Behind the ground-level throngs of fans and photographers, models stood on six-foot risers, wearing hot pink Prada sunglasses and bright white tent dresses with graphic prints of L.A. landmarks on them: the Hollywood sign, Grauman's Chinese, the Beverly Hills Hotel, a postcard shot of Malibu. Most of the fans barely paid attention to the glamazons; they were more interested in catching a glimpse of their favorite Hollywood starlets arriving for the premiere of *The A-List*.

"Fairy Princess!"

"Fairy Princess!"

Even though Amelie wasn't in the movie, her fans knew she was coming tonight. Clusters of little girls waved homemade, glittery signs proclaiming their high-pitched love for her Kidz Network character, Fairy Princess. Amelie leaned back in her seat, pushing a red ringlet from her turquoise eyes.

Across from Amelie, her mother's face broke into the wide, voluptuous smile that Amelie had inherited. Helen Adams's own red hair was shorter—shaped into a face-framing chin-length bob by Mario, her one-name-only personal hairdresser for the last ten years—and her eyes were a dark hazel, but otherwise she and Amelie could have been mistaken for sisters.

"Have fun. And remember, you'll get it next time." She winked one heavily mascaraed eye and smoothed her strapless violet Carolina Herrera gown over a flat stomach courtesy of a three-week fitness boot camp in Studio City.

Amelie's gloss-lacquered lips formed a grimace. She'd been up for the part of Emma Hardy, *The A-List*'s lead, but had lost the role to Marlee Aces, a blonde with one screen credit in a sexy indie, *Rock My World*—about a lesbian heavy metal band in Mormon Utah. The producers had deemed her "more mature" and therefore better for the part. The Emma character had a sex scene, and while Amelie knew that a jump from petting winged ponies to heavy petting would've been a risky career move, sometimes she longed to do *something* that wasn't G-rated.

"No scowls." Helen leaned over to kiss her daughter on the cheek. "And have fun. I'm going to take a quick meeting about your Christmas special, but I'll find you at the party later."

Amelie reached back, giving her mom's hand a squeeze, as two tuxedoed valets reached in to extract her from the limo.

"Fairy Princess! Fairy Princess!"

Amelie stepped out of the limousine, plastering on the same magical grin that had sold four million T-shirts with her face on them. Her new white patent Miu Miu wedges sank into the plush carpet and she gracefully adjusted the hem of her silver Jovani flapper-inspired dress. Her character wore pink *exclusively*, so it was nice to not feel like human cotton candy for once.

She made her way down the row of crazed fans—the younger ones near tears—signing glossy pictures, massive posters, and *BOP* magazines in her trademark swirly script. After each autograph, she flourished her pink Sharpie with Fairy Princess's signature wand wave. *Elbow left, wrist swish, elbow right, wrist swish.*

At the far end of the red carpet, cast members from *The A-List* mingled with other actors about her age. Raven-haired Kady Parker and milky-skinned Moira and Deven Lacey, twins whose trademark sexy scowls had helped them get parts on *School of Scandal*, a new CW show, shot her curious glances and then returned to their conversation.

Used to being ignored by her Hollywood peers, Amelie sighed, signing a talking Fairy Princess doll with bubble gum pink hair and glittery accessories. She knew she was lucky to be seated at the helm of a multimillion-dollar empire at only sixteen, but sometimes she just wanted to move up from the kids' table. She was growing up, but no one besides Mary Ellen, the on-set stylist who'd had to let her Fairy Princess wardrobe out in the chest, had really seemed to notice.

Amelie smiled at a white-blond seven-year-old in a replica of Fairy Princess's Winter Festival ball gown. She held up a shirt for Amelie to sign. "Is it true you're playing a new kind of fairy in *Class Angel*?" the little girl asked, awestruck.

"You got it," Amelie answered, shooting another dazzling smile that almost outshone her dress's sequins and crystals. Filming started on her new movie, *Class Angel*, the day after tomorrow. It was PG, and more mature than her Fairy Princess role, but she still played a teenager's guardian angel rather than an *actual* teenager. It was like calling Pinkberry ice cream.

Amelie leaned over the metal barricade railing to sign the shirt, her face inches from the little girl's.

"Mommy!" The little girl pointed at Amelie, then yelled, "Mom, Fairy Princess has boobies!"

Amelie felt the blood rush to her face. Well, then. Maybe people *were* noticing her growing up, after all. . . .

Amelie stood bathed in the sapphire-blue lights cast by the Nokia's looming facade. She'd barely paid attention to the ninety-minute movie, mentally replaying her red carpet humiliation instead of focusing on the film. Not that she could have focused even if she'd tried. She'd given up her primo reserved seat to an agent who'd brought his grandmother, and had wound up seated next to three fifteen-year-old girls who'd driven in from the Inland Empire after winning tickets on KROQ. They'd snuck in cans of Coors Light with them, and Amelie had struggled to hear the movie over their giggly conversation about the cute slacker who'd sold them the beer at 7-Eleven. She stretched her tired neck from side to side, wishing she could skip the afterparty and head home. Unfortunately, she knew she had to put in an appearance, or her absence would be chalked up to sour grapes.

Now she stood just outside the outdoor party area,

watching people trickle out from the theater. Stars donned their occasionally misguided interpretations of the invite-specified "sexy *A-List* evening wear": skin-baring miniskirts, long glittery gowns that looked like expensive prom dresses. Security was already manning the makeshift entrance to the afterparty area, to make sure that people like Amelie's drunken underage seat-mates didn't crash.

She'd do one turn around the party space, meet and greet with some studio bigwigs, smile big, look sweet, and get the heck out of there. Amelie had an early call time tomorrow to shoot a music video for the Kidz Net-work site, anyway. It was the perfect excuse to trade her painful wedges for her Paul Frank monkey slippers. Add a bowl of Häagen-Dazs and her *Veronica Mars* DVDs, and she was set for the evening.

Someone tapped her on the back. "Hey, do you mind walking in with me?"

Amelie turned. Kady Parker was standing by herself, her wide sapphire blue eyes shimmering beneath the fringe of glossy black bangs that framed her heart-shaped face. "I always feel weird walking into a party alone."

Kady Parker was her costar in *Class Angel*. Since get-ting into the business as a twelve-year-old, Kady almost always played the sassy tomboy who gets kicked around by bitchy prom queen types but gets the guy in the end. Amelie nodded, half surprised that Kady—whom she'd met only briefly, at a table read—was being so friendly.

"Cool," Kady said, flashing her wristband and leading the way. The movie premiere might have been open to the hundredth caller, but the afterparty was strictly by invitation only, and you needed a "Get *A*-ed" wristband, which of course they both had. "Hot dress, by the way."

"You look great too," Amelie replied. Kady's feminine-cut black Armani tux fit her slightly rebellious movie persona and her petite frame.

"Thanks. Let's hit the bar—you can meet some of the other girls from *Class Angel*," Kady half-shouted over the new Santogold song, leading Amelie into a courtyard area, where four bars were set up in a square. The platform models now wore opaque white Prada one-piece swimsuits and the kind of sultry yet bored expressions mastered only through lots of practice. They danced languidly to the music as guests loaded their plates with food from the catered buffet. Three twentysomething brunettes hovered at a cocktail table, congratulating themselves for getting in without wristbands.

Kady paused, standing on the tiptoes of her already-high cherry red Christian Louboutin stilettos, searching the crowd for her friends. "I don't know what they'll be drinking tonight," she said.

The four bars were all serving drinks inspired by the characters, and behind each was a backdrop featuring a glamorous publicity shot of one of the *A-List* actors. The Emma bar was serving classic cocktails like Manhattans and martinis, and rare Opus One wine in an exclusive *A-List* vintage. A bar for Peter, Emma's on-and-off-again love interest, was serving twenty microbrewed beers in frosted glasses. The bar for Sarah, a super-rich character with movie star parents (allegedly based on young director Sam Sharpe), offered Cristal, Veuve, and Dom Pérignon champagnes, while a bar for Dahlia, the wild child with a mean streak, served potent vodka, rum, and tequila combos.

"There they are," Kady said, grabbing Amelie's arm and leading her to the Dahlia bar. A group of bored-looking girls stood around a shiny silver cocktail table. The Lacey twins slouched on stools, sipping identical Grey Goose and cranberry cocktails. They were mirror images of each other, with endlessly toned legs, thick caramel hair, and the same "don't mess with us" expressions. (Though rumor had it that three-minutes-younger Deven was actually a sweetheart.) Next to them stood DeAndra Barnett, a former child model who'd made her foray into acting in the massive Kidz Network hit *West High Story*. She had luminous toffee-colored skin, a lean, athletic body, and short curly hair that highlighted her sharp cheekbones. She wore a strapless D&G dress in a wild lily-and-leopard print that kept falling down her skinny chest.

"You guys know Amelie, right?" Kady gestured to Amelie as though she were a showcase prize on *The Price Is Right*.

DeAndra squinted as though she barely recognized Amelie, gracelessly pulling up her dress. The twins smiled faintly. "*Fairy Princess*, right?" they said in unison. Amelie nodded.

"*Fairy Princess*, and *Class Angel* with me and DeAndra," Kady corrected. "And now Hunter, too."

Hunter?

Amelie thought she was hearing things. Kady could only be talking about one Hunter. Hunter Sparks. The guy so hot his role in *West High Story* had propelled little girls from their "I hate boys" phases directly into their "I heart Hunter" obsessions.

"Wait, Hunter Sparks is in *Class Angel*?" Amelie

fought to sound casual as her brain hyperventilated: *HunterSparksHunterSparksHunterSparks!*

Amelie had starred in her first feature with him, when she was eleven and he was fourteen, before her Fairy Princess reign began. He played her older brother, who died trying to save Amelie when aliens invaded Chicago. Even though he treated her in a brother-sister way the whole shoot, she'd fallen totally in love with him. She still had script pages covered in hearts filled with loopy cursive musings: "I love Hunter," "Mrs. Hunter Sparks," and "Mrs. Amelie Adams-Sparks." For five years, she'd barely run into him, even at Kidz Network headquarters. And, yet, just glimpsing his face on a *West High Story* poster or hearing his name was enough to make her heart thud in double time, the way it did now.

"I thought our lead was Raleigh Springfield," Amelie hastily added, naming the actor who was originally slated to play the role.

"Nope, he's out." Kady shrugged. "Said he wants to do an indie instead, but I think it's just rehab. The producer called in a favor and Hunter's in."

"Cool." The twins nodded and drained their glasses. "He's yummier anyway. Raleigh has that greasy hair."

A delightful tingle worked its way through Amelie's body. Her stars were falling into place, *Fairy Princess* style.

"Anyway, this party blows, K." The twins looked at Kady like two dogs begging their owner to take them outside.

"Okay, then," Kady said, processing the info. "We could hit the Standard, the downtown one on Flower." She turned to Amelie. "Have you been? The rooftop bar has waterbed pods and great bottle service. And no wannabes." She glanced at the uninvited brunettes in Payless heels at one of the bars.

Before Amelie could answer, she felt a hand on her shoulder.

"Hi girls." Amelie's mom's voice strained over the noise. Amelie flushed with embarrassment. "Amelie, honey, they moved up the call time for tomorrow by a few hours. The limo's waiting out front."

Amelie turned back to Kady, who'd probably never brought her mom to a premiere before. She shrugged. "Thanks for the invite, but it looks like I've got to call it a night."

She made an apologetic face, though secretly she was thankful for the interruption. Party hopping was fine if you wanted to end up with a has-been rep and a drug habit by age twenty-one on *E! True Hollywood Story*, but Amelie intended to be the industry's anti-Lohan, thank you very much.

"No worries," Kady said, hugging Amelie. "I'll see you on Sunday."

"For sure," Amelie said, waving at the other girls as she grabbed her clutch off the cocktail table.

Helen led the way back through the crowd, walking with her perfect Pilates posture. "They seemed nice. You might have fun on this movie."

Amelie grinned. She and Kady didn't have to get matching BFF bracelets, but at least Kady didn't seem like the kind of crazy costar who'd put Nair in Amelie's shampoo bottle. Plus, a movie where she didn't have to match dance steps with whimsical sprites? One that might even have Hunter Sparks?

Amelie was definitely ready for her close-up.

DELAYED GRATIFICATION

Myla Everhart stood in the LAX baggage claim, wishing she hadn't worn her thigh-high, yellow Aztec-print Pucci Sundial dress—every time she sat down, the back of her legs touched some invariably sticky surface.

The first daughter of America's hottest on- and off-screen couple craned her neck, looking toward the doors to the street. Ash had said he'd park and come inside to help shield her from the paparazzi and carry her bags. Granted, she'd internationally overnighted everything via Luggage Concierge, but he could certainly carry her plum Marc Jacobs tote full of French *Vogues* and her cashmere travel blanket.

Myla fished her emerald-adorned iPhone from the bottom of her bag. One fourteen. Ash knew she landed at twelve thirty. What was the freaking holdup?

But then . . . that was Ash. Her Ash. Laid-back, easygoing Ash.

She softened, just thinking of him. Long before they'd gotten together, Ash Gilmour had been her best friend and the only guy who *got* Myla. It wasn't easy going through puberty as the child of Barkley Everhart and

Lailah Barton—*People*'s Most Beautiful Couple, 2001, 2002, 2006–present. Most Inattentive, too, by Myla's standards. They'd adopted Myla as a baby after spending time on-set in Thailand, filming an Adam and Eve–inspired love story that had grossed some ungodly amount. It had been just Myla, until four years ago, when they'd brought home four-year-old Mahalo from Bangladesh on her twelfth birthday. They'd just returned from a *Babel*-meets–*Independence Day* shoot and decided to bring back a souvenir. At least that's how it seemed to Myla.

Then one day in the eighth grade, she and Ash were waiting for his dad, Gordon Gilmour—a record producer who spent more time coddling whiny rock stars than taking care of his only son—to pick them up from the ArcLight after they'd gone to see the new *Harry Potter* movie together. They hadn't told their friends, who said the movie was dorky. That was okay though; it was their secret. Myla was in the middle of a rant about how she sometimes hated the ArcLight's assigned seats—the Hogwarts-uniformed senior citizen in the seat next to her and Ash had reeked of asparagus and Old Spice. That was when Ash leaned over and kissed her, right in front of the Cinerama Dome. They'd been Hollywood's youngest golden couple ever since.

And they were inseparable.

But Myla's parents—Barbar, as they were called by the press—had insisted on a family vacation this summer. "Vacation" meant a whirlwind tour of the third world, doing United Nations aid work at their older children's adopted countries: Thailand for Myla, Bangladesh for Mahalo, and Madagascar for Bobby, now six. Myla had to share a room with her two brothers—next to her parents and the three recently adopted toddlers—often in villages so small and remote she couldn't get a cell phone signal or Internet. She couldn't indulge in online retail therapy, take a real shower, update her Facebook status, or, more important, communicate with Ash. It was *torture*.

Granted, she could have called Ash every second while she was in Paris last week, visiting her old friend Isabelle, who'd moved there in fourth grade. But she'd been in the city of love without the love of her life—thinking about him too much would have depressed her. In a way, she also thought the waiting was romantic. Being someone who never had to wait long for anything she wanted, Myla enjoyed the way her heart beat when she thought about her and Ash finally being together again.

She punched a string of numbers into her phone, twirling a lock of her long ebony hair around her index finger. She smiled, catching a glimpse of the shiny, emerald green streak that fell along the left side of her neck. It had been Ash's idea, and Myla had initially been revolted, but now she loved the secret burst of color.

Isabelle picked up on the third ring. "*Ma chère amie*, I missed you too."

Myla could hear the clinking of silverware and wineglasses in the background. Even though it was after eleven there, Isabelle was probably just eating dinner now, before hitting Paris's nightclubs.

"Stop that, Guillaume!" Isabelle squealed delightedly to her boyfriend. "Sorry, he's being a total perv. Shouldn't you be with Ash?"

"He's late." Myla fiddled nervously with the plastic

Green Lantern bubble gum machine ring she wore on a Tiffany gold chain. She and Ash had traded rings from a bubble gum machine in ninth grade, and she had worn it on her neck ever since. Myla fully planned to hire Mindy Weiss, the best wedding planner in L.A., to work the cheap rings into the ceremony when they got married.

"Better he's late than you are, if you know what I mean," Isabelle said bawdily, before cracking up. "Oh, that's right! You haven't done it yet. *Quel dommage.*"

Myla rolled her eyes. "We can't all be French sluts like you," she teased her friend.

A woman in a *Jesus Saves (Ask Me How)* T-shirt rumbled by, scowling at the dirty talk.

"I know, you're waiting for the right time." Isabelle yawned. "Just make sure to take advantage of being young and hot. Now go moisturize before he gets there."

Isabelle hung up with a giggle, probably to stop Guillaume's wandering hands again, and Myla hung up too. Two girls walked by arm in arm, wearing matching Fairy Princess T-shirts and glittery purple leggings.

Myla sighed. Even if they were only ten, you had to start learning the basic rules of fashion *sometime*. She yanked the pile of dog-eared *Vogues* from her bag and thrust the magazines into the taller girl's arms.

If thoughts of "stranger danger" occurred to either girl, they didn't show it. They studied Myla's round cheeks, smooth skin, and almond-shaped, shamrock-colored eyes. Recognition flashed across their surprised faces. They must have seen her photo in *People*, helping Barbar hand out care packages in the Philippines. And here she was again, doing charity work of her own.

Ash Gilmour was late for everything, a habit he'd never wanted to develop but had learned from his record impresario father. "Early means eager. Eager is weak," he'd always said.

But when it came to Myla Everhart, Ash *was* weak. And he'd wanted to be waiting at LAX when she'd landed. He wanted to watch her come down the escalator to the baggage claim, to see whatever impossible shoes she was wearing, followed by her long legs with the little birthmark below her right knee. Then her slim little body, and her tumble of hair with the green streak just for him. And then that face—lips that reminded him of the cherries on top of a sundae and eyes that always looked a little sleepy but saw every little thing.

Ash parked his vintage black 1969 Camaro and stumbled out, half-running across the wide one-way street reserved for shuttle buses and taxis. Safely on the sidewalk, Ash composed himself, shoving his shaggy dark blond hair off his forehead and smoothing his vintage Zeppelin tee. He stepped through the automatic doors. The air-conditioning swallowed him, but he saw no sign of Myla on the benches or near the baggage carousel. He checked the arrivals board. Her flight had made it. Oh, shit. How late was he? Had she left without him?

Read the rest of
THE A-LIST: HOLLYWOOD ROYALTY
Available now

Spotted back in NYC:
Blair, **S**erena, **N**ate, and **C**huck

And guess who will be there to
whisper all their juicy secrets?

i will always love you

^a gossip girl

novel

An all-new special hardcover edition,
featuring the original cast.

Coming November 2009.

Welcome to Poppy.

A poppy is a beautiful blooming red flower
(like the one on the spine of this book). It is also
the name of the new home of your favorite series.

Poppy takes the real world and makes it
a little funnier, a little more fabulous.

Poppy novels are wild, witty, and inspiring.
They were written just for you.

So sit back, get comfy, and pick a Poppy.

poppy

www.pickapoppy.com

gossip girl   THE CLIQUE   THE A-LIST

 the it girl   SECRETS OF MY
HOLLYWOOD LIFE   POSEUR